ACHILLES PORT

Book 1: The Anomaly

Julian Nicholson

Book Cover by the author

First edition. 2024

For my daughters

1

In the centre of the grandiose entrance lobby on Orbital C there is a large and extravagant fountain. The sight and sound of so much moving water is soothing as well as surprising, particularly after the faintly nauseous experience of the shuttle, and he usually stops to take a look.

At the top of the fountain, an impressive square-jawed man enjoys the company of three women carved from the same marble. The man is understandably preoccupied with their feminine charms and so presumably fails to notice the water that spurts and sprays in all directions from the rocks below them. Otherwise he might be tempted to climb down one day and do something about it.

But it is the two fish women that live in the main pool at the base that are the real attraction of the fountain. They are sitting quietly at the edge this morning, their fishy tails sending gentle waves across the water. When they see him watching, they dive into the pool and complete a couple of circuits beneath the surface, blonde hair streaming out behind them. Then they pull themselves out, their bodies glistening with moisture, and they sit on the edge again, smiling and giggling. He knows from experience that if he approaches, they will be back in the water in an instant, so he stays where he is. If he is lucky, he might hear them sing, a sound so beautiful it makes his hair creep.

One of the women beckons him with her hand, inviting him to come closer. He checks the lobby behind him to be sure she had not meant the gesture for another man, but seeing him look around, she laughs and motions to him again.

He approaches her until he is near enough to see the individual droplets of water on her eyelashes and on the taut nipples; close enough to smell the wet stone of the pool basin and the evaporation inhibitor, and to feel the slight chill the liquid imparts to the air.

The fish woman pouts her lips at him playfully. ‘Do you want to kiss me?’ she asks him.

He keeps quite still, not daring to speak, expecting her to dive back into the water.

‘You’ll have to come closer,’ she suggests.

He imagines for a moment what it would be like to kiss her, feeling the dampness soak through his clothes as he holds her body against him, the smell of her wet hair in his nostrils.

‘What’s your name?’ she asks him when he does not move.

‘Charlie,’ he tells her.

She is studying him now, her head tilted to one side as she looks up through her long lashes.

‘You’re not afraid of me are you, Charlie?’ she teases.

Her voice is musical even in speech and he wonders if he can ask her to sing to him instead because she is unlikely to let him get close enough to touch her.

She raises her face to him, pouts her lips again and closes her eyes, and he has just begun to think he might really try to kiss her, when a security guard appears discreetly at his side, or as discreetly as the baton, body armour and conspicuous side arm allows.

'Step away from the pool, Sir,' the guard orders.

'Okay,' he tells the guard, 'I'm going.'

Charlie takes a step back, but the guard remains at his elbow, the baton in his ribs.

'Okay,' he says again, 'I'm going.'

The fish woman shrugs, waves her fingers at him sadly and slides back into the pool. Her companion laughs and joins her in the water.

He has been told they are copies of something called 'mermaids', although where women like these lived – if they ever did – he has been unable to find out.

'Step away,' the guard repeats, jabbing him again with the baton. 'If you have some business here it's time to get to it now.'

Reluctantly, he turns to go. He knows better than to give the guard an excuse to get rough. A man with a stick in his hand has a natural urge to hit something with it, and having done it once the man is apt to want to do it again.

So he walks and the guard says nothing more, but he does not leave Charlie's side until they reach the passenger tubes.

Getting in a car, Charlie states his destination and then waves his fingers at the guard, just as the fish woman had done to him. He regrets his action immediately, fearing what might happen if he meets the same guard on another occasion. The guard flushes and tries to jam his baton between the doors to stop them closing, but he is too late and the car speeds away.

Charlie tries to forget the guard and to think instead of the fish woman, but all he can see wherever he looks is his own reflection. The walls of the car are mirrored on all sides with a faintly bronze sheen. For a light-skinned man wealthy enough to live on Orbital C the multiple reflections will confirm what the occupant already knows: that he is tanned, healthy and successful. By contrast, his own reflections confirm that the security guard had been correct in his assumption that he has no right to linger anywhere on the orbital. Despite the bronzed mirrors he looks decidedly pale, unhealthy and badly dressed.

He closes his eyes and tries again to conjure up the sight of the fish woman's wet breasts, but his heart is not really in it. He is sorry though he did not hear either of the women sing. It really is the loveliest thing he has heard. When they stopped singing the last time he heard them, he stood for a long time letting the music slowly fade in his head, until another man hurrying across the lobby bumped into him and broke the spell.

It is said that the women of The Breakaway States could sing and that their song was so pure it could drive a man crazy, but men say lots of things. They also say that the women of The Breakaway States were the most beautiful ever known, the way men do when they get talking with that wistful, faraway look in their eyes. The legend has it that the men and women of The Breakaway States were quite unprepared for the future that dropped onto their country one morning out of a clear sky, but he has no idea if any of it is true. The women of The Breakaway States are long gone, no more than a memory, and perhaps not even that. Perhaps they are just a story men tell each other after an evening of drinking.

Most men will also swear that a Synthia is better than any biological woman, and when they do so Charlie always agrees with them. He would be stupid not to, given that he earns his living by selling them, but it is not only the prospect of commission which prompts his enthusiasm; he is genuinely proud of the product he represents because his company make the very best examples.

To the average man who knows no better, any femdroid is a 'Synthia' or a 'Syn', but the real Synthias, one of the early brand names, are still the best. 'The Original Syn' the company sometimes boasts in its brochures as though it is a joke of some kind, although if it is, the joke is lost on Charlie.

Synthia Corp makes a wide range of models. It even made the fish women in the fountain and in the early days the company produced a few male models too. They were not illegal then. Mostly, however, his business lies in selling the basic workhorses, the tried and trusted models, the ones you find in hotels and clubs and factory recreation rooms. They are more expensive than the domestic models, but they are reliable and virtually indestructible. They will give you a good time and can keep doing it again and again.

More exciting than the workhorse Synthias, however, are the high-spec models and the Limited-Edition Specials. They really are something he can enthuse about. There is a range and a model to satisfy every desire and it is a shame so few individuals can afford them, certainly not someone like him on the commission he earns, so they mostly sell to high-class clubs and to wealthy private collectors. Even so, Charlie can get that wistful faraway look when he imagines having one of them of his own.

Like most men, Charlie has never had sex with a biological woman. A quality biological in prime condition costs more than one of Synthia Corp's very top models. In addition, a biological will not stay in peak condition very long – whatever the growers claim about artificially slowed development after maturity – which further increases their value and scarcity. The popular assertion that Synthias are better than biological women is just a positive spin on reality and the result of clever marketing.

The car tells him he is approaching his destination, and it slows to a careful stop. It has a nice voice, not quite as arresting as that of the fish woman, but soft and feminine and something about it prompts him to thank it. Perhaps his reaction owes something to his encounter with the security guard. It has left him a little ruffled and discomposed, like the feeling of a small foreign object in his shoe, or the nagging worry he has his shirt on inside-out or his trousers unfastened.

'You're welcome,' the car says, a standard response, but he detects a faint note of surprise in its reply.

He steps out of the car, grateful not to be moving, and leaves the passenger tubes to enter a spacious private atrium. A nameplate announces that the apartment belongs to Sly Barrest, in case anyone should worry they had mistaken the number.

Marie is already at the door, the house Synthia, to greet the visitor. The car will have called ahead and alerted her to his imminent arrival, although he is expected, has been invited – 'summoned' might be more accurate, given their respective importance and status – summoned here by Sly himself.

'Hello, Sir,' Marie says. 'How nice to see you again.'

'It's nice to see *you* again,' he tells her truthfully.

Sly is a serious collector and has dozens of fantastic women, both femdroid and biological, any one of which would keep a discerning man satisfied, and more than a few who would make most men very happy for the rest of their natural. Sly's own tastes, as they say, do not run in that direction, but it does not stop him from having a good eye in choosing his specimens. Sly collects them in the way that men collect rare artefacts, for the pleasure of possession and for the look of envy in other men's eyes. Charlie thinks it is a waste, but he would never say so to the man's face.

Marie is not one of Sly's collector's items. She is for form's sake, for the benefit of guests like himself, but she is an expensive model and really quite lovely, and she must make a good impression on all the men who call. Sly's collector's pieces are safely stored and hidden from casual view, but Sly is quite generous in displaying Marie's charms. Apart from her silk slippers, Sly has her dressed in only a string of golden bells at her waist. A closer inspection reveals she also wears some bangles on her wrists and small decorations in her ears, but perhaps she has chosen these herself.

Marie shows him into the day room, although he has been here enough times to know the way.

'Will you please wait in here, Sir?' she says, as she always does. Up close, she has a lovely warm scent.

'"Charlie",' he tells her, as she begins to back away from him and out of the room. 'My name's "Charlie", remember?'

'Yes, Mister Charlie,' she says, nodding.

'Not "Mister" Charlie,' he tells her patiently, 'just "Charlie".'

She gives him a broad smile and a wink and backs out of the room.

It is a routine they repeat each time he comes. He knows that she remembers every encounter precisely; she is incapable of forgetting. It is a game, therefore, and perhaps she does something analogous with all the men who come. Sly has probably instructed her to do something of the kind while not allowing her to become too familiar, but it is a pleasant and probably harmless fantasy to think there is something more to the smile and the wink, even if she is another man's property, or perhaps because she is.

With Marie gone the room seems less bright and less alive. It is a beautiful room, however, and large. There are real works of art on the walls, some pieces of nice furniture and ancient carpets on the floor, but nothing can compete for attention with the window which occupies half of the far wall. You could buy a great many apartments like the one he owns over on the less desirable Orbital B for what a window like this one would cost. He goes over to it and looks at the view.

Standing in front of it, the window fills his entire field of vision, and the effect is dizzying. Although it is placed in the wall at right-angles to the orbital's centre of gravity, the window is currently looking directly down onto the surface of the planet below. It is a little like the moment when the shuttle separates from the orbital: he feels a moment of light-headedness, as though his head is moving away from his feet, along with the peculiar sensation in his insides that disturbingly, but not altogether unpleasantly, reaches all the way down to his groin. He breathes deeply and lifts his arms, letting himself fall in his imagination into the immensity of blue. As he hangs there, apparently in freefall, his eyes trace the contours of the landmasses and then the clouds, including the swirling pattern of a major storm out over the ocean.

He has never been down to the surface. He knows no one who has. You need to be very well connected to get a visa and stupendously wealthy or equally powerful to get a residency permit. But in the alternative future that he often fantasises about, the one in which he somehow makes lots of money, Orbital C is where he invariably chooses to live. Once he is wealthy, he will be able to go down to the surface from time to time to see it for himself, and of course he will have a window in his apartment just like this one.

Sly could perhaps afford to live on the surface, but it may be that he has other reasons for living where he does. Security is good on C, it is one of the features the orbital pushes in its promotional material, and for Sly that might be an important consideration. A man does not get to be as rich as Sly is without being quite ruthless, and that inevitably makes a man enemies.

At a small sound behind him he lets his arms fall to his side and turns to see his host.

'Charlie!' Sly greets him expansively, his own arms spread wide. 'Always a pleasure.'

Sly comes over to join him at the window, looking as tanned and as wealthy as ever.

'Great view, isn't it?' Sly says. 'I never tire of it myself.'

Sly looks a little soft and flabby up close, but he never lets that fool him. Sly's eyes are harder than the marble of the fountain in the lobby and just as cold, despite the smile and the courteous hospitality.

'Thank you for coming,' Sly says now, turning back from the view. 'Come over here and take the weight off.'

He follows and sits in the chair Sly offers him, facing the huge window.

'I've asked Marie to bring us something to drink,'

Sly tells him. 'Can she get you anything to eat?'

Charlie thanks his host but says not.

'Have you ever heard the fish women sing?' he asks. The question is in his mouth before he really thinks about it.

'The fish women…?' Sly replies vaguely.

'In the fountain,' Charlie explains, 'in the entrance lobby.'

'Oh … I see,' Sly says, catching on at last just as Marie comes in with their drinks.

'No, I can't say I have,' Sly decides after a moment.

Charlie watches Marie as she bends low to serve the drinks, making the little bells tinkle.

'Why?' Sly asks him over Marie's head, evidently thrown off guard by Charlie's question. 'Have they malfunctioned or something?'

That is the thing about Sly: the man has no soul.

'No,' he reassures his host. 'They're as lovely as ever.'

'Good,' Sly nods absently, clearly wondering now what Charlie is up to. 'Good.'

As Marie serves his drink, her back to Sly, she gives Charlie another wink. Does she feel under-valued by her present owner? Does she hope that he will steal her, recognising him as a man who would more fully appreciate her feminine qualities?

But letting his thoughts run in that direction plays too neatly into Sly's hands, a distraction just before they get down to business. He takes a swig of his drink. It is good, but he reminds himself he must keep a clear head.

He has no doubt that when he is alone Sly is served by his other house synthetic, the one with the altogether more androgynous physique and the complete and fully functioning male anatomy. That is Sly's business of course, but Charlie still finds it puzzling. He cannot really complain though; the purchase of Marie from Synthia Corp – which had been perfectly legal and accounted for – and of Jan, from a more discreet source – which had been very definitely illegal and clandestine – had both earned Charlie a nice commission.

'Sing, you say?' Sly asks suddenly, sipping his own drink, but evidently still pondering Charlie's question.

'Extraordinary!' Sly adds after a moment.

When Marie is satisfied they have everything they want, she gracefully bows from the room and closes the doors on them, and he knows the talk will now turn to business and whatever it is that is on Sly's mind.

2

'So, how's business?' Sly begins, as Charlie expected he would.

He shrugs. 'I'm keeping busy.'

'Demand still buoyant?'

'There's always plenty of interest.'

'But it's closing the deals that counts,' Sly says wryly.

Charlie agrees that it is.

'Sold anything special recently?' Sly asks, looking down and swilling the drink around in his glass. 'Anything particularly juicy?'

'I've just sold a nice Special Edition,' he admits, seeing as yet no reason to conceal the truth.

'Tasty?'

'I think she'll make the customer a happy man,' Charlie smiles.

'He hasn't taken delivery yet?' Sly asks.

'No, not yet: a few more days. Delivery is pretty quick.'

Both men sit for a moment in silence, each apparently contemplating the view afforded by the window.

'There's no danger of the Syn going missing I suppose, before the customer gets it?' Sly asks.

The question seems casual, but Charlie knows it is anything but that.

'I mean,' Sly shrugs when he gets no immediate answer, 'if she's that tasty, she's presumably a very desirable piece of merchandise.'

This question seems safe enough to answer, even if it is not the one Sly is really interested in.

'She's very desirable,' he agrees.

'Yeah, of course,' Sly says, 'but besides the obvious attraction, I mean she's presumably a very valuable item?'

Charlie nods.

'I know that I've paid quite a bit for the ones you've sold me!' Sly adds with what Charlie guesses is meant as a chuckle.

Charlie nods again, looking in Sly's direction.

'I imagine that a man wouldn't have any difficulty finding another buyer for this Special Edition,' Sly suggests, 'were it to come into his hands – unexpectedly as it were – rather than into those of the intended customer?'

Charlie takes another sip of his drink and tries to look inscrutable. Then he tells his host that Synthia Corp is very good at protecting its products.

'Yeah, so I believe,' Sly agrees slowly. 'Still, even so, I imagine that some Synthias must slip through the cracks? In my experience things have a habit of going missing occasionally, particularly valuable things.'

Charlie reminds himself that he must go easy on the drink. Sly has hardly touched his own, merely swilling it around in his glass.

'The tracking device is very effective,' he tells Sly evenly.

'Is it?'

'Yes, and…'

'And what?'

'And it can't be disabled.'

'Really?' Sly muses.

'Really.'

'Well, that's good to know,' Sly nods and there is a moment of silence between them again.

'So, according to Synthia Corp the tracking device can't be disabled,' Sly repeats slowly.

'Yes,' Charlie agrees.

'Can't be, or just that it would be difficult?'

'Can't be, not without deactivating the Synthia.'

'Not to doubt their technical expertise for a moment,' Sly counters, 'but they would say that though, wouldn't they?'

'That doesn't alter the fact that it can't be.'

Sly nods thoughtfully. Then he says, 'So… if for the sake of argument, someone took a fancy to Marie and sought to permanently deprive me of possession, she could be traced wherever she was, so that I could get her back?'

He wonders if Sly has read his thoughts or if he merely saw the way he looked at her just now.

Charlie nods. 'And as most Synthias still belong to the finance company that loaned the money for the purchase they've all got their own tracking services too.'

'Really?' Sly muses again.

Charlie nods again. He thinks it unlikely that any

of this is news to Sly.

'Of course,' Sly goes on after a moment, 'some enterprising young man – someone like yourself, for example – might see it as a challenge. Tell a man like that something is impossible, and he won't just say, "Okay". He'll say, "How long will it take?" or "What will it cost?"'

Charlie waits. There is no reason to say anything just at the moment.

'You do understand me?' Sly asks him, looking at Charlie directly for the first time.

He holds Sly's gaze but remains silent.

There is a discreet knock at the door and Marie enters. Charlie is unable to tell if this is by prearrangement or if Sly has some means of signalling to her.

'Get the man another drink, will you?' Sly instructs her.

'No, really, I'm fine…' Charlie protests.

'Don't listen to him,' Sly countermands good-humouredly. 'Give the man another drink.'

Marie nods and comes forward to take Charlie's glass.

'You see, Charlie,' Sly begins once she has left, 'I have a little problem and I thought – I hoped – you might be able to help.'

Charlie waits. There will be a time to react, when he has the full picture.

'In fact,' Sly goes on, 'I think we might both benefit.'

'I'm listening,' he confirms when Sly hesitates and seems to need some kind of response from him.

'Good. You see, there's this bloke. He runs a club over on Orbital B – your neck of the woods as it happens. Luc, his name is, Luc Vos. You know him?'

Charlie shakes his head. He has not heard of the man, although he probably should have.

'Well, I helped him overcome a couple of obstacles in the way of running this club of his, and the upshot is that he owes me a considerable sum, but thus far he hasn't shown much willing to pay me back. Says business isn't that good and he hasn't got the wherewithal.'

Sly pauses, but Charlie continues to wait, letting the man speak.

Sly says, '*Now* I hear, as a man that likes to be informed, he's just ordered a very expensive item from Synthia Corp, and not for the club, but for his own entertainment.'

Sly glances at him to check that he has understood. Then Sly continues, 'Moreover, it appears he didn't need finance. Would you believe it? He paid for it outright, just like that!'

'He didn't order it from me…' Charlie interrupts quietly.

'I know that,' Sly stops him quickly, holding up a hand, 'I reckon he knows that you and I do business and that's why he used a more "direct source" shall we say, trying to cover his tracks, although by rights you've got prior claim to the deal. Anyway, it leaves me with a problem. In fact, I should say it leaves both of us with a problem.'

So, this is it, the connection that links or is meant to link him to this Vos and whatever it is that Sly wants. He knows that Sly is applying subtle – or maybe not-so-subtle – pressure here. Whatever it is that Sly wants and whatever he is going to offer in the way of incentive, there will also be this: the suggestion of a common problem to be solved, so that it will not simply be whether he is hungry enough to accept the task Sly is going to offer him, but also whether he is man enough to deal with this personal slight.

Marie knocks again, waiting in the doorway with a small tray with his glass on it. Sly gestures impatiently for her to enter. As she bends to give Charlie his drink, one nipple lazily grazes the top of the glass while it is still on the tray. Her eyes meet Charlie's for a second and he is certain the action was deliberate.

'The way I see it,' Sly continues when Marie has left them alone again, 'is that by rights this Syn that Luc has ordered – and has no doubt been salivating over for weeks – has been bought with my money.'

Charlie resists the temptation to drink from his glass, even from the spot where Marie's nipple has wiped a trace of the misting from the rim.

'Do you see what I mean?' Sly asks him.

Charlie nods.

'Now, of course,' Sly continues, apparently confident he has Charlie's attention, 'Luc might meet with some horrible accident that means he'll never properly enjoy this new Syn of his, or any other Syn for that matter, but that would be a shame because I think on balance he's got a promising career ahead of him.'

Charlie waits, still unsure exactly where the conversation is going.

'Alternatively,' Sly continues after only the briefest of pauses, 'and this strikes me as the more clever option, delivery of the Syn might be interrupted or delayed.'

When it is obvious that Sly is waiting for something, Charlie nods again to show he is still listening.

'So that Luc has to *wait*,' Sly says now, 'before he takes possession of his new toy: wait until *after* I've received the money he owes me. Then if he really can't or won't pay, I'd have goods of his with which to offset my losses. You see what I mean?'

Charlie does see, and he nods again, although he is far from happy with the turn the conversation has taken. He sips from his glass, and then drinks more deeply.

'Of course,' Sly goes on, as if what he is proposing is perfectly reasonable, 'as far as Synthia Corp is concerned, she must be delivered safely to the customer, or they'll be liable to supply a replacement.'

Charlie opens his mouth but can think of nothing suitable to say so he closes it again.

'Which wouldn't exactly help us,' Sly concludes.

'No.'

Sly looks at him expectantly.

Charlie's thoughts are racing, struggling to see how the problems involved in what Sly is proposing might be overcome and wondering just what he is walking into.

'It needs to be done cleanly,' Sly says, 'but I think it ought to convey the right message to the priapic Vos.'

'Yes,' Charlie nods cautiously.

Then he says more positively, 'Yes, I think it will,' knowing that right here, with these words, he is stepping off the edge and without any idea how far the drop is.

'You'll look into it for me, then?' Sly asks him, adding, 'Unless you think it's too much for you?'

First the request, and now the challenge. Charlie swallows another generous mouthful of his drink.

'No,' he says again, with as much confidence as he can muster. 'I mean, okay.'

'Excellent,' Sly concludes, finally emptying his own glass in a single swallow. 'Excellent.'

Charlie sips at the remains of his drink, his mind still reeling. Perhaps this will be the turning point. It is the first time Sly has asked him to do anything like this. If he carries out this job successfully, he might find himself properly on the inside, trusted with further business and finally on his way to greater rewards. There has been no mention of what Sly will give him in return. He supposes he has to prove himself first, but he wishes the task had been different. He had not been untruthful when he told Sly the tracking cannot be disabled without deactivating and thus destroying the Synthia. He is used to talking up the difficulty of something in order to increase the price – of including some feature a customer wants perhaps – but he has not exaggerated the problems involved in this. He believes what he said.

Sly rises from his chair. 'You don't have to rush off, do you?' he asks him, signalling that the discussion is at an end, but also hinting at what is to follow.

'No,' Charlie confirms.

'It's just that I've got something I want to show you,' Sly says, 'something I think you'll appreciate.'

'You have a new addition to your collection?' Charlie guesses, trying for the moment to put the conversation they have just had to the back of his mind.

'You know I value your opinion,' Sly admits.

Although Sly allows few men to see his collection, he is nevertheless keen to show off his acquisitions to someone: to see confirmation in the eyes of another man that the women he possesses are the beautiful and desirable creatures he believes them to be. It is no doubt for this reason that Sly has shown him several of his collector's pieces, and all of them have proved to be exquisitely beautiful.

'I regret to say I had to pay rather more than I wanted to for this one,' Sly tells him confidentially. 'But… well, see for yourself.'

Charlie puts down his empty glass and rises to follow his host, already intrigued.

3

'What do you think?' Sly asks him, watching his face closely.

He says nothing. He had known she would be a beauty, they all are, but even so he is unprepared and somewhat caught off-guard by the sight of her.

'Where did you find her?' he asks eventually, not able to take his eyes from the woman.

'I'm sure you don't expect me to tell you that, Charlie!'

'No, I suppose not.'

'I have my sources. You know I'm always on the look out for something special – if you think she *is* something special…?'

'Oh, yes,' he agrees quickly, 'she's quite special.'

She stands in the centre of the room on a small rotating stand under the lights, completely naked except for two delicate bands at her wrists that hold her.

He continues to stare.

'She's… amazing,' he says after a while, shaking his head in disbelief.

'I'm glad you approve.'

'She's biological,' he tells Sly, 'she *has* to be. I mean, any man can see that.'

'Perhaps,' Sly admits, not giving anything away.

Charlie will occasionally say that a woman is biological even when he knows that she is a synthetic, in order to flatter the owner, especially in pursuit of a sale. There is no doubt in his mind in this case, however, even before he has taken a closer look.

He takes one of her hands. Its range of movement is limited at present by the restraining band at the wrist, but he waits for her to let it go limp and then he turns it softly as far as he can to examine the fingers and the nails and then the palm. Then he lets it go and puts a hand under her chin, raises her head a little, and examines her face. She *is* amazing. Her hair is brunette, long and thick, pulled back from the face in a single, magnificent plait that hangs down her back. Until this moment he has favoured blonde, but now he is ready to abandon this prejudice. No man could fail to be dazzled by this woman. In fact, he is more than a little intimidated by her and hardly dares look into her eyes – eyes that are a shade of vivid green – and he quite quickly moves down to her mouth. Her lips are truly exquisite, not coloured with make up, but delicate and naturally pink.

'Open!' he commands.

Her eyes flicker and her nostrils flare a little, but she opens her mouth and he looks at the perfect white teeth, at her tongue gently moist with saliva. Then he drops his hand to her breasts. They are not too large, but beautifully rounded and firm, just filling his hand as he cups one, just as he likes them. He brushes a nipple with his thumb and then steps back and does a circuit in the opposite direction to the rotation of the stand, his eyes never leaving the woman before him.

He realises then what it is that has been nagging at him from the moment he first saw her, and he whistles softly.

'She's not farmed, is she?' he says, hardly able to believe it, but also suddenly certain it is true.

For a moment Sly says nothing.

'I told you she was something special,' Sly reminds him after a moment.

'Farmed' means cloned and commercially produced, as all biological specimens are. That is expensive.

Not farmed means she is an original, naturally reared and one of a kind – unique – and therefore so rare as to be difficult to *begin* to put a price on, even for someone like Charlie. He has never seen a biological that is not farmed. He has only heard men talk about them, men who have never seen one either or known anyone else who has. Charlie doubted any really existed.

If she has a grower's mark – a model and a serial number – they will be on the inside of her left wrist, at present concealed by the restraining bands, but he doubts he would find anything there even if he were able to look.

His original question now returns to him with far greater force. *Where* has Sly found her? Certainly not through any legitimate dealer.

When Charlie was first told what natural rearing meant he thought he was being teased.

'You mean, all you have to do to get *more* women,' he said after it was explained to him, 'is to have sex with them?'

He knows now that all farmed biologicals are infertile. It is illegal to produce a woman capable of biological reproduction; although it seems unlikely anyone would try to do so. Basic economics rule the market, even if the law can be stretched.

He knows the chances of finding an unfarmed woman, let alone a truly exceptional specimen such as this, and in such perfect condition, are so slim as to be almost impossible to work out; as is the price Sly must have paid for her.

'I've never seen anything like her,' he says, truthfully. 'I can't imagine what she must be worth.'

'Yes, I'm quite pleased with her,' Sly admits.

'There's nothing,' Charlie repeats, shaking his head, 'nothing to begin to compare with this. Nothing.'

Sly seems amused. 'I'm glad you approve.'

Charlie gets down on one knee to get a better look at her legs and feet and to look up at her as she rotates. He is still wondering where Sly might have found her, and despite the evidence before him, he is still wondering if it is even possible that she is not a commercial clone. He is on one knee, gazing at her, but some sense makes him suddenly pull back and start to rise. The blow when it comes a fraction of a second later catches him on his shoulder therefore, rather than full in the face. He is thrown backwards with a powerful jolt before he fully realises what is happening.

'Yes, she's a little unpredictable,' Sly observes dryly as Charlie sits up and rubs his shoulder.

It was a powerful kick and quite a shock. But now he has his proof; no farmed biological – and certainly no femdroid – would ever do such a thing. It is impossible.

Charlie stands and looks at her again, but her back is toward them now, the muscles in her buttocks and legs relaxed as she rotates docilely on the stand once more. His shoulder hurts. Had the kick caught him in the face he is sure it would have done quite a lot of harm and he imagines himself giving her a good slap across those buttocks in repayment for the kick. Then the moment passes and he is once more simply in awe of her beauty and perfection. It might indeed be fun to slap those perfect buttocks, but not in anger, just a little playfully – but she would need to be tamed first.

'It's almost a pity…' Sly says quietly.

'A pity?'

'A pity that she must be frozen.'

Like all true collectors Sly wants his specimens to remain in the condition in which he has acquired them; that way they will not lose their value. With the femdroids it is fairly easy. For the biological specimens, despite the wonders of science, there is still really no alternative to suspended animation and Charlie knows all Sly's other biologicals are safely 'frozen' in this way.

'You can re-heat her from time to time,' Charlie suggests.

'Yeah, of course,' Sly admits, but they both know

he will never do so.

As she slowly turns towards them again on her stand the woman fixes him with a defiant stare, her hands clenched in tight fists below the restraints. She is impossibly beautiful, perfect in every respect, but it is her eyes – what he sees in them, as well as the disquieting way she looks at him – that finally holds his attention, and it unnerves and challenges him. There is something in those narrowed eyes, a ferocity and an intensity, he has never seen before and which he is sure could never be replicated in a synthetic, not even in the very best of Synthia Corp's quality models – although as a salesman he would never admit that to anyone.

It *is* a pity to freeze her, more than a pity, and he knows it is a sentiment Sly rarely has time for.

4

It is a couple of days before he makes it back to the small box he calls home. Cheryl greets him warmly as he enters the apartment.

'Charlie!' she calls, coming over to him at once, eyes wide with excitement.

She puts her arms around his neck and pulls him to her, then holds her face raised to him expectantly until he kisses her. When he has done so she puts her head on his shoulder and holds him tightly. She seems genuinely pleased to see him, but then she always does. He imagines it is part of her basic programming.

'You hungry, Charlie?' she asks, raising her head. 'You want me to make something for you?'

'No, I'm not hungry.'

'Okay. You want a drink?'

He is unsure what he wants, but a drink is the easiest to accept. 'Yes. Make it a big one.'

She goes into the tiny kitchen area and busies herself preparing his drink, happy to have something to do for him. She is not a new model, not as up to date as Marie, but she has been fully factory-reconditioned and as a salesman he got a good discount. She is therefore a much better model than he could have otherwise afforded.

'You're not wearing any clothes,' he points out when she brings him his drink. She has no need of clothes of course and she looks very nice without them. So far as he knows she never feels the cold and her skin is perfectly functional, but he likes her to wear something as it makes it more special when she is naked, and he has found that new outfits help to keep things fresh and exciting. He bought a little string of bells for her to wear, like the ones Marie wears, but he would not want her to wear them all the time. At present she is wearing nothing more than a pair of slippers.

'It is time for application of *Forever Young and Supple*,' she explains.

'Oh, I see.' He sits and takes a mouthful of his drink.

Cheryl uses all the products Synthia Corp recommend for the maintenance of their femdroids. 'Forever Young and Supple' is the special shine and preserver they sell to keep the Synthia skin just that: supple and in perfect condition. It has a great, sexy smell and Cheryl likes to put it on at least once a week. Sometimes she lets him apply it and rub it in for her.

'You just in time to help,' she says, waving the bottle at him invitingly.

'In a minute,' he tells her.

She looks disappointed at this lack of enthusiasm.

'I promise we won't miss any part of you,' he tells her.

'My eyes,' she reminds him seriously, 'you must

miss my eyes.'

'I know, you've told me often enough.'

'Men not remember.'

'This one remembers very well.'

'Okay, Charlie. When you finished your drink you will be more relaxed. Then Cheryl will make you forget *everything* except Cheryl.'

'That sounds good.'

It does too. She has learned how to read his moods well.

When he has finished the drink she does as she promised, seeking to make him forget the world beyond the apartment, and for a while she succeeds.

They start with the skin conditioner, Cheryl stretching and making appreciative noises as he rubs it in, but still careful to make sure he does it right and misses no part of her.

'You missed bit here, Charlie,' she admonishes him when he is already impatient to move on to the next stage. It is not just that she takes her maintenance seriously, she likes to tease him and to make him wait, and he knows that ultimately it is part of the fun and helps prevent him getting bored with her.

There are a few slight scuff marks on her skin the shine and preserver is unable to remove, but he thinks she worries about those more than he does, particularly at moments like these. He tells her they are a part of what makes her his Cheryl. She thinks about that for a while, clearly not sure what he means and so he kisses the marks for her.

Although he does not know if she ever really

sleeps, she lies quietly beside him, keeping him warm after they have finished making love. As he often says, it would be hard to ask for more. He is a lucky man.

The next morning he is feeling relaxed and quite content. He would not really swap Cheryl, he thinks, not even for one of the Limited Edition Specials, and his box is much too small for a threesome. He feels for her hand and holds it, grateful for the way she has made him forget about everything.

After a moment he turns over to kiss her. He looks into her dark eyes, but today all he sees is his own face reflected there. He kisses her quickly and turns away. Her eyes are quite realistic, and they look now as they have always looked, but this morning he sees Cheryl's eyes for what they really are: the eyes of a machine.

He gets up and makes himself some coffee.

'I could have got that for you,' Cheryl says, anxious as ever to look after him.

'I know,' he tells her. 'It's okay. You stay in bed.'

He has to think, as if he has not spent the last two days doing just that. He does not return to the bed, but sits on one of the uncomfortable so-called 'easy' chairs, wishing he has a window, even a small one, fighting a sense of claustrophobia and confinement while Cheryl watches him. He closes his eyes, recalling the view from Sly's window and wonders whether it is night or day on the surface below. He realises he has no idea what direction 'below' is. There is only the world in his head, a world that at present revolves endlessly around the same thoughts, around and around, like a woman on the display stand in Sly's apartment.

There are stories, a myth no doubt, a legend he has known for as long as he can remember. There are rumours and whispers that go about, always slightly different, yet essentially the same.

He sips his coffee and rests his head back against the grey plastic wall of the apartment.

Sometimes, when men tell the story, she has been captured and frozen and then lost. Sometimes it is her own people that had frozen her, to preserve her as the perfect example of their race or to save her till a better future comes along. Sometimes she is a daughter who has a daughter who has a daughter and so on, so that her descendants are around, somewhere, if you only know where to look. But most often she lies still frozen, forgotten or hidden in some private collection. Sometimes the stories have her carefully trained and taught in the arts and skills of love before she had been frozen, so that she is the most accomplished lover that ever lived. Sometimes she is still a virgin, untouched and pure, waiting for a man to claim her and to bring her to life.

When men tell the version in which she is a virgin, safely frozen somewhere, there is a different look in their eyes he thinks, still wistful and faraway, but it is not really sexual. It is as though – he knows it sounds silly – it is as though they want her, always young and always pure, to cradle them between her perfect breasts not as a lover, but as a mother. Perhaps that is not so silly really, for none of them has ever had a mother and can only imagine what it would have been like to have one.

Always though, the stories are about *her*, about the woman variously named Sabella, Isobel or Isabelle. Whatever name she is given, she is the Lost Princess, the only survivor of her kind, the last of the legendary women of The Breakaway States. Of course, they are just stories, just every man's wishful fantasy, but they persist.

Synthia Corp makes a range of Synthias called the Goddess range. Actually, they are on the Mark Six version now, and even she comes with a range of options, but if there was a *real*, genuine goddess, it would be Isabelle. She is the one the creators of every synthetic and biological woman consciously and unconsciously try to emulate; she is the mythical standard by which they are all to be judged; the most beautiful and the sexiest woman who ever lived. No one has ever actually named one of their femdroid models or range of biologicals after her. It would not make business sense. How could you improve on it? How could you have the Isabelle Mark Two? That is the point: you cannot improve on perfection.

So, it is not very likely that the biological Sly showed him is really *her*, really Isabelle, but – and it is this 'but' that really torments him – how likely is it that Sly would have found any unfarmed biological woman? Three days ago he would have said their existence was also just wishful fantasy.

'What is it, Charlie?' Cheryl asks him from the

bed. She is still watching him. She can tell there is something wrong.

'I'm just thinking, honey,' he tells her.

She pulls her long, blonde hair back and ties it up behind her head. 'You look worried,' she says.

The commercial models have detachable hair. They can be blonde one minute and dark the next. It is safer, and more practical in the harsh reality of the clubs, but it is less realistic. The domestic models like Cheryl have fixed hair. It was replaced when she was reconditioned and it is now full and luxurious, with a lovely sheen. Of course, there is a range of products to help keep it in good condition and Cheryl makes him buy them all.

'I'm just thinking,' he repeats. He ought to be thinking about what he has agreed to do for Sly, but for the moment Sly's new collector's item has driven everything else from his mind.

'Are you hungry, Charlie?'

'No,' he says automatically.

'You not eat last night,' she reminds him.

Actually, he is hungry and so he allows her to make him breakfast. Then she sits and watches him while he eats.

'What is mark on shoulder, Charlie?' she asks.

He had seen her looking at it the night before.

'It's nothing,' he tells her.

'It not nothing, Charlie,' she says. 'You damaged.'

'I'm not *damaged*!' he tells her angrily. 'I'm not a goddamned …,' but he leaves unfinished what he had been going to say.

'It's a bruise,' he says instead, adding more gently. 'It'll go.'

'How you get it?'

He says the first thing that comes into his head. 'In a fight,' he says.

'Men fight you?' she asks, eyes wide.

'No not me. Other men fight. I mean other men were fighting, and I had to stop them.'

When he had bought her they told him the reason her English is the way it is – heavily accented and broken – is that her previous owner, the one who had bought her from new, had specified some language other than English and that she has since learnt English for herself. Charlie had asked the technical guys at Synthia Corp if they can simply erase that now and give her normal English, but they told him it is not that simple. Once a Synthia has learnt a language it is embedded in her. Sure, they could teach her to speak perfect English, but it would take a while and it would cost a great deal.

Charlie had decided that it is not worth it. It will take him long enough to finish paying for her as it is and he is hardly buying her for her language skills. Actually, he now thinks her accent is cute and in a way quite sexy. It is just hard to know when she fails to understand something whether it is because of her English, or because she is just a femdroid.

'So you tough man, big hero?' she asks now, sounding pleased at the idea.

He shrugs.

'Yes, I think you big hero, Charlie,' she says brightly.

Then she grows serious again. ‘You must be careful, Charlie.’

It is good advice, the advice he has always given himself in the past, but he has been cut adrift now and he is struggling to find his bearings.

5

He wastes the next couple of days sniffing around rather than doing any lucrative work or thinking about what he has agreed to do for Sly. He looks obsessively at every advert and catalogue for biological women he comes across or can find anywhere, on any system, current and archived. He searches particularly through the models offered by the boutique growers, the ones that offer only very limited numbers of each of their ranges, editions that are often sold out long before the women themselves are ready for sale. He searches for anything that comes even remotely close to the woman Sly showed him. He is unsure whether he would be disappointed or relieved to see her face – or an identical one – looking back at him from a catalogue or advert. But he finds nothing that alters his original impression, or that challenges his conclusion, however incredible. The woman Sly showed him is a one-off, like no biological he has ever seen, and not a commercially produced clone.

He then spends hard-earned commission buying drinks for anyone who has time to spare, for any man who will talk to him. He is trying to find out if anyone has heard anything, if there is even the vaguest whisper about Sly's new acquisition or about where she might have come from. He is sure that someone must know something, but at the same time he also knows that if they do they are probably unlikely to say anything, unless they are either very stupid, or very drunk.

He also wants to talk about the stories that involve Isabelle. He no longer has any feeling for what is likely and what is merely fantasy. He really needs to get some kind of feedback about whether men think there is any truth or substance behind the myth. In this he has to tread even more carefully, forced to couch his inquiries in joking terms, obliged to make light of the idea in case anyone thinks he is serious for heaven's sake. Not surprisingly perhaps he draws a blank there too. His last conversation is probably the most depressing and perhaps the most predictable.

'What are you worried about?' Gel says when he introduces the subject.

Gel tends the bar in one of the clubs he sometimes frequents, sometimes in pursuit of business, sometimes just for a drink. Gel occasionally puts business his way in return for a backhander. He has also been known to forget to charge for a round of drinks, but he has been no help on either account today.

'Even if she does exist, there's only one of her, and there's…' Gel breaks off. The man has been drinking all afternoon at Charlie's expensc. Gel is not good with mathematical concepts like number or quantity at the best of times, and certainly not after a few drinks. 'You'll still be able to sell *lots* of Synthias,' Gel concludes.

'Anyway, the likes of you and me wouldn't get so much as a glimpse of her,' Lars observes, 'even if she was ever found. It would be kept so quiet you'd be able to hear a femdroid fart.'

Lars can be pedantic, admittedly, but he is an acknowledged expert at retro-customising a Synthia.

'Can you imagine what she'd be *worth*?' Gel says staring glassy eyed at them, clearly trying, but once again failing to do some sort of mental arithmetic.

'If you found her you'd never have to work again,' Lars nods.

'You could hire her out,' Gel agrees, 'just a few hours a week, and still make enough to live like a king for the rest of your natural.'

'It wouldn't be right,' Vern says suddenly.

Charlie had thought Vern was asleep or simply unconscious.

'How do you mean, "Not right"?' Gel challenges him.

'It wouldn't be right for one man to have her as his private. She ought to be the property of all mankind,' Vern declares expansively with the generosity of the inebriated, 'available so everyone can have her, at least once.'

Vern stood briefly in order to make his point. He collapses onto his stool again now, nearly falling off the back and almost sweeping a bowl of snacks off the bar as he flails his arms in an attempt to regain his balance.

'Yeah, right on, Vern!' Lars scoffs.

You have to look quite carefully to see that Lars has drunk as much as the rest of them. He is still sitting straight and upright, which means he would dwarf Vern even if Vern was not sprawled across the stool and the bar like a pair of discarded overalls.

Charlie watches Gel absently pick up a few spilled snacks from the surface of the bar and put them in his mouth. The bar is slick with drink, but Gel does not seem to notice, or perhaps he prefers the snacks a little damp.

Vern is clearly puzzled by Lars' reaction to his contribution to the conversation. With effort, Vern manages to bring both eyes together again and tries to focus them on Lars.

'What's wrong with that?' Vern asks, his words only a little slurred.

'Apart from the fact that the world simply doesn't work like that,' Lars tells him patiently, 'do you have *any* idea how many billions and billions of men there are, and how long she would have to live for every man to have just five minutes with her?'

Gel looks as though he is going to try to work it out, so Charlie decides to take his leave.

He turns from the bar and notices a group of Synthias owned by the club. There are no other customers at this time of the day so they are just sitting around. Until he had been able to afford Cheryl, all his sexual experiences had been with club-owned Synthias like these. It had been the only thing he had really wanted to spend his first wages on, but it had taken him several weeks to save enough and to work up sufficient courage to ask a Syn to take him into one of the club's recreation rooms. The sex itself had been all too brief, a result of a combination of too much anticipation and nerves. He had rather stupidly told the Synthia afterwards – probably as a result of his nervousness – that it was his first time and so she had insisted he stayed for a while. It would not have been what her owner wanted. He would have wanted her to kick him out and get another customer in because a commercial Synthia is a serious investment and she is there to make her owner a profit. But this one had held him and stroked his hair and told him how handsome and strong he was and eventually his desire and his strength had been rekindled, and the second time it had been much more sustained and more pleasurable. In all, the encounter was nothing like he had expected and when he thinks back to it now the experience has a kind of unreal quality, as though he might have merely imagined it. When he left the recreation room that day he had been pleased with himself, feeling he was a man at last.

He had spent much of the following week reliving the experience. As he left the club he had told himself that he would see a different Syn the following week, one who knew nothing of his over-eager and unsatisfactory first performance, but before he finally got to sleep that day he knew he wanted only to see Shirley – she had told him that was her name – and what had stayed with him throughout that week was not the sex itself, nor even his first explorations of a femdroid's body, but the way she had comforted and held him, had murmured reassuring words in his ear.

There had been no sign of her when he entered the club the next week, but he guessed she was with another client and he waited and resisted the invitations of the club's other Syns. Late in the evening, when he still had not spotted her he asked where she was, speaking first to the other femdroids and then, when they could give him no satisfactory answer, to the barman. He had not been able to understand what the barman told him, the shock was too great, so the barman had called the owner to come and speak to him.

'Shirl's gone, son,' the owner told him, not unkindly. 'Why don't you try Anita over there? If you think you're man enough!'

'But where's she gone?' Charlie asked stupidly, 'What's happened to her?'

'Traded her in,' the owner said simply, 'helped bring down the price of Anita. I expect Shirl's been deactivated and broken up by now; recycled. Getting a bit long in the tooth was Shirl.'

It is an expression he has never understood, but he knows it means 'getting old', although he does not understand why. A man's teeth do not grow longer as he gets older, and a Synthia's teeth naturally remain exactly the same as when installed. They can be replaced if they get damaged because men sometimes take a swing at a Syn when they are angry or frustrated.

He had been both disappointed and surprised to learn Shirley's fate. Unless you know what to look for it is hard to tell how old a Synthia is. Parts of her might degrade, there might be visible evidence of damage or wear and tear, but her looks do not change. She remains as young and as pretty as the day she was made, even if she does not possess all the features of a more recent model.

He had not tried Anita, not that evening. After the club's owner told him about Shirley he had been forced to leave in a hurry, afraid someone might see the disappointment he felt or the way his eyes were stupidly and stubbornly moist, although he knew it was ridiculous. His first experience with a Syn had been a little humiliating. He did not like to think how it would feel for one of them to think he had actually been crying because Shirley had been deactivated.

What strikes him now – once he has cleared from his mind the unsettling memory of that first time – is that the Synthias in the club appear to be talking to each other. They are not performing in any way; there is no one to perform for. He has seen some of the same femdroids performing here on previous occasions and normally he would find it hard to look away and concentrate on a conversation while they did so, but just now he doubts if they could do anything that would really distract him sufficiently.

They are not doing anything this evening; they are just sitting there, talking quietly to each other and passing the time – just as men would do. It is a simple observation, hardly worth noting, but just then it seems significant in some way. Unfortunately, he is unable to quite put his finger on what it is that might be important about it. He has had too many drinks.

It is not until he is outside the club that he finally realises what it is that struck him about the behaviour of the Synthias: they talk to each other. That is it: the Syns talk among themselves. Probably most of what they say to each other is pretty boring and predictable. He would be the first to admit that most of what men say to each other is also pretty boring and often very predictable, but they also share information, pass on ideas and spread gossip. Very little of it will ever be directly repeated to a Synthia, even if much of what men say to each other is about femdroids, as individuals and in general. But men speak quite freely in front of them. The Synthias must therefore overhear and observe a great deal, and it suddenly seems obvious to him that if they talk to each other they must also share the things they hear and observe.

Feeling increasingly the worse for wear, he heads back to his apartment. The two days might have been a waste of time for him, but Cheryl has been pleased to see him return each evening. When he is working he sometimes fails to return for several days.

'Charlie, you back again!'

'So it seems, honey.'

'You want a drink, or you want to eat now?' She of course is as fresh and energetic as always.

'Let's sit down,' he tells her, untangling himself from her embrace. 'I want to talk to you.'

'Oh.' She looks worried. 'There is problem? I do something wrong?'

'No, you not do anything wrong – I mean, you haven't done anything wrong. I want to ask you something.'

'What you want me to do for you?' she asks encouragingly, with an expression that reminds him of the fish woman in the fountain. She has her hair pinned up and she is wearing one of the shiny one-piece suits he bought her, with matching sandals on her feet. He thinks in passing that she looks very elegant and appealing.

'No need be shy with Cheryl,' she says when he just sits silently looking at her because he does not know how to begin.

'The other day a man showed me something,' he says at last, feeling foolish for trying, for even talking to a Synthia in this way.

Now she looks uncertain. 'What kind of something?'

'A woman, a new woman he had bought.'

'Oh.' She stops gazing at him and looks away.

'A biological woman,' he tells her.

'You like her?' she asks, her face still averted.

He says, 'Yes, she's very… very beautiful.'

'I see, and you want to change Cheryl now?'

'No!'

'What then?' she asks, looking at him again, but with a puzzled frown. 'You want me to be like her? To do something for you like her?'

'No, it's nothing like that.'

Cheryl seems to have exhausted her ideas about what he might want and she sighs now.

Then she says, 'This woman,' before he can start to explain, 'she made you happy, yes?'

'No… I just looked. I told you; the man had just bought her and he showed her to me.'

Cheryl shrugs. 'So why you tell your Cheryl about her?'

'It's… There's something different about her. I think she isn't a clone. I think she isn't 'farmed' like most… like every other biological woman I've ever seen.'

'Oh,' Cheryl says without expression.

He has no way of knowing whether she understands what he is saying. His head is starting to ache in a way that is increasingly hard to ignore. A second day spent drinking in bars is beginning to take its toll, and he knows the idea of talking to Cheryl had been stupid in the first place. How can a Synthia know anything, or even comprehend what he is talking about? But for some reason he cannot let it go. Perhaps it is only that he is desperate to talk to anyone who might listen, and because he knows he can never utter a word about what he has seen to another man.

So he asks her now, 'Do you understand what I mean?'

'Yes,' she nods, 'like Lost Princess.'

That startles him. 'You've heard about her?'

'Of course,' Cheryl says seriously, 'I think every man think about her. Especially when he is tired of Synthia and he wants a different woman.'

If he thought it was possible he would say that she looks unhappy. He is uninterested in that, however.

'Do you think she really exists?' he asks.

Cheryl frowns. Despite his preoccupation, his habitual responses are still functioning at some deeper and more instinctive level and he finds himself a little aroused by her, not only by her presence beside him or by her appealing smell, but also by the way they are talking like this.

'What you mean?' she asks him after a moment.

'I mean, do you think – do other Synthias think – there's a real Lost Princess, an Isabelle, somewhere?'

She shrugs. 'Men believe many things that aren't true or possible.'

'They do?'

She pulls a face. 'Men not logical like Synthia.'

'Okay, but do you think it's logical for me to think that the woman the man showed me recently could be her?'

'What this man say, her new owner?'

'Nothing, he wouldn't tell me anything.'

'You are certain she not a clone?'

He hesitates. 'Yes.'

'Then maybe she is Lost Princess.'

He shivers. Just to hear those words on another's lips, even a Syn's, makes his spine tingle.

Cheryl is watching him. 'Yes,' she warns, 'but "maybe" is not same as certain.'

'No,' he agrees, 'I know'

'First point,' Cheryl says, holding up a finger, 'If she just very good clone, then she cannot be Lost Princess.'

'No, that's obvious.'

'Second point,' she continues, producing another finger, 'if there are no not-farmed women in world then there can be no Lost Princess.'

When he has understood what she means he sighs. 'No.'

'But,' she says, 'if even one exist, maybe she is

Lost Princess.'

'Yes!'

'*Maybe*,' Cheryl repeats, waiting for him to show that he accepts this.

He nods.

'Or,' she says, holding up a third finger, 'maybe there is more than one not-farmed woman in world. Then if you find not-cloned woman, maybe she not Lost Princess even if she not farmed.'

He has to think about what she has said for a long moment before replying.

'Yes,' he nods at last, 'I think I understand that.'

'Good. You want me to get you drink or make something to eat now?' she asks him, but he is not ready to be diverted just yet.

'What would make it more likely that the woman I saw is the real Isabelle?'

Cheryl's look suggests she is concerned about him, but she seems to be thinking about his question.

'This man,' she says after a moment, 'this man who show you the woman, he very rich and powerful? Other men afraid of him?'

'Yes.'

She nods slowly. 'Then maybe she is real Lost Princess. If he is poor and not very powerful he is either very lucky man or she is just farmed, like other women, even if she is very beautiful.'

He has to admit that what she says makes sense, more sense than he has heard on the subject for the last couple of days. If the men he knows make less sense than a Synthia he probably needs to get out more and meet some new people.

'*Now* you want a drink or something to eat?'

He finds himself smiling. 'Nothing to drink, but I'm very hungry.'

Cheryl gets up and goes to the kitchen area.

'You know you must never, *ever*, speak to anyone about what I've told you?' he asks her, watching the way the one-piece suit covers but also reveals every part of her. 'No matter what happens, no matter who asks you.'

'Yes, of course, Charlie,' she says, doing a good impression of being offended. 'And who does Cheryl talk to?'

He shrugs. 'Other Synthias?'

She turns to look at him. 'Your Cheryl is not stupid like man, Charlie,' she says seriously. 'I know if woman you see is real Lost Princess it is *big* danger just to see her, just to know where she is.'

'What…?' he begins.

He was going to ask, 'What do you mean?' But he thinks he knows exactly what she means.

'Can you imagine what she'd be *worth*?' Gel had asked.

He can still recall the look of wonder on the man's face as he tried to grapple with the concept. What is it they say? *Out of the mouths of drunks and idiots…*

He has tried imagining what she might be worth, but has been unable to get anywhere close to a figure. Actually, a figure is impossible. Even if she is 'just' naturally reared, and not Isabelle, with her looks and in such condition she is virtually priceless. Yes, that makes her 'big danger' as well as impossibly beautiful.

He has been unable to think about anything else since he saw her, but now for the first time he feels the cold and harsh invasion of reality into his thoughts and with it comes a sudden understanding of the dangers involved in going down the route he has been fantasising about.

He sees out of the corner of his eye that Cheryl is watching him. When he looks at her she goes back to preparing his food and his mind inevitably slips back to her.

Where did Sly find her? And why did he show her to him? He can almost wish now that Sly had not done so; it would have been easier, much easier to simply continue with his life not knowing she existed. But now that he has, can he really wish that he has not seen her? The vision of her body and of her face haunts him, becoming more not less vivid with the passing hours, like the bruise she has given him on his shoulder.

He thinks he knows at least why Sly showed her to him. It is the same reason he has shown him the others: Sly has to show her to someone; he has to get another opinion; he has to see if his own evaluation is anywhere near the mark, and he can never show her to another collector. Not even Sly could risk that. If he has even half an idea what his new acquisition is he will know that to do so would be very stupid indeed. And Sly is not stupid; he will know that wars have been fought over much less.

He fails to sleep much that night, even after Cheryl's energetic and inventive ministrations have left him spent and exhausted. Then, as the hours when he should have been sleeping drain away, the business Sly wants him to 'look into' begins to vie for attention in his churning mind with his thoughts about Isabelle and the look that she gave him through her narrowed eyes.

He has wasted a couple of days. Now he wonders just how many hours are left before the Synthia will be delivered, or if it has been delivered already…

6

Mat works in Orbital B's dock area, in the office that handles incoming and outgoing freight. That makes him a useful contact, all the more useful because Mat's boss is rarely to be seen, leaving Mat to handle everything. Mat seems not to realise just how useful his position is, which makes it all the easier for others to exploit it, but perhaps Mat is simply happy to help his fellow men if it does not inconvenience him too much. Mat is about the same age as he is and more intelligent than some of the other men he knows, but on the surface at least, Mat appears content with his life and in Charlie's experience that is rare.

Figures and information about consignments and deliveries expected, completed or mysteriously 'mislaid' flash all over the three-dimensional displays that form the walls of Mat's office, but they have to compete with the other uses Mat has for the display. When Charlie arrives this morning about half of the space is occupied by a slowly changing sequence of slightly dreamy images of some new femdroid model, as well as other large and disturbingly graphic images of various features possessed by models in the range. He finds it hard to concentrate, compelled despite himself to keep looking around as the images steadily morph into new ones.

'How's it, Charlie?' Mat greets him amiably.

Mat is sitting back in his chair, feet propped up on an empty crate, looking relaxed and untroubled by any work that might need his attention.

'I'm good,' he tells Mat.

'Haven't seen you in a while.'

'Too much work, not enough business.'

'That so?'

Charlie looks at the pictures for a while. In general he prefers the more dreamy ones, showing the women's perfect smiles and lovely flowing hair, looking young and fantastically healthy while showing off a variety of outfits or none. At the moment, however, all women remind him of only one, and in comparison with her these femdroids, as clever and lovely as they are, seem to be merely toys.

'Anything in particular?' Mat asks him. 'Although naturally I'm always pleased to see you.'

'I'm just checking up on a delivery to a customer,' he says, turning back to Mat. 'Would you mind looking to see whether it's turned up yet or is expected soon?'

'Surely can,' Mat nods without moving from his chair.

'The customer is Luc Vos.'

'Delivery from Synthia Corp?'

'Yes, of course.'

'Just thought I'd ask,' Mat says. 'You might have been talking about some sideline of yours.'

'No, no. Like I say, it's just regular work.'

'The crate will be in the dock in seventeen hours and thirty three minutes,' Mat tells him.

Mat has not moved from his chair or so much as

glanced up at any of the displays that might contain this information.

'You need to check that?' Charlie asks him.

'Nope.'

'You're not kidding me?'

'Nope. You're the second guy has been down here this morning asking about the same delivery. I pulled the info earlier, that's how I know when she's expected.'

'Vos?' he guesses.

'I imagine so. Never seen the guy before, but he seemed keen enough to be the intended recipient. Sort of excited, if you know what I mean.'

'Well, he's ordered something quite special.'

'So he says.'

'Once the crate is here I'll need to take a look,' he tells Mat, 'just to make sure everything's okay.'

Mat looks at the changing display. It is unclear whether he is looking at the freight information or at the attractively posed femdroids and their various features, but Charlie is willing to bet it is not the lines of consignment numbers and the associated dates and times that have Mat's attention.

'Not supposed to let you do that,' Mat says after a moment, without altering his gaze.

When the displays are dimmed you can see through the walls into the cavernous body of the dock below, a huge space filled with crates of every size as well as conveyor belts, cranes, sleds and loaders that shift the freight around, often at alarming speeds. The walls are opaque now, but Charlie remembers his first visit to the floor of the dock; it had been both awe-inspiring and utterly terrifying.

'I'm sure you can stretch a point a little, Mat,' he says now, 'for a friend.'

'You know, Chas,' Mat says slowly, 'last time you were here asking about something similar, you happened to have a few containers of something that needed drinking.'

He has found that with Mat it is better to let him suggest the pay-off. That way he does not make the mistake of offering more than he needs to. Nobody calls him 'Chas', not twice anyway, and Mat should know that, but he lets it go this time.

'Now you mention it,' he tells Mat, 'I think there's another six or seven I've been trying to get rid of. I might as well give them to you if you'd like them.'

'They're good,' Mat concedes slowly. 'Question is, are they quite good enough on this occasion,' he says, adding, 'On their own, if you see what I mean.'

This is something new, but Charlie is prepared. 'Oh,' he says, sounding as disappointed and perplexed as he can. Then he sighs. 'Well, I do have...'

He lets it hang there and Mat's eyes flick away from the display for a second.

'A new advid, a YO,' he finishes.

'Wouldn't be that one you gave me about a year ago?' Mat queries.

'No. This one's just been released. Haven't even watched it myself yet.'

This is a lie on two accounts. The advid is an old one or he could not have obtained a copy, however devious he was. And he has already viewed it half a dozen times.

A 'YO' or a 'Your Eyes Only' is a special advid available only to Platinum customers, and only after they have deposited a sizeable sum with Synthia Corp, redeemable on their next purchase. Mat will never know if it is a new one or not and the copy will be time limited. Once it is uploaded to the system in the office Mat will have to watch it immediately and in one go or it will expire, and he hopes that this will ensure Mat is not tempted to check up on what he will be doing while he is down on the floor of the dock.

'Tomorrow morning,' Mat says after a moment, 'That'd be a good time to look her over. It'll be nice and quiet then, and she won't be delivered to the customer's local freight reception area till the afternoon.'

'Thanks, Mat. I'll come back tomorrow morning.'

He had worried at first that if Mat ever found out just what a pushover he is he might cease to be so useful. Now he thinks the man might have the right attitude. Mat has an easy life and does not appear to be consumed by a desire for more. Perhaps he could have learnt from Mat once, but it is too late now.

So, he has discovered that the Synthia has not yet been delivered. With that worry out of the way his next call has to be to see Lars.

Lars rents a space in the orbital's enterprise zone, a surprisingly spacious lock-up where he conducts his semi-legal business retro-customising femdroids, putting in features that were not installed as part of the original spec, either because it had been unavailable as an option or because the original customer had not wanted it; or simply because it is illegal.

When he touches the button on the communicator panel beside the door a voice barks a sharp 'Yeah?' but no visual appears on the tiny screen.

The panel has been broken for as long as Charlie can remember. He gives his name and there is a faint click and a green light indicates the door is now unlocked. Inside, in the centre of the space beyond the door, a Synthia is lying on her back on the workbench directly under the bright lights. Beyond the circle thrown by the lights the workshop is dark. Lars is wearing a magnivisor and has his head down between the femdroid's legs.

'What brings you down here?' Lars asks without looking up.

'It's good to see you too,' Charlie says, his gaze directed toward the femdroid on the workbench. She has a nice body. It is probably no better than Cheryl's, but the fact that it belongs to another Syn means his eye is instantly drawn to it. It does not seem to matter how many beautiful women a man sees, he always wants to look at one more.

'I'm pretty busy at the moment,' Lars tells him.

Apart from the femdroid there are several tools on the workbench and a couple of small boxes that contain spare parts, including one box with parts he thinks he recognises.

'Don't touch!' Lars says sharply without looking up. 'Don't touch anything.'

Lars is not only tall, he has a sort of chiselled,

almost machined look. The dark patches of stubble that cover the lower facets of his face, and which no amount of shaving seems to dispel, blend now into the deep shadows cast by the harsh work lights. It would be difficult to read his expression, even without the magnivisor.

Charlie planned to be casual about his question, but he can see such an approach is not going to be easy, not right off. So he tells Lars what he has just seen on his way over from Mat's office. He has not quite come to terms with it yet and he wants to talk about it anyway.

There had been some kind of an accident with one of the tube cars. When he got out of his own car at the nearest stop to Lars' workshop there had been security men and medics and a small crowd gathered around something lying on the floor, two somethings in fact, things that ought by right to have been just the one, but which lay separated now with clear floor between them. There had been a lot of blood too, and when he turned around he had seen that it extended over the outside of the tube itself and the outer doors he had just come through. It looked as though someone had been throwing buckets of it.

From the muttering, shocked but fascinated crowd he quickly learned what had happened. A man had apparently tripped and fallen as he was leaving one of the cars. There must have been a system failure of some sort because even though the man's body blocked both the outer and inner doors, they had closed, cutting the unfortunate man in half.

'Cut him clean in half,' a man repeated to Charlie

with a dazed expression.

A quick glance at the remains suggested it was more like a seventy-thirty divide, rather than an exact halving – sixty-forty at best – but the effect had been the same and Charlie had not corrected the man.

'Do you know who it was?' Lars asks him now.

Charlie had seen enough of the bloody face to recognise the man. 'Yeah,' he says. 'It was Tan Lee.'

'Him too?' Lars says.

'Him too, what?'

'One of them it's an accident, just maybe. Not very likely, but maybe. But both of them, it stinks rotten.'

'What do you mean,' he asks Lars, '"both of them"?'

'Nils. You didn't hear what happened to him earlier today?'

Charlie shakes his head. 'No.'

'He was getting on a shuttle, or getting off. Not sure which. Seems something went wrong and the system thought there was a problem with the connection between the shuttle and the dock, so the airlock closes, but something also went wrong with the airlock – another system failure – and Nils just happened to be the only one in it at the time.'

'He's dead?'

'Took a couple of hours to hose him off the inside of the lock is what I hear.'

Charlie shudders involuntarily at the idea, the images in his head all the more vivid after what he has just seen.

'What's the connection with Tan?' he asks Lars,

although he knows of at least one.

'Gel says he and Nils had been spreading it about a bit in the last couple of days, like they had done some really lucrative deal recently.'

That is a different connection from the one he had thought of, but then Lars adds, 'Tight as a femdroid's arse about what it was, but word has it that it had something to do with your pal, Sly.'

That is the connection that had immediately occurred to Charlie, and of course he also has an idea about what the particularly lucrative deal might have been, if it involved Sly. In the past, Nils and Tan have been known to supply Sly with women for his collection.

Charlie feels suddenly cold, as though the temperature control in the shop has stopped working.

'Really?' he says and his voice sounds a little too high and too tight in his head.

'Yeah, really,' Lars says. 'You want to watch your step, Charlie boy. I don't know whether they double crossed him, or if they just knew too much. Either way, Sly's rich and powerful enough to expend a couple of guys that are suddenly more useful dead than alive.'

Charlie says nothing and looks round instead at the shelves which line the walls. It is too dark beyond the lights over the bench to make out the details, but he can make out a couple of spare limbs.

'What's on your mind?' Lars asks when the silence has gone on too long.

'Nothing.'

Lars makes a noise that says he does not buy that.

'Where should a man go if he wanted to disable a Synthia's tracking device?' Charlie suddenly blurts.

Lars looks up at him for a second and then resumes whatever it is he is doing.

'Now why would you, of all people, want to do something like that?' Lars asks, his eyes fixed on whatever he is working on.

'I'm just saying, hypothetically, if a man were to ask.'

'Hypothetically then, I would answer such a question by saying that the man should go to Syn City.'

Charlie is intrigued, puzzled and disappointed in equal measure. Syn City is a luxury resort that occupies an entire orbital. It is incredibly expensive, but if the advertising is to be believed it is populated by armies of beautiful femdroids of every kind who are just waiting to ensure that a visitor has an unforgettable experience every minute of his stay.

'Why should he go there?'

'Because at least he will have a good time and he won't be wasting his money.'

It takes him a second to work out what Lars means. 'You're saying it can't be done?'

'What did they tell you when you did your training?' Lars asks him, looking up from his work again.

'That it can't be done.'

'There you are then.'

'But you hear stories…' Charlie persists.

Lars looks up again and then takes off the magnivisor. 'They're stories,' he says finally.

'It really can't be done?'

'No, and I'm still a little worried that you're even asking.'

'Thank you for your concern,' he tells Lars, 'but as I say, my inquiry is just hypothetical.'

'Yeah, and you have your answer. And that isn't hypothetical.'

Charlie squirms. This is not good news. He has been counting on Lars to help him out, even if Lars is only telling him what he already knew.

'I just can't believe there isn't a "but" that you're not telling me about,' he says.

Lars says dismissively, 'What you can and can't believe isn't my problem.'

Charlie says nothing and Lars works on again in silence. There is something straightforward and basically honest about Lars. It is true the man does not mind bending the rules and breaking the law, like most men, but every man knows the law is there for breaking; breaking it does not mean a man necessarily stops being essentially decent. He wonders what Lars would say if he told him what he really plans to do, besides stealing a Synthia. Lars would not want to know, of course. Just to know is dangerous, as Cheryl has warned him and as two recent fatal accidents seem to demonstrate, but he would have liked to be able to discuss it with Lars. His crazy idea is steadily eating away at his brain, dissolving all the familiar parameters of his world like some kind of corrosive fluid that got into him the moment Sly showed him his new acquisition.

Lars looks up at him a couple of times as though

Charlie's lingering presence bothers him and is interfering with his concentration. Finally, Lars sighs and puts down his magnivisor and the tool he has been using. Then he beckons his friend to follow him.

They go into a small room off the shop. It serves as an office, but there are more parts and tools in here as well. Once they are inside Lars reaches across and closes the door. Charlie assumes Lars is worried about the Synthia overhearing their conversation. The door has a transparent panel in it so whoever is in the office can still see whatever is going on in the workshop.

'Okay,' Lars says, keeping his voice low, 'first off, it's not really a tracking device. I mean, whatever Synthia Corp might like you to think, they can't tell where any Syn is at any moment. Sure, the system works well at short range, and they've got readers all over, but it's really more of an ID. It gives every model a unique serial number. They can probably log the ID of most Syns on an Orbital say, and get the system to flag up the ID of any particular Syn they're interested in.'

'So?'

'So, like they say, you can't disable the tracking device. You can't stop them reading the serial number, not without destroying the Syn.'

'But?'

Lars sighs. 'The guys at Synthia Corp aren't stupid. They've invested tons in making it foolproof.'

'Yeah, but what?'

Lars shrugs. 'But nothing's really foolproof, is it? They didn't think it would be possible, but you can change the serial ID if you know how.'

'Ah!' Charlie says after a moment. 'So she will still show up in a scan or to a reader, but…'

'But she shows up as a different Syn, yes.'

'That would do it,' Charlie says, relieved.

Lars is watching him with a slightly pitying expression.

'I mean,' Charlie adds hurriedly, 'if that's what a man wanted to do. Does Synthia Corp know about this?'

'What do you think?' Lars asks him.

'Yeah, they know about it.'

'They just haven't found a way to prevent it, yet. But they will. Meantime, you have to change the ID to a genuine one issued by Synthia Corp, but one that's no longer in current use, or it won't work.'

'You wouldn't be able to tell it's been done?' he asks Lars. 'I mean, it doesn't reduce the value of the Synthia?'

'You wouldn't be able to tell from a physical exam, only by cross-checking the serial number with the company's records.'

Lars steps back and turns in the small space to sit on the only seat, carefully steadying the chair which appears to have a castor as well as most of the padding missing.

'Sounds… straightforward,' Charlie suggests hopefully, perching on a crate, the only other surface available to sit on.

Lars twists around without having sat down. 'Sure,' he says, 'anyone could do it, but they'd probably end up destroying the Syn.'

'Okay,' Charlie says soothingly, 'I guess it's not that easy.'

Lars sits in the chair, not looking at him. After a pause Lars says, 'You go in through the Achilles port and establish a connection that way.'

'That stands for the "Ankle something" port,' Charlie offers, groping for the answer.

'I hope your knowledge of the rest of Synthia anatomy is better than that!' Lars scoffs. 'You should have paid more attention in class.'

'Okay, so I forget what it stands for.'

'Firstly, it's in the heel, not the ankle, and it's named after some bloke that died.'

'Really? Why's that?'

Lars shrugs. 'Beats me.'

'How did he die?' That seems like the obvious question.

Lars shrugs again. 'Happened a long time ago is all I know. He had something that made him practically invincible, some sort of body armour I guess, something that protected him from any sort of harm or weapon. Apart from his heel, for some reason. So that's how he died.'

'Why didn't it protect his heel?'

'How would I know? Maybe the armour was made on a Monday morning when everyone was still hung over. You know how it is. Anyway, he died and the Achilles port is named after him.'

He has to hand it to Lars, it is surprising the things his friend knows.

'I suppose you can see it as a weak spot in a Synthia,' Lars adds, 'because it allows you to connect straight into the sub-systems.'

'Right, so you can do that, can you?' Charlie asks.

'Nope.'

He sighs with frustration. There is so little time and they seem to be going around in circles. 'But you know someone who can, right?'

'You're sure about this?' Lars asks.

'Yes.'

'Really sure?'

'Yes!'

'Okay, tell him I sent you,' Lars says. 'But do you think you'll be able to remember his name and where to find him if I tell you?'

'Why not?'

'It's just that you seem a little on edge, anxious maybe, and you're clearly going crazy or you wouldn't even be asking me about doing it.'

'I'm just tired, overworked and under-rewarded. Nothing new in that. Listen, you say that you wouldn't be able to tell that the ID has been changed from a physical examination. But you could tell it's been changed?'

Lars nods. 'If you run a sub-system diagnostic it will show up, yes. That's why I hope you know what you're doing, because I sure wouldn't want those Synthia Corp security blokes up my arse. And when it all goes horribly wrong, you don't tell them I even had an idea who might have been able to help you. Understand?'

7

His home orbital has never aspired to the glitzy, luxurious opulence of its neighbouring orbital. It was designed as a home for ordinary men, not wealthy and successful men like Sly, and it has no pretentious fountains, parks or artificial beaches. Charlie had never seen a plant until he went over to C, or more water than can be contained by the basin in his sanitation cubicle.

Orbital B is smaller than Orbital C but has four times the number of inhabitants. It also has far fewer basic resources per capita. Even excluding the fountain and the artificial beach, Orbital C has almost three times as much water for each of its inhabitants as that available to the men on its more lowly neighbour. Every time you drink a glass of water on Orbital B you know that the same water has not only already been drunk by every other man on the orbital, it has also been a part of the water some other man has showered with and flushed through his waste evacuation unit only that morning. You just hope that the purification system is not one of the systems that is currently off line due to a fault of some kind. That is one of the reasons Charlie rarely drinks the stuff.

He is also convinced the air quality is better over

on C, that the oxygen levels are higher at the very least. He has been told this is not the case, that the oxygen levels are the same on both orbitals, but it does not mean that the air extraction and purification systems are equally efficient.

He has never been more conscious of the difference in air quality than he is this morning in the part of his home orbital where Lars has sent him. Here the air is foul tasting and he feels heavy and sluggish almost as soon as he gets out of the tube. There are faulty lights flashing in the overhead and pieces of litter lying underfoot. It has a neglected, forlorn look that makes his own neighbourhood seem almost respectable. He thinks a man could live his whole life on Orbital B and never have a reason to come down here.

He eventually finds the number of the apartment that Lars has given him, and since the intercom is obviously bust, he bangs on the door to get attention. After a moment it opens a little, but not enough so the inhabitant will have to part with any of his air.

'Lars sent me,' he says through the gap.

The door opens some more and he squeezes into the apartment beyond. Then he just stands there looking at the woman who has let him in.

After a moment there is a noise behind them and a man's voice says sharply, 'What can we do for you?'

Charlie turns. The speaker is a man wrinkled and stooped with age. No more ancient than your average planet, but very definitely no longer young.

'Lars sent me,' Charlie repeats uncertainly,

convinced now that he has come to the wrong place. 'Are you Hans?'

'That's right.'

Despite his age the man's eyes are still bright and they regard Charlie coolly.

'Lars suggested you might be able to help me.'

'Help with what exactly?'

'Disabling a Synthia's tracking device.'

'You've wasted your time, young man. It can't be done. Lars should know that. Good day to you.'

The old man starts to shuffle away, a little short of breath. Charlie knows how the man feels; the air quality down here can do that to a man whatever his age.

'Lars says you can change the serial ID,' he says to the man's retreating back.

Hans turns around and nods slowly. 'Whether or not that's possible, I have to ask why you would want to do that?'

'Why? What do you mean?'

'I know who you are,' Hans tells him. 'You're a company man. Normally I don't ask questions; a man's business is his own, after all. But that's normally. In this case I'm wondering more than a little about your motives.'

'You're worried this might be a set up?'

'Call it what you want. It's just that I know what Synthia Corp's security men are like and I don't want them after me.'

Charlie wonders what he can tell Hans, and he wishes men would stop going on about Synthia Corp's security arm. It is starting to make him nervous.

After a moment he says the first thing that comes into his head. 'Do you think there's any possibility that the stories about Isabelle are true? Do you think she really exists? That someone might find her one day?'

Hans looks at him for a moment. Then he lowers his shoulders and says, 'Why don't we sit down and have a drink.'

The old man gestures in the direction of some easy chairs. They look as old as Hans himself and Charlie sits gingerly in the one nearest him, but although it sinks a little under his weight it proves to be surprisingly comfortable. More comfortable than the ones he has in his own apartment.

The woman disappears out the back somewhere and returns after a moment with a bottle and three glasses. Charlie's immediate reaction is to look around for a third man, but then the woman joins them, settling slowly into another of the chairs, and he realises that one of the glasses is for her. He had forgotten that biological women eat and drink just like men.

Charlie finds himself looking at her again.

'This is Will,' Hans says, taking the bottle and the glasses from her.

'Will?'

'It's short for something longer, but I forget what now,' Hans explains.

In different circumstances, with a different woman – a Synthia certainly – Charlie would make a joke out of it and suggest "Willing", but that seems entirely inappropriate in this instance.

'Wilhelmina,' the woman says in a soft voice, following this with a little smile.

'I guess you already know my name,' Charlie says.

Hans nods and looks across at the woman. 'Charlie,' the old man tells her, as if she might be interested.

Then Hans hands them each a drink and says, 'I'm old fashioned enough to think that a man doesn't double cross someone he's enjoyed a drink with.'

'I'll drink to that,' Charlie offers.

'I'm old, but I'd like to end my days in peace, if possible,' Hans declares, and then they drink.

Whatever it is they are drinking it is new to Charlie and he examines the contents of his glass.

'This is also quite old,' Hans explains, holding up the bottle. 'You may be forgiven for not knowing it, young man, but some things get better as they get older.'

'It tastes pretty good to me,' Charlie agrees, but his gaze keeps returning to Will. When he first saw her he was unsure even that she was a woman. It is not that she is masculine, it is just that she is so…

'What's the matter?' Hans asks him suddenly, but not unkindly. 'You've never seen an old woman before?'

'No,' Charlie admits honestly. 'I haven't.'

Hans nods and Will gives Charlie another of those smiles, but less timidly this time. He thinks she must have been beautiful once. Her skin is wrinkled in the same way the old man's is, and her hair, which might have once been dark and glossy, is now almost white, tied up at the back of her head. Her hands are marked with brown spots and there are prominent veins showing on them. He tries to imagine what the rest of her must look like under her clothes, and then he wishes he had not done so.

'I can't tell you exactly how old she is,' Hans says, 'we don't know, but I've had her for…' He breaks off to ask, 'How long is it now, Will?'

'Almost forty-four years,' Will supplies.

'Of course, she wasn't young then, or not in her prime anyway, but then neither was I.'

Will smiles again at this and Charlie is unsure what to say.

'Do you know what they do with women – biological women, that is?' Hans asks him. 'When they're past their prime and their owner wants to trade them in or get another one?'

Charlie has no idea. A Synthia can be refurbished, or she will simply be broken up and her parts recycled. He shakes his head.

'They send them to the mining colonies. A biological is something of a novelty in those places and after a long shift and on the wrong side of a few drinks a miner isn't too particular.'

Charlie nods slowly, unable to think of a suitable reply.

'And how long do you think the women last once they get there?' Hans persists.

Charlie shrugs. 'Five years?' he guesses.

'Six months, buddy,' Hans corrects him, 'six months at the very most before they're worn out to the point of death or fatally injured. But what does it matter? They're cheap and expendable because no one wants them.'

Charlie has no idea what to think. It is clearly something Hans feels strongly about, but every man wants a woman who is young and beautiful. That is a given surely? He glances at Will and sees she is still smiling at him. Looking at her and at the expression in her eyes, he feels adrift and finds himself recalling Shirley, the Synthia he had been with that first time in the club, and of the way she had cradled his head in her lap and stroked his hair.

'So you're interested in Isabelle?' Hans asks him, changing the subject.

Charlie shrugs. 'Isn't every man a little curious at some time?'

'So you'd like to see her, if she is found?' Hans' eyes are very bright as they look at him. Maybe it is whatever they are drinking.

'Of course! Definitely.'

'It's always said she's a real beauty.'

Charlie nods. 'That's what they say. "Impossibly lovely",' he quotes.

'But supposing when they find her – assuming for the sake of argument she really exists – supposing she turns out to be already as old as Will here? How will you feel then?'

Charlie does not answer.

'Or don't you think she'll age?' Hans asks him. Then when he gets no answer Hans says, 'She's supposed to be a naturally reared woman, don't forget, not a commercial clone, so there's no reason why she won't age just as quickly as any man.'

'But if she's frozen…' Charlie suggests.

'Ah, yes, in all the stories she's frozen and still young and fresh. But what will happen when you reheat her, when you wake her up so that you can start to enjoy her youth and her beauty? What then, huh?'

Charlie thinks about the real Isabelle, the one he knows anyway – he is unable to think of her in any other terms. She is probably already safely stored as the jewel of Sly's collection would be, in suspended animation. It is not the fate Charlie wants for her, but how *will* he feel if and when she grows old, as Will has done: as she inevitably will if he succeeds with his plan?

It is hard to imagine his Isabelle as an old woman. Would he be happy to see her traded in once she is old, to see her shipped off to a mining colony somewhere to face the kind of end Hans has outlined? Of course not; it is unthinkable. He would go to great lengths to save her from such an end, but then she is a special case, unique and precious. No man who has seen her could think otherwise.

He realises with a start that Hans is asking him something.

'What did you say?' he asks the old man.

'I said: how do you know Will here isn't the real Isabelle?'

For a moment Han's question comes as a shock and he is unable to answer. Then an answer comes to him, one he very nearly blurts out.

'Because I've met the real Isabelle,' is what he

wants to say, but fortunately he realises the danger in time and stops himself.

The old man chuckles. 'Don't worry. I'm just messing with your fantasies. You go on imagining her as a young woman.'

Charlie gives a wry smile, acknowledging what Hans has said, and then empties his glass.

'Now, do you want me to top up your glass while you tell me what it is you want me to do for you?' Hans asks him more soberly. 'And then I'll tell you whether I can, and if I'm prepared to do it.'

8

The door beside the one to Mat's office provides access to a lift that goes straight down to the floor of the dock. Charlie has vivid memories of his first visit to the dock and in his mind the door is not simply a door; it is a portal from one dimension into another. On one side there is the familiar, man-sized, man-shaped world he inhabits, the one he has known his whole life. It is a space tailored more or less to suit a man's bodily and mental needs. On the other side lies a realm shaped by very different requirements and created on an entirely different scale. The first time he had been through this portal it had frankly terrified him.

'Yeah,' Mat had said with a grin, seeing his expression as they descended in the lift, 'it takes some getting used to.'

When Charlie steps into the lift now he likes it even less, but he is not going to let the old man see how he feels. The lift is really no more than a wire cage open on two sides – the one through which they have entered and the opposite one through which they will alight at the bottom – with only a single rail on the open sides to prevent passengers from tumbling out.

The lift swings slightly as he and the old man enter it and he reaches for the handrail on the opposite side, but the rail is attached at one end by a length of chain and at the other by a hook on a swivel and it moves away from him when he grips it, moves out over the abyss. Charlie pulls back sharply and knots the fingers of one hand through the mesh at the side of the lift instead. When Hans has attached the rail behind them he touches the button and they start the descent.

Mat has not offered to accompany them. He is clearly eager to view the advid. Nor has Mat asked who the old man is and he wonders whether Mat simply has little curiosity or if he just knows when not to ask questions.

Hans seems perfectly at ease in the lift and stands looking out over the rail while it begins to drop at an alarming pace. The view of the dock is breathtaking, provided one does not look down. The air is noticeably cooler as they descend, as though someone has left one of the giant airlocks open, but he knows that in reality, if that ever happened, the pressure of the air inside the orbital would push it out into the vacuum of space, carrying with it most of the inhabitants and everything not very securely fastened to the structure. After what he has learned from Lars he is unhappy about any reminder of the existence of airlocks or of the perilous vacuum that lies beyond them.

The dock itself is so huge the curved nature of the orbital's geometry is apparent, the floor climbing perceptibly towards the far wall, and the wall itself seems a little indistinct and less sharp than the things closer to them, as though it is only an illusion or some projection on a giant screen.

Mat said that it will be quiet this morning, but it is clearly a relative state of affairs. There are still crates of every size flying around on the conveyors and loaders or suspended under the giant cranes, or moving on the self-propelled sleds that appear to defy gravity. Lights flash and claxons blare deafeningly, although the operations in the dock are fully automated and apart from the two of them there appears to be no one to hear or see any of these warning signals. Sometimes it looks as though there must be a mid-air collision, but the crates and machinery continue their colossal three-dimensional ballet without incident.

As they near the bottom of the drop it looks for a moment as if the cage will simply smash onto the metal deck, but at the last moment it brakes and comes to rest with only a minor jolt. The descent in the lift has been so great that he expects to feel appreciably heavier as they step out. Down here they are further from the orbital's centre of rotation than most of the habitat levels and the effective gravity must therefore be greater, but perhaps the unsteadiness he feels in his knees is simply a result of the ride in the lift.

'I take it you know where you're going?' Hans asks him, raising his voice over the noise.

Charlie assures the old man he does, but with more confidence than he really feels. He is glad to be back on solid ground, but now he is aware of a new source of unease. He has spent his life in small, confined and defined spaces, with walls and ceilings almost – if not actually – within reach, and he feels uncomfortable in this huge cavern. It is not only an awareness of the masses moving above him that makes him choose to set off along the edge of the dock. He knows there is a ceiling up there somewhere, between the floor of the dock and the centre of the orbital, but it is far above them and he concentrates on looking ahead of him instead.

Somewhere out in this giant field, among the towers of stacked crates containing freight and supplies of every kind, there is a small one containing what they are after. Mat has given him a gadget that will guide them to it, but he stays close to the cliff-like walls for as long as he can, feeling that at any minute some giant mechanical hand will crash down onto them or scoop them up into the air. In theory, the gadget is supposed to protect them by signalling their position to the computer that controls the movement of the loaders moving around the floor and the overhead cranes and flying sleds, but it is hard to put his trust into something so small when the machinery in movement all around them is so huge and so powerful. This does not feel like a place for men; it is a field on which huge mechanical giants play as though squaring up to fight, feinting only at the very last minute just when they appear to be about to land a mortal blow. As mere men he and the old man could be crushed in an instant and the machinery would fail even to register the impact.

Eventually they are obliged to head out toward

the centre, and he is pleased the crate they want proves to be shielded by high stacks on all sides, stacks that not only provide the illusion of safety from the machinery, but which will also conceal what they are doing from casual observation or prying eyes.

Charlie checks the reading on the crate's panel and then produces his key. He had been given a 'spare' Synthia Corp crate key some years before by a man who worked in the shipping department. It had cost Charlie a generous backhander, but it has proved useful on more than one occasion, although he has never used it to do anything as criminal as what they are about to do.

He inserts the key into the slot beside the display panel, ignoring the desire to look around for Synthia Corp security men as he does so. The lock indicator stays red and Hans looks at him questioningly.

Charlie tries to remain calm while he withdraws the key, wipes it on his clothing and tries again. This time the lights cycle through orange to green and he relaxes a little. Then he touches a button, and the hinged lid opens gently to reveal what is inside.

'Nice,' Hans says softly, 'very nice.'

The Synthia lies on her back in a shaped and padded recess. She is wearing a white dress with a short ruffled skirt and a gauzy, sleeveless bodice. Her face is partly obscured by more of the white gauze. Her tanned, bare arms are folded in front of her and her skin looks fresh and firm and yet obviously supple, and so alive it is hard to believe it is not real. Her chest gently rises and falls as though she is breathing, a feature Cheryl does not possess. He has always thought it an unnecessary refinement, but he has to admit it is certainly effective. The Synthia holds a bouquet of white flowers in one of her hands. She is wearing white stockings and on her feet she has a pair of white satin shoes. Her blonde hair is luxurious and beautifully curled, with a small circlet of flowers on her head to match the ones she holds in her hand. Her breasts can just be made out under the gauzy swell of the bodice which is drawn tight at the waist, accentuating its narrowness. Her eyes are closed as though in sleep, and below her cute little nose her lips are a glossy, pink bow.

From inside the crate there comes a delicate fragrance, some perfume the Synthia is wearing, together with another smell, equally pleasant and alluring, a smell he thinks of as ‘newness’, the hard-to-pinpoint but unmistakable aroma of something freshly created and not yet exposed to everyday life.

‘Do you want me to get started?’ Hans asks when Charlie just stands there looking at her.

He had been imagining what it would be like to open the crate knowing the woman inside was intended for him and not this Luc whom he has never met and about whom he knows very little, and in his mind he had been about to bend forward and lift the white gauze out of the way and gently kiss the pink lips to bring the Synthia to life.

Perhaps it is the sound of the old man’s voice that triggers it, but just then the Synthia opens her eyes anyway, without any kiss. She blinks at them and even under the veil Charlie can see the irises are a startling shade of blue.

'Hello,' she says.

He finds his mouth is suddenly dry and he is unable to reply.

'Are you Luc?' the Synthia asks, looking directly at him.

He shakes his head. 'No,' he tells her.

'Luc is my new owner,' she tells him seriously. 'I'm waiting for him.'

'You'll meet him soon,' Hans assures her. 'We just need to check something.'

The Synthia is unable to turn her head very far, held as it is by the padding, but she seeks out the old man with her eyes.

'Okay,' she agrees without protest, once she has located the source of the voice.

'Can you do it while she's in the crate?' Charlie asks.

'Not really. If we can get her out perhaps she can sit on the top.'

Charlie would prefer to keep her in the crate for the moment, but he can see it is not really practical.

'Get out of the crate,' he says to the Synthia.

The Synthia blinks at him and frowns a little, but then she sits up.

Hans gives him a look and asks the Syn, 'What's your name, my dear?'

'What does it matter what her name is?' he asks the old man testily, but Hans ignores him.

'I'm Poppy,' the Syn tells Hans, 'I'm pleased to meet you.'

'I'm pleased to meet you too,' Hans says, 'and that's a pretty name you have.'

Poppy has focussed her attention on the old man now and Hans has all but pushed Charlie aside.

'Thank you,' Poppy says graciously, favouring Hans with a smile as pretty as her name.

'Would you mind getting out of the crate for a moment?' Hans asks her gently. 'Then when we've closed the lid I'd like you to sit on top of it.'

'What are you doing?' Charlie challenges him. 'We don't have time for you two to get acquainted.'

But Hans continues to ignore him, and Poppy gracefully stands inside the crate. Then Hans takes her hand and helps her to step up and out of it, as if the pair are acting a scene from a history dramvid, as if they have all the time in the world.

'You're really very lovely, my dear,' Hans tells her, looking her up and down.

'Thank you,' Poppy says again. 'I hope Luc thinks so too.'

'There's something wrong with him if he doesn't,' Hans assures her.

Now Poppy looks worried. 'Is there something wrong with him?' she asks, the frown once again furrowing her brow.

'Not that I know of,' Hans says, shaking his head slightly. 'If he ordered you, I'm sure he's a fine young man with everything in perfect working order.'

Charlie has never seen anyone behave in such a way with a Synthia and he shakes his own head in disbelief. Hans must see the gesture, but he ignores it.

'Can you close the lid,' Hans says, addressing him now, 'and then lift her up so that she's sitting on the top?'

Charlie hesitates, some unspoken words partly formed in his mouth, but he puts his hands around Poppy's waist and hoists her up onto the crate. The feel of the Synthia's narrow waist under his hands excites him.

Poppy sits now with her legs together over the side of the crate. 'Is this all right?' she asks Hans.

She sits very properly and demurely, her back perfectly straight, her hands in her lap, cradling the flowers.

'That's perfect,' Hans tells her, 'but I need to remove one of your shoes, if I may?'

Charlie is on edge and understandably nervous. He wants it done and finished with and he wants to get away from here, out of the dock and away from the scene of the crime, and something about the way the old man is speaking to the Syn feels at odds with their purpose. They came here to steal a Syn from her crate and Charlie had not stopped to consider what she would be like; or even that she would have a name.

'Can we just get on with it?' he says, unable to articulate what he is feeling even to himself, but Hans and Poppy ignore him.

'Sure. Go ahead,' Poppy tells Hans in answer to some question Charlie has not even heard the old man ask. She is looking down as Hans kneels and carefully eases the shoe over her heel.

'And you'll have to remove the stocking too,' Hans tells her now.

Charlie watches as Poppy lifts the hem of her dress and rolls down and then removes the white stocking; watches while Hans busies himself with some of the equipment from the little bag he has brought with him, and then as he begins to probe the back of Poppy's heel with a thin connector.

Charlie has nothing to do at this point. He cannot hurry the process along; he can only look on.

The connector is attached by a wire to a small device, a gizmo Hans has taken from the bag. It has the look of something Hans has built himself.

'How's it going?' he asks the old man after a moment.

'It is necessary to be a little patient,' Hans tells him, watching the screen on his box while fiddling with the connector.

'That doesn't bother you?' Hans asks, looking up at Poppy.

'No,' she says, shaking her head and making the blonde curls dance.

Charlie counts silently to himself, wondering if the old man is deliberately trying to annoy him.

The previous day Hans explained how the system works and what is involved in changing the serial number. It had sounded complicated and involved and he had been dismayed to learn that it could take up to an hour, and possibly two.

The first step, what Hans is presumably doing now, is to establish a connection, and then, because they do not have it, they will have to crack the Synthia's security code. When he asked how long this would take, Hans had merely shrugged.

'It'll take what it takes,' the old man said. 'We won't know until we start. Then there's no way to hurry it. We might get lucky, or we might cycle through a few billion possibilities before we crack it.'

Assuming this is achieved, Hans will then find and copy the existing serial ID on to an external device that will broadcast the serial number and respond to queries in a way that mimics the Synthia's own system. Only when that is working can they introduce the new number into the Synthia.

Hans has explained to him that the ID number is not contained in a single device within the Synthia but spread throughout its entire body. That is why you cannot simply disable it. The number is encoded onto millions of microscopic chips capable of replicating themselves, chips which float freely in the Synthia's system fluid. Hans will enter the new number – he said this is the tricky part – and this will then be transmitted to the chips, each of which will begin to synchronise with every other chip they encounter that also has the correct security code, and so the new number will spread until it has been taken up by the vast majority of chips in the Synthia's body. A few rogue chips might remain with the original number and some probably already have a slightly different number, but Hans said this is not unusual and not a problem. 'Not normally a problem' was his exact phrase.

Again, Charlie demanded, 'How long?' and again Hans had shrugged.

'Anything up to an hour,' had been the old man's distressingly vague reply.

Once the process is completed the Synthia will have a new serial number – or rather an old one, since it has to be a number already generated by the Synthia Corp computers.

'There,' Hans says now, after what has already seemed like an age. The display on the gizmo has come to life.

Poppy blinks her eyes and looks surprised.

'You can feel that?' Hans asks her.

Poppy nods. She looks a little anxious.

'It's nothing to worry about,' the old man assures her and picks up the small box and starts to scroll through the information on the screen, tapping it to move into various sub screens until he finds what he is looking for.

Poppy looks at Charlie now while Hans is working. Perhaps she is trying to distract herself from whatever Hans is doing. He supposes it is a little like having a shot or your blood pressure taken. She is studying him and he can almost feel her eyes on him as she runs them over his various features. He wishes again he had something to do.

When Hans seems to have found what he is after he puts the little box down and removes something else from the bag. It is only about a third of the size of the first device. Hans connects the two gadgets with another lead. Then he sits back, watching the screens.

'What are we waiting for now?' Charlie asks.

'We're waiting until it has cracked the security code.'

'Does it look as though it will take long?'

Hans merely shrugs. It is clearly a habit the old man has.

'It depends how good Synthia Corp's encryption

is these days,' Hans says after a moment.

Then Hans stands, apparently to relieve the tension in his back and legs.

'Can't you make it go any faster?' he asks the old man.

Hans shakes his head. 'No,' he says. 'I told you that yesterday.'

Hans stands with his hands on his back and looks at Poppy, examining her appearance.

'I don't think you need to worry, my dear,' Hans tells her once again, 'I'm sure you'll make your new owner very happy.'

'I hope so,' Poppy says seriously. 'I want to make a good impression on him.'

'Shouldn't you be doing something?' Charlie asks the old man when he can no longer keep silent.

'I am doing something,' Hans assures him. 'I'm waiting patiently.'

Finally, the device emits a small beep and Hans kneels beside it again and examines the screen.

'Yes?' Charlie asks eagerly.

'We're in,' Hans tells him.

'What now?'

'We copy the serial ID onto this little beacon here – along with the message you want it to display,' Hans tells him, indicating the item he holds in his hand, 'and then we enter our new ID into this young woman. Then save the changes and exit from the sub-system menu.'

That sounds reassuring, but then the old man adds, 'And then we wait to see what happens.'

At that moment a huge overhead crane

approaches them, displaying flashing yellow lights and emitting an ear-splitting warning horn as it passes over their heads. Suspended beneath it is something larger than Charlie's apartment. Poppy puts her hands to her ears and looks up at it with interest.

'Loud, isn't it?' Hans shouts to her.

'Yes, it is,' she agrees watching its progress with her hands still clamped to her ears.

'Are you doing this on purpose?' Charlie asks the old man as soon as the noise has died down sufficiently for him to make himself understood.

'Doing what, exactly?' Hans asks him levelly.

'Chatting to the Syn. All this, "How lovely to meet you," and "Isn't it a lovely day?" stuff, rather than doing what we came here to do. What I'm *paying you* to do.'

Hans takes his arm in a surprisingly firm grip and pushes him back from the crate some distance before Charlie can stop him.

'Listen, young man,' Hans says under his breath, 'we go to enormous lengths to create these things to be just like real people, with personalities, with desires and wants of their own; with the ability to feel pleasure and pain, with feelings. The least we can do is treat them like the people we designed them to be.'

'Are you trying to teach *me* about Synthias?' Charlie asks, narrowing his eyes and trying to shake the old man's hand from his arm.

Hans just looks at him for a moment. Then he says, 'No, I guess I'm trying to teach you how to treat women in general.'

Charlie finally shakes his arm free from the old

man's grip.

'What will you do if you really meet your fantasy woman,' Hans asks him, 'your Lost Princess?'

Charlie is breathing heavily, but the old man seems not to have exerted himself.

Receiving no reply, Hans answers his own question. 'You wouldn't have the first idea how to behave with her.' His words are scathing, but his tone is gentler now. 'I know it's probably not really your fault. I doubt anyone has ever taught you anything different.'

'Can we please just get on with it?' Charlie asks, rubbing his arm.

The old man shrugs and returns to Poppy and his equipment. Eventually, Hans removes the connector from Poppy's heel and announces. 'I'm done here.'

'That's it?'

Hans nods and then hands him a small device. 'As far as Synthia Corp's tracking is concerned this is now Poppy.'

'So we can put this in the crate?'

'It would be stupid to take it with us.'

'Okay, I'm just checking you're finished with it.'

'Would you like to step down now?' Hans asks, turning to Poppy.

'If you're finished with me,' she says demurely.

'I think I'm strong enough to help you down,' Hans tells her, 'even if I couldn't have lifted you up there.' Then he swings her down gently as if she were no weight at all.

With the Syn off the crate Charlie opens the lid again and puts the object Hans has given him into the recess of the crate where Poppy had been lying. He is careful not to touch the sensor that turns on the display. It would not be hard to hide the device between the padding and the exterior of the crate, but he wants Vos to find it and to activate the display. In fact, he needs Vos to remove it from the crate before it is sent back to Synthia Corp. Then he closes the lid and uses the key to lock it again, checking to see that the red light is once again illuminated.

'Okay, we can go now,' he announces.

'Like this?' Hans queries, gesturing at the Syn. 'I think she'll be a little conspicuous dressed like that.'

'Oh, yes,' Charlie agrees, ready to kick himself. 'I nearly forgot.'

He has no idea why, but almost all new femdroid models – and certainly every Synthia – is shipped in a variation of the white outfit Poppy is wearing, including the gauze over her face and the artificial flowers she is holding. No man he has ever met keeps his femdroid in this outfit once he has taken delivery, not unless he is a collector like Sly who wants to keep them just as they were sent out from the factory. But perhaps that is the point: delivering the femdroids in such an impractical and unusual costume no doubt boosts sales of clothing, and of course Synthia Corp produce a wide range of clothing designed specifically for their models. It makes good business sense and nobody would dress their Syn in the sort of clothes men wear.

He takes out the one-piece suit and sandals he has borrowed from Cheryl's closet. 'Put these on,' he says to the Syn.

Hans flashes him a look and so he adds, 'Please.'

'You want me to change my clothes?' Poppy asks, turning to Hans. She has apparently decided he is the more senior of the two men.

'Yes, please,' the old man tells her. 'We'll dress you again properly before you meet your new owner. It's just we don't want you to spoil that lovely dress and those shoes.'

She looks uncertain, but then she says, 'Okay,' and reaches behind herself to unzip the dress, but Hans is already there to help.

'Thank you,' she says.

Then the old man turns his back as the Synthia starts to step out of the dress. Charlie is looking forward to seeing Poppy without her clothes, but Hans pulls him around, muttering, 'Give her some privacy!'

'What?'

He is unable to believe what he is hearing, 'I'm not supposed to look?'

'She's not yours to ogle. How would you feel if you were changing?'

'I wouldn't mind if my Syn was looking.'

'Well, she's not yours and you're not the new owner she's been prepared for.'

Charlie allows himself to be tugged around so that he is looking the other way, feeling ridiculous, but without the energy to argue.

After a moment Poppy announces she is dressed and they turn back to look at her. She has removed the flowers from her hair and the gauze from her face. She still looks beautiful in the zip-fronted one piece and sandals, but Hans is right; she will not be nearly so conspicuous now. She just looks like any other classy femdroid. An expert like him would see immediately she is something special, but he has discovered that most of the time men do not really notice much beyond the obvious, not unless it is pointed out to them.

Hans puts the white dress and the shoes into the bag that Cheryl's clothes were in, together with the gauze that had been over her face. The Syn seems reluctant to part with the outfit, but the old man assures her they will not lose anything. Then they retraced their steps back to the lift with Poppy following.

At one point, Charlie looks behind him to make sure the other two are keeping up and he notices that Hans is holding the Syn's hand. She seems to be nervous about the movement all around and above her, but she seems interested too, pausing to stop and look up from time to time. Hans is talking to her, but Charlie cannot hear what the old man is saying.

He shrugs. He has heard that a man's brains can get a little soft in old age but has never seen it for himself until now.

When they step out of the lift Mat has another man with him in his office, a man Charlie does not recognise, and they are able to slip past without either of them noticing their passage. He had a story ready to give Mat if he had seen the Syn with them, but he is pleased not to have to use it. He knows it was feeble at best.

'This is where I take my leave of you,' Hans

announces once they reach the main transit level.

'It was lovely meeting you,' he says to the Syn. Then he wishes Charlie luck. 'And take care of Poppy,' he adds. 'Everything is still very new to her.'

Charlie grunts something noncommittal and the old man sets off, carrying his little bag of equipment under his arm. The Syn watches the old man go without expression and then she turns expectantly to Charlie, realising perhaps she is now in his care.

'Come on, this way,' he says to her and starts forward. Then, as an afterthought he turns to look at the retreating back of the old man.

He calls as loudly as he can without shouting, 'Thank you.'

He thinks he is too late and he will not be heard, but Hans turns, inclines his head and smiles. Then the old man gestures with his hand, half wave and half salute, before turning again and walking on.

9

‘What she doing here, Charlie?’ Cheryl asks him before they have even entered the apartment. ‘We not need her.’

She makes no attempt to give him the usual greeting. She simply stands in the doorway, blocking his way and staring at the other Syn.

He is too taken aback at first to reply.

‘Why you bring her here, Charlie?’ Cheryl repeats. ‘We not need her.’

‘Will you just let us in?’ he says angrily. He has had more than enough stress already this morning and he is in no mood for this bizarre behaviour from Cheryl. The last thing he wants is a scene in the corridor that will draw attention to his return and advertise the fact he has a new Synthia with him.

‘I’m not going to stand in my own doorway arguing with a Syn!’ he tells her and steps forward.

Cheryl moves aside and they go in and he thumps the touch pad to close the door behind them, not because it makes the door close any faster, but out of frustration and from sheer relief they have made it back to the apartment without incident.

'I am your Synthia, Charlie,' Cheryl tells him fiercely as soon as the door has closed, her face very close to his. 'You belong to me.'

'Damn it!' he snaps, turning on her. 'Why couldn't I at least get a Synthia that speaks English?'

He is worked up, but even in his agitation he is aware that this is something new. He has never known Cheryl like this; he had not even known she was capable of this kind of behaviour.

'I speak English,' Cheryl insists. 'I learn it myself.'

'Well, you didn't learn it very well, did you?' he tells her, knowing that this is unfair, but he needs to work off the pent up anxiety.

'You're my Synthia, and *you* belong to *me*,' he tells her, pointing at her and then thumping his own chest to emphasise his point.

'Yes,' she agrees. 'You are my man and you belong to me.'

'No!' He says sharply. 'You *don't* understand. You're a Synthia and women don't *own* anything. Only a man can own something, and so *you* belong to *me*.'

'That is what I say,' Cheryl says, but more quietly.

'Whatever,' he shrugs. The argument is over and she has backed down, but it is still a marvel to him that she had contradicted him at all. 'I guess you'll never understand properly,' he says in an effort to end the matter and to have the last word.

'I understand,' Cheryl tells him. 'But I not understand what she is doing here.' Cheryl points at the other Syn, at 'Poppy', as he will have to start thinking of her. Poppy is standing meekly just inside the door and waiting to be told what to do, as any good femdroid ought to do.

'Not that it's any of your business,' he says to Cheryl, 'but she's only here for a little while. Probably just for one night. Then she's going somewhere else.'

'You not keep her?'

'No, I not keep her, but if she doesn't stay here tonight she has to spend more time in her crate.'

He collapses into a chair, trying to ignore Cheryl and to start to get the details of what he is going to do straight in his mind.

Cheryl looks at him and then at Poppy. 'I remember crate,' she says quietly. 'It is better not to be in crate.'

Then she goes over to the other Synthia and examines her closely, feeling her hair and her skin and looking into her eyes.

'But why she here?' Cheryl repeats more quietly, turning back to him. 'What you do, Charlie?'

He does not answer her. He sees no reason to explain what he is up to, particularly when he is not at all sure he understands it himself.

'She is new Synthia,' Cheryl pronounces once she has looked Poppy over completely. 'Special Edition.'

She looks to him for confirmation, but he remains silent. Then she says, 'And I think she not delivered yet.'

He tries to ignore her, but he finds himself

watching the scene despite himself, but with detachment, as though it is something he is not involved in. His brain seems to be disengaged.

'But why is she wearing my clothes, Charlie?' Cheryl asks suddenly. Then she looks into the closet where her outfits are kept. What she sees, or perhaps does not see, confirms her suspicion.

'Why she is wearing my clothes, Charlie?' she repeats with something like indignation, her English growing even less reliable.

'She's borrowing them,' he tells her, his own irritation forcing him to speak again when he has resolved to stay silent.

'Cheryl is only Synthia and of course I not understand anything,' Cheryl says with considerable irony, 'but explain me why she not wearing own clothes.'

'She couldn't wear them.'

'Why?'

'Because she couldn't, okay?'

When he remains silent and unmoving, Cheryl turns to Poppy instead. 'Where are your clothes?' she asks.

'They're in this bag,' Poppy tells her, picking up the one he has dumped beside the door. 'The men asked me to change out of them. They gave me this to put on.'

Poppy pulls uncertainly at the one-piece suit.

'The men?' Cheryl queries.

Poppy looks at Charlie. Then she shrugs. 'They did not tell me their names.'

'This man,' Cheryl tells her, pointing, 'this man

is Charlie.'

'There was another man,' Poppy says, 'But neither of them are my new owner. They aren't the man I was expecting to see when the crate was opened.'

'So, you have clothes?' Cheryl asks her.

'Yes, but I don't want to get them messed up,' Poppy explains quietly.

Cheryl looks at her. 'Show me,' she says.

Poppy opens the bag and carefully brings out the white dress and holds it in front of her. 'I am supposed to be wearing this when I meet my new owner,' she says.

Cheryl looks at the dress. 'It is beautiful dress,' she agrees. 'You have shoes as well?'

'Yes.' Poppy holds the dress with one hand while she removes the white satin shoes from the bag. 'I had flowers too, but I don't know where they are now.'

Cheryl examines the shoes. 'Yes, they very lovely too. You have lost flowers?'

Poppy looks across at Charlie before answering. 'I don't know,' she says. 'But I don't have them now.'

'Where are flowers, Charlie?' Cheryl demands.

He shrugs. 'How should I know?'

'I think flowers are lost,' Cheryl says, and Poppy looks disappointed.

'No need worry,' Cheryl tells her, 'We make you look nice again when you go to meet your man.' Then she asks, 'So, what name do you have?'

Poppy tells her, repeating what she had said to

Hans down in the dock, 'I hope my new owner will be pleased with me.'

'You don't worry about that,' Cheryl assures her. 'If he is man, he will be very happy. I think new owner will be very happy man, even without flowers.'

'I hope so,' Poppy says seriously.

'We hang dress up while you here.' Cheryl takes the dress and puts it carefully on one of her hangers. 'You can put shoes in cupboard too.'

'Should I return your clothes now,' Poppy asks.

'It is best keep clothes on while man here,' Cheryl tells her with a glance at Charlie, 'and you always have to be careful not to damage your skin. Sometimes even *Forever Young and Supple* cannot make marks disappear.'

'Okay,' Poppy nods solemnly.

'But please, come with me,' Cheryl says now.

She takes Poppy's hand and leads her back to the door, opens it, and tells Poppy to go outside. Charlie realises at the last minute what is happening and snaps out of the semi-trance he has been in, leaping to his feet.

'What are you doing?' he cries as the door begins to slide closed with Poppy on the other side.

'We talk, Charlie,' Cheryl says.

'But she'll escape!'

'Escape?' Cheryl does not seem to understand the concept.

'I mean she'll wander off and get lost,' he says, annoyed again at Cheryl's inability to understand the simplest of concepts.

Cheryl looks surprised and opens the door again

to reveal Poppy standing exactly where she has been told to wait.

'See, she not go anywhere,' Cheryl says. Then speaking to Poppy, she adds, 'You not let any man take you away.'

'I will wait just here until you tell me to come back in,' Poppy assures her.

Cheryl closes the door. Then she says. 'What you do, Charlie?'

'It's complicated,' he tells her, feeling the unreality of the situation, not just the fact that he has embarked on a course of action that takes him to an entirely new level of law-breaking, but that he should be explaining himself to his Syn.

'It only complicated if you are man,' Cheryl tells him. 'Synthia is logical, not like men. Cheryl will understand.'

The morning has been so unusual that he wonders if he is dreaming. However, he can no longer discuss what he ought to do next with any of his friends. He can never breathe a word of it to another man. Lars and the old man already know too much as it is, so he shrugs and says, 'The man who ordered this Syn owes another man a great deal of money. This man, the one who is owed the money, he asked me to help him get the money back.'

'So you steal Synthia before she is delivered and you keep her until man pays?'

'No,' he says, 'I mean, yes,' surprised that she has understood so quickly. 'I'm just looking after her until the debt is paid,' he adds.

This last part is not entirely true. It is not even

vaguely true.

'You know about tracking of Synthia, Charlie,' Cheryl tells him seriously. 'Synthia Corp will know she is here in apartment, in *your* apartment, Charlie.'

He sighs. 'It's okay. We changed her ID. Synthia Corp will think she's still in the crate.'

'Why they think she in crate when she is outside apartment?'

He sighs. He knew it would be difficult to explain it to her.

'We left something in the crate with her ID on it,' he says patiently, 'The tracking will show her being delivered to the customer's local goods reception area. Once he acknowledges receipt and opens the crate it isn't Synthia Corp's problem anymore, but if anyone checks the tracking record they'll think she has been delivered.'

He does not try to explain the other part of it. It had taken him a while to understand it himself when Hans explained it to him, but when he had finally grasped what the old man was suggesting he liked the idea a lot. It is undeniably neat and it will no doubt make Vos livid when he discovers that he himself now shows up in the tracking log as the missing Syn.

Concealed in the sensor that activates the small display on the gadget they left in the bottom of the crate are a myriad of microscopic hypodermics. Once in contact with human skin they will inject dozens of self-replicating ID chips, just like the ones that circulate in a Synthia's system fluid. Hans told him that for the chips there will be no difference between the blood of a man and a Syn's system fluid. The chips will migrate into the bloodstream and once they have multiplied in sufficient quantities the chips will answer a query with the ID that Synthia Corp assigned to Poppy at her inception, and in a pattern very similar to that of a femdroid. Over time tiny errors will occur in the replication and without the femdroid's system code against which chips are regularly checked and inconsistencies eliminated, the ID will slowly become fragmented and distorted. But for the moment Vos will in one important detail have become the Syn he has been waiting for.

Cheryl is looking at him. She appears unconvinced by his assurances. 'Even if that possible, Charlie,' she says, 'customer will complain. I think this Synthia must be very expensive.'

'The man he owes money to also knows things about him, things he has done that he will want kept secret. He won't make a fuss. He can't.'

'Okay. This much I understand. I not like, but I understand. But why you bring her here, Charlie? Why you not hide her somewhere else?'

He hesitates. 'I want her to help me with something.'

Cheryl nods slowly. 'So,' she says after a moment, 'this is part of Lost Princess business?'

He sits down again, suddenly exhausted by the effort of it all and once again surprised she so quickly grasps the truth.

'What is plan, Charlie?' she asks him.

He says nothing. He just looks at her. He is thinking that it is unnecessary, surely, to make a femdroid quite so smart.

Cheryl repeats her question as if she thinks he has not heard her, so he tells her his plan, in so far as he has it worked out. It sounds wild to him even as he explains it, a crazy idea that only a mad man would take seriously. When he has finished Cheryl is silent for a moment.

Then she says, 'That is very bad plan, Charlie. Certain way to go to prison colony. Likely way to die. In fact, it is really quite stupid, Charlie.'

He sighs again, and rubs his hand over the back of his head. 'Well, I can refine the details, but right now it's all I've got.'

'But why you do this, Charlie?'

This is the thing he does not really understand himself. He just knows it is something he cannot let go of now that he has seen her.

'I just *have* to. All right?' he says. 'You won't understand. I don't really understand it myself.'

Cheryl looks at him. Then she says, more softly, 'I understand. You like small piece metal, Charlie. All men are small pieces metal and this Lost Princess, even if she is only fantasy, she *big* magnet. Very powerful magnet. So you not able to help yourself. Metal just drawn to magnet.' She shrugs. 'It not able argue.'

'But only certain kinds of metal,' he points out, just for the sake of finding fault with her analogy.

'Yes, Charlie, Cheryl know difference between ferrous and non-ferrous metal.'

This is a new surprise. 'You do?' he says.

He would have been forced to scratch around in the less frequently aired parts of his brain for that answer.

'Very early Synthias have ferrous metal chassis,' Cheryl tells him. 'It proved big mistake. Now Synthias not contain any ferrous metal. In fact, no metal anywhere.' She holds out her arms and even raises a leg and points to it as if demonstrating her point.

Now he has gone beyond surprise; he is astonished.

'How the hell do you know any of that?'

'I read material Synthia Corp give you,' she says. 'I watch the edvids they want you to look at.'

'But why the hell would you?'

The company had given him the edvids as part of his ongoing training. They are rather technical and boring and he has watched very few of them, and he certainly has not read most of the other material that he is supposed to have looked at, but he will not admit that his Syn knows anything he does not also know.

She shrugs. 'I am by myself lot of times' she says, 'and most of channels on screen only good for stupid men with no brain. I can use time to learn better English, but I have no one to talk with.'

'I talk to you,' he protests.

'Actually you not say very much, Charlie,' she tells him. 'You say only "Do this", "I'm hungry", "I not hungry", "Not now", "I want drink"…'

'Okay,' he stops her. 'That's enough!' Then he remembers Poppy.

He swears and leaps to his feet and punches the control for the door, certain that she will be gone, but as the door slides open it reveals the Synthia standing exactly where they left her.

Poppy smiles. 'Do you want me to come in now?' she asks sweetly.

'Yes,' he hisses, 'quickly!'

She steps into the apartment and he reaches past her and closes the door. She is very close to him now and he sees her as though for the first time, sees what ought to have been obvious to him from the moment he opened the crate. It is not just that he was anxious about what they were doing when they took her from the crate, although he had been acutely conscious of the consequences of their actions if they were discovered – either then or subsequently. Nor is it simply that the Synthia is not and never will be his. He is perfectly capable of appreciating the qualities of a woman of any sort whether or not he will ever have the opportunity to enjoy them. He had simply not wanted to become aware of her as an individual. He had not wanted to know anything about her that would distinguish her from any other examples of her kind. As he has just explained to Cheryl, he plans to use this Syn to help him with something, and ultimately to exchange her for something else, something that he hopes will help him with his plan, and he knows that he will find that much easier to do if she remains in his mind simply the Synthia that Vos ordered. It is for that reason he had not even wanted to know her name.

But now he looks at her properly, at the careful way she holds herself, as though conscious that someone will always be looking at her. He sees the perfection of her figure, revealed as it is by the clinging one-piece suit he has told her to wear: the shape of her breasts, the narrowness of her waist and the swell of her buttocks. He sees the long legs and her dainty, minutely detailed hands and feet. He takes in the exquisite beauty of her face, of her ears and her neck. He sees that she is lovely in every respect and that any man would desire her. It is what she has been created for after all, and yet at the same time there is – and here he struggles to find the right word – an *innocence* about her, a trusting lack of experience combined with an eagerness to please, to do the right thing. Hans has told him that everything is still new to her. He supposes that men will find that appealing too.

Who is he kidding? It *is* appealing, and he finds it painfully so. She will look up to a man, will rely on his superior intelligence and experience. She will be eager to learn from him as well as to please him.

He sighs.

She is looking at him now a little anxiously, her face able to convey even very subtle emotions. He can see from her expression that this is not the immediate future she expected, but he is a man and so she will adapt, and she will do whatever he tells her to do.

'She's just a Syn!' he tells himself, but this fails to provide the salve to his conscience that he hopes it will. He remembers, a little guiltily, that it is more or less what the club owner had said when he told him what had happened to Shirley.

'Cheryl will look after you,' he says, searching

for something to say.

Poppy is still looking at him, studying his face intently and standing very close to him. He guesses that she is programmed to become attuned to men's expressions, to learn to interpret them as well as what men say and what they do; to anticipate a man's wants and desires.

She has really quite amazing eyelashes he notices when her startlingly blue eyes blink and her pupils grow fractionally larger as she studies him, and all the time her chest rises and falls gently just a hand's length away from his own chest. He can feel the subtle warmth her body radiates. Some delicate fragrance that has been applied to her skin comes to him together with the warmth. The impression that here is a biological, breathing woman is hard to dispel, even this close, even though he knows perfectly well what she is. The illusion is as effective and as convincing as he has ever seen. She seems to be as real, and her effect on him as powerful as was that of the woman Sly showed him a few days ago. He is in danger of losing his bearings.

'Ask Cheryl to show you her fish,' he says, turning away and returning to his chair again.

He said the first thing that came into his head in an effort to break the spell. It was either that or he would have pulled her gently towards him and kissed that inviting mouth. And she would have let him of course. She would have been eager to learn just how it feels and how it should be done. She seemed to be waiting for him to do it, but it would have been the first time a man has kissed her, and Hans is right: she is not his Syn and that privilege is not his to claim. And Cheryl is watching too and for some reason that makes no real sense to him it would not feel right to do it in front of her.

He risks a glance at Cheryl now and then back at Poppy. The latter is exactly where he left her, just inside the door. He remembers the feel of her narrow waist in his hands as he had lifted her up onto the lid of the crate. She was not heavy, but solidly real and alive. He wonders how it would feel to put his arms around her and pull her close so that he can feel her body pressing into his own.

He looks back up at her face. A new frown creases her forehead.

'What sort of thing is a fish?' she asks carefully, clearly having failed to make any sense of what he said to her. She looks first to him, and then over to Cheryl when it appears that the man is not going to help her with this.

'I show you,' Cheryl says to Poppy, coming to life and taking charge again, much to his relief.

He bought Cheryl the fish as a present to mark the fact that it was a year since he took delivery of her. He felt a little foolish, but of course Cheryl was delighted, or she acted as if she was. It had been surprisingly hard to find something to give her. There were plenty of things on offer, but most of them were really just more toys for men, things they could use with their femdroids or their femdroids could use with them. He wanted something that was clearly just for her, something she could enjoy when he was absent, not something that would merely enhance his experience of her.

The fish in its transparent tank of water had intrigued him, and of course its association with the fish women in the fountain, who have just the same kind of tails, had clinched it for him, as well as the fact that it is supposed to be a genuine biological creature.

Cheryl takes the business of looking after the fish very seriously. She talks to it too, naming it what sounds to him like 'Riba', but he does not know whether the fish can hear or understand what she says, particularly when she speaks to it in that other language, the one he does not understand, the one her first owner had spoken.

The following year he bought her a plant in a container and she acted just as pleased, and to be fair she takes just as much care of that as she does of the fish. The plant has actually grown bigger since he gave it to her, although it does not seem to do anything else. The fish hangs motionless in its tank for much of the time, but it comes to the surface when Cheryl approaches and it nibbles at her fingers when it wants her to feed it.

Poppy seems entranced by the fish and listens intently as Cheryl tells her what is involved in caring for it. He sees Poppy's hand go toward the tank as though to tap on it and he knows what will happen. Cheryl did the same thing to him when he tried to tap on the glass. The speed of her reaction surprised him, as had the firmness of her grip as she took his arm and prevented his knuckles reaching the tank almost before his brain had instructed his hand to move in the first place. He allowed her to explain to him that the sound waves created by his tapping on the glass would travel through the water and hurt the fish, but he had only half-listened to what she told him. He had looked at her face and thought how lucky he was to own her. He found her action in grabbing his arm exciting; her protective behaviour towards the fish, the gift he had given her, had been a turn-on.

Now it is Poppy's face he looks at as she gazes intently at the fish, glancing back at Cheryl as she explains about the shock waves in the water. Poppy is clearly anxious to learn and to absorb everything she can, and he finds that a turn-on too.

'I'm going out,' he announces, making towards the door. He wants to get on with his plan, but he has work to do, real work that is. He has appointments with customers and potential customers he made before his visit to Sly, before his world changed shape. The meetings are a nuisance now he has something else he wants to do, but he figures he ought to keep the appointments and to make it appear he is simply carrying on with his life, that it is business as usual. And a sale would not hurt; he could do with the commission.

Tomorrow, he promises himself, tomorrow he will set things in motion.

Cheryl looks up. 'You not want food before you go, Charlie?'

'I'll get something,' he tells her.

Cheryl's face is not as expressive as Poppy's, but he knows how to read it and he sees she looks worried. It is her job to feed him after all.

'You sure, Charlie?' she asks coming over to him.

'Yes,' he says. Then they just stand there looking at each other for a moment. It seems she wants something from him, which is ridiculous. She is there for his benefit and surely it ought to be the other way around.

'I'll be back later,' he says at last. 'You can give me food then.'

'Okay, Charlie.'

'Your job at the moment is to look after Poppy,' he tells her.

'Okay, Charlie,' she repeats, before adding, 'You be careful, Charlie.'

Then she comes towards him and gives him a kiss, tentatively at first, but then more confidently.

He feels better suddenly, as though the world is the right way up again, and feeling reassured, he touches the door control and goes out.

10

When he wakes the next morning, he finds himself pressed uncomfortably close to the wall, his nose almost touching the shiny surface which is now glistening with moisture from his exhaled breath. He half rises and half turns in order to see why Cheryl should be taking up so much of the bed, when she is normally careful to leave him a generous half of the available space. This morning he finds that she and Poppy are sharing the other two thirds of the bed. The Synthias are lying facing each other, their arms entangled and they both appear to be sleeping, Poppy's chest rising and falling very gently, just enough for him to make out in the dim night-lighting. He sees that by contrast Cheryl is perfectly still and he experiences a moment of panic, alarmed that something has happened to her before he remembers that she has never possessed that feature. He has never missed it or even thought about it before, but now she looks lifeless in her motionless state, whereas Poppy by comparison appears to be merely at rest and peaceful. Looking at what he can see of Poppy's face he envies the man who will wake up and see it at the start of each new day.

Cheryl lifts her head and looks at him, her eyes

instantly focused.

Seeing that he is awake she smiles and says, 'You want me to get up and make coffee, Charlie?'

'In a moment,' he tells her.

He slides off the end of the bed to attend to a biological function that does not trouble either of the femdroids. While he is in the tiny cubicle he showers and shaves, examining his face thoughtfully in the small mirror.

The previous evening he arrived back at his box to find Cheryl and Poppy trying on clothes and discussing the merits of various care products designed to maintain Synthias. They were chatting easily with one another and he felt a little jealous. It seemed to him they shared something he could not, but they had quickly broken off what they were doing and given him their full attention, Cheryl eager to demonstrate her abilities in making drinks and preparing food for her man, while Poppy had been just as eager to observe and to learn, and to help when allowed to do so. It proved to be an enjoyable evening.

There had been an awkward moment when he wanted to retire and the inevitable question of who would sleep where had led to another question, put to him by Cheryl, about whether he wanted sex and with which if not both of them. He had resolved the matter by declaring himself to be very tired, just wanting to sleep, and there being no other space available the three of them shared the bed. It might have been by chance that Cheryl ended up between him and Poppy, but he thinks it was more than that, but he was relieved. In reality he had not felt particularly sleepy and it was not only worry and the endless planning and scheming that his mind seemed unable to stop that kept him awake. He even considered going into the cubicle and taking matters into his own hands under the guise of answering a different kind of biological urge, but eventually sleep had come, a sleep filled with all kinds of vivid and disturbing dreams. Perhaps the one that involved him being confined in the padded recess of a crate designed for a Synthia owed something to his cramped position on the bed.

When he emerges from the cubicle the day-lights are on and both the Synthias are in the kitchen alcove preparing coffee and breakfast for him. Cheryl seems to have got over her initial jealousy and the two of them appear to be getting on well together. As he sits at his small table waiting for them to serve his breakfast he wonders for a moment if he is doing the right thing. Not so long ago he would have considered his present situation an impossible and unattainable fantasy.

After he has eaten he moves to one of his two easy chairs while Cheryl tidies away the remains of his breakfast. Poppy does not seem to be involved in this and she stands for a moment as though unsure what to do. She is wearing a lacy blue top with short sleeves that he bought for Cheryl some time ago. He has not seen it for a while. Poppy has teamed it with a short but full-cut, rusty red skirt, below which her legs look fabulous. The legs end in short white socks and a pair of sandals. He does not know if she chose the ensemble herself or if Cheryl helped her. He thinks it may have been Poppy's own idea, for the look is different from any that Cheryl has ever put together. The top clings to Poppy's figure, emphasising her breasts and her slim waist. It makes her look soft and innocent and incredibly sexy at the same time.

As he watches her she runs her fingertips over the edge of the table in a distracted manner and then drifts over towards him, apparently intending to pass by so close that the skirt will brush against his face as she does so. He grabs her wrist when she draws near and she stops and turns to look at him. He holds her hand in his own, examining its delicate and finely detailed fingers while she looks down at him through her long lashes. He cannot read her expression.

He turns the hand over, marvelling at the fine lines on her palms and the underside of her fingers, comparing them with the markings on his own hands. He gently bends one of her fingers, noting the way it moves and the way the skin creases. She puts the tip of her forefinger to the end of her thumb and then does the same with the tips of each of the other fingers in turn before reversing the sequence. Perhaps she wants to show him what her hand can do or perhaps she is simply entranced by her own dexterity, as if she is still getting used to her body and what it can do. She sees him looking and, a little shyly, she lets her hand go limp again in his own.

The skin on her palms is different to that on the backs of her hands. In the places where he has hairs on his arms and on the backs of his hand and fingers, her skin has an almost downy texture, suggesting fine hairs that he cannot see and which are almost certainly not there. He runs his finger lightly up the outside of her arm and then down on the inside, noting the changing feel of it. Poppy follows his actions with her eyes, eyes that grow larger as his finger rises higher up her arm.

Without any warning she sits on his lap, at right angles to him, her legs swinging very gently for a second against the side of his right shin. Then she turns and studies his face while he in turn looks at her. She shifts her position slightly, as though seeking a more comfortable pose, but perhaps she knows what effect this has on him for he sees the trace of an amused smile on her lips.

Now that she is sitting on him with so much of her legs in view below the short skirt it is the skin on her thighs that captures his attention. He puts a hand on her knee and she twitches slightly at his touch, as though it tickles, but she watches his hand with the same amused expression. Again, the skin on her thighs seems softer and smoother on the insides. He runs his hand gently up the inside of her thigh, watching as her eyes widen even further, but he stops when he reaches the hem of her short skirt. He is afraid to go beyond this limit and he knows that no good can come of doing so.

He is minutely conscious of the feel of her on his legs and in his lap, of her weight and supple solidity. She is looking at him with that same amused expression, but she is waiting too, waiting to see what will happen next, her chest almost but not quite stilled, still rising and falling, but so fractionally that he has to watch for it.

'What are you wearing under the skirt?' he asks her, knowing that he should not, that this is dangerous, but he is curious. She arches her eyebrows and then lifts the skirt to show him. She is wearing a pair of white panties with a tiny bow in the front at the waist. They must be hers, for he has never bought anything like that for Cheryl, but he wonders now why not. Not hers, he tells himself; the panties, like the wearer, belong by rights to Vos or perhaps to Synthia Corp.

'Shall I take them off? Poppy asks him quietly. She means the panties and he realises he has simply been staring at them.

'No,' he says, more loudly and more forcefully than he intended, but she does not appear upset.

'No,' he repeats more gently. 'Thank you, but I have to go and do some work now.'

'Do you want me to get off your lap?'

He tells her he does, and they both stand.

Cheryl has finished her work in the kitchen, and he sees that she is watching them. He thinks her eyes flick to his crotch, noticing with her acute vision the increased tension on the fabric of his trousers at that point.

'I have to go,' he tells her.

She makes no reply, but he finds that he cannot just leave, not like that, not without exchanging some words with her. It is rather like it had been the day before when he had made to go. He wants to say something, yet he has no idea what to say or even what he wants from her. But he does want something, even if he cannot be sure what it is.

He approaches and she watches him with her eyes, but otherwise remains motionless. He wonders what she is thinking and what it is like to be her. Her eyes do not only register his presence, she is looking at him, she who probably knows him better than any other being ever has. Her eyes are those of something other, not quite those of a human, but there is a thrill in being observed by them, because she is other; because she is not him, because she is different and separate, and he might never fully understand her. It is true they are the eyes of a machine, but she is much more than that, much more perhaps than he has hitherto understood.

She is his property – owning her costs a fair percentage of his monthly commission, but he is – has made himself – vulnerable to her, both emotionally and physically, sharing his apartment and his bed with her. There are all kinds of safety features that mean she will never harm him, but she is an autonomous and powerful thing.

He puts his face near to hers and kisses her gently on the cheek. She looks surprised. It is not what she expected. It is not something he has done before, and he realises at last what it is he wants. He wants some assurance that the intrusion of Poppy into their hitherto simple arrangement has not changed things. He does not want it to change the way he feels about her, or the way she behaves towards him.

Something has changed in him though, and he knows it, and it is not just Poppy. He is still haunted by those narrowed eyes and the defiant look they contained. He knows he dreamed of her again during the night although he can no longer recall the substance of the dream, only the way he felt when he started awake, his shoulder throbbing anew as though she had only just delivered that surprisingly powerful kick. He thinks too that his dream of being in the Synthia's crate had morphed from an earlier one in which he had been lying on his back, held down by restraints, while tubes steadily replaced his blood with icy conserving fluid, a fluid that had brought with it a gradual numbing darkness that had felt like a creeping death.

The panic he felt in the dream brought him awake, although he must have drifted back to sleep again quite quickly, but the memory of that feeling helps him now to drag himself from the two Syns and from the cosy, rather feminine world of his apartment, to continue with his planning and preparations for the crazy idea.

11

The man he is looking for does not have an office, not even a lock-up in the enterprise zone like the one Lars has. It is said that the best way of finding him is to start in the bars and clubs and to make discreet inquiries. There are places that he frequents more often than others, but he likes to move about – or so it is said by those who claim to know something about him. A man who is regular in his habits, they point out, is too easy to find.

As Charlie is going into the second club that morning, he is hailed by another man apparently intent on entering after him.

'Charlie!'

He turns and the man says, 'I didn't expect to see you out and about.'

'Why's that?'

He knows the man slightly and that his name is Peet. He is shorter than himself with a round face and rapidly thinning hair.

'A man as has just got himself a new Syn tends to stay in his apartment rather more than usual,' Peet says with an attempt at a wink, 'if you get my meaning.'

'A new Syn?'

Charlie's mouth is suddenly dry and his pulse quicker than it has any reason to be. He tries not to look anxious or guilty. He tries for a little puzzled instead.

'I saw you bringing her back yesterday morning,' Peet tells him with a grin. 'Very tasty little number I thought, but you're in the business. I expect you get the pick of the bunch. Traded in your old one, have you?'

Peet's apartment is not far from his own. He had thought that no one had seen him when he returned from the dock with Poppy, but he should have known that it could not be that easy.

'Oh,' he says, trying for relaxed now, the temporary and understandable puzzlement over, 'No, she's not mine. She's… a demonstration model,' he says.

He realises he ought to have had a cover story prepared.

Peet nods slowly. 'Oh, I see,' he says, sounding uncertain what to make of this claim.

'Yes, she's on loan from Synthia Corp to show to a customer,' he tells Peet, getting into the story now. He laughs wryly, 'You wouldn't believe how complicated and involved the protocols are just having custody of her for a couple of days. I'm supposed to keep it quiet too, in case everyone thinks they can come and have a look or try her out. She's not been released yet and she's still… she's still unused, if you know what I mean and I have to return her in the same condition.'

Peet shrugs and asks slyly. 'Would they know? I

can't believe that you haven't tried her yourself.'

'Oh, they can tell,' he assures Peet, 'and they'd just have to ask her, wouldn't they? I mean, she isn't going to lie about it.'

'No, I suppose not,' Peet says slowly, sounding disappointed.

'I'm sure you'll understand if I ask you not to tell anyone about her,' he explains to Peet as casually as he can, 'or everyone will have the same idea you did and I won't get a moment's peace until she goes back.'

Peet says nothing.

'I'll spend the rest of my working life paying for her,' Charlie says, 'if anything happens to her while she's with me.'

'Really?' Peet does not sound too concerned. 'Well, we all have our problems, don't we?'

Then Peet turns and enters the club.

Charlie is tempted not to go in after him, but he reasons it might look odd if he failed to follow the man in, since he was clearly going to do so when Peet called to him. The last thing he ought to do now is to draw more attention to himself or to act suspiciously in any way. He has no idea whether Peet believes his story, but then Peet has no reason to doubt it. The real question is whether he will keep it to himself.

In the main room of the club he finds the floor show is holding the attention of all the men present, including Peet. For the moment what the femdroids are doing to each other will probably keep Peet distracted, but he suspects that the moment it is over Peet will be talking about the demonstration model, the tasty Syn he had seen his neighbour with the previous morning.

Perhaps he should have just agreed with Peet that he has acquired a new Syn for himself. The story he invented offers no more protection if it eventually gets back to Vos or to anyone from Synthia Corp. In fact, any man sent by Synthia Corp will know instantly that the company does not loan models in that way. Protocols or not, it would be far too difficult to control. But it is too late now and he knows that any story involving a Syn is likely to spread throughout the entire orbital given sufficient time. He just hopes that enough time elapses before the story gets to Synthia Corp for him to have executed his plan. By then it will no longer matter: he will be far away, or else he will be under arrest, or simply dead.

He watches the floor show for a while, unable to draw his eyes away. The show is like the free snacks they keep in bowls on the bar. The snacks are salty and they make you thirsty and so encourage a man to buy more drinks. The performances by the Syns are meant to encourage a man to pay to take a Syn back to one of the recreation rooms, or two Syns maybe, if you can afford it. The idea is that the shows will make a man think about sex, but he thinks that most men think about little else.

When the show is over he buys a drink. When it is put in front of him he asks the barman if he has seen the man he is looking for. The man is known as ‘Gen’, but no one seems to think it is his real name. The barman looks him over carefully before answering, the answer a barely perceptible shake of the head.

'Not for about a week,' the man says under his breath and without looking directly at Charlie.

He nods and thanks the man.

At the fourth place he goes into the barman answers his question with one of his own, 'You buying?'

That is the answer he has been waiting for.

'Yes, sure,' he says, 'what does he drink?'

The barman tells him and Charlie resists the urge to comment that business must be good for Gen if he can afford that stuff.

When he has paid for it, the barman says quietly, 'Third door on the right.'

No drink is produced. The charge is just the price of the admission ticket.

The corridor is poorly lit, the walls a dark red, walls that seem to muffle and absorb the sound of his footsteps. It is typical décor for a club, although a man headed back here with a Syn will probably not notice it, not consciously anyway. His mind will be on other things, or maybe just switched off completely. He finds the door he wants and knocks, hoping it is not another punter in the room behind it.

After a moment the door slides open and a voice says, 'Come in.'

It is very dark inside and the reddish glow from the corridor does little to help. He hesitates, but before he can decide how to proceed he is blinded by a sudden and powerful flash of light. He puts his hands up to cover his eyes, but it is too late.

He swears. 'What the hell was that?'

'Come in,' the voice repeats more forcefully.

He can see nothing now, no matter how much he blinks or turns his head from side to side, but he stumbles blindly a couple of steps forward, his hands out in front of him.

'What was that?' he repeats.

'There's a chair one step to your right,' the voice says by way of reply, 'Sit on it.'

He feels for it and sits and he hears the door closing behind him.

'What's that you just flashed in my eyes?' he asks again. 'I can't see anything.'

'Can't be too careful,' the voice says calmly, 'but you're clean: no weapons, no electronics and you're not a synthetic. So what do you want?'

Sight of sorts is returning slowly, but everywhere he looks he can see only a patch of bright green, vaguely square-shaped, the after image of whatever was directed at him. He puts his hands in front of him, blinking and shielding his eyes.

At first he was scared at finding himself suddenly blind and helpless. He was afraid of what would come next, but now he is starting to feel aggrieved instead.

'It's not permanent,' the voice says. 'It'll pass.'

'I certainly hope so,' he says. Then he asks, 'Are you the one they call "Gen"?'

'I'll repeat *my* question,' the voice says firmly, 'What do you want?'

Charlie tells him, adding, 'Including all alterations from the original, modifications of any kind, changes to the floor plan, installations, cameras and other security devices. And the location of any freezing cabinets, you know, for biologicals. Hypothetically, of course.'

'Yeah, hypothetically,' the voice says. 'And where hypothetically is this apartment?'

He tells him.

'That's more difficult.'

'But you can still get it?'

'It'll just take a bit longer, which means it'll cost more.'

'Okay,' Charlie agrees with more confidence than he feels.

The light in the room seems very low, and it has a yellow cast to it, but that may just be the after-effects of the scanner beam. He thinks he can see a small figure a little way in front of him now, silhouetted against the light. He thinks he can smell him too, as though moving around as much as he does the man has few opportunities to wash. The voice sounds unwashed too, as though he needs to clear his throat. Maybe that is due to the expensive liquor he drinks. If that is the case it might be better to risk the water.

'Hypothetically,' the voice asks, 'who owns this apartment you're interested in?'

He tells him.

'You know,' the voice says, its tone more conversational now, 'there are cheaper and more pleasant ways to kill yourself. Are you really sure about this?'

Charlie nods and the voice is quiet for a moment.

'The first results I get will most likely be a blind,' the voice says almost as if it is talking to itself, 'difficult to find, but not so protected I can't get to them. But they won't be worth shit. The real info will be deeper and much harder to reach. Probably a trip wire or a data mine as well, as a backup in case anyone gets close.'

Charlie knows the voice is not really talking to itself. He is a salesman too, and he also knows when to talk up the difficulty of obtaining something for a customer.

'The guy's not just very rich,' the voice says now, 'he's not stupid either, not from what I hear, but I'm not so sure about you.'

'But you can get the info?' Charlie persists.

'Do you know about women?' the voice asks, rather than answering his question. 'About Synthias?' it adds.

Charlie shrugs. Then he says, 'Yeah, I do. Quite a bit, actually.'

The voice says nothing, so he says, 'And you know about information?'

'You have a good line in silly questions,' the voice tells him. 'Maybe your customers like them. Maybe not.'

Then the voice tells him its price, what it wants for obtaining the info Charlie has requested. It is an opener, but he does not have half that much, not even a quarter, but he has not come prepared to pay with money, no matter how little. He tells the voice so.

'So, what have you got?' the voice says, apparently neither too surprised nor noticeably disappointed by his response.

He asks the voice what it means and it says, 'Payment in kind, seeing as Syns are your business,

Charlie.'

'You know who I am?'

'There you go with the silly questions, again,' the voice tells him. The voice seems to be coming from a different part of the room now and he tries to see if the shape that he took to be the man has moved. He thinks not. Either there are two men, or what he took to be the man is something else, just a shape perhaps.

'If I hadn't known who you were in less than ten seconds of you appearing in the doorway, we wouldn't have been having this conversation,' the voice says. 'Does that answer your question?'

'I guess it does,' Charlie says, turning his head to see if he can locate the source of the voice more accurately. Things in the room have not got much clearer and he hopes that it is just because the light in there is very low.

'So,' the voice says, 'you got anything to offer, or not?'

He tells the voice what he proposes. It is a subject he can talk about with some confidence and the voice listens.

'Two hours doesn't cut it,' the voice says dismissively as soon as he has finished, 'not even if she's as tasty, and as inexperienced and virginal, as you say she is.'

'Four,' he counters. That earns Charlie a sound he thinks is meant as a laugh.

'Twenty-four,' the voice says.

'Can't be done,' Charlie says sadly, 'I have to return her to Synthia Corp.'

At least he is used to haggling about prices and

making deals. That kind of lie comes easily to him.

The voice is silent for a moment. Then it says, 'You bring her to me the night after next and collect her the same time the following morning.'

Charlie remains silent now. Sometimes silence is better than anything a man might say. Then he says, 'Okay, but that's awfully tight timewise. If I don't give her back to the guy from Synthia Corp on time, we'll both have their security arm after us.'

'That's your problem. They won't be after me, Pal,' the voice says coolly.

'They'll know where the Syn is though, and where she's been. It won't take them a moment to track her.'

'You need to check that?' he asks when the voice fails to answer.

'You'll get her back, don't worry,' the voice says soothingly. 'I'll just have to wake her up real early in the morning – if she gets any rest at all.'

'Where do I bring her?'

The voice tells him. It is a bar, not a club, and it has no femdroids of its own to offer customers. That makes sense; it will not be so unusual therefore for a man to bring one in with him.

'Be there around eight,' the voice says.

'You'll have the info for me then?'

'No,' the voice says. 'I've just been wasting your time and mine.'

The lights come on then and Charlie has to close his eyes for a second against the sudden brightness. When he is able to open them again, he is on his own and he sees that there is a second door, a way out the back. The guy, whoever he is, is very careful and extremely cautious. Charlie has to give him that.

On other occasions the room is clearly used as a recreation room, somewhere where one of the club's Syns can do her stuff, or you can do yours with her. There is a bed, a couch, a small table, and the chair that he has been sitting in, placed just inside the door that leads in from the club. In front of that chair is a cloth thrown over another chair. This is what forms the shape he took to be the owner of the voice. The chair is of a type he remembers from other rec rooms when he made use of clubs in the days before Cheryl. It is adapted for various games a man might play with a Syn, or she with him, and only for sitting on if you really can think of nothing else to do.

Apart from the memory of the rasping voice, only the man's smell remains now as proof that someone has indeed been in here with him. It is a rank odour of unwashed hair and body, and maybe of bad teeth too.

12

In Speaking to Gen the day before, he has finally made a start at putting his plan into action and the coming day and the next can be devoted to putting the rest of the pieces in place. After a good breakfast he leaves the apartment with a purposeful stride, turning over in his mind who to see first and how exactly to handle the various conversations he plans.

He has gone no more than ten steps – his body propelling him along the walkway with little if any conscious direction from his brain – when a man walking towards him abruptly stops and accosts him.

‘Hey, you’re Charlie, aren’t you?’ the man says, grabbing his arm.

There is nothing overtly threatening in the man’s action; it is almost as though the man expects to be recognised, but Charlie feels his heart leaping about uncertainly in his chest.

The man’s appearance suggests he is a visitor to the orbital; the expensive looking suit, the confident manner, even the tanned and healthy complexion, all distinguish the man from the majority who call Orbital B their home.

Charlie is fairly certain he has never seen the man before.

But the well-dressed visitor insists, 'You are Charlie, aren't you?'

Then the man flashes a hologram ID at him. It indicates that the bearer is an agent of Synthia Corp's security arm.

The sight of the ID shoots adrenaline into Charlie's blood stream in a painful spasm, but then, confusingly, the agent puts out his hand and adds with an enthusiastic smile, 'I'm Steev.'

Charlie shakes the proffered hand, puzzled now as well as fearful, hoping that Steev will not notice the clamminess of his palm or the sweat that has broken out on his upper lip and forehead. He tries to return Steev's easy smile, but he suspects the attempt merely pulls his face into something like a grimace. But if Steev notices any of this he is careful to conceal it.

'It's always good to meet another company man,' Steev says now, with every sign his pleasure is genuine.

'What brings you out to this floating piece of junk?' Charlie asks, with an attempt at good humour. For the moment the fear makes him more loquacious, but it also threatens to make him do something stupid before very long.

'Oh, we're here to sort out some mess with a unit that's gone missing,' Steev says, as though this is of no importance.

'Really?' Charlie says, his mouth dry. 'I thought you boys had security pretty tight?'

'Oh, we do,' Steev assures him, 'and don't worry, it's not one of your sales.'

Charlie frowns and attempts to look puzzled, rather than scared. Steev has effectively just confirmed that it is Poppy he is here for, not that there had been any doubt in his mind.

'I know,' Steev says, holding up his hands defensively. 'It's your patch, so by rights the sale should have been put through by you. But there's something pretty screwy about the whole deal, if you ask me. But I can't tell you anything about it, as I'm sure you'll understand.'

Charlie nods, not really understanding much just then, but he tells Steev insincerely, 'I hope you get it sorted.'

'We will, have no fear of that,' Steev assures him, 'but listen, that's not why I've come to see you.'

'Oh,' Charlie says, weakly, but fortunately Steev does not really seem to need him to say anything.

'I have this thing, Charlie,' Steev says now, as though he is confessing to something. 'Call it weird if you want, but… well, I'll just come right out with it.'

'Okay,' Charlie says cautiously.

Steev pauses and says nothing more for the moment. Either the man is hesitant about admitting to whatever this 'thing' is, or he is playing some very sophisticated game.

'I really like the old Diana series,' Steev admits finally, the words tumbling out in a rush, as though the man is expecting to be ridiculed.

Whatever Charlie might have expected Steev to confess to, it was certainly not this.

'I know,' Steev says, raising his hands yet again, as though in expectation or acknowledgement of protest. 'The later series have improved so much and there's a lot that the Diana range simply doesn't have.'

Charlie nods slowly.

'As a salesman, I know you'll be able to list all the things they don't have,' Steev goes on, 'but there's just something about the Dianas that I love.'

Charlie nods again. It seems a fairly safe response, but he still has absolutely no idea where this is headed.

'Anyway,' Steev says with a shrug, 'I do a routine scan whenever I'm in a new zone, you know, just to see if I can find any examples of the Diana range still around. Most of them have been decommissioned and those that haven't have often been modded in some way that completely destroys their original beauty.'

Steev gives every sign of being sincere about his passion for this range of outdated Syns, so Charlie tries to look suitably sympathetic and equally bemused at the sheer stupidity of any man crass enough to mess with the original specs of the Dianas. In reality he knows nothing about the range and suspects that they pre-date his own time as a salesman by a decade at least, perhaps more.

'So, you can imagine how delighted I was when I found a Diana show up in the scan this morning,' Steev enthuses.

This brings Charlie's mind back into focus. There is something about what Steev has just told him that is alarming, but for the moment he is struggling to understand exactly what it might be.

'But I wasn't surprised,' Steev says, 'when I realised that she was in the possession of another company man!'

Charlie has been several steps behind Steev all the way, but now he makes the connection, and his stomach reminds him that keeping his breakfast in place is not a given.

The false ID code that the old man implanted into Poppy had originally been assigned to one of these Diana models. That has to be it. It is Poppy, therefore, that showed up in the scan Steev conducted this morning, and it is Poppy that has brought Steev to him, and to within a few steps of the missing 'unit' hidden in Charlie's apartment.

Apparently unconcerned at having received no response thus far, Steev continues, 'I said to myself, this Charlic is obviously a fcllow connoisseur.'

'They are pretty special,' Charlie allows, his mind meanwhile desperately seeking some means of escape.

Steev has stopped speaking now and is looking at Charlie, clearly waiting for something, and he has a horrible idea he knows what it is.

'So?' Steev asks when he can evidently contain himself no longer, 'are you going to let me see her?'

The man is almost wetting himself now in his excitement.

'I know that a lot of them have been customized,' Charlie says, playing for time and putting as much regret into the words as he can muster.

'It's criminal isn't it?' Steev agrees. 'Last time I thought I'd found a unit it turned out that she'd been given a really amateurish shop job, and you'll never guess what they'd done to her.'

It is true. Charlie is unlikely to guess, not unless he is extremely lucky and at this moment he does not feel lucky at all. In fact, he thinks he is probably the unluckiest man on the orbital, but Steev does not need him to guess. He is going to tell him.

'They'd reworked her face!' Steev says, breaking the suspense. Steev actually looks close to tears as he recalls this monstrous act of vandalism.

'It's hard to credit what some men will do,' Charlie nods sympathetically.

'Tell me your unit at least hasn't been customised,' Steev says, and finally, Charlie sees an escape route.

He makes what he hopes is an apologetic gesture and tries to look both a little sheepish and sad at the same time. Then he shrugs as well for good measure.

'I know just how you felt,' he says, his voice full of a regret as synthetic as any femdroid. 'I guess they're so scarce now that it's going to be hard to find one in its original configuration.'

'Tell me they haven't changed the face at least…' Steev pleads.

Charlie pulls a face of his own. 'Do you want to come and see?' he offers, turning to look back towards the door of his apartment. He knows this is risky, but it is probably less risky than a simple refusal to let Steev see the Synthia. 'It isn't pretty,' he warns.

'No,' Steev says sadly, 'not if she doesn't have the original face.'

'I can't imagine what they thought they were doing,' Charlie says, so convinced now by his own deception he feels genuine disbelief at the changes that have been made to the Synthia.

'She's still a Diana,' he says quietly, 'underneath the poor re-con job, but you'd never know.'

'No, I'd rather not see,' Steev says, sounding increasingly horrified. 'I'd rather not see what they've done.'

It is Steev who trembles a little now, perhaps realising how narrowly he has missed a traumatic and distressing encounter with a disfigured Diana

Then the man adds sadly, 'I'll just keep on looking and maybe I'll find one eventually.'

'She's worth it,' Charlie tells him. 'You keep on looking, and if you find one I'd love to see it.'

Steev brightens at this. 'Okay, Charlie. I'm disappointed, but it's good to meet a fellow enthusiast. I'll certainly let you know when I find her. I know she's out there waiting for me somewhere.'

There is a kind of rapture in Steev's eyes as he pictures the Syn waiting for him.

'Don't give up,' Charlie tells him.

Steev sighs and nods. Then, with a visible effort to bring himself back to the present, Steev says, 'I'd better let you get to work now. Another day, another sale and all that.'

'You betcha,' Charlie agrees.

'And good luck with the missing unit,' he calls as Steev walks briskly away.

Steev turns and waves his hand dismissively. 'Don't sweat,' he calls cheerily as he strides off back the way he had come. 'We'll find it, we always do, and we'll nail the bastards responsible.'

He watches Steev go, unable for the moment to decide what to do next.

Perhaps it is all bluster, the fabled reach and ruthless power of the Synthia Corp security arm: no more than a myth. What has he been worrying about?

It is just that no more than forty-eight hours after he and Hans took Poppy from her crate, one of Synthia Corp's agents has grabbed the arm of the very man responsible for her disappearance. Steev knows both who he is and where to find him. A simple scan has unerringly taken him to no more than ten paces away from the missing Syn.

If Charlie had lingered only five more minutes over his breakfast, Steev would have come to the door of the apartment looking for him and would probably have seen the missing unit the moment the door opened.

On the other hand, it is all a horrible coincidence, just a matter of luck, or the lack of it. Steev was looking for an old Diana model. He is just a guy who has a thing about an old range of Synthias that have not been produced in years.

Or, they are just toying with him...

'I know she's out there waiting for me somewhere,' Steev said.

But perhaps he did not mean an example of some outdated range in its original configuration. Perhaps he meant the missing Syn, the thing that really brought him out to the orbital. These guys are so sure of their success in finding it that Steev was just playing with him.

Charlie feels a thin, ice-cold fluid replacing his warm blood. It is travelling rapidly throughout his body and it is making him feel weak, his legs wobbly. Of course, they are on to him. Would any man really take seriously for a minute the story Steev gave him? Would a man like that really be obsessed with the face of a discontinued Syn?

Yes, because men are like that. Men have dreams and moments of madness. They become obsessed. It has happened to Charlie, and it has thrown him off balance as surely as the kick had done. Just a look from a pair of narrowed eyes has altered the course of his thus far perfectly predictable and relatively safe existence.

But, on the other hand...

On thc other hand, he has been horribly, terrifyingly close to discovery, and he is either terribly unlucky, or astonishingly fortunate. He cannot tell which it is, but at least he is not being interrogated or already on his way to a penal colony far away in an inhospitable part of the solar system. Some men say that if you are sent to a penal colony you are lucky: it means that you survived the interrogation, and some men apparently last as many as ten years in the colony before the harsh conditions finishes them. So it is not all bad.

He looks down at himself. There are no wet patches on his trousers. Perhaps it is his lucky day after all.

While he is still standing where Steev left him, wondering whether he should carry on with what he planned for the morning, he is accosted a second time. This time he recognises the man.

'Sly wants to see you,' the man says in little more than a whisper. 'Says it's urgent.'

The man is turning his head and not looking directly at him. He is shorter than Charlie and rather small, as though his growth has been stunted in some way. It is the sort of thing that men claim is the result of having sex by yourself too often. He does not believe the stories, but he supposes that for a society whose chief source of income comes from supplying women it might be a useful fear to instil in men.

He has never learnt this diminutive man's name, but Sly always contacts him this way, not trusting more conventional methods that might be intercepted and which would leave a trace.

'Okay?' the man asks now, wanting to be sure that his message has been understood, although it seems fairly clear. The man's eyes dart about continually and Charlie is never sure if and when they are focussed on him.

'Tell Sly I'll be with him as soon as I can,' he tells the messenger. 'I'll add him to my list of appointments,'

The little man shakes his head. 'No, it has to be now, Charlie. Sly was very clear about that.'

He has no wish to see Sly just now for all sorts of reasons. He has a plan to put into action and time is precious, and then there is the nature of what he is plotting. On the other hand, it is natural perhaps that Sly should want to see him. Perhaps Sly has heard from Vos.

He sighs. ‘Okay,’ he says and the diminutive messenger sidles away, apparently satisfied.

Charlie remains where he is a moment longer, thinking the day is already in danger of turning out to be a waste of his time. Then he sets out in the direction of the shuttle port.

13

'The next shuttle leaves in five hours and forty-two minutes,' the man at the desk tells him.

The clerk has answered his inquiry without looking down to consult his screen and with more precision than was really required. The shuttle runs every six hours, so the man is telling him the shuttle has just left, eighteen minutes ago. Perhaps that accounts for the slight smirk the man is not trying very hard to conceal.

Sly will have to wait.

'Do you wish to reserve a seat?' the man asks him, his tone suggesting he does not really care either way.

'Yes, I guess so,' Charlie agrees, his thoughts already elsewhere.

'Your name?'

Charlie is forced to ask the clerk to repeat the question. He had been trying to decide how to fit everything in and still meet the man known as 'Gen' the following evening in order to hand over Poppy.

Once he has understood what the clerk is asking he gives his name and the man's demeanour changes instantly.

The clerk says, 'Oh, you need to go up to the next

level, Sir. They're expecting you.'

'They are?'

For a moment Charlie has no idea what the man is talking about, but then the news alarms him because he assumes the man means men from Synthia Corp are waiting for him. But he can still play for time while he works out what to do.

'Who are?' he asks innocently. 'Who's waiting upstairs?'

'Your shuttle is ready for you, Sir,' the man explains brightly.

So, not that, then. They are not about to arrest him, not yet at least, but this is another surprise. It seems Sly really is in a hurry to see him.

'Shall I take you up there, Sir?' The man asks, his previously offhand manner replaced by this new version of himself, all smiles and eager to be of assistance.

'No, that's okay,' Charlie tells him, 'I think I know the way.'

He has never taken one of the VIP shuttles. They run for the benefit of wealthy men who are in a hurry or wealthy men who simply prefer not to travel in the company of their less wealthy fellows. The shuttles do not follow any schedule, but operate at the convenience of their passengers. He never expected to travel on one, but he thinks he knows where they depart from.

There is an attractive Synthia waiting at the VIP shuttle desk on the floor above. She regards him coolly as he approaches her. He supposes he does not look like one of the VIPs she is used to dealing with, but when he gives her his name she rewards him with a wide smile.

'Welcome, Sir,' she says as though his arrival has made her day complete. 'Would you like to follow me? We are ready to depart, if you are?'

He shrugs and follows her. The air lock has none of the alarming utility of the larger one that leads to the commercial shuttle. There is nothing that overtly proclaims its purpose or the potential if theoretical dangers that attend its use, or the harsh reality of the space beyond that demands its existence. The floor is carpeted and the recessed doors at either end have been made to look innocuous and to blend in with the décor.

'This way please, Sir,' the Syn says when they reach the door into the shuttle. She steps aside, gesturing for him to enter. She is wearing a pleasant little uniform that enhances her figure and shows off her bottom, and then does the same for her lovely legs, a generous amount of which are visible below the short, tight skirt. As he passes her and steps into the shuttle he catches a whiff of her perfume. It is like walking through her smile, as though the smile hangs suspended in the air like a warm and gentle breath.

He ducks his head in order to pass through the hatch. It too has been made to blend into the décor and the floor of the cabin beyond is carpeted with the same material as in the airlock.

The interior of the shuttle is smaller than he expects and has only seven seats, three on either side and a simpler, smaller one facing towards him in the middle at the front. There are windows too, small apertures beside each of the wide and deep seats. He is used to the large cabin in the commercial shuttle which has no windows and is tightly packed with rows of small seats.

The Syn follows him inside.

'Where should I sit?' he asks her, all of the available seats being still vacant.

She smiles again and gives a little shrug. 'Sit wherever you please, Sir,' she suggests.

He selects the front seat on the left-hand side and as soon as he is seated she comes over and helps him fasten the straps of his harness, bending low and giving him a glimpse of the tops of her breasts and favouring him with more of the perfume. It is her eyes and their long lashes that he notices though, while she fusses about him expertly securing the straps. She has her name displayed on a small badge on the breast of her uniform. It tells him that it is 'Lisa'.

'You're not one of ours, are you?' he says to her.

He asks his question before he has thought about it and not surprisingly perhaps she is puzzled.

'I'm sorry, Sir?' she says stepping back from him, 'I am afraid that I don't understand your question.'

'It's just that I was wondering who made you.'

'Oh.' Now she seems not only surprised by his question, but a little affronted too, although he has no idea why she should be. For a ridiculous moment he thinks that she is going to ask who made him.

'I work for Synthia Corp,' he explains 'so you could say it's just a professional interest.'

'I see, Sir,' she says, her words, like her lips, a little tight and compressed. Her reaction makes him feel as though he has asked her something improper, has said something offensive, but he is sure that men must say all sorts of things to her every day, must make the kind of lewd suggestions and demand the kind of favours that all men want, and wealthy men expect from a Syn.

'It doesn't matter who made you,' he says quickly, trying to win another of those smiles of hers and trying to make up for any offence he might have caused, 'I'm very glad that I'm flying with you this morning, Lisa.'

'Thank you, Sir' she says, appearing to relax a little. Then she says quietly and a little stiffly, 'I was made by the Paradise Corporation, Sir. I am one of their Angel models.'

'And very lovely you are too,' he tells her, giving her one of his own smiles. 'But you don't need to call me "Sir". I'm not the kind of man who normally travels by VIP shuttle. It seems that someone wants to speak to me urgently, but I'm just a regular guy, as I'm sure you can tell. Please call me "Charlie".'

Her expression softens and she smiles again now, not quite as broadly as she had when he first announced himself at the desk, but he thinks this smile is more genuine.

'Okay, Charlie. Are you ready to depart?'

He looks around at the other seats, which all remain empty. 'Don't we have to wait for the others?' he asks.

'Are you expecting someone to accompany you,

Charlie?' she asks him.

He shakes his head.

She smiles again, 'You are our VIP this morning, Charlie. The shuttle is booked for you.'

'Okay,' he says. 'Then I'm ready.'

Lisa closes the hatch at the rear and then straps herself into the seat at the front facing the rest of the cabin, from which position she can keep an eye on all the passengers, or could do had there been any others.

He looks out of the little window at his side. All he can see at present is a section of the wall of the dock. It is almost within touching distance were he able to open the window and reach out. He reminds himself that this unremarkable wall is the outer surface of the orbital, the divide between the ordinary world that he lives in and the vacuum beyond. He thinks it ought to look scarred, dirty perhaps, to bear some evidence of the brutal and inhospitable nature of space, but it merely looks clean and functional.

He is aware of a slight movement, a faint jolt and a low sound as the shuttle disengages from the airlock. Then they drop from the confines of the dock and suddenly there is nothing to see out of the window, only the blank emptiness that the orbital itself floats in. It is like the lift down to the floor of the dock, only more so, as though the mechanism has failed or the steel ropes have snapped and they are hurtling towards the bottom in free-fall, his head just a little behind the rest of his body as they plummet.

The shuttle rolls a little and his stomach follows fractionally later, the straps of his harness first tugging at him and then releasing him into the seat back that now presses him from behind as the shuttle's main thrusters burn briefly. Then there is only that dizzying, light-headed sensation that he remembers from his previous trips on the commercial shuttle, the feeling that he dislikes so much, his arms and legs rising a little of their own accord, no longer held down by their own weight. He looks at Lisa and she smiles encouragingly at him, her own hands folded neatly in her lap, her legs crossed at the ankles below her seat as though held in position by invisible straps.

For a moment he has a view of the surface of the planet below. He turns his head to look through the windows on the other side and sees the orbital, looming large and yet fragile, lit by the rays of the distant star. When he turns back to his own window he sees the star itself visible over the curve of the planet whose leading edge seems to be on fire, a thin crescent of yellow-orange marking the boundary between the day and the night.

The shuttle rolls again and the view is gone, to be replaced by the black and then increasingly by the stars, which seem to be both incredibly close and yet so far away that they belong to some other realm or some other reality.

Lisa is watching him as he looks intently out of the window, bending his neck and peering as far as he can in every direction.

'You don't get a view on the commercial shuttle,' he explains.

'No?'

He shakes his head. 'I wish I had a window in my

apartment.'

She frowns. 'Is that possible?'

'The man I'm going to see has one, a large one in his living area.'

She looks suitably impressed and perhaps a little sad. 'Yes, that must be nice,' she says.

He wonders where she spends her time when she is not on the shuttle. If she is owned by the shuttle company he supposes she might simply divide her time between the shuttle itself and the company offices. Unless an employee takes her home with him – and he thinks it unlikely that the company would encourage such a thing – she has probably never seen the inside of an apartment of any sort, not even one like the tiny, utilitarian space that he has.

'Why don't you move to one of the other seats so you can look out properly?' he asks her.

'I am supposed to remain here so that I can observe the passengers,' she tells him seriously. 'I am here for your comfort and safety.'

He smiles. 'I won't tell anyone, and there aren't any other passengers.'

She says nothing, so he adds, 'And you may not get another opportunity.'

He sees the inner conflict reflected in the flickering emotions that play across her face. He thinks it is obvious that she takes pride in performing her duties and no doubt this includes obeying her owner's instructions. When he considers this he realises that she has nothing else, no other identity or purpose, only this role as shuttle hostess.

She hesitates and then she undoes her harness and

pushes herself toward the seat on the opposite side, where she manages to pull herself gracefully down into the seat and fasten the harness. She looks at him briefly and then turns to the window and after a moment he sees she is as engrossed in the view as he is.

He sighs with a mixture of contentment and not a little wonder. His day has certainly taken an unexpected turn, more pleasant this time than his encounter with Steev had been. He is starting to get used to the weightlessness now and he has plenty of room so that he can stretch out his legs, can move his arms without fear of incurring the displeasure of passengers on either side of him, and he has the rare pleasure of the window and the small but wonderful glimpse it affords of the universe. He imagines recounting this adventure to Cheryl when he returns home – and to Poppy too, he remembers – and then he wishes they were here with him, able to see it for themselves. He turns to Lisa and sees she is turning her head and looking up and down and then in front and behind as far as she can, just as he has been doing. Perhaps she can see the orbital from her side of the shuttle. Seeing her evident and unselfconscious absorption stirs something inside him, produces an emotion he cannot name. He smiles at her, but without knowing why. It is not as though she is looking at him, so she cannot see his smile, but he does not want anything from her at the moment, not even her good opinion of him.

Making the journey on a VIP shuttle is pretty special and a treat he is unlikely to repeat, unless he really does achieve the success and wealth he fantasises about. Making the journey as the only passenger seems too amazing to believe and he is glad that he has invited Lisa to look out of the window. It seems only right that she should share his treat.

Then an idea strikes him, strikes him as forcibly and as unpleasantly as though the shuttle has been hit by a piece of space debris. He has heard that can happen, and with potentially devastating results.

Is it not just a little too amazing that he is the only passenger? Sure, men who are wealthy enough, men with a sufficiently inflated sense of their own importance might seek to make the trip in splendid isolation with only a Syn to keep them company. But can Sly really be that anxious to speak to him that he has paid for the shuttle to make the trip solely for the purpose of meeting with Charlie just a few hours before the commercial shuttle would have got him to Orbital C, and far more cheaply – and at Charlie's own expense?

Lars' words echo unbidden in his head. 'One of them it's an accident, maybe. But both of them it stinks rotten.'

Two freak accidents and two deaths, both the result of events that ought not to have happened at all: an airlock fails in some way and the sole occupant is killed; both the inner and the outer doors of a passenger car in the tube malfunction and a second man, again the sole occupant, is cut in half – approximately in half at any rate. The two men worked together on something for Sly, men who almost certainly knew what Charlie also now knows.

He still knows, but who else knows besides Sly himself?

Two down, one to go.

Simply to know such a thing is 'big danger' Cheryl said.

A shuttle might explode on its way between orbitals – a freak accident certainly, but not impossible – a collision with space debris perhaps, or a malfunction of some kind, even a sudden decompression of the cabin would be enough, and the sole passenger would be killed in an instant.

And then there are none.

'We've got to go back!' he says suddenly, turning to Lisa and trying to unfasten his harness. 'We've got to turn around and go back!'

She turns to look at him, her expression suddenly composed and professional once more.

'What's the matter, Charlie? Are you feeling unwell?'

She is gently undoing her harness as she speaks while he is still frantically fumbling with his own.

'We've got to turn around and go back to the orbital immediately. There may not be much time,' he tells her.

'It's okay, Charlie,' she says soothingly. 'Everything is okay. You are perfectly safe.'

She is at his side now, holding the edge of his seat to steady herself, but he has freed himself from the harness and he kicks up and forwards, away from her. Then he bangs his fist on the front wall of the cabin.

'We've got to attract their attention,' he insists, 'get this thing turned around.'

'Everything is okay, Charlie,' Lisa repeats in the same professionally soothing and neutral tone. 'Please return to your seat.'

'How do we attract their attention?' he asks, turning to face her and fending her off with his arms and legs.

'Attract whose attention?'

'The pilot, whoever flies this thing.'

'There's no one else, Charlie. It's entirely automatic.'

'Automatic?' he repeats stupidly. 'There's just the two of us on board?'

'Yes,' she agrees, but he can see that she is playing for time. She is planning something.

'Please,' she says gently, 'there is nothing to worry about. Please return to your seat.'

She is swimming towards him again, a hand outstretched, but he manages to get past her, using his legs to push off from the wall of the cabin towards the rear where the hatch is.

Then he turns to face her again. 'There must be some way to attract attention,' he says, 'to tell someone that we have a problem.'

'There is no problem,' she says gently, reaching out with her hand to his face.

He fails to notice what she has in the palm of her hand until it is too late. When he does so he frantically pushes her arm from him and tries to move out of reach, but he is not quick enough. She catches him on the side of the neck, a glancing touch that grazes him. He feels a slight pain and then he knows that everything is going to be all right. He is suddenly quite calm and relaxed and he knows that all he has to do is to sprawl in his seat and let the day and its excitement wash over him.

'Everything will be okay, Charlie,' she is saying again.

Her voice is soft and lovely and he wants to agree with her, but his mouth fails to cooperate. A little of the blackness has got into the cabin with them. It must have come in through one of the windows. Had he left his own window open after he had reached out and touched the wall of the dock?

No, that is ridiculous! He opens his eyes again and sees she is tugging him back to his seat, trying to refasten the harness.

'No!' he manages to shout at last. He sees she has another of the little black discs in her hand and he struggles desperately, spinning them around so that his back bounces off the front wall of the cabin, taking them both in a slow arc off the ceiling towards the back again. Her hand is coming for his cheek or his neck again and he kicks out as hard as he can, pushing her away.

He thinks the shuttle must have been making some adjustment in course, must have been accelerating or turning, for although he only strikes the front wall quite gently Lisa slams into the rear of the cabin and the hatch with obvious force. He had kicked at her quite hard, but that ought to have pushed them apart at a similar velocity. He is slightly winded, but he sees Lisa crumple and roll before bouncing off the hatch. She puts out an arm to cushion her impact and when she rolls and turns towards him again he sees that it now hangs at an awkward angle. She clutches at the injured arm with her other one.

'I am damaged,' she says. Her voice is flat and without inflection, but her face shows surprise.

She is in a state of shock, he thinks, just as a man would be, but she uses her feet to manoeuvre and he sees she is going to come at him again, another of the black discs in her good hand.

'No!' he shouts, 'Wait.'

She looks at him warily.

'Your arm is hurt,' he says.

'It does not matter,' she tells him, still waiting for her chance, still determined to tranquillise him and get him back into his seat.

'Of course it matters,' he says angrily. 'I'm sorry. I really am. I didn't mean to hurt you.'

She says nothing and he tells her, 'It can be repaired.'

'Yes,' she agrees, her voice still flat. 'Everything will be okay. Please return to your seat.'

One of her feet finds the back of a seat and she pushes off towards him again.

'Wait!' he pleads 'Please listen. You don't understand. Somebody is trying to kill me.'

'Nobody is trying to kill you,' she says, but he thinks he detects a trace of doubt now in the professionally cool voice. Then the blackness is rising up off the floor, washing around him and he feels light-headed. His eyes flutter and then close again for a moment.

'He's killed two others already,' he tells her, forcing his eyes open. She is closer now, and he sees that she is waiting for a chance to inject him. The first attempt was only partially successful. He puts a hand to his neck and sees blood on it when he looks. The disc has torn at his neck, the needles leaving a shallow, ragged tear and he has not received a full dose of the drug. He would be unconscious now if he had.

'The first man was killed because there was a problem with an airlock,' he tells her, his words sounding a little slurred, but he thinks he sees her take notice. No doubt she has heard about the incident.

'It was made to look like an accident,' he tells her, finding it an effort now to make his mouth form the words. 'The second man was cut in half when the inner and the outer doors of a passenger tube car malfunctioned.'

He realises that he has closed his eyes again. When he opens them he sees she is closer still and her hand is ready with the black disc.

'Please,' he begs, 'you've got to listen. Both of those men worked for the man I'm on my way to see. They knew something, something it is dangerous to know.'

She waits, watching and listening. Yes, he thinks, listening. She will know the probabilities involved, will be able to understand the likelihood of two accidents like that.

'You know that I'm not the kind of man who travels by VIP shuttle, and look,' he gestures with his arm, 'there aren't any other passengers. There's just me, and if something happens to the shuttle this morning the man's secret is finally safe.'

She makes no comment so he continues, 'I didn't question it, but it doesn't really make any sense, does it, to pay for a shuttle just to get me to see him a few hours earlier than I would have done on a commercial shuttle?'

She remains silent, studying him.

'I'm sorry about your arm,' he says again.

'It does not matter,' she repeats. 'I am here for the comfort and safety of the passengers.'

'It matters to you,' he tells her quietly, 'and it matters to me.'

'What is this secret that you know?' she asks after a moment. Perhaps she is simply keeping him talking. Perhaps it is what she has been trained to do.

'You've heard of the woman they call the Lost Princess?'

She sighs, a little wearily he thinks. 'Yes,' she agrees but without much interest. 'She's what all men think about.'

'I know where she is,' he says and she looks unimpressed. 'I've seen her. The man who's trying to kill me showed her to me.'

He sees her eyes widen a little at this. She might not be a genuine Synthia, but she is quite sophisticated and lovely nevertheless, and he likes her. He really is sorry about her arm.

'Look,' he says, 'there might not be much time. We've got to turn around and go back.'

'We can't,' she says simply. 'There is no way to

do so.'

'But there must be a way to contact the orbital if there's a problem.'

She shrugs and he thinks she winces a little. Perhaps her arm troubles her. 'Everything is automatic. If there is a problem the shuttle will automatically inform the orbital.'

'So they'll know if it blows up, but that'll be too late, won't it?'

She is silent again, but then she says, 'You should return to your seat and remain calm. I will look after everything.' Her voice is soothing and professional again, her training kicking in once more.

'I don't want to die,' he says simply.

The words appear to cut through the training, and she seems to realise at last that he is serious, and he sees she is considering something now, considering what she ought to do.

'What?' he asks urgently.

'There are evac suits, for an emergency,' she says slowly, 'if the passengers have to abandon the shuttle.'

'Where?' he demands. 'Show me where.'

She points to the floor below him, but when he looks in the direction she indicates he realises that it is to the ceiling she is pointing, to a hatch that ought to be above their heads. He does not know if it is the drug she has injected into him or just the absence of gravity that has disorientated him. She pulls herself down to the hatch and tugs at the lever. When it does not move, she tries to bring her other arm to bear on it and he sees what he is sure is a wince flash across her features as the damaged arm flops uselessly near her other arm.

'Here,' he says, pulling her away and twisting at the lever himself. It requires the combined force of both of his hands to shift it. Then he is able to lift the hatch easily, as if it weighs nothing, which just then it does. Lights flick on beyond the hatch, activated by the action of opening it. The air that comes out at him smells different to that in the cabin. It is very cold too. He propels himself into the space beyond the hatch and sees there are suits as Lisa has said, arranged three on each side, just as the seats in the cabin are. One for each of the passengers. Lisa follows him inside and he realises that it would be very cramped in this space with six men all trying to don the suits at once.

Lisa is fiddling with a panel on the arm of one of the suits, touching the large icons. She sighs impatiently and moves on to another suit.

'What?' he asks.

'Oxygen level,' she says. 'There's very little left in that one.'

While she works he looks around and locates the outer hatch in the wall above him – or is it below?

'Here,' Lisa announces suddenly, 'this one is good.'

She helps him into the suit, putting the collar over his head and guiding his limbs into the arms and legs as best she can with her one good arm.

While they work at it she asks him, 'Do you own a femdroid, Charlie?'

'Yes,' he admits, wondering what lies behind her

question.

She shows him how to fasten the layers of the suit's opening.

'Do you love her?' she asks him.

At first he thinks she is asking if he has sex with his Syn, but he quickly realises that she means something more than that. She is looking at him, hoping for an answer, but it is too difficult a question for him to get his mind around now. His fear and the effects of the drug are making it hard to concentrate.

'There's more oxygen in the buoy,' she tells him, her voice professional and dispassionate again, 'if the suit's supply runs low.'

She points to a large white cylindrical object that takes up much of the space and shows him how to connect a hose from it to his suit. Then she checks that his suit is securely connected to the buoy. The connection takes the form of a thick, flat coiled strap. He listens to her instructions and explanations, but the other half of his mind is preoccupied now with her question.

'When the outer hatch opens you launch the buoy here,' she tells him, indicating a button on the cylinder, 'then you follow it outside before the tether pulls you out...'

'Wait,' he says, interrupting her, a sudden realisation dawning upon him, 'you're coming with me, aren't you? In another of the suits, I mean?'

'It is better if I operate the controls from inside the passenger cabin. It is designed that way.'

'But there are other suits here,' he protests, 'you must come with me. There's no need for you to…'

He does not know quite how to finish what he wants to say, but his meaning is clear.

'They will not repair my arm,' she says quietly. 'I am an old model. They will just replace me.'

'I'll get it repaired,' he tells her urgently. 'It's my fault.'

She shakes her head. 'I belong to the shuttle company,' she says quietly.

'I'll buy you from them.'

She smiles. 'You're just a regular guy, Charlie,' she says. 'You told me so, remember? You cannot afford to buy me and no company will finance the purchase of a damaged femdroid.'

'You don't know that...' he says, but she cuts him off.

'We must hurry,' she says, 'there may not be much time and it is better this way.' Shc takes the suit helmet and lowers it over his head. At first he thinks she has made a mistake because the face visor is to his left and he is looking into the side of the helmet.

'Help me turn it,' he hears her say, her voice muffled so much that he barely understands what she is saying.

He puts his hands either side of the helmet. They are huge and clumsy inside the gloves of the suit, but he manages to twist the helmet so that the face visor is in the front and he feels it lock smoothly into place on the collar of the suit. She is talking to him again, but he can no longer hear her, only the sound of his own breathing. He brings up a hand to his ear and shakes his head. She nods and he sees her indicate the hatch from the main cabin. He tries to watch her go, but it is difficult to manoeuvre the helmet to follow her progress. When he has located the hatch in the field of view afforded by the visor she has already returned to the passenger cabin and he can see her face through the window in the hatch. The face is suddenly very small. She appears to be trying to get his attention and pointing with her good hand.

At first he cannot understand her meaning and then he realises she means him to lock the hatch. He nods slowly and half-swims, half-pulls his way to the hatch and grasps the lever. He gets both hands on it, but it will not budge until he realises he is pulling it the wrong way. A light changes to green and he sees Lisa make a sign of some kind with her fingers and thumb. His mind cannot resolve the shape into any meaning; some of the black appears to have followed him into the suit. Finally, he sees that she means 'okay'.

Unable to form the same gesture with the gloved hand of the suit he nods his head as far as the suit allows. She nods too. Then he sees her put the palm of her hand flat against the glass, holding it there and he raises his own hand within the glove of the suit and places it against the glass on his side of the panel. It is huge in comparison with her dainty hand and almost completely covers the small window.

He thinks he can hear the air as it escapes into space, but perhaps it is only the sound of his own breathing. The space around him does not change in any way that he can detect, but his suit notices the changing pressure. He hears it creak and rustle around him and feels it grow more rigid. The idea that he is now surrounded invisibly by that very vacuum, that emptiness, that lies outside the shuttle is a little terrifying. He hopes the suit is securely fastened and will not leak.

He can no longer see Lisa's face at the window so he turns awkwardly to the outer hatch and sees that it is now open, forming a perfectly circular discontinuity, a rent in the fabric of the shuttle, a singularity through which the infinite vastness of space can be accessed from the confines of this enclosed and limited area.

His breathing seems to be very loud in his ears, his heart thudding painfully fast in his chest. He approaches the buoy, tugging at the empty suits on their racks in order to propel himself into position, and then after only a moment's hesitation he presses the launch button. Nothing appears to happen at first, but then the buoy begins to slide on its rails towards the hatch and then it is outside in that fearful emptiness, reflecting back at him some blinking light on the outside of the shuttle and growing perceptibly smaller as it moves slowly away from him. He sees his suit tether begin to uncoil rapidly and he pushes off with his feet towards the open hatchway and then pulls himself a little clumsily outside.

At first he tries to hold on to the shuttle, reluctant to let go and let himself simply drift away, but then his tether wrenches him free and the shuttle shoots away from him. After a moment he passes the buoy, the tether snaking out until it yanks him back again. He looks down between his feet and sees only stars and he is terrified, terrified of the sheer emptiness and terrified that he will simply fall. He is too afraid to move, holding his body tense and rigid, but after a moment he rotates without any effort on his part and he finds himself staring up at the surface of the planet and his heart redoubles its efforts to climb out of his chest.

14

He longed to see something of what lies beyond the enclosed world of the orbitals, what there is beyond his own and the infinitely more glamorous and luxurious one on which Sly lives, but he envisaged doing so through a window and from a position of safety. To view it through the visor of the suit is entirely different, and if the orbital's dock area is frightening in its apparently unconfined spaciousness, his present situation is too overwhelming to contemplate. Yet, he has the uncanny feeling that there is a wall or a floor or a ceiling just out of sight, behind, below or above him, just beyond what he can see without moving his head, but whenever he turns there is nothing, nothing remotely close to him in any direction.

The shuttle is already quite distant, no more than a point of light, and he knows he is more alone than he has ever been in his life. He dearly wishes Lisa had come with him, or that he had simply stayed with her. He knows he would have found her presence comforting, and he liked her. She is attractive and sexy, but she carries her sexiness very differently from the way in which a femdroid at a club does. She had not tried to attract or to seduce him, she had not used her beauty in any way. It is just an incidental feature of who and what she is.

He cannot quite believe now that he has voluntarily abandoned the shuttle. It is very unlikely that Sly would really try to have him killed. Now that he is no longer on the shuttle the certainty he had felt has evaporated, has bled into space like the air from the airlock. Sly trusts him, and that is surely why he showed Isabelle to him, why he entrusted him with the task of stealing Poppy. He half remembers something the old man said to him, something about preferring to believe that a man with whom he has shared a drink will not betray him. But his mind shies away from considering it further. Either way – whether or not he was mistaken in his fear – the subject is too difficult to consider just now, given the enormity of the decision he has made. He is trying not to succumb to outright terror and trying to second-guess his decision is not going to help. He tries closing his eyes, but that only makes it worse.

So he tries to think about his position rationally. Firstly, he wonders what there is to stop him falling immediately to the surface below. There is nothing holding him up. Away to his left he can see the orbital, his home. It looks very small to him now, not just because it is so far away, but also in comparison to the bulk of the planet. What holds the orbital up? Does it have engines of some kind, like the shuttle? He is sure Lisa could have answered his questions, but he is trying not to think about her or what he caused to happen to her arm, or what will happen to her now. He tries not to think about her small face as it appeared to him through the tiny window in the hatch. But of course, that is futile. His mind perversely insists on feeding him the very images and ideas he least wants to see or to contemplate.

He remembers Lisa's question, in fact a part of his mind has been preoccupied with it since she asked it.

'Do you love her?' she asked.

The question would have come as a surprise at any time and on anyone's lips. It certainly caught him off guard, but his response seemed important to her in their last moments together, although he had been unable to come up with an answer.

Does he love Cheryl, and what does it even mean? It is not a word men use very frequently, and then only as a synonym for something else, for sexual desire or lust, but he is certain Lisa had meant more than that.

When he thinks about Cheryl now he remembers his surprise at the way she argued with him recently, her insistence that they did not need Poppy and the way she had tried to block his entrance into the apartment. He hears again her verdict that his plan to steal Isabelle is a stupid one and likely to get him killed. But he also remembers the way she grabbed Poppy's arm in order to protect the fish, and her pride in the plant, the two presents he has given her. He remembers the suggestive look she gives him as she waves the bottle of the skin preserver at him and invites him to help her apply it. He remembers her greeting and the embrace she gives him whenever he returns to the apartment; her lingering kiss and the feel of her body against his own when he has sex with her. He is used to her now and the novelty of the first weeks and months after he bought her has faded, but perhaps it has been replaced with something else, a new feeling that is connected to her very familiarity.

Images of Poppy flood into his mind now, her face when he is trying to think about his feelings for Cheryl. He can see again the way Poppy's chest rises and falls as though she is really breathing, the inquiring way she turns her head to look at him, the way her eyelashes flutter as she studies his expression, trying to learn what he wants, what will please him. He wants to protect her, to shield her, although to protect her from what he is unclear. From the hurts and disappointments of life, he supposes. Yet he knows this feeling, this wish to keep her safe, is not entirely pure. It is dangerously close to his desire to have sex with her. He would like to have been able to protect Lisa too, to hold her gently and try to comfort her, and he would have tried to get her arm repaired. Perhaps Lars could have done it. Perhaps he still can if nothing happens to the shuttle and they both get safely back to the orbital. He hopes so.

Then he is seeing Poppy's face again, looking up at him expectantly, her eyes blinking at him. He had almost kissed her right there in the apartment in front of Cheryl, but the knowledge that Cheryl was watching had stopped him, and then the following morning when Poppy had sat on his lap it had taken a tremendous effort of will not to go very much further than mere kissing, and to refuse her offer to remove those white panties. Cheryl was watching that time too.

Cheryl. Yes, it will be very good to see her again. When he gets back to his apartment he is going to give her such an embrace he will be in danger of crushing her. He knows that with her arms around him he will feel safe once more, that her touch will soothe him and dispel the memory of the terror he feels now.

If he can only have one of them – if he has to choose between Lisa, Poppy and Cheryl – he can really only choose Cheryl. He cannot lose her, and apart from anything else the look of hurt in her eyes if he chose otherwise would haunt him for the rest of his life. He does not know if that answers Lisa's question.

The sudden light blinds him. The visor of the suit darkens automatically, but not quickly enough. As the light expands and spreads out it dims slowly, or perhaps the visor simply begins to filter it out. Then there is just a sort of greenish after-glow that might be in his eyes, and this fades more slowly and then is gone. The flashing light that had been the last evidence of the shuttle's position is gone now too.

He feels numb, unable to comprehend the reality of what has just happened, not that the shuttle has exploded, that Lisa is gone – evaporated along with the shuttle itself – but that the explosion had been meant for him. It feels so brutally personal, and though he had suspected it, the confirmation of that suspicion is still a shock. He feels betrayed and wronged and unbearably diminished by this assault upon him.

His mind is still a blank as he notices without much interest that a black spot has appeared on the white tether where it snakes out beside him. Then there is another, larger one, and then one right at the edge of the tether that frays the edge, forcing him to see that these are not spots, not patches of discolouration, but holes.

He swears. He knows very little about space, but he has heard of space debris. He can recall a drunken afternoon when Lars or one of the others had told him how foolish he is to take the shuttle given the amount of rubbish there is flying around out here, tiny fragments that can pass through the shuttle or almost anything else that gets in the way, and with awful results. The shuttle, the one that he has just got off, has now added to the total of the debris circulating about the planet, and the explosion has hurled some of it straight at him.

He grabs the tether and frantically begins to haul himself towards the shelter of the buoy, afraid that at any moment the tether will be cut completely. He tries not to think about what will happen if a piece goes through his suit, or perhaps straight through him at the same time. He realises that the explosion of the shuttle might kill him yet. Maybe it will even be some fragment of Lisa that does it. At this idea he angrily tells his imagination to be quiet, unless it has anything useful to contribute.

He reaches the buoy without the tether breaking and he tries to position his body so that it is in its shadow. It seems a miracle he has not been hit. He can feel the impacts on the buoy, but the debris seems to be moving too fast for him to see it as it shoots past him. He wonders what will happen if one of the oxygen tanks in the buoy is punctured. Will it explode? But there is no point in worrying about that. He is better off sheltering behind it, and if he is going to have any chance of being rescued, it is the buoy with its radio beacon and tanks of additional oxygen that will save him.

There is no gravity to work against, but it is a continual effort to hold his body in position. There are grab handles to hold on to, but he cannot seem to get a boot of the suit to lodge in one and the slightest movement sets him in motion, pivoting about the hand holding on to the buoy and making some part of himself dangerously exposed again.

Aftcr a while he thinks it ought to be safe. He reasons that all the particles from the explosion hurled in his direction will have passed him at about the same time. Then he wonders if larger fragments will travel more slowly. He decides not, given that there is no resistance from air to hold them back, but there is still inertia to consider, although he does not know if this is relevant in an explosion. As Lars told him recently, he could have paid more attention during his instruction and training programs. He cannot put any faith in his analysis, therefore, and he worries about simply sticking his head out to take a look.

He wakes to find himself floating some distance from the buoy. At first, he is afraid the tether has snapped, but he is still attached, for the moment. He hauls himself in again and tries to anchor himself by wrapping the tether around his legs. He is afraid of drifting off to sleep again or perhaps simply passing out.

The next time he wakes from some troubled dream he is being plagued by an annoying noise and someone is talking irritatingly and insistently into his ear.

Eventually he surfaces sufficiently to understand what the voice is saying.

'Oxygen level critical,' the voice is saying, or something like it, and he realises the annoying noise is an alarm inside the suit.

He is relieved to discover he is still close to the buoy. Wrapping the tether around his legs has apparently worked, but he has to unwrap it now in order to work his way around the buoy until he finds the hose outlets that Lisa showed him. He pulls out a hose and connects it to the suit as she had instructed. It is difficult to manage with the limited dexterity afforded by the suit gloves, but after stabbing the hose at his chest a few times he manages to make the connection and the annoying noise cuts off at once.

The voice in his ear changes its message. 'External oxygen supply connected,' the voice says matter-of-factly, as though this is of no consequence.

He is unable to tell if it is the lingering results of the drug that Lisa injected into him or if he is just astonishingly tired, but he keeps drifting in and out of consciousness. Even the memory of someone telling him that if the space debris does not kill you the radiation you are exposed to on every shuttle journey probably will, cannot keep him awake. He is too tired to care any more. He is cold and scared and very alone, and he tries to tell himself that if he is out here long enough for the radiation to be an issue he will run out of oxygen or become dehydrated anyway, although he has no idea how long it will be before any of these issues become critical.

There is something more urgent than any of those things, something that is already critical, and in the end he just has to let go. It feels very much better after he has done so, but then he worries that he might drown in his own urine. He is certain it would be a horrible way to go. He tells himself that he ought to keep his feet pointing downwards, and then he laughs at his joke, laughing harder and for longer than is warranted by his attempt at humour. Perhaps he is hysterical, or it is a sign that he is running out of air or something.

After a while he decides the suit must have some means of dealing with bodily excretions because he cannot feel the urine sloshing about inside it. So that at least is something positive.

Eventually, when he has lost all idea of time, he begins to sing to himself. He even tries to remember the song that the fish women had sung, but the tune remains stubbornly elusive when he tries to hum it.

15

'You're a very lucky man, Charlie.'

'I am?'

'I should say so, wouldn't you?'

He thinks he might have been luckier if he had not needed to leave the shuttle, if it had not exploded, and if someone was not trying to kill him, but he does not say any of this.

'The shuttle you're travelling on explodes, virtually vaporises,' the man says, using his hands to sketch an explosion in the air, 'but you manage to get into one of the suits and launch the buoy unscathed.'

Charlie touches his neck automatically, at the place where Lisa grazed him with the tranquilliser disc, but the wound is covered now with a sterile patch.

'Yes,' the man adds quietly, seeing his action, 'apart from the small wound on your neck. It doesn't bother you now?'

Charlie shakes his head. 'No,' he says, 'no, not really.'

'Remind me,' the man says, as if the answer is of no importance, 'how did you come by it?'

Charlie has so far failed to say anything about it and he shrugs now. 'I must have grazed it getting through the hatch from the cabin,' he suggests.

'Yes,' the man agrees slowly. 'Yes, it was probably something like that.'

Charlie makes no reply. He knows better than to add to his explanation.

He is in the infirmary back on Orbital B and he has been judged fit enough to speak to this policeman who has dropped by, just to see how he is. It is just a courtesy call really. The man is not wearing a uniform, so he is either not on duty or he is from the investigation branch. He has said his name is 'Wes', but has offered no more than this. It has all been very casual and low key, so much so that Charlie is not really sure who he is talking to, but he is smart enough to understand that casual or not, he is being interrogated, and he is too much of a salesman to let Wes' informal approach fool him.

He feels at a disadvantage because he is lying on the treatment gurney while Wes is standing and free to walk about while he talks, or as free as the cramped conditions in the cubicle allow. He had sat up when Wes came in, but the man told him to lie back again.

He knows he has to say as little as possible about what happened. Anything he says is liable to lead to discussion of all kinds of things he does not want to talk about, things that will almost certainly get him into all manner of trouble.

'I understand that maybe you don't feel ready to talk about it yet,' Wes says, man to man, 'but I'm just a little puzzled about what happened.'

Nobody can take exception to that, surely? Wes seems to be suggesting.

Charlie says nothing.

'I get it that there was some kind of accident and the shuttle exploded,' Wes says, 'but what I can't quite understand is why you got into an emergency suit and launched the buoy before it exploded.'

He lets that one go. There is an obvious reply and Wes gives it to him anyway, as Charlie suspected he would.

'Okay, so there wouldn't have been much point in leaving the shuttle after the explosion, because you would've been dead, blasted into tiny pieces.'

Charlie gives an involuntary shudder.

'Yeah, it's a scary thought,' the policeman nods sympathetically, seeing his reaction, but it was not fragments of his own body Charlie was thinking of.

'But you see,' Wes says, 'the question that's bugging me is how did you know that you needed to get off the shuttle? Did you know it was going to explode?'

Charlie looks surprised, or at least he hopes this is how the policeman will interpret his expression.

'No, I had no idea there was anything wrong,' he tells Wes innocently. He shrugs, 'I don't really know anything about shuttles or any other spacecraft.'

'No,' Wes agrees readily enough. 'Who does? I mean, apart from the men who design them.'

Charlie says nothing. It needs no reply. Wes is just talking.

'Femdroids,' Wes says now, 'or Synthias to be more precise: that's your area of expertise I believe?'

Charlie nods. This is probably safer ground.

'The shuttle hostess, the Syn, she stayed on

board?'

Wes knows that she had.

'I tried to get her to come with me,' he says. 'There was a spare suit. I couldn't see any reason why she should stay behind and be…' He shrugs again.

'Oh, I wouldn't worry too much about that,' Wes assures him soothingly, 'the shuttle company will have been insured against the loss of the Syn.'

'I liked her,' Charlie protests, 'and she…' He stops, his breath catching in his chest. 'She saved my life,' he says simply, as soon as he is able to speak again. It is a fine performance, but he is genuinely upset about what happened to Lisa.

'Yeah,' Wes agrees slowly. 'That's something, isn't it?'

Charlie leaves this piece of bait dangling where the policeman has left it for him and Wes goes on, 'I imagine you'll be able to get free drinks retelling the story.'

Charlie gives this a wide berth as well, but if Wes is disappointed he does not pick it up and run with it, the policeman is careful not to let it show.

'When I heard about the terrible thing that happened to you, I did a little research,' Wes confides instead, as if his curiosity is really something to be a little sheepish about, and certainly nothing to do with his job.

'Do you know how many shuttles have exploded?' Wes asks him conversationally.

'No,' he admits. 'Does it happen a lot?'

Wes looks at him. Perhaps he has spoiled the policeman's next line.

'That's what I wondered,' Wes says, proving that he is good at this game and can come right back. 'Shall I tell you the answer?'

He is unable to think of a reason for saying no, and in truth he is a little interested, so he nods, the professional straight man giving the comedian his cue.

'None,' Wes says with a flourish, showing that the box that ought to contain the glass with the drink in it is now miraculously empty. The Syn has not been sawn in half after all.

'No shuttles have ever exploded,' Wes says, 'before yours did, that is.'

Charlie says nothing. He is tempted to point out it was not his shuttle, but it might appear too pedantic.

'It's never happened before,' Wes adds, in case his somewhat unresponsive audience has missed the trick.

Charlie nods slowly and raises his eyebrows for the policeman, to signal he is duly impressed.

'So I also checked to see how often passengers have been obliged to use the emergency suits and the buoy,' Wes says.

Why not go the whole way while we are about it?

'You know, like you did, Charlie,' Wes adds.

'And?' he asks, just to keep the act going when Wes pauses a little too long.

'They never have,' Wes says at last, shaking his head almost sadly. 'They never have.'

'Really?' Charlie says, although he is not surprised. Lisa's examination of the suits gave him the impression they had not been used or checked in a long time.

'Impressive safety record,' Wes admits judiciously, like a hesitant customer acknowledging the virtues of a Synthia being offered to him.

'There've been a few collisions with SDPs,' Wes feels obliged to disclose now in the interests of openness.

'That's Small Debris Particles to you and me,' Wes explains.

Charlie nods. 'Right.'

'"Small" here means too small to be detected in advance,' Wes supplies, in case his audience is unfamiliar with the terminology.

'What happens if the shuttle gets hit by the particles?' Charlie asks. He genuinely wants to know, and he has to keep up his end of the conversation sometimes. He has to appear cooperative.

Wes shakes his head again. 'Nothing, apparently. The shuttles have a hull that's able to cope. There's some inner layer sandwiched in the middle that's self patching, and there's another layer that absorbs the velocity of the particles and catches them before they can penetrate the cabin,' Wes tells him, adding, 'And the passengers of course.'

'Right.'

'Pretty neat, huh?' Wes says.

Charlie nods.

'It's wonderful what science can do these days,' Wes muses slowly. 'But you'd know that, being an expert on Synthias,' he adds, once again offering him the ball.

Charlie nods. He is in danger of sustaining a neck

injury from all this nodding, but it is safer than talking.

'So, I guess you use these VIP shuttles a lot in your line of work?' Wes ventures.

It is a good pass, but he is sure Wes knows the answer to that one already.

Charlie shakes his head. At least this seems to use a different set of muscles.

'I suppose you thought you'd give yourself a treat,' Wes suggests. 'Hell, I bet you thought you'd earned it!'

Charlie decides to sit this one out entirely. Maybe if he keeps quiet long enough Wes will talk himself out. It is quite an act he has going, but it is wearing rather thin.

'No, that's right,' Wes corrects himself. He really must do something about his memory. 'You tried to use the regular commercial shuttle, but it had just left.'

Charlie wonders idly whether Wes is recording this conversation somehow and if so whether his performance is intended for a wider audience. Or maybe he just wishes he had chosen a different career, as an actor in the dramvids perhaps, instead of as a policeman.

'I suppose you were in a hurry and couldn't wait for the next one?' Wes hazards. 'That would be, what? Another four hours?'

'Nearly six hours,' he gives Wes. It is not much. It cannot hurt to concede that point.

'Six hours.' Wes nods seriously. 'Yeah, that's a stretch. Six hours is a long time when you're trying to close a deal, huh?'

Charlie says nothing.

'You have to put these things in perspective, don't you?' Wes suggests. 'Some men might object that it's half their monthly salary, but that's missing the point, isn't it?'

Charlie lets that one go past him too.

'What do they charge for the trip, by the way?' Wes asks, trying a more direct approach.

Charlie shrugs. 'You'd have to ask the man who booked it.'

'That's right,' Wes corrects himself again, all but slapping his forehead this time. What is he going to do about his memory?

'You didn't book it yourself,' Wes says.

This is not even a rhetorical question and Charlie sees no reason to answer.

'In fact, by all accounts,' Wes continues, 'you weren't even aware the shuttle had been booked for you.'

No need to respond to that either. Wes is still just talking, revealing how much work he has already put in on this.

'So, why do you think he did it?' Wes asks him.

Here it is at last, the first question to which Wes does not already have the answer.

'Why did he book the shuttle for you, Charlie?' Wes says quietly.

'I suppose he was just in a hurry to see me,' he tells the policeman. 'He wanted to talk to me.'

Wes looks surprised and this time it appears his surprise is genuine. This is not part of the routine.

'He booked the shuttle over to Orbital C for you because he wanted to talk to you?' Wes repeats slowly.

Charlie nods. It is after all what he himself assumed.

'Okay,' Wes says slowly.

Wes is surprised by his answer. There can be no doubt about that, but why? Had Wes expected him to say he thinks it was just an elaborate assassination plot; that it was because Sly wanted him out of the way? Sly's name has not been mentioned, but Wes has to know who booked the shuttle.

'So, let's go forward a bit,' Wes says, his manner different now. Let's just cut to the chase it seems to say.

'So, you're on your way, out there in the big nothing, admiring the view out of the window or maybe just admiring the hostess. What was it that made you decide to get off the shuttle mid-flight?'

16

By the time he finally escapes the infirmary and takes a passenger tube car in the direction of his apartment it is almost exactly twenty-four hours since he checked in with Lisa at the VIP shuttle desk the day before. He has lost a day of his life, but at least he is still alive.

Even after Wes left him he was told he had to remain for more tests or the results of tests. It was not quite clear which and he suspects it was a ruse, that they were just holding him for as long as they could. Perhaps Wes left instructions to this effect. Perhaps it was tests the policeman or his colleagues were conducting that the medic was referring to.

He knows Wes did not believe for a moment that the explosion on the shuttle was an accident, but there is no evidence Charlie was responsible. Nor can Wes disprove his story that it was Lisa who finally persuaded him he was in danger and that his only chance of saving himself was to use the emergency evacuation suits. Charlie eventually admitted that the mark on his neck resulted from Lisa's attempt to tranquillise him, but he told Wes it was because he had not shared the Syn's belief that something was wrong with the shuttle, that he had not wanted to get into one of the suits as she was insisting he should.

'I was terrified,' he told the policeman, 'And I thought she had simply malfunctioned in some way and would get me killed.'

Wes was silent for a long while after that and Charlie had remained silent too, not giving in to the temptation to add to his story or to try to embellish it.

'All the shuttle systems appeared to be operating normally, apart from the signal indicating that the emergency buoy had been launched,' Wes said quietly, 'right up until – presumably – the moment of the explosion, when contact with the shuttle suddenly ceased.'

Receiving no response, Wes added, 'How about that?'

Charlie simply shrugged.

'It doesn't look as though the Syn malfunctioned,' Wes told him, looking him directly in the eye. 'It looks as though it knew about, or detected a – a problem shall we say – that did not show up in the shuttle's diagnostics. What do you think that suggests?'

Charlie shrugged again, holding the policeman's gaze. 'I think it means that Syns are probably cleverer than we think. As I say, this one saved my life.'

Wes nodded slowly. Then he smiled, and Charlie thinks it was a not unfriendly smile.

'Spoken like the salesman you are,' Wes said. 'Maybe you should ask Synthia Corp for a raise. They made the one on the shuttle, didn't they?'

'No,' he told the policeman, 'it was a Paradise Corp model, one of their Angel range.'

He thinks this last question, almost a throw-away line delivered as Wes was getting up to leave, was a test of some kind; a test of his honesty perhaps. The policeman will have known exactly what kind of Syn Lisa was.

'But I have to admit that I was quite impressed with her,' Charlie added, 'even before she saved my life.'

Wes turned and smiled again and then departed, leaving him alone in the cubicle.

Now he feels mentally exhausted, but his experience does not seem to have harmed him physically. He is just a little hyped, as though he has drunk too much coffee. It might be the result of some drug he was given at the infirmary, or it is simply because he is trying to come to terms with the idea someone has tried to kill him. He alternates between feelings of betrayal and hurt and blind anger. On the whole, the anger is easier to bear than the sense of betrayal.

At last, he reaches his apartment and presses the communicator. Mid-morning or not, he is ready for a drink, for several perhaps.

Nothing happens; the door does not open and there is no response from the communicator panel. He presses it again and thumps the door for good measure. He wonders what the two of them can be doing in there.

When neither of these actions produces a response, he presses the unlock button, using the fingerprint scanner. The panel beeps, but instead of opening the door it displays a helpful message for him.

'Scan failed. Please enter your passcode.'

This has never happened before and he does not know if he even remembers the code. He thumps the door again, wondering what has gone wrong. He shouts again too, more loudly this time.

'Cheryl, let me in!'

But there is no response. There are no sounds of movement from inside or any answering call. A part of him is anxious now, but mainly he is just irritated. He breathes deeply and racks his tired brain for the entry code. At the third and final try permitted by the system he obtains a green light. But the door still fails to open.

He gives a shriek of frustration and kicks the door and finally it slides back, but slowly.

'Cheryl!' he shouts as he enters, 'Why didn't you…' and then he stops.

He does not need to search the apartment to know that neither of the Synthias are here. It is no more than a box really with nowhere for them to hide, but he looks in the tiny sanitation cubicle nevertheless, and then opens the closets for the clothes. He sees now that the other cupboards are already open, their contents spilled onto the floor and his easy chairs have been overturned. He tries to think what might have been taken. He does not have much, but he sees that the edvids from his employers are gone. A panel on one wall has been prised off, revealing some controls for air or water presumably, controls he did not even know were there. The only things he has lost are the obvious, the only two things that matter, and even one of them is not really his.

He stands for a moment, his brain unable to give his body any clear instructions about what to do next. Then he goes into the kitchen alcove and finds a bottle of drink in one of the cupboards. He finds a glass on the floor and pours a generous measure into it from the bottle. He drinks it down without noticing its taste or the reassuring burning in his throat after he has swallowed. Then he is sick, vomiting violently over the floor and over one of the upturned easy chairs. He looks at the mess, realising vaguely that it is a long time since he ate anything.

He goes into the sanitation cubicle and washes out his mouth and splashes water onto his face before drying it slowly on a towel. When he returns to the main room he sees that the door to his apartment is still open so he goes out into the hallway and looks around. There is no one to be seen in either direction, and certainly no sign of the only two things he is really interested in seeing.

Returning to his apartment he considers that there are two possibilities, two explanations for the present state of things. Perhaps there are more than two, but he is unable to come up with a third just at the moment.

Option One is that Steev and his colleagues have worked out who stole the missing unit and came looking for him. Finding him not at home they retrieved the stolen property and confiscated Cheryl. If that is the case it is only a matter of time before he is picked up and interrogated. If, as is probable, he is sent to a penal colony all his property will be forfeit and Cheryl will likely be deactivated and recycled. Poppy they can probably sell as a reconditioned unit. Vos will get a brand new replacement. Everything will have been neatly tidied away. He is not quite sure why Steev and his men searched the apartment, nor can he guess what they might have been looking for, but that is a minor detail.

Synthia Corp and its employees may have thought that he was dead when they came to his apartment. This is really Option One-Point-One. In this option they took Poppy and Cheryl anyway, and they will soon discover that he is not dead after all and therefore it is still only a matter of time before he is picked up and interrogated, unless that is, he can escape from the orbital somehow and hide out somewhere. Neither possibility seems likely and certainly not both, not for any length of time.

Or, and this has to be Option Two, Sly sent someone to his apartment knowing he would not be there and that he would not be returning any time soon for the simple but compelling reason that he was on a one-way shuttle ride and would soon be dead, if he was not dead already. In this option Sly wanted to retrieve what he sees as his property, namely Poppy, and either he ordered his men also to take Cheryl or they took her for their own purposes, ransacking his apartment in the hope of finding something else worth taking. In this option, it will also soon be known that he is not dead, and it will therefore only be a matter of time before another attempt is made to kill him or he is captured and taken to Sly. As with Option One, the possibility of escaping and hiding somewhere might be a temporary if not permanent solution, but hiding from Sly is probably no easier than hiding from Synthia Corp. Steev and his colleagues have the law on their side, but Sly has money and power and, as recently demonstrated, Sly is ruthless.

He realises now that he can think of a third possibility, and he is quite pleased with this refinement because it combines both the other options. Steev and Sly's men came looking for him, and it does not matter much in which order this occurred. The first callers took Poppy and Cheryl and the second group ransacked the apartment, annoyed at not finding what they really wanted. As with the first two options, his future – to put it no more strongly – does not look hopeful.

So, now he has it sorted in his head. That is a start. But he cannot keep up the pretence he is capable of thinking about the problem rationally and of devising, never mind actually carrying out, a sensible and workable course of action based on such an assessment. He is angry, scared and frankly beside himself with worry about what might be happening even now to Cheryl, if not also to Poppy. He stares around the apartment not seeing anything and not knowing even what to look for.

After a moment his brain registers something. At first, he has no idea what it is, but his head turns back to look at whatever it is that triggered the response. There is nothing there. There is just an empty space. Then he realises this is the point and he looks again. There is a shelf in a recess in one wall of the apartment. Cheryl keeps both the fish in its tank and the plant on that shelf. Neither is on the shelf now, nor are they on the floor below and a quick scan of the apartment reveals that they too are missing.

He tries to see how this fits into Option One. Perhaps Cheryl refused to leave without the plant and the fish. He can easily imagine her protests at being asked to leave them behind, but he cannot really believe that Steev and his colleagues said, 'Okay, bring them with you' or that Steev said to one of his men, 'Here, you carry this for her.' If they took Cheryl it is because they are confiscating his property and she will be deactivated. They will not worry about humouring her attachment to a plant and a small fish.

Nor can he assimilate the taking of the plant and the fish into Option Two. Even less so, he thinks. It just cannot be made to fit into the story at all.

So perhaps there is an Option Three – number Four actually, if Three is a combination of One and Two – even if he is unable to think what it is. All he can come up with is the certainty that if Cheryl was allowed to take the plant and the fish it suggests that she left without too much of a struggle, but he is unable to get further than this in inventing a scenario to explain how and why she and Poppy left, and more usefully, where they might be now. But there is a gap, a small one admittedly, through which a slim hope might squeeze.

He remembers his recent judgement that Lars is an essentially decent individual, even if the man stretches the law sometimes. He cannot tell his friend very much, but perhaps Lars can still give him some useful advice. He can think of nothing else to do.

17

Persuading the apartment door to close again is as difficult as getting it to open had been and he almost decides to leave it. There is nothing left in the apartment that matters, but leaving the door open invites curiosity and signals that something is very wrong, and it is hard to break the habit of closing and securing the door after him. It is impossible to kick the door now it is retracted into the wall, so he kicks the wall instead and this works quite well.

There is a man some way off down the hallway. Charlie thinks the man was watching him as he wrestled with the door, but when he looks now the man is walking away. Maybe the man will report him for vandalism, but his life can hardly get worse, and he has far more important things to worry about.

At the passenger tubes he gets into a car and

gives his destination as the enterprise zone where Lars has his workshop. As the doors begin to close, he happens to catch sight of a man a little way off. Perhaps he had been looking in Charlie's direction. The man is turning now, about to walk away, but something about the man is familiar somehow and as the car begins to move, he realises it was the man who had been watching him outside the apartment. His tired brain does little more than register this fact, tucking it away for storage in case it should ever be pertinent.

After a minute or two during which he has almost drifted off to sleep, it occurs to him that the man is following him. His first instinct is to reject the idea as unhealthy paranoia, but there is a growing list of men and their associates who might have their reasons for wanting to see what he is up to and with whom he meets. On this list are Synthia Corp, Sly and now the police. After a moment's indecision while he worries what if anything he should do, he gives the car a different destination and he feels it switch routes without complaint.

As he sits there, impatient for the car to reach its destination, he feels irritated and frustrated that he now has something else to worry about. He has lost enough time already and he wonders why other men cannot leave him alone. He has a plan he is trying to put into action and he wants to get on with it. He does not have the time to deal with men from Synthia Corp pestering him or with other men trying to kill him, or the police interrogating him about exploding shuttles. And now he has to find Cheryl and Poppy before he can begin to do anything else. And as if all of that is not enough, it looks as though he has a man following him so that he is forced to make a detour and waste yet more time instead of going directly to see Lars.

He reminds himself that he has to remain calm and discovers that reminding yourself to keep calm is actually no less irritating than having someone else do it for you. How can he keep calm, he wants to shout at himself, given everything that is going on?

He gets out in the leisure zone where most of the clubs and bars are located. He does not look around or attempt to see if the man has followed him, but sets off purposefully towards the area where most of the big clubs are concentrated. Then he enters almost the first club he comes to. It is dark inside, the air thick with drink and the odour of too many men who do not wash frequently enough, men who are now sitting together in a confined space. There is a floor show in progress featuring two Syns, one with her arms bound behind her and with something in her mouth. The other femdroid is dragging her across the stage into the circle of light.

He has no interest in seeing what will happen next. In any case, he is more interested in the audience and who might be joining it very soon. He sits at the first table that has a free seat. One of the men already seated at the table begins to protest, but Charlie makes a sign to the man to be quiet, gesturing behind him with his eyes. The man nods, an almost imperceptible motion, and then turns his attention back to the floor show.

Someone comes into the club. There is a brief

increase in light from the area of the door, a light that just as quickly fades, and there is also that slight change in the air and sound quality that occurs whenever an outer door is opened into an enclosed space. He keeps his head facing the show, leaning forward over the table to make himself less conspicuous, but his senses are straining to detect what is happening behind him, not what is going on on the stage. The newcomer passes him after a moment, the man's head turning slowly from side to side. The man might just be looking for a seat, but it is too much of a coincidence if that is the case, because it is the same man that was outside his apartment and again at the station for the passenger tubes. As the man passes the table there is a sudden shout of appreciation or encouragement from the audience, and taking advantage of the distraction Charlie stands and slips out the way he came in.

Outside, he goes a little way down the passageway and then ducks into the doorway of another club. An illuminated sign above the door proclaims that its name is Venial Syns. It is an odd name, but he has more important things on his mind at present. There is a small recess, a kind of foyer, that allows the club's personnel to screen customers before they are allowed to enter or are turned away as either too drunk, too dishevelled or perhaps simply too poor.

Charlie stands just inside the foyer. Then he puts his head out to look back the way he has come.

'You coming in, mate, or not?' one of the bouncers asks him.

‘Maybe,’ he tells the bouncer. ‘I’m waiting for someone.’

Charlie puts his head out into the walkway again, but ducks it quickly back in again. The man who is following him has come out of the club and is looking in his direction.

‘Been making a nuisance of yourself,’ the bouncer asks him, eyeing him suspiciously, ‘or are you just playing hard to get?’

Charlie gives the bouncer a look and then puts his head out again. The man is going away now, but walking slowly. As soon as his pursuer has rounded the corner, Charlie leaves the club’s foyer and walks briskly off in the opposite direction. Then he makes for the nearest stop for the passenger tubes and this time takes a car all the way to the enterprise zone.

When he reaches Lars’ workshop he presses the communicator panel outside.

‘Yeah?’

From his offhand tone it sounds as though Lars is busy.

He gives his name, expecting the click of the lock and the green light to follow.

Instead, Lars gives another more cautious, ‘Yeah?’

‘It’s Charlie, let me in.’

He knows the screen no longer works so Lars will not be able to see him, but his friend must recognise his voice.

The lock clicks and the green light finally appears, and he pushes the door open and goes in, but before he has taken more than a step, something is thrown over his head, hitting his shoulders hard and effectively blinding him. At the same time his right arm is seized and wrenched painfully up behind his back.

He cries out in surprise and protest and the thing is taken off his head. It is a small crate and it is no wonder it hurt, but his arm and shoulder are hurting more.

'Charlie!' a voice says behind him, its tone somewhere between surprise and disgust. The voice belongs to Lars, however, and Charlie's arm is released.

'What are you doing here?' Lars asks as Charlie turns to face him. 'You should be in the mortuary along with the other dead men. Walking around like this you're liable to stink after a day or two.'

He asks Lars what he means, massaging his shoulder and neck, and feeling aggrieved as well as shaken.

'The news is you're dead, blown to little pieces when the shuttle you were on exploded.'

Charlie is not ready to deal with that yet.

'Why did you jump me when I came in?' he asks instead.

'I don't get many social calls from dead people,' Lars says, looking him over, 'it's not healthy.'

While Charlie struggles to think of a suitable reply, Lars asks, 'Were you followed?'

'Yes, but I lost him.'

'Who was it?'

Charlie shrugs and Lars opens the door into the passageway and looks in each direction before closing the door again and making sure it is locked.

'Well, I hope you're right,' Lars says finally, 'but there's no one hanging about outside at the moment.'

'Who says I'm dead?' Charlie asks, finally understanding what Lars told him.

'Everyone. The police especially. They're making out it's an accident of course, like the ones that happened to the others.'

'I got off the shuttle before it exploded,' Charlie explains.

'Yeah, I figured it was something like that,' Lars says. 'Either that or it's a very good reconstruction job. I can't even see the joins.'

'You don't seem surprised I was nearly killed.'

'I'm not,' Lars says. He is still looking at Charlie with a wary expression. 'I was more surprised when it seemed someone wanted me out of the way as well.'

Before Charlie can ask him what he means, Lars indicates a man lying in a corner of the workshop.

'Is he dead?'

'His heart is still doing its beating thing, if that means anything, and there wouldn't have been much point tying him up if he was dead.'

Charlie asks what happened.

'I hit him with this.' Lars picks up a leg that had once been part of a femdroid.

Charlie noticed the leg when he was here before. It was sticking out of a box.

'I kept it because I thought some of the parts might come in handy one day,' Lars says. 'I'm glad I did.'

'What kind of Syn was it?'

'I think it was an old Desiree model.'

Lars inspects the thigh joint, where various connectors protrude from it. 'A Mark Four model, I think. They made them to last.'

'Why did you hit him?'

'He became distinctly unfriendly,' Lars says, putting the leg down again.

Then he picks up a second something from the work bench and offers it to Charlie.

'And he came at me with this.'

Charlie is reluctant to take it, uncertain how to hold it safely. 'What's it for?

'They might issue them to military personnel I suppose, but I can't think of anything good you can do with it, not unless your food at El Torro is really tough one night.'

Charlie turns the thing over slowly and asks Lars what it is made of. 'It's not metal.'

'No, it's some kind of synthetic alloy. Makes it harder to detect I suppose. Anyway, the guy just touched me with it, and it opened me up pretty good.'

Lars holds up an arm and Charlies sees now he has it bandaged from the wrist up to the elbow.

'Did he say what he wanted?'

Lars shrugs. 'Pretended at first he was a customer looking to get some work done. That's before he got out the blade, but I knew there was something funny about him right off. Maybe he just has a problem with his eyes, but they kept darting around the workshop like he was looking for something, or somebody.'

'What do you think he was looking for?'

Lars just looks at Charlie for a moment and then

suggests they go into the office. This time Charlie gets to have the chair, while Lars pulls out the empty crate.

When Charlie sits, the chair almost tips him off again.

'You should have remembered about the missing castor,' Lars tells him.

Charlie balances the chair and scoots it back to the wall. Provided he does not let the chair roll forwards it is stable like this. The greasy mark on the wall suggests Lars regularly does the same thing.

'So, what's the story?' Lars asks him when he is settled.

Charlie gives him an edited version of his experience.

'I realised it was a set up,' he says finally.

Lars nods. 'But you only realised that when you got bored with asking the hostess to show you the things you can do with the seat harnesses, not right away.'

Charlie ignores this, and Lars says, 'I warned you you were dealing with dangerous men.'

Charlie says he remembers. 'I think you saved my life, you and the Syn both.'

Lars gives a dismissive grunt. 'You heard about Mat?' he asks after a moment.

'What about him?'

'Official version is he fell out of the lift on his way down to the floor of the dock, day before yesterday it must have been. Whatever really happened, he reached the bottom far too quickly for his own good, and made quite a mess by all accounts.'

'It's a long way down,' Charlie says, his mouth suddenly dry. 'But why Mat?'

Lars shrugs. 'You ask that, and it suggests you have a good idea why someone might want *you* dead. So do you?'

Charlie does not reply, and Lars just looks at him.

'That's what I thought,' Lars says finally. 'So you tell me why someone might want to kill Mat. Did he work for your pal Sly?'

Charlie is thinking, or what passes for thinking with him at the moment. He cannot imagine any direct connection between Mat and Sly. The only connection he knows of is indirect, via himself, and that leads to all kinds of possibilities that make his head ache more than it already does, so he lies to his friend and says no.

'You had dealings with Mat recently?'

Charlie hesitates and then tells Lars lots of men have dealings with him. 'You know that.'

Lars just looks at him again and they sit in silence,

'What are you going to do now you're dead?' Lars asks him when the silence has lasted too long.

'But I'm not dead.'

'Not yet anyway,' Lars says, 'but it might be safer to stay dead for the moment.'

Charlie asks him what he means.

'Well, it might help with your taxes, but I was really thinking of your long-term health. Someone's liable to try again when they hear you're still ambulatory.'

Charlie sighs. He is unfamiliar with the word and is too tired to pretend otherwise.

'It means you're walking about more than is usual for a dead man,' Lars tells him.

Charlie sighs again. He is not in the mood for wise cracks. He is shocked about Mat, and he needs time to think about the timing of this latest death.

'I'm trying to find my Synthia,' he says, feeling unable to sit here any longer. 'Someone's been to my apartment and searched it. My Syn's missing, and so is …'

He stops himself, remembering no one is supposed to know about Poppy.

'The other one,' Lars finishes, making it clear he already knows. 'She's cute, I'll give you that. Must be a Special.'

'You know about her?'

Lars ignores the interruption. 'But that Cheryl of yours, she's a fierce one. Nearly took my head off.'

'What do you mean?'

'Wouldn't even let me in. Blocked my way and I think she'd have damned near killed me if I hadn't backed off.'

'You went to my apartment?'

'Yeah. I figured if you were dead or just in some kind of trouble someone should look out for you. First thing either the police or your enemies will do is go to your apartment...'

'Where are they now?' Charlie demands anxiously, 'Cheryl and Poppy?'

'It's okay,' Lars says soothingly. 'They're safe,'

Charlie feels himself relax a little. 'Where are

they?'

'Like I say, I couldn't persuade that Cheryl of yours I was a friend and was just trying to help, so I went to get the old man. I guessed the other one was the Syn he'd helped you with, after you came here asking about disabling a Syn's tracking device. Just hypothetically, of course. Anyway, she recognised Hans right off and greeted him like they were old pals, and after a bit she persuaded Cheryl he's a friend of yours. So they're both with him now, him and the old woman he has.'

'They're with Hans?'

Lars nods. 'Yeah, like I told you, and the plant and the fish thing in the tank too. Cheryl wouldn't leave without them.'

Charlie thinks about what Lars has told him for a while, or maybe he is just too tired to absorb the information quickly.

Then he says slowly, 'So, you were what, looking out for me?'

'Yeah, that's nice, I must say!'

Lars sounds offended. 'I was trying to help. You ought to know that if you're dead they'll take the Syns away; if whoever wanted you recycled hadn't got there first. And it isn't as if that Cheryl of yours would let another man near her.'

Charlie says nothing. Then he asks what Lars was searching for.

Lars looks puzzled, before voicing the conclusion Charlie has already reached for himself. 'So someone went to the apartment after Hans and I left.'

Charlie says nothing.

'What do you think they were looking for?'

Charlie shakes his head. He genuinely has no idea.

'If they ransacked the apartment, I guess it wasn't Poppy they were looking for,' Lars says. 'There's nowhere to hide a Syn in your apartment; nowhere that requires a search of any kind. I also think that whatever it is, it's probably what the guy sleeping it off out there in the shop was after.'

Charlie nods, but he is struggling to fit the facts into any kind of coherent explanation.

'What are you mixed up in, Charlie?' Lars asks.

Charlie is wondering that too. Neither of the scenarios he considered while surveying the wreckage of his apartment seem adequate now, not on their own.

'They're still saying I'm dead?' he asks, instead of answering Lars' questions.

'I haven't heard otherwise.'

'Why do you think that is? Why would they do that?'

Lars scratches the back of his head. He says the police must know it was not an accident, and they must know the other deaths were not accidents either. 'Maybe they're trying to flush out the man responsible. Something like that.'

'Maybe,' Charlie agrees.

'What did you tell the police?' Lars asks him. 'I'm guessing they didn't just welcome you back and ask how your trip was.'

'I didn't tell them anything. I said that the Syn on board thought something was wrong with the shuttle and made me get into an evac suit.'

'They believe you?'

Charlie shakes his head. 'But they can't prove I'm lying.'

'I'm presuming you didn't just steal the other Syn, Poppy or whatever her name is, no matter how cute she is. You must know you can't get away with it long term.'

Charlie hesitates. He knows that.

He tells Lars agents from Synthia Corp's security arm are already on the orbital. 'I met one of them yesterday morning.'

Lars looks worried. 'They questioned you about the missing Syn?'

'It was just a coincidence. They weren't looking for me. I mean, they didn't think I'd stolen the missing Syn, not really.'

Lars shakes his head. 'Not really,' he repeats in a mocking tone.

'It's complicated,' Charlie tells him and Lars shrugs again.

'Whatever you say. My point is I'm guessing you stole Poppy because someone asked you to.'

Charlie hesitates and then agrees it was something like that.

'Mat help you with it?' Lars asks quietly.

Charlie wants to ask what that has to do with anything, but he knows what Lars is suggesting.

'Re-routing the Syn must have pissed someone off mightily, and my guess is that was the point.' Lars nods to himself. 'But Tan and Nils weren't involved in that. Whatever the deal was they were talking about before they died it must have been way bigger than that.'

It is a statement, not a question and Charlie feels no need to comment.

After a moment Lars says, 'It's possible that somebody was attempting to squeeze information out of Mat. They could have dangled him over the drop to persuade him to talk, and then helped him get to the bottom faster because he didn't cough, or maybe even if he did, just to cover their tracks. Or maybe it just went wrong.'

Charlie remembers the elevator and the drop only too well. It is a horrible idea.

'You arrange to have a man contribute to the small particle debris and you don't stand a chance of learning much,' Lars muses, 'but what happened to Mat might be different.'

'I can't really think straight at the moment,' Charlie says. 'I need to go and get Cheryl and Poppy now.'

'Where are you going afterwards? I wouldn't go back to your apartment.'

He tells Lars he will figure something out. He is unable to think about the next steps until he has seen for himself that Cheryl and Poppy are okay.

'What are you going to do about the guy who attacked you?' Charlie asks. 'You can't…'

'Can't let him go, you mean? Or I can't kill him?'

Charlie's expression gives Lars his answer.

'It would be stupid to let him go, but no, I can't kill him. If he had stopped breathing after I got him acquainted with the inner thigh of the Desiree's leg, I wouldn't have cried too much about it. I was pretty pissed off with him, and bleeding all over the floor to boot.'

'What will you do?'

'A guy I know deals in second-hand biologicals,' Lars says.

That is the thing about Lars: he always knows someone.

'I figure he may have a spare suspender unit where we can freeze the guy until we think it's safe to let him out, or until the unit's needed for a woman.'

'Will he be all right afterwards?'

Charlie has a new interest in the effects of suspension.

'From what I hear he may feel lousy for a while and have a tendency to vomit when he thaws, but there won't be any lasting problems. Depending on how long the unit's free it may just be that he's become younger than the men he used to hang out with.'

'Do you need any help?' Charlie asks, 'getting him over to your friends' business, I mean?'

'No, you go and find your Syns,' Lars tells him. 'I can manage. There's a freight tube stop just down the hall. I'll go over and get an empty crate and then we can shift him over there pretty easy.'

Charlie thanks him. He is glad his help is not needed.

Lars nods. 'Just remember, friends look out for each other, or there isn't much point to our sorry existence.'

18

Hans proves no less cautious about admitting a man presumed dead than Lars had been, and Charlie reflects that being dead could seriously affect a man's social life.

As before, the door is opened only a fraction when he knocks, just enough to allow one of the occupants to ask, 'Who is it?'

He announces himself and hears some exchange of words inside together with sounds of movement. Then the door opens some more, but leaving the gap tight enough so he has to squeeze through it, preventing him from rushing at anyone inside or several men entering at once.

He is met by the two of them, Hans and Will. Both face him with what look to be some kind of weapon directed at his chest, devices that have a crude, home-made look. Cheryl is standing to one side, trying to shield Poppy by placing herself between the other Syn and whatever might be coming through the door.

For what feels like a long moment no one speaks. Charlie seems unable to make the first move. They can see it is him, and he lets them adjust to the change in his status: from dead to merely feeling lousy.

It is Cheryl who breaks the silence.

'Charlie!' she says, coming towards him. 'I say you not dead. I say not Charlie, he too clever to be killed!'

The old couple smile at him, and Hans takes the weapons and tries to hide them.

'We didn't know what to expect,' Hans says. 'The news is you're dead, but it's true your Cheryl wouldn't accept it. She refused to give up on you.'

Cheryl has stopped short of him. She looks at him intently but seems unsure what to do.

'She's fiercely loyal to you,' Hans tells him when none of them moves, 'but I guess you know that.'

'Anyway, we're all mighty glad to see you,' the old man adds when everyone else seems tongue-tied and unable to speak.

'Thanks,' Charlie says at last. It is inadequate, given the lengths to which Hans has gone, but it is all he can manage at present.

'Why don't you embrace each other,' Hans says, looking from him to Cheryl. 'You don't need to be shy in front of us.'

The truth is he does feel inhibited. He remembers deciding the first thing he would do when he returned was to hold his Synthia in such a fierce embrace he would be in danger of crushing her, but he cannot do it in front of the old man and his woman. It is the sort of thing a man might do in the privacy of his own apartment.

Hans asks when he last ate. 'You look pretty done in.'

Charlie struggles to remember and then realises it

had been breakfast the day before.

'It's been a while,' he admits, 'but we really ought to go and get out of your way.'

'Nonsense,' Will says.

Charlie is surprised she feels able to say such a thing to a man – and to a man who is not her owner – however kindly it is meant.

'Hans and I will get you something to eat,' Will tells him, 'And you can get re-acquainted with your lovely ladies. Then I'm sure we all want to hear what happened to you.'

He feels overwhelmed, but guesses he is simply suffering from a mixture of a lack of food and delayed shock.

'You're very kind,' he tells her.

'Nonsense,' Will says again. 'And we've really enjoyed having Cheryl and Poppy visit. Cheryl and I have had such a lovely long talk.'

Charlie can think of nothing to say.

Hans is nodding at him and smiling and the whole scene feels unreal, as though he has become a character in some dramvid, the kind in which characters speak to each other using stilted and unlikely lines, living lives that are equally unlikely and full of emotions that none of the men he knows would ever admit to experiencing.

Hans eventually tells him to sit down before he falls down, with what feels like more realistic common sense. Then the old man and Will disappear out back somewhere.

When the old couple have gone, Cheryl comes closer and he takes her hand. She pulls him into the tight embrace he imagined giving her. She does not hold back now the three of them are alone, as though she had not wanted to embarrass him in front of Hans.

'Charlie,' Cheryl says into his neck. 'I told you, you must be careful. Why you not listen to Cheryl?'

'I did listen, honey,' he tells her, 'That's why I'm still alive.'

Over Cheryl's shoulder and through strands of Cheryl's hair he spies Poppy standing uncertainly in the far corner, unsure what she ought to do. He smiles and beckons to her to come over, and she comes forward eagerly, but he is reluctant to disentangle himself from Cheryl's embrace, so he simply takes one of Poppy's hands in his own and squeezes it.

The feel of Cheryl's arms around him begins to ease some of the tension, but he is trembling now.

'Come,' Cheryl instructs him, raising her head from his chest. 'You come and sit.'

He collapses into one of the easy chairs, grateful as it takes his weight, but he does not let go of Cheryl's hand. She is wearing a dress he has not seen for a while, with a short, full skirt and a low-cut top with straps over her shoulders. It goes well with her hair and skin. Perhaps she has chosen it because she noticed the way he responded to the outfit Poppy chose the previous day and is wearing now.

'Come here,' he says quietly. He tugs at Cheryl's hand and gestures for her to sit on his lap, and she sits across him with her legs over the arm of the chair. Then she puts her arms around his neck and leans back, looking up into his face.

He bends to kiss her, but she pulls back and puts

a hand to his cheek.

'You need shave, Charlie,' she says, feeling the stubble on his cheeks with her fingers. 'And maybe shower too.' She wrinkles her nose to emphasise her point.

He smiles and nods. 'I guess,' he says, but for the moment he wants only to sit here like this with her. They have not done anything like this in a long time, not since the early days, when she was still a marvel to him.

'Why men grow hair on their cheeks, Charlie?' she asks, letting his arms take her full weight while she studies his face.

He shrugs. 'I don't know,' he says. 'You don't like it?'

'I like it when you have shaved and your face smell of the shaving cream, and the skin is tight and smooth. Then it is sexy.'

'Sexy, huh?'

He is used to telling her what he finds sexy about her own body or the things she does. She never tells him whether she likes something or not, and he has not thought about her preferences or tastes, has not considered that she has desires of her own, beyond an inbuilt desire to please a man in whatever way he wants.

He bends and kisses her forehead and then the tip of her nose. 'You're always sexy,' he tells her.

'That is Synthia's job, I think,' she tells him seriously, and he tells her she does her job very well.

'It is easy with you, Charlie,' she says simply. 'You are good man and Cheryl like to make you happy.'

He wonders if he is a good man, and whether Cheryl really thinks so.

'If you had died, Charlie, I would be recycled, and I would be glad because I not want new owner. Cheryl want to live only with you.'

He finds his eyes growing embarrassingly moist, but he knows he is in a weakened state and needs proper sleep and food. He blinks away the tears and hopes she will not notice them.

'But I more glad you not dead,' she says, snuggling her face against his chest.

'I'm glad too, honey,' he says, and they sit quietly like that for long minutes.

'What is point of men, Charlie?' she asks him suddenly, her voice a little muffled by his shirt.

'What's the point of men?' he repeats. 'What do you mean?'

She looks up. 'Point of Synthia is to make men happy,' she says. 'Men make Synthia for sex, to give them food and maybe for friend. But what is point of men?'

'To make Synthias happy?' he suggests with a smile.

'No, Charlie,' she says. 'You make Cheryl happy, but you cannot say point of Synthia is to make men happy and point of men is to make Synthia happy. It is not logical. It is like circle. Men explain Synthia, but not other way round.'

He blows out his cheeks. 'I'm not sure I understand.'

'Even if you are careful and other men do not kill

you, Charlie, you still get old like Hans and then one day you die. Then everything you have is finished, is gone. So, I wonder, while I wait to see if you are dead, what is point?'

'Oh, I see,' he says. He does see, but he cannot begin to answer her question. Perhaps no man could. He is reminded of what Lars said to him about men's sorry existence, but friends helping each other is surely not a sufficient explanation of man's existence.

'But you not dead yet,' Cheryl says, her face once again buried in the folds of his shirt. 'And that make Cheryl glad.'

He kisses the top of her head. 'No,' he says softly. 'Not dead yet.'

They sit quietly again, without moving or talking and he thinks he might drift off to sleep, but then Cheryl sits up and says, 'Now I think you sit with Poppy.'

He wants to protest; he is happy sitting here like this with Cheryl.

'You must have turn with Poppy,' Cheryl says firmly, and she gets off him and stands.

He is unable to say anything. He holds on to her hand for as long as he can, but she pulls away and goes over to the other Synthia.

'You sit with Charlie now?' Cheryl asks her.

Poppy says nothing, but after a moment she nods. Then she keeps her head down, not meeting his eyes as she comes over to him and sits on his lap as Cheryl had done. She lays her head against his chest, her legs over the arm of the chair.

Tentatively, he puts an arm around her. He can

smell the fragrance on her, the same perfume that he had been aware of when she sat on his lap a couple of days before. He buries his face in the curls of her hair. It is fine and springy, and it has its own appealing smell.

Poppy changes her position slightly and snuggles into him more closely, but he does not think she does this in order to arouse him, not this time. She seems to want to be reassured, to simply feel safe in his presence and confident of his affection. He pulls his arm around her more tightly and takes one of her hands where it rests on her lap and holds it in his own. Then he lays his head on the back of the chair. He is suddenly very tired, and he sleeps like that, the gentle weight of the Synthia pressed against him and keeping him warm.

When he wakes again, Poppy is shaking him. She is still sitting on his lap, but Hans and Will are holding plates of food before him and there are drinks and more food on the low table. He feels quite a bit better and realises he is very hungry.

'We let you sleep for a while,' Will tells him, 'But we think you ought to eat something as well.'

It is a novelty for him to share food with others. There is some passing of dishes between them, and discussion of the various ingredients and he enjoys the social aspect of the meal. At first, he tries to hide his hunger out of politeness, until Will tells him that she wants to see him eat. The food is not simply for show, she tells him. Cheryl and Poppy can only watch, of course, and neither Hans nor his woman will allow either of them to help in anyway.

'You're our guests,' Will tells them, 'And we don't often have visitors.'

It is also a novelty for him to be in the company of a biological woman, young or old, and to see just a little of how Hans and Will interact and share their lives. In many ways it is not so different from the life he shares with Cheryl, apart from the fact that Will also eats and drinks. What is different is the extent to which they appear to be almost equals in the relationship, but perhaps it is because of her advanced age that Hans appears just as likely to wait on Will as she is to serve him.

Cheryl is very quiet, as though she thinks it is not her place to speak in this company, but he sees her watching intently, absorbing everything that goes on and listening to whatever is said. Hans tries to draw her into the conversation but has more success with Poppy and this is also interesting for Charlie has barely heard her speak. Her conversation brings home to him what Hans told him, that everything is still very new and strange to her, but she talks quite freely with both Hans and Will and is not afraid to ask questions whenever she encounters something she does not know or understand.

After they have eaten Charlie tells them the story of what happened to him on the shuttle. Unlike Lars, this audience is keen to hear a lot more about how and why he was on the VIP shuttle and then about what occurred during the trip as well as after he got into the evacuation suit and left the shuttle. He tries to describe the view from the window of the shuttle and then through the visor of the suit and what it was like to find himself floating free, with nothing below, around or above him, except for the bulk of the planet. He sees Poppy's eyes grow wide when he tells them how he saw the orbital from outside and tells them that it had looked small in comparison to the planet below.

'Were you falling?' Poppy asks him uncertainly, clearly more shy about speaking to him than she is with the old man.

He opens his mouth to reply but hesitates, and he is glad when Hans steps in and explains that Charlie would have been in orbit about the planet, just as the orbital itself is, and what this means and why it meant Charlie had not been in any immediate danger of falling to the surface below.

'It felt as though I ought to fall,' he tells Poppy when Hans has finished, 'even though I knew I wouldn't.'

He is not going to let on that Hans' explanation is as new to him as it is to her. He is a man, and he ought to have known and understood what being in orbit meant. He has after all spent his whole life in that position.

It is perhaps natural that both Poppy and Cheryl are particularly keen to hear about Lisa and the role she played.

'She was very pretty, this Syn?' Cheryl asks him, and he agrees she had been.

Poppy appears more interested in the fact that Lisa supervised him boarding the shuttle and in the proper use of the seat harness, and in the fact that it was Lisa who showed him how to get into the suit and how to launch the buoy.

'That was her job,' he tells her. 'She had been given training in how it all worked and what to do if there was an emergency. She was responsible for the safety of the passengers.'

'And there was no man on the shuttle?' Poppy asks him.

He shakes his head. 'No, I was the only passenger, like I told you.'

Poppy hesitates. 'But there was no man in charge, to look after the passengers and the shuttle?' she persists.

'I think what Charlie is saying,' Hans says, 'is that there didn't need to be. Lisa knew exactly what to do. She was capable of handling any situation.'

'Lisa's job was also to have sex with passengers and to give them food?' Cheryl suggests.

'No,' Charlie tells her. 'I'm sure men will have tried to get her to do all kinds of things for them, but it wasn't what she was there for.'

There is something behind their questions he does not understand. He thinks he has explained it clearly enough and he supposes there is always a point when a Syn cannot understand what is clear to a man.

He is reluctant to talk about the fact that Lisa stayed on board rather than come with him when he left the shuttle, nor does he want to reveal the reason that Lisa gave him for doing so. It is not that he wants to spare them. It is simply that he still feels guilty as well as saddened about his part in her demise.

'She had to operate the controls,' he says simply, 'and she could only do that from inside the cabin.'

All four of them greet this part with a long and slightly awkward silence. He also omits to tell them about the question Lisa put to him while he was donning the suit.

'She was obviously very brave,' Hans comments eventually.

When he has finished his story, Charlie says, 'I don't know how to thank you both.' He looks from Hans to Will, still finding it awkward to speak to Will in the way he would to a man. Then, before they can make any comment, he adds, 'I think we really need to go now and leave you in peace, and I have someone I have to meet later.'

'Where're you going to go, son?' Hans asks him. 'I don't think it's wise to go back to your apartment.'

He shrugs. 'I'm not sure, but I'll sort something out.'

'Why don't you stay here for the moment?' Will asks him. 'Then when you go to your meeting, you'll know that Cheryl and Poppy will not be left on their own.'

'That's very kind,' he tells her, 'But there's really no reason why...'

'She'd like you to stay,' Hans interrupts, 'and so would I, given you don't seem to have anywhere else to go at present. If someone's gone to quite a bit of trouble to try to kill you – and it certainly looks that way – there's every reason to think they'll try again.'

'You'll have to make the best of sleeping in this room,' Will says, 'but I'm sure that we can do something with the chairs.'

'Just give in, son,' Hans says with a smile when

Charlie tries to protest. ‘Learn to know when you’re beat. It’s not as if Cheryl and Poppy are any trouble.’

‘I don’t know what to say,’ he says truthfully.

‘I guess that’s a new experience for you,’ Hans tells him, ‘As a salesman.’

19

When it is time to leave to go to meet Gen, he says casually, 'I need Poppy to come with me.'

He is careful not to meet the eyes of the others. Hans gives him a look but does not try to interfere. Poppy looks uncertainly at Cheryl, seeking guidance about what to do.

'You go with Charlie if he asks you to,' Cheryl tells her neutrally.

Once they are out of the apartment Poppy walks quietly beside him and he tries not to look at her or to think about what will happen when they meet up with Gen. When he first conceived his plan, he convinced himself what he was doing was perfectly reasonable. It is true Poppy is not his to make use of, but what Gen wants from her is surely no more than the Synthia was made for.

He had not met her when he began to formulate the plan; he had not known her, had not seen her face, known the colour of her eyes or her name; she was just the Syn that a man called Vos ordered and that Sly had asked him to 're-route', as Lars put it.

He tells himself nothing has really changed since then, and he needs the information he has asked Gen for if he is going to go ahead with his plan, and he is still going ahead with it. He is more and not less determined to do so now Sly has tried to kill him, and in any case, it has never really been about himself and what he wants; he has a task to perform whose significance and importance goes far beyond anything else he has ever known, and anything can be justified if it is necessary for the plan to succeed. Almost anything.

They take a car at the passenger tubes to the area where the venue that Gen had named is located. When they alight, he gets his bearings and then starts in the direction of the bar. Poppy is looking about her now with interest, at the men milling about – many of whom slow to give her appreciative looks – and at the signs and entrances for the various establishments.

He finds the business he wants without much difficulty. From the outside 'High Spirits' does not also appear particularly 'high' class, not if the men entering and leaving are a reliable indication of its habitual clientele. He understands the double reference implied by the word 'spirits' but as they enter it occurs to him that 'high' also refers to the fact that the bar, like the orbital itself, floats far above the planet below.

The lighting inside the venue is subdued, but more than bright enough for the customers present to notice and enjoy the sight of Poppy, and he feels the eyes of all the men on the two of them as they squeeze their way through to the bar. Poppy looks innocently around, and several men raise their glasses at her with a smile. That is okay. It acknowledges the fact she is pretty, but it does not overstep the mark.

A large man turns to look at Charlie and then slowly and deliberately turns his gaze to Poppy.

'Evening, Gorgeous,' the big man says, giving Poppy a wink and raising his glass and keeping it there for a second or two longer than is required.

That is not okay. It is a calculated insult, not to Poppy, but to himself. It is the kind of thing that can provoke trouble. Most men get touchy if another man makes any kind of attempt to muscle in on his Syn. Fights can easily break out that way, fights that can quickly turn ugly. If you want any attention from a femdroid – even the right to talk to her – you ask the owner first, and if you want to do more than talk, you pay him for the privilege.

Poppy knows none of this, however, and she smiles happily at the man and replies with a pretty, 'Good evening.'

Charlie keeps his expression neutral while he glances at the man, careful not to stare or to catch the man's eye. He has other, more important things to do this evening than get into an argument, but a man cannot afford to let too many insults go unchallenged on his home orbital. His glance tells him the man is not simply large. A good part of the bulk is muscle rather than fat, and Charlie guesses the man could easily handle any trouble he might try to give him.

He decides to ignore the insult and turns to the barman instead. He asks for Gen, using the formula he used at the previous locations when he had been searching for him. As before, he is obliged to pay for an expensive drink, one that is not produced.

Holding Poppy's hand, he leaves the bar in the

direction indicated to him by the barman, stepping into a poorly lit corridor. The barman told him Gen is in Room Three. Charlie peers at the room numbers and then finding the one he wants he knocks, careful to stand back this time and keep his eyes closed in case he is blasted with the scanner beam.

Nothing happens, so he knocks again, and when this produces no more response than it had the first time, he tries calling to the man.

'It's Charlie,' he announces, but softly because he does not want the men in the bar to hear.

Getting no response and hearing no sound from beyond the door he tries calling again a second time, more loudly. Unless the man is very deaf, he ought to be able to hear.

Nothing happens. He tries the button beside the door, expecting it to be locked from inside, but he gets a green light and the door slides open. The room beyond the door is dark as it had been before and Charlie hurriedly puts a hand over his eyes, but there is no sudden beam of brilliant light.

He reaches inside, feeling for a button to turn on the lights, but he hears men coming along the corridor from the direction of the bar, so he quickly pulls Poppy inside and closes the door behind them. The men pass along the corridor outside, the sound of their low voices fading as they continue on to wherever the passageway leads.

When it is quiet outside again, he finds the switch beside the door panel and risks putting on the lights.

It is suddenly very bright inside the room, but the light does not reveal much. There is a bed – no more than a couch really – an ordinary chair and a second chair much like the one he had mistaken in the dark for the man himself the last time the two met. This time, however, there really does appear to be a man seated in it. The chair faces away from the door and is positioned in front of a small table in the far corner of the room. Charlie can see the top of the man's head over the chair's back, but not much more.

'It's Charlie,' he says, but the head does not move.

'Gen?' he calls.

He realises now there is a sickly smell in the room. There is the faintly nauseating smell of the unwashed man he remembers from before, but something else too, something vaguely familiar and equally unpleasant. He pushes Poppy back against the wall beside the door and tells her to close her eyes.

'Don't move,' he tells her firmly, 'and don't open your eyes again unless I tell you.'

He takes a couple of steps towards the man in the chair and notices something he ought to have seen before. There is something on the floor, quite a lot of it, mostly pooled around the chair and under the table, and it is the source of the smell, which he now recognises as that of spilled blood. The man in the chair is sitting very still but also too upright if it is his blood on the floor. The ghastly sight of the man cut in two at the passenger tubes ought to have prepared Charlie, but the memory does nothing to lessen the shock value of so much livid red fluid now.

Careful not to tread in the blood, Charlie approaches for a better look. The man's shoulders and head are held fast to the chair back. The chair has been designed for all kinds of uses and it easily handles the task of keeping the body in such a position. The man's hands are strapped to the arms, while both his feet are kept planted firmly on the floor thanks to the thoughtfulness of the chair's designers.

No matter how loudly Charlie had called, the man could not have answered, much less have got up to open the door. Even without the restraints, Gen will never again be capable of movement. His eyes are open, as though staring at what is on the table, but Charlie hopes the eyes had not seen what is there, and it was arranged this way after the eyes had grown sightless.

Two small circles have been drawn on the surface of the table with spilled blood, with a curving line in more blood. The curving line is below the circles when viewed from the position of the man in the chair. Between the circles and the line there is an object taking the place of the nose in this grisly smiley face. The sight makes Charlie want to be sick. He is fairly sure Poppy will never have seen such a thing and will not yet have been introduced to any of the various uses a man might have for it and he does not want her education to begin with the sight of this one, so out of place and out of context. The death of the man is obscenity enough, without this gruesome mutilation. The man known as 'Gen' – a man who had been so careful – had somehow not been careful enough on this occasion.

There is something else on the table, besides the face. It is a small black disc, not much thicker than a man's thumbnail and not much larger. It has been deliberately shattered, the result of a blow from some hard and heavy object. Charlie has not seen one quite like this, but the information Synthia Corp gave him was held on discs quite similar.

Whatever data this disc held it will never now be extracted. The disc might have contained the information Charlie requested, and he experiences a second wave of fear and revulsion at the thought that his witness to this death is almost certainly no coincidence. He is ashamed of the disappointment he feels when he realises he will not now get the information he wants, but it is a serious blow nevertheless, even if it is nothing in comparison to what has been done to the man in the chair.

He knows that he and Poppy have to get out and quickly, but something has caught his eye. He thinks the pocket on the breast of the dead man's shirt hangs away from the shirt itself very slightly more than is consistent with the weight of the fabric alone. He can see nothing in the pocket, not even when he tries to look into it from above, but he suspects something is there. He is reluctant to touch the shirt for all kinds of reasons, so he hesitates, but then he gently inserts two fingers into the recess. The tips of his fingers encounter something hard in the bottom of the pocket, and a further probing reveals it to be not one but two small objects, almost certainly two more of the small data discs.

Extracting the discs is fiddly, not least because he is panicky and increasingly nauseous in the presence of the blood and the body and what is on the table.

His fingers alone refuse to grasp the discs sufficiently to pull them out against both gravity and the tug of the fabric of the shirt, but it is hard to get his hand far enough into the small pocket for him to use his thumb as well.

He is tempted to simply rip the shirt, but finally he manages to get the objects out. As he suspected, the objects are two more discs just like the one on the table. One of them has some markings, something printed or written by hand in a dark colour, not so different from the colour of the disc itself. He holds it under the light, rotating the disc until the light catches it in just the right way. The markings are really no more than slightly more reflective patches of the same colour as the disc itself, but he is eventually able to make out the letters C.H.A.8. Then he decides it is C.H.A.S.

As an acronym it means nothing to him, but the letters are familiar to him as the shortened version of his own name, even if he never lets anyone use it. It might be a long shot, but he feels a surge of hope and puts both of the discs in his own shirt pocket. He wants to thank the dead man, but can think of nothing more to do than carefully close those staring eyes.

A quick escape is what is required now, and he sees that beside the table is another door almost concealed in the wall. The room provides a means of egress that does not involve going back through the bar, as had the room in which Charlie met the man the previous time. It is a further sign of the caution exhibited by the dead man while he was alive.

A release for the door is located on the panel

itself and when Charlie presses it the door clicks open, swinging back into the room on concealed hinges. He cautiously puts his head out and sees that the door leads directly into an alleyway. To his right it joins the passage from which they entered the bar. He goes back in and takes Poppy's hand.

'Keep your eyes closed,' he tells her firmly, 'and don't open them until I tell you.'

'Okay,' she says without protest.

He guides her to the door, and then having checked there are no men in the alley he helps her to step outside. There is no means of closing the door from the outside, but he is reluctant to leave it open.

'Stay here,' he says, and letting go of Poppy's hand he reaches back inside and pulls the door in an attempt to close it, but he does not get his arm out in time and the door merely bumps against it and the door swings open again. He repeats the procedure with the same result, so he goes back into the room once more, looking for something that might help. He picks up the empty chair. It is rather light, but it will have to do. Holding the door, he balances the chair against it so that it rests on only two of its legs, its weight being taken by the door. Then he slides through the narrow opening and when he is safely outside he lets go of the door. It closes behind him with a soft but encouraging click. Once it is closed it is almost invisible and when he tries it, the door will not open.

Taking the Synthia's hand he walks them both briskly to the main passage where they merge with the men walking there.

A man going in the opposite direction brushes against Poppy and she asks, 'Can I open my eyes?'

He tells her she can, but they keep walking.

After a moment she asks him, 'Did I do everything right?'

He answers her roughly, not wishing to talk about it. He is still in shock at what he has seen. It is not just the fact of the violence alone, it is also the fact that he had been forced to confront it up close, almost intimately so, so that the brutality and the ugliness of it was unavoidable.

'Yes,' he says at last, answering her question more gently this time.

'Are you angry with me for some reason, Charlie?'

'No,' he tells her, stopping and turning to look at her, 'of course not. You did exactly what I asked you to do. It's just that there was something in the room that I didn't want you to see.'

Tugging her gently he begins to walk on again at a quick pace.

'Why didn't you want me to see it?' she asks, walking rapidly to stay beside him.

'Because it was horrible.'

'Oh.'

After a moment she adds, 'There was an unpleasant smell in the room.'

'Yes,' he agrees. 'There was.'

'What was the smell?'

He waits until there are no other men close to them before he says, 'There was a dead man in the room.' He does not tell her that the man had smelled unpleasant even while he was alive.

'Oh,' she says again, and she grips his hand more tightly.

'Why was he dead?' she asks when he says no more.

'Because someone killed him,' he tells her.

'Does it have something to do with the man who tried to kill you?'

'Maybe,' he agrees. 'It might.'

'Can I ask why you wanted me to come with you?'

He hesitates, wondering what to say.

'The man wanted to talk to you,' he tells her eventually.

Her question is inevitable, but at least he has had a second or two to consider his answer.

'I told him you're very beautiful and very lovely, and he wanted to see you for himself.' The lie is easier because it is close to the truth.

'Oh,' she says quietly, 'but because he is dead he could not see me or talk to me. I am sorry.'

'Yes,' he agrees, 'so am I. I'm angry too, at the man or the men who killed him.'

She is silent then and he wonders what she can make of it all. He supposes the world of men will always be something of a mystery and a surprise to her. He squeezes her hand and turns to smile at her.

'What is it?' she asks him, seeing his expression.

'I'm just glad that you're here with me,' he tells her.

'Are you?' she asks and the doubt in her voice is so clearly genuine it distresses him.

‘Yes, very glad,’ he assures her.

He hopes one of the discs he found in Gen’s shirt might contain the information he asked for, but even if it does not he is relieved Poppy is returning with him. In fact, the greater the distance he puts between them and the mutilated corpse the greater his sense of relief becomes. He is almost happy.

He knows it is because of the guilt he felt at what he was going to ask Poppy to do, a sense of shame he tried to conceal even from himself. He looks again at Poppy now and cannot help smiling again.

He squeezes her hand once more. ‘Very glad,’ he repeats. Then he stops and turns to kiss her gently on her cheek.

She puts two delicate fingers to her cheek, perhaps expecting the skin to feel different when she touches it.

‘Does that mean you like me?’ she asks him seriously.

‘Yes,’ he agrees, ‘it means that I like you very much.’

She regards him for a moment, and he says again, ‘I like you very much. You don’t need to doubt it.’

Then they continue on towards the passenger tubes to take them back to Cheryl and the others.

20

He hears the music even before the door is opened. It is muffled and faint through the walls of the apartment, but he can tell what it is and because he does not listen to music very often it comes as a surprise.

He knocks and announces himself, adding, 'And Poppy.'

It seems that Will never opens the door more than she really has to and he lets Poppy go through the narrow gap first.

Will greets them with a smile.

'Come in,' she says, a little breathlessly, closing the door behind them, 'I'm glad you're back.'

Inside, the music is much louder. The furniture has been pushed up against the walls, the low table placed on top of one of the chairs. In the now quite large and clear space, Cheryl is dancing. He guesses that Will has been dancing too.

'I can't keep up with her.' Will says admiringly. 'I know that I'm old, but I wouldn't have been able to even when I was young.'

'I suppose she doesn't get tired,' she adds.

She sounds wistful, he thinks, and younger, but he says nothing.

When Charlie makes no comment, Will turns to him to gauge his reaction.

'But doesn't she dance beautifully?' Will asks him.

Cheryl has her eyes closed while her body is moving gracefully and sinuously to the music, sometimes with her arms raised above her head and sometimes extended out in front or beside her. She appears unaware of his presence. When she spins on her feet the short skirt of the blue dress flares out around her thighs. Her face wears an expression he finds complex and not easy to read. She seems totally absorbed in what she is doing, unselfconscious, and… happy.

'Why don't you dance with her?' Will suggests.

'Oh, I don't dance,' he tells her quickly.

Most men do not dance. It is something the femdroids do in the clubs for the entertainment of customers, and occasionally a man, if he is drunk or just larking about, might get up and dance or pretend to dance with them, but always in a self-conscious way. The moves men make are normally no more than a parody of the dancing of the femdroids.

'Go on,' Will encourages him.

Cheryl opens her eyes suddenly. When she sees him, she stops and smiles.

'Charlie, you back!' she says excitedly. She comes over and puts her arms around his neck with no trace of her former inhibition in front of Will. She smiles up at him but says nothing for the moment. If she was a biological, he might think she had been drinking.

'You look happy,' he tells her.

'Yes, Cheryl very happy,' she agrees, still smiling. 'Cheryl like to dance, but there is no room in apartment. Here there is plenty of room and Will like to dance too.'

'I'm glad you're happy,' he tells her, kissing the tip of her nose. He thinks she has never looked more beautiful, and yet he knows that her looks do not change. What men see depends upon what is inside them as much as on the reality around them. He supposes it is why men can often be so blind.

'Come and dance, Charlie,' Cheryl says. 'And then you can have shower.' She wrinkles her nose again.

'I don't know how to dance,' he tells her.

He has no intention of making a fool of himself, and he has not yet shaken off the gruesome scene that greeted him in the back room of the bar. He has the unpleasant sensation that violence and disaster are drawing ever closer to him, threatening everything he cherishes and values. His plan meanwhile – his crazy idea – seems hardly any further forward. He needs to see if Hans knows how he can read the data discs he has brought back with him, and he needs a drink. He feels the disconnect between his own present mood and preoccupations and that of the women, and at this moment the gulf seems unbridgeable.

'Poppy will dance with you,' he tells Cheryl. 'Teach Poppy to dance.'

'Okay, Charlie,' Cheryl says sadly, 'but one day Cheryl will get you to dance.'

He leaves her and goes in search of the old man.

'You brought Poppy back with you?' Hans asks him.

Charlie nods. 'Yeah,' he says, 'of course.'

Hans makes no comment, but he can see in the old man's face thoughts unsaid and questions left unspoken.

He shows the discs to Hans who takes one and peers at it.

'Haven't seen one of these in a while,' Hans says after a moment.

'Do you know how I can access the data on it?'

Hans says, 'I think I might have a reader somewhere. Come with me.'

He follows the old man out the back and sees that, as he suspected, the apartment is a large one. There is a whole room rather than just an alcove for the kitchen area and a separate sleeping room and another smaller one for sanitation, a whole room when he has only a cubicle. When Hans keeps going through a further door he thinks it is almost like two apartments.

'You've got a second apartment here,' he tells Hans as they go through into a large space that is clearly used as a workshop.

'Don't go telling anyone,' Hans smiles. 'There was an empty space next door to us, not an apartment, it was used by maintenance, but you'll have seen that there hasn't been much of that in this area in quite a while, and this space was empty for a long time, so I installed a door and sort of annexed it. Shame to let the space go to waste.'

'And the door in here from the main passage?'

Charlie does not remember seeing anything in the wall beside the door to the old man's apartment.

'I disguised it,' Hans says lightly, 'blocked it off. I used some of the wall panels I removed to make the door in from the apartment.'

'Neat,' Charlie says admiringly.

The old man potters about looking on shelves and opening drawers in benches before he finds what he is looking for.

'There you are,' Hans says. 'You may need to charge it, but it should be able to read that disc. Keep it for as long as you need it. I don't really have a use for it at the moment.'

'Thanks.'

The reader is unresponsive when he tries it, with or without one of the discs he has brought back with him, so Hans sets it to charge, and Charlie goes back into the main room.

Cheryl has evidently finished dancing and the furniture has been put back. There is still some music playing, but more quietly and softly.

'Come with me, Charlie,' Cheryl says, getting up and advancing towards him.

When he asks her where they are to go she says, 'I think you have shower now.'

She takes his hand and turns to go out the back, but he protests that he needs to check that it will be okay with Hans first.

'It is arranged,' she tells him. 'Will say it is okay. We can do it.'

'Will?'

'Come, Charlie,' she insists and gently leads him

into the sanitation room and closes the door behind them. The action of closing the door turns on the overhead lights.

As he has already seen, it is a complete room with separate facilities for washing, showering and waste evacuation.

'I think you start with shaving,' Cheryl says.

'And I think I know how to look after myself,' he tells her, increasingly exasperated at being told what to do.

She merely smiles and hands him a razor and shaving cream. She also has some towels.

He takes off his shirt and washes his face. In the large mirror over the basin he looks at her reflection as she watches him. He has the impression there is something going on that he is not understanding, but she is right: he needs a shave.

When he has finished he turns to her and says, 'Okay, if you go out now I'll have a shower.'

'I stay and help,' she tells him.

'I think it's better if you just go out and leave me to it,' he says.

She puts her hands to his cheeks, running her fingers over the now smooth surface of his skin. Then she raises herself up on her toes and kisses him.

'I think it better if I stay and help,' she says.

'Help how?'

'Take off trousers and shoes, Charlie,' she instructs him.

'I know how to have a shower!' he protests, but he sees that she is lifting the dress over her head. Underneath the dress she is wearing a pair of panties like the ones Poppy had been wearing.

'Where did you get those?' he asks, but she merely smiles a little mysteriously.

The sight of her body with her pert breasts cuts through his tiredness and the anxiety. It has been a few days since he last had any sex.

'You can take them off if you like,' she tells him, meaning the panties, 'if you take off your trousers and shoes and get under shower.'

He hesitates, wondering what has happened recently to affect her behaviour. He removes his shoes and the rest of his clothes, and then he steps into the cubicle and closes the door. The water feels good and he has to admit that she is right: he needs a shower. It has been a few days at least since he washed and now he also needs to rinse away what he saw and smelled in that back room at the bar. After he has let the water run over him for a while he opens his eyes, looking for something with which to wash his hair. He starts when he finds himself face to face with his Synthia. She is holding out some hairwash for him, the water cascading over her. She has her hair tied up at the back and he sees that she has removed the panties herself.

'For hair, Charlie,' she says, showing him the hairwash.

'What are you doing?' he asks her in some alarm.

'We take shower,' she tells him, and I help to give you wash.' Her expression is very like the one with which she invites him to help apply the Forever Young and Supple skin product.

'But should you be in here?' he asks her,

perplexed.

'Synthia is waterproof, Charlie,' she says seriously. 'You must know that.'

He does know, of course he does, but he experienced a momentary panic at the sight of the water glistening as it runs down her body in rivulets and drips from her face. She puts a hand on his chest, the one that is not holding the hairwash, and rubs it gently. Then she moves her hand down and continues the motion below his waist. She stops when she reaches his genitals and looks up at him.

'You wash hair, Charlie,' she says. 'Then we wash everywhere else, and we not miss any part of you.'

She is echoing what he says to her when they talk about applying the skin product to her body.

'You have to miss my eyes, Cheryl,' he tells her. 'You must miss my eyes.'

Cheryl smiles, showing she understands the joke.

During what follows he learns that she understands a good deal more, more than he has guessed and probably more than he himself does. The experience is so novel and so wonderful that he wonders why they have never done anything like it before. He supposes it is partly because there is not the space in his own apartment.

He is more than ready for the sex once he is thoroughly clean. He would have turned off the water, but Cheryl tells him to leave it running and he has to admit that it certainly adds a new dimension to things. It seems to have been a long time since they last did it together, and of course, even if his body is tired,

Cheryl is as athletic and as energetic as always. She is obviously keen to please him, but he thinks somehow there is more to it than that.

At one point she says, ‘Slowly, Charlie, wait. We don’t know if you will manage second time.’

When they resume he is alarmed when her body becomes tense and rigid for a moment, while her eyes apparently roll back in their sockets, her eyelids blinking rapidly.

‘Are you all right?’ he asks her anxiously.

She opens her eyes and smiles a little vaguely. It is as though she is coming back to him from somewhere, re-booting almost.

‘Yes, Charlie,’ she says, smiling more broadly. ‘Cheryl okay. Now we take you to finish.’

Afterwards they dry each other with the towels, Cheryl reminding him that he must not rub too hard in case he marks her skin. For Charlie it is like the first days and weeks after he bought her when every part of her and everything she did was special and magical. When they are dry he wraps one of the big towels around them both and kisses her.

‘Where did you learn… that?’ he asks, gesturing with his head towards the shower cubicle.

‘I learn much from talking to Will,’ she tells him. ‘She is wise, Charlie, and she know many things about men.’

‘Well, I’m still learning things about Synthias’ he smiles. She looks different with her hair wet. There are some drops of water on her cheeks and he wipes them gently away with his fingers, thinking again how lucky he is to have her as his own. His mind perversely flashes up an image of Lisa. He is not sure why he should be thinking of her now as he looks at Cheryl.

'And Will told you that I might find that fun?' he asks, indicating the shower again with another nod of his head.

She frowns. It is not quite as sophisticated a facial gesture as Poppy might manage, but it is cute nevertheless.

'Why you think Will said it would be fun for *you*, Charlie?' she asks him, her eyebrows raised.

After a moment she smiles, and he smiles too. He is trying to remember if it is the first time that she has made a joke quite like that. He thinks it might be, but perhaps he has simply not noticed when she has done so before. He has certainly known her to be ironic and she made a kind of joke earlier about not missing any part of him. He just goes on smiling at her, not having anything to say. He is feeling warm and tender towards her, and increasingly aroused again.

'Charlie,' she says, pulling their bodies closer together, 'I think you manage second time.'

When they are ready to leave the sanitation room, Cheryl says, 'Charlie, Cheryl ask you something.'

'What, honey?'

'Your plan,' she says, and he immediately feels himself tense.

'You say you "swap" Poppy,' she says quietly, perhaps worried that someone beyond the door might be able to hear.

'Swap' is the word he had used. He guesses she is not familiar with it.

'You give her to other man so he gives you another femdroid that you need for plan,' she says, showing she understands well enough what he meant.

He says nothing. Her words are a statement not a question, but she seems to want him to answer her.

'Well?' he says, his voice tight.

'You not do it, Charlie,' she says, 'you not give Poppy to other man when you not know what happen to her afterwards.'

'Don't tell me what I can and can't do!' he snaps. 'That's not your place.'

'No, Charlie,' she says quickly, putting a hand to his chest, 'I not say that, I say…'

'You say what?' he asks sharply before she can explain any further.

She is quiet then and looks at his face instead.

'Cheryl not say what you must do,' she says patiently, 'but what you can't do. I say you can't give her to other man.'

'And what's the difference?' he asks her. He knows that his tone is not pleasant, but he cannot have her interfering. It is hard enough as it is.

She is frowning again now, clearly struggling to find the right words to make him understand.

'I mean you not able,' she says. 'Cheryl think it not possible for you to give her to other man, not now when you know her. She belong to you now and you are good man.'

'She doesn't "belong" to me,' he says, 'as you very well know.'

He says the words even though he knows they are unjust and inaccurate. He has a pretty good idea that what she means by "belong" is something different from the meaning in law. He remembers her telling him he belonged to her when he brought Poppy back with him. She had meant then that there is some kind of contract between them, a kind of bond, and she means now that an attachment of sorts has been formed between himself and Poppy. He has become responsible for her. Poppy wants his approval, wants to know he 'likes' her. That much had been obvious to him even before her question this afternoon. Cheryl is suggesting now that Poppy is no longer just an anonymous Syn to Charlie.

But Cheryl has seemed to want him to form a bond with Poppy. She has practically pushed the two of them together. Only this afternoon she insisted Poppy sit with him when he would have been happy just to sit with Cheryl.

'That was your plan, wasn't it?' he says to her now.

'What you mean, Charlie?' she asks him.

'You wanted me to get to know her so that I wouldn't give her away,' he says nastily, 'so that I will keep her. Maybe because it will take the work load off you a bit.'

He both feels and believes what he is saying and yet also knows it is not really the case, that it is cruelly unjust, but he seems unable to stop himself.

'No, Charlie!' she protests. 'Cheryl not make plan. I only say what I think is true. You good man, you not able to give her to other man now.'

'You don't know what I'm able to do or not do,' he says crossly, not making any effort to keep his voice low. 'And that's an end to it. I'm not going to discuss my plans with my Syn!'

He opens the door and goes out, leaving Cheryl alone in the sanitation room. She can pick up the dirty towels and his dirty clothes. That is her job after all, not telling him what he can and cannot do.

He is cross and irritated. He is cross that she has made him cross, and he knows she is right, and that only makes it worse. She has correctly identified his weakness. He is soft and allows sentiment to cloud his judgement. He is not really the right man for the task he has set himself; he is certainly no hero. He knows that if it comes to it he cannot simply hand Poppy over to someone else, and not even because he wants to have her himself – although surely there would be nothing wrong with that? – but because he could not bear the thought of her being treated badly and callously and used for who knows what ends.

He knows also that he did not handle the situation very well just now and he is cross about that. It is such a shame when they had been having such a good time, but a man should not base his happiness or peace of mind on a mere machine. He has been weak and foolish and allowed himself to feel all manner of sentimental feelings, and look where it has got him.

But he does not really believe that either. He certainly has no wish to believe it, and it only makes him even more irritated, with himself and with Cheryl: with everything, damn it!

Perhaps it is all Sly's fault, for showing him that cursed woman in the first place. But he cannot really cling to that either, not as an explanation or as an excuse.

Cheryl had gently run her fingers over the now fading bruise on his shoulder while they were in the shower, but she had not said anything about it. The woman who had given him the bruise has also marked him in other ways that are not fading. He touched her; he handled her hand with his own; he put his hand on her chin and cupped her breast, actions that now in retrospect make him uncomfortable, and she in turn had also touched him, not only with the heel of her foot, but with the look. And like the microscopic ID chips that must have been implanted in Vos when he handled the device left for him in the crate, the look the woman gave him is growing inside him. There are times when the thing sleeps and he can forget it, when he can almost persuade himself he should just continue with his life and be happy. He felt that way in the shower with Cheryl just now. But then the thing stirs, shifts its position and nudges him painfully in the ribs, bringing him awake or stopping him in mid thought.

He tries to clear his head. He imagines the reader Hans has lent him ought to be charged sufficiently now and he goes to try the disc in it, but when he pats the pocket of his shirt it is empty and he panics before remembering that he is wearing a clean shirt now, one Cheryl had thoughtfully brought with her from the apartment when she and Poppy left it. The discs had been in the pocket of the dirty one, the shirt he left on the floor of the sanitation room.

Cheryl is not in the sanitation room when he goes back, and neither are his clothes. He finds Cheryl and

Poppy in the main room with Will and Hans.

'Where's my shirt, Cheryl?' he asks, interrupting whatever she had been saying to Will.

Cheryl looks at him for a second and says, 'It is in cleaning machine, Charlie, with other things. The shirt was very dirty.'

'What?'

'And it smell bad too,' Cheryl says.

Charlie puts his hands on his head in frustration.

'Those discs,' he asks Hans, 'will they still work if they've been washed along with the shirt?'

Hans shrugs. 'The water probably won't hurt them, but the electrical charge in the water will probably destroy the data.'

'You idiot, Cheryl!' Charlie says, turning on her and giving vent to all the pent-up anger and frustration that has been building up for days. 'You stupid, dumb Syn!'

He knows the others are watching him and he feels their shock and disapproval like a sudden drop in the air pressure or temperature.

'What has Cheryl done that is stupid, Charlie?' she asks him levelly.

'You wouldn't understand,' he says dismissively. 'How can you? You're just a stupid machine.'

'What is problem, Charlie?' she persists in the same level voice.

'There were some things in the pocket of my shirt, very important things that I went to a very great trouble to get, and you've destroyed them.'

He shrugs his shoulders. 'Just like that,' he says quietly. He knows what they must be thinking, but it feels surprisingly good: terribly wrong, but good.

'You couldn't help interfering,' he adds, savouring the senseless cruelty of the words, like spicy food on his tongue. 'Damn it!'

No one says anything, while he simply breathes hard and stands where he is, his hands hanging at his sides.

'You mean the data discs, Charlie?' Cheryl asks him after a moment.

'Yes!'

He cannot believe that everything, every last little thing can be so against him. He thought for a moment that he had gained a bit of an edge; he might even have got the information he needs without giving anything away, but no, even that is taken away from him!

'You mean these, Charlie,' Cheryl says. She is holding something in her hand, but he cannot see what it is from where he stands. She comes across the room and puts them in his palm.

'Yes, I only machine, Charlie,' she says quietly, 'but I not stupid.'

She makes to return to where she had been sitting, but he grabs her arm.

'What now, Charlie?' she asks, still turned away from him.

He opens his mouth to speak but cannot form the right words. He cannot form any words. The knowledge that Hans and Will have witnessed the scene, have heard every word is humiliating. He is ashamed and he is angry. He is angry that he has made a fool of himself, that he has once again handled a situation so very badly, and so soon after the last time. He was wrong and unjust, and more than that, he was cruel, deliberately cruel. He knows that Cheryl is not stupid. She is a machine he supposes, but he used the word in an attempt to belittle her.

And he is not on his own. He is not even in his own apartment, which only makes it harder.

He realises too that Poppy has also witnessed the exchange. He sees that she is sitting very still and looking down at her hands.

He knows that most Syns will hear and see very much worse during their operational existence. They are after all made for the benefit and comfort of the men who own them, and all men vent their feelings and get angry from time to time. He is no different from any other man, but that makes it no better.

Cheryl remains where she was when he grabbed her. She has turned to look at him now, but he cannot read her expression. What he will do next appears to hang in some delicate balance; a nudge in one direction almost too small to measure and he will apologise and probably embarrass the others even more, while a similar, almost imperceptible shift in the opposite direction and he will simply shrug it off and ignore the whole thing. He knows that Cheryl will not mention it again.

She is still looking at him.

'I was wrong,' he says finally. 'I was scared that the discs were ruined, and I'm tired and worried and I really don't know what to do.'

'I know, Charlie,' Cheryl says gently.

'But none of that makes any difference,' he tells her. 'I was cruel and unjust, and you don't deserve that, not in the least.'

She approaches and embraces him, her action as gentle as her words had been.

'I'm sorry,' he says over her shoulder, finding what seems like the right word at last. 'I'm sorry,' he says again.

'It's okay, Charlie,' she says into his chest.

'No, honey,' he says, 'it's not okay. And I was wrong earlier as well, in the sanitation room. You were right and I wouldn't listen. You know me too well. I'm weak, as you pointed out, and Poppy does "belong" to me now, just as you told me she does.'

He knows the others are listening and watching and he feels vaguely ridiculous. The sight of a man apologising to his Syn would no doubt be greeted with incredulity and derision by most men, but he thinks that of all the people on the orbital Hans and his woman are the least likely to laugh at him.

Cheryl is still holding him, and he has no wish for her to let him go.

'You're not stupid, not in the least,' he says. It feels ridiculously sentimental, but just then he does not care. 'You're very precious to me. I don't deserve a Syn like you.'

She hugs him even tighter.

'I think...' he starts to say, but then he stops, and he whispers into her ear instead. He does not want the others to hear, not these words. There are limits to how stupid a man can afford to appear in front of other men.

'I love you,' he says into her ear. He is not entirely sure what it means even now, but he believes it is true. He meant what he said about her being very precious to him, and the knowledge that he has treated her badly hurts him almost like a physical pain. He thinks if that is not love then he has no idea what is.

'Cheryl knows that, Charlie,' Cheryl says, her voice still muffled by his shirt. 'Cheryl has known it for a while. You are only man, but you are good man, Charlie.'

'I'm sorry,' he says again, and they continue to stand together like that, not moving or speaking.

It is hard being a man, he thinks, very hard. Perhaps it is easier being a Synthia, but he remembers that Syns are the ones who bear the brunt of men's outbursts; they are the ones who experience the bad behaviour, the scathing language and the physical violence which is so often the result of the frustrations, the disappointments and the shame that men feel, and still men expect their Syns to cater to their every need and desire, without either protest or reward.

His thoughts, like his emotions, seem to have become terribly soft. He wonders what is happening to him and if he is losing his mind, but it is so very good having Cheryl hug him fiercely like this, although he knows he does not deserve it.

21

His plan – he doubts it has ever been sufficiently developed and considered to really deserve to be called a 'plan' – always involved swapping Poppy for something else. He has no other means of payment likely to cover the price of what he wants, or thought he wanted, just as he did not have sufficient money to pay for the information he required from Gen. He thought too there was a certain symmetry in the idea of using the Syn Sly asked him to steal from another man in furtherance of the theft of Isabelle from Sly himself.

He has learnt a lot from his association with Sly over the past few years and from the various pieces of business the man has put his way. The sale of Marie and a couple of Limited-Edition Specials from Synthia Corp each earned him a good commission. Those deals were straightforward, but as he began to gain the other man's trust he learned where Sly's real interests lie, as a man rather than as a collector. Thus he was eventually given a commission that led to the procurement of Jan, a commission that introduced Charlie to all kinds of illegal enterprises and activities the existence of which he had previously been completely ignorant.

He obtained the androgynous Jan from a man named Dex. Dex's business – his real business rather than the dummy activity behind which he hides – is illegal in all kinds of ways and it had proved hard to track down anyone who could supply what Sly was after. Sly is too careful to have made a direct approach or to be seen searching for that kind of thing himself.

Even when Charlie obtained Dex's name and went to see the man, had told Dex what he was after, Dex had at first denied that he could provide anything of that sort.

He mentioned the name of the man who finally put him on to Dex, thinking that it would gain Dex's confidence, but it provoked Dex's associate and business partner, Len, to lunge at him and pin him to the wall.

Dex is so slight and insubstantial that he looks as though he might need to wear especially thin and lightweight clothes. Len, on the other hand, looks as though he could carry a man of Dex's size under each arm and still look around for something else to carry, rather than waste time coming back for it.

That first meeting with the pair had been difficult, particularly when Charlie suddenly found himself with both feet off the floor, his nose squashed painfully to the wall panel, while he was quickly and deftly searched – one-handed – by the over-sized Len. The man finished the examination with a painful squeeze of his testicles and Charlie's cry of pain seemed at last to satisfy the giant, and Len dropped him to the floor.

Dex suggested – without too much conviction, Charlie thought – that Len had perhaps been a little over enthusiastic in his search, but the giant merely grunted that a man can never be too careful.

When Charlie asked what Len was looking for, Dex shrugged and said, 'Well, the obvious, really.'

This apparently meant weapons of any kind, recording devices or cameras and a check to see that Charlie was not a synthetic.

Whilst the supply of male synthetics is strictly illegal, the police are not above using them to entrap men engaged in various activities. The evidence so obtained – the droids can stream visual and audio direct to the police – can send a man to the penal colonies without further interrogation or investigation.

The fact that male femdroids – or simply male 'droids' – are illegal no doubt has more than a little to do with the fact that no one seems entirely sure what to call them. Some men call them femdroids despite the fact that they are not really women of any kind. He has heard the term 'androids' used, but for some reason it is not in general use and he has found that it often produces a frown from other men if he uses it. Those who have reason to worry whether a man they are dealing with might actually be one, tend to simply call them 'synthetics'.

Once Len had established Charlie's bona fides, Dex led the way to another space behind his office where he conducts his true business. There, Dex showed him a couple of sample synthetics that Dex thought might be what Charlie was after. He found them distinctly disturbing, and repeated what he had told Dex already, that he was acting on behalf of a client, insisting again that his own tastes are very different. Dex simply smiled and he is not sure if Dex entirely believes him even now. He finds the way Dex looks at him almost as disconcerting as the appearance of the androgynous droids. They are clearly perfectly functioning males and yet also in some way feminine at the same time. However, Charlie was sure right away that they were the kind of thing Sly was looking for and he took information about them back with him. Any transmission of such information other than carrying it personally was too much of a risk.

Before he left on that first occasion, Dex – a little shyly – pointed out that other varieties of male synthetics are available, depending upon one's personal preference, and Charlie was forced to repeat once again that he was only acting on behalf of a buyer.

'I'm just making sure you know,' Dex told him. 'You can have one like Len here,' he added, 'if that's more to your liking.'

'Len's a synthetic?' Charlie asked, looking more carefully at Dex's partner.

'He's all man,' Dex said, 'I can assure you of that, but he's man-made too and it isn't blood that pumps through his system.'

'He must have been expensive?' Charlie hazarded, looking Len over with a new eye. The other synthetics Dex showed him were all the same size and roughly the same build as a femdroid. Len, on the other hand, was clearly made to a different scale and to an entirely different pattern.

'Yes,' Dex sighed in answer to his question, 'very, but you can't put a price on it, can you?'

Charlie supposed not.

After the procurement of Jan for Sly, he has been able to sell a couple more of Dex's synthetics to other customers. As Dex suggested, his work for Synthia Corp is the perfect cover. In general, however, Charlie prefers to bend the law in other, more orthodox ways.

Until Isabelle, that is. He is sure that it would take a stronger man than him to resist the challenge contained in that stare. He spent the first few days after he saw her in a kind of trance, but he soon realised that he has to act on the challenge it seemed to contain, to try at least, whatever it costs him.

The plan that he hatched in the days and hours after Sly showed her to him involved the acquisition of something similar to Jan, but adapted so that should Sly have sex with it in any of the various ways Dex and common gossip suggest that a man might, Sly would be anaesthetised by a drug, either injected into him through microscopic hypodermic needles like the ones in the device Lisa used on him, or by contact with a substance secreted by the droid at the relevant locations.

The use of a droid of any gender in this way is not an original idea. It features in stories that circulate at the bar in pubs and clubs, stories that are probably mostly myth, but memories of which can come back to terrify a man when trying out femdroids from less well-known or less orthodox sources.

Charlie intended to pay for the customised male synthetic by selling Poppy, or, if possible, by means of a straight swap. The plan was probably unlikely to succeed, but he convinced himself that he could make it work. He realised that Sly would be highly suspicious of any sudden gift of a new synthetic like Jan from any source, and certainly from an unknown one, but he had rather fancifully thought that he could drop in on Sly one evening – although he has only ever been to Sly's apartment by prior appointment and always at the invitation of Sly himself. He would ostensibly be on his way to another appointment. He would ask if he might leave the synthetic in Sly's apartment while he keeps this mysterious appointment, and if Sly shows any interest he will be careful to be vague and offhand about the synthetic and the intended customer, perhaps letting slip that the customer merely wants to see it before considering a purchase of this or one similar to it.

There are all kinds of potential difficulties with the idea, he knows that, but none of them matter now because the plan is essentially scuppered and for three compelling reasons.

The first of these is time. He knows that the more time passes since the theft of Poppy the greater is the chance that he will be discovered. When he considers it, he is surprised that he is not already in custody. Time is also critical in another way: he needs to get Isabelle out of suspended animation as soon as possible or it will be more difficult and will take longer to bring her round sufficiently for him to smuggle her away. It will no doubt be difficult once she is fully awake again, but it will be very much harder if she is still only semi-conscious and unable to walk. The shuttle fiasco and the subsequent search for Cheryl and Poppy has cost him more than twenty four hours. If he had known what was to happen he would have immediately abandoned any attempt to carry on with business appointments, but of course he had not known and as things stand now he has not even had time to approach Dex and has no idea how long it will be before Dex can supply him with what he wants, if indeed the man can or is willing to do so.

The second reason is the steady invasion of cold reality into that part of his mind that entertained the idea in the first place: a growing realisation of how unlikely it is that this plan can be made to work. Cheryl told him it is a stupid plan, and he finds it increasingly difficult to argue with that assessment, particularly now he understands how ruthless a man Sly is and the lengths to which he will go to protect his secrets.

The third reason is the one that Cheryl correctly identified after their time together in the shower. She knows he is essentially weak and sentimental and that he cannot part with Poppy and abandon her to whatever fate might follow thereafter. Whatever that fate is, it is unlikely to be an easy one. He has no idea how Vos would have treated her, but at least the man was buying a new Syn for himself and for which he paid full price. As a stolen unit with a false ID Poppy can never be resold for anything like as much. She will still command a good price, but the uses to which she will likely be put are very different from the private, publicly admitted and exclusive use that Vos no doubt had in mind for her. By stealing her from her crate Charlie has irrevocably altered Poppy's fate and he is responsible for her now. And he likes her. He likes her a lot. She is very appealing and lovely, and her very vulnerability is a part of the charm, but it is not simply that he would like to have her for himself. Cheryl is right; now that he knows her, he simply does not have the toughness of spirit or the courage to use Poppy as a bargaining chip. Now that he is responsible for her, he has to do everything he can to protect her.

So, now he needs a new plan, a different approach entirely, and he has to come up with it fast, but whenever he considers the problem, his brain keeps following the same, endless circles that lead to the same dead ends and blind alleys. He has no useful ideas about how to achieve his goal, none that bear even a moment's scrutiny, but he has an idea at least who can help him.

When it is time to retire and with Will's help, he and the two Synthias do their best to turn the main room of the apartment into a bedroom, using the cushions from the chairs to create a makeshift sleeping area on the floor for the three of them. Once the old man and his woman have turned in for the night and left them on their own, he and the Syns converse in quiet voices. It is obvious to him that Poppy should hear what they are planning because she will be involved or at least present for most of it, and since he is not now parting with her, he does not need to conceal his plans from her. He explains that he intends to steal a biological woman and he explains to her what a suspender unit does – even if he has no idea how it works.

Poppy seems pleased to be involved and makes some sensible comments and neither he nor Cheryl mention his earlier ideas about her role in the scheme.

Gen's search for information appears to have been as thorough as the man promised and the disc taken from the dead man's pocket contains everything Charlie asked for. Lying between Cheryl and Poppy on the makeshift bed he tells his fellow conspirators what the disc reveals about the layout of Sly's apartment and its various features.

'This man very rich,' Cheryl comments when she understands the full extent of the accommodation.

As he suspected, Cheryl's ideas are both bolder and more simple and direct than his own.

'The more complicated the plan the more likely it will go wrong,' Cheryl tells him.

And as he listens to her talk, he thinks Cheryl's idea might even work.

When he is too tired to talk any more, he kisses each of them and then pulling them close, he sleeps.

He wakes once in the night and finds his thoughts preoccupied with the information on the other disc he took from the dead man's pocket and with the question of who might have requested that Gen search for it, and why.

22

'You want the Syns to travel in the cabin?' the man asks doubtfully.

If he wants Cheryl and Poppy to sit with him on the shuttle, he will have to pay for a full ticket for each of them. The alternative is for them to travel in the pressurised freight hold below the cabin, strapped to the wall in the harnesses provided for conveying femdroids and biological women. The two of them will not come to any harm down there and it will be much cheaper that way – about half the price of a single ticket, even for both of them – but the booking clerk has misjudged his customer.

'Yes,' Charlie confirms brightly, ignoring the note of incredulity in the man's question, 'of course.'

After the VIP shuttle the seats are not exactly luxurious and there is no view to be had, but he wants Cheryl and Poppy with him, and it will be a new experience for both of them. Whatever its final outcome, he intends to treat this trip as a kind of holiday or adventure.

He considered touring the main shopping areas before they depart, but their trio has attracted a fair amount of attention, and he does not want to run into Steev and his colleagues – assuming they are still on the orbital – or any man sent by whoever employed the one who had followed him yesterday. He judges it will be safer to conduct their sightseeing on Orbital C, and the shops over there, like everything else, are much grander and more impressive than those on his home orbital.

He is a little worried the police might still be taking an interest in him and that he might be prevented from leaving the orbital, but he pays for the shuttle trip without a problem, once the clerk accepts he really wants tickets for all three of them.

He has timed their arrival at the shuttle port carefully and they are able to board almost immediately. All the other passengers are men like him. Charlie has never seen men bring Syns with them onto the shuttle and as they board many of the passengers look at Cheryl and Poppy and then at himself with interest, and perhaps a little envy.

The shuttle seats are relatively narrow, but neither of his lovely ladies – as Will refers to them – takes up much room and he places one on either side of him. Cheryl has a small bag that she wears on her back. He stows it and shows the Syns how to strap themselves in, smiling reassuringly at Poppy who is apprehensive. He supposes his own recent experiences have not encouraged her.

'Yours?' a man asks, taking a seat across the aisle.

'Yes,' Charlie says, nodding, as if it is the most natural thing in the world.

'Lucky devil!' the man comments with a grin, adding, 'The name's Kam.'

Charlie shakes the proffered hand and after he has given his own name he says, ‘This is Cheryl.’ Then, leaning back so that Kam can see her, he introduces Poppy.

Kam looks surprised. ‘Pleased to meet you both,’ Kam says after a moment, not meeting the eyes of either Syn.

Cheryl nods at Kam and smiles politely. Poppy leans forward and says, ‘Hello,’ holding out her own hand for Kam to shake.

Kam hesitates and then takes her hand, letting go of it quickly as though it might burn him.

Regaining his composure, Kam asks, ‘Do you mind if I ask you what kind of Syns they are?’

Charlie considers suggesting that Kam ask them himself, but he remembers Lisa’s response to his own clumsy question about the identity of her maker.

‘The lovely kind,’ he tells Kam.

Kam blinks and then smiles. ‘Of course,’ he says nodding slowly. ‘Yes, indeed.’

Charlie says they have Synthia Corp to thank for the existence of the two Syns, telling Kam at least a part of what he wants to know.

‘Ah,’ Kam nods slowly, ‘Synthia Corp still seem to have the edge, don’t they?’

Charlie says nothing. He just nods and grins like an idiot or a drunk, smiling first at Cheryl and then at Poppy.

Kam says, ‘I’m with Paradise Corp myself. I’m hoping to make a sale today to a potential customer over on C.’

‘I met a Paradise Corp model recently,’ he tells

Kam slowly. 'One of the Angel models.'

'That's going back a bit,' Kam suggests dismissively. 'We've made a few improvements to our range since then.'

Charlie tells him he thought the Syn was lovely, and Kam looks surprised, caught off guard again by the direction of the conversation.

A salesman ought to treat any man as a potential client and be able to hide his surprise at whatever the man says, but Charlie does not tell Kam this.

'We can give Synthia Corp a run for their money,' Kam comes back eventually.

'I think it was her personality I was really impressed with,' Charlie says, trying to find the right way to express what he is thinking, 'who she was as an individual, although she certainly looked very pretty and sexy.'

'Oh,' Kam says, and now Charlie feels sorry for him.

He has not been trying to wrong foot Kam and to be fair to the man, his comment about Lisa's personality is not the kind of thing anyone has ever said to him when he is extolling the merits and qualities of the products he represents.

'I don't know whether you can build that into a Syn?' he wonders aloud, giving Kam an opening.

'We have our basic personality traits,' Kam tells him, raising his eyebrows and nodding slowly, 'you know, submissive mostly, but to be honest I don't really know much about what makes them…' he shrugs, 'what makes them individuals, I guess.'

Charlie nods too. He has not thought about it

much either, not until recently. Now he thinks it is the most important thing about a Syn, for they are all lovely to look at, and all are equipped one way or another to provide a man with physical satisfaction. He supposes he has simply been lucky with Cheryl. He bought her on the strength of her looks and the features included in the range, and – inevitably – because of the price. He still thinks she looks fabulous, but the declaration he whispered into her ear yesterday has only a little to do with his appreciation of her appearance or how good it feels when they have sex together.

'I suppose you'd say these two have different personalities?' Kam ventures, indicating Cheryl and Poppy with a nod at each of them.

That is easy to answer. Charlie agrees with a ready smile and says he would. 'Definitely.'

'Interesting,' Kam says slowly, before adding, 'You know, no one's really asked me about that side of things.'

Kam sits back in his seat now, looking contemplative.

Cheryl watches Kam for a second and then turns and looks at Charlie, a smile on her lips, and he wonders what she is thinking behind those lovely dark eyes. As soon as they are alone again, he will have to ask her.

When it is fully loaded and the hatch has been closed, the shuttle slides out sideways from the dock. The movement can be felt through the floor and through the seats, but without windows the passengers are blind to whatever is happening beyond the curved walls of the cabin. From the inside, the shuttle appears to be a simple tube divided along its length by the floors of the passenger and freight cabins. Charlie has no idea what it looks like from outside, but perhaps it is merely a larger version of the VIP shuttle.

A hush descends in the cabin. Some of the men probably use the shuttle on a regular basis, but every man experiences to some degree a reminder of his own fragility whenever he leaves the security and comforting familiarity of the orbital. Poppy tentatively slips her hand into Charlie's, and he gives it a reassuring squeeze.

Once the shuttle separates from the docking cradle it merely falls for a while, spun away from the orbital by the orbital's rotation, and the shuttle and everything in it is instantly weightless. He sees that each of the Synthia's eyes grows a little wider as they experience the sensation.

'It was like this sometimes in the crate,' Poppy says after a moment and Cheryl agrees that it had been.

'But this is nicer than being in crate,' Cheryl says seriously, 'even without windows.'

Then the shuttle's thrusters fire and it feels for a moment as though gravity has been restored, even if the shuttle now appears to be vertical, with the front of the cabin lifted high into the air above them. When the acceleration is complete, they are once again weightless, held in their seats only by the harnesses. An object floats up from one of the seats in front and a man's hand shoots out trying to grab it, but misses.

Poppy catches it easily as it floats towards her, apparently surprised at the speed of her own reaction. She turns to Charlie for guidance and mimes handing it back to the man in front, and he nods encouragingly.

Poppy holds it over the back of the seat, saying, 'I think this is yours, Sir?'

A hand takes it, and a voice says, 'Thanks.' Then the owner of the voice can be heard unbuckling his harness before rotating in his seat to look over the top at Poppy. The man opens his mouth to say something, but then he turns to the man he presumes to be her owner.

'Your Syn just caught my reader and gave it back to me,' the man says.

Charlie nods. 'She has good reflexes.'

'Thanks,' the man says, adding, 'She's very pretty.'

'Yes, she is,' Charlie agrees. 'You can tell her that.'

The man says nothing, but he turns to look at Poppy. The man smiles cautiously with his lips pressed tightly together, and then turns slowly around and pulls himself down into his seat again and they hear him refasten the harness.

Charlie grins at Poppy. 'Well done,' he tells her quietly.

They arrive at the shuttle port on Orbital C without incident, the familiar and comforting illusion of gravity returning as the shuttle matches the orbital's rotation and attaches itself to the docking cradle.

Once they are through the dock he leads the way into the main lobby, a Synthia on each arm. As on his home orbital, he feels the eyes of other men on the three of them. He knows that however humble and lowly he himself might appear, both Cheryl and Poppy can hold their own anywhere. Men will instinctively turn their heads to admire them and will not be disappointed by what they see.

He walks slowly, not in order that men might admire the women, but so that Cheryl and Poppy might turn their heads and take in the splendour of the lobby. Then he steers the now uncharacteristically silent Syns towards the fountain, stopping just a little way back from the main pool while men hurry by on either side of them preoccupied with their own thoughts.

He still finds the fountain impressive even though he has seen it many times before. To Cheryl and Poppy he knows it must seem incredible. Neither of them speak at first, but he sees them studying it intently, their heads as well as their eyes moving as they examine the rocks and the figures carved from them, and the constantly flowing sprays and cascades.

'Where does the water come from?' Poppy asks him after a moment, and he explains there are machines that suck it up from the large pool at the bottom and spew it out again at the top.

Then, without warning, the two fish women rise out of the water immediately in front of them and cling to the edge of the pool, water running and dripping from their arms onto the floor. Charlie senses Poppy and Cheryl stiffen beside him, while the fish women study the two Synthias in return. It is a full minute before one of the fish women breaks the silence.

'Hello, Charlie,' she says in her lovely, musical voice.

It is the one who invited him to kiss her. He is pleased somehow she remembers him, although he supposes it is not a very difficult feat for her. Cheryl turns to him and raises an eyebrow.

'She knows you?' she asks.

'I've stopped to speak to them,' he tells her.

'Are these your Synthias, Charlie?' the fish woman asks.

He agrees, and he sees her study each of them some more.

'They're very pretty,' the fish woman decides at last.

'So are you,' he tells her, and she smiles and shrugs.

'Is this the first time you've brought your women here?' she asks him.

He agrees that it is. 'But I'm going to take them everywhere with me now. I want them to see and experience everything for themselves.'

'That's nice,' the fish woman says, nodding sadly.

He realises now what he has said. He is talking to a woman compelled to spend her life in this one spot, limited to the pool around the base of the fountain, a world more constrained and circumscribed even than Cheryl's has been until now, waiting for him in his tiny apartment, waiting for him to return at his convenience.

'If you had legs I would take you with me,' he tells her, and Cheryl turns and gives him a look.

'I would like that,' the fish woman says seriously, water still trickling down her torso in rivulets wherever her long hair clings to it, 'but the security guards would probably arrest you.'

'Yes,' he agrees, remembering his previous encounter with them.

He would like to ask her if she would really have let him kiss her, if the guard had not stopped him, but he decides against doing so with Cheryl and Poppy beside him.

'Will you sing for us?' he asks her instead.

The fish woman looks at her companion and it is almost as though the two of them can converse with each other without speaking.

'For you, Charlie,' the woman says after a moment, some agreement apparently having been reached between them, 'yes.'

She smiles and they both disappear under the water, and he thinks for a moment she was just playing with him, but they reappear in the middle, pull themselves out of the pool and sit on the rocks at the base of the fountain, in a spot clear of the cascades. Water drips from every part of them while they arrange and compose themselves. Then they begin to sing.

He sees men stop and turn, arrested for a second in the midst of whatever they are doing. Some men merely hurry on again once they see what is happening, but a few stop and listen as the voices of the fish women fill the lobby, soaring up to the great lights suspended from the ceiling, echoing from the walls and from the pillars, flowing around the space, and around and through every being present, an invisible but palpable energy that is impossible to ignore.

He still thinks the sound is like nothing he has ever known. It does something to him he cannot really describe. He hopes it will last forever, although he finds it makes his eyes moist, and after a moment he feels the moisture spill over onto his cheeks. He is unable to wipe it away because he has both of his arms entwined in those of his women.

The singing stops eventually, as of course it must, and he is unsure if the singing continued for a long time or only very briefly.

He disentangles his arm from Cheryl's and discreetly wipes at his face with his fingers, feeling foolish and a little sad, but happy.

'Thank you,' he calls to the fish women.

They bow, their smiles as bright as their glistening and brilliantly green tails. The one who spoke to him blows him a kiss and then they both slip back into the water.

He puts his arm through Cheryl's again.

Poppy turns and lifts her shoulders, unsure perhaps how to express what she wants to say.

'That was nice,' she says at last, managing to imbue the small and mundane little word with everything she feels.

Charlie agrees that it was. Looking at her he finds that he wants to kiss her, not in a passionate or sexy way, but just because. Because of what he finds it harder to say, but with his arm entwined in Cheryl's he can only smile at Poppy instead.

'They have to stay here all the time?' Cheryl asks, meaning the fish women, 'in water under fountain?'

Charlie nods. 'I guess they do.'

'Hmm,' Cheryl says, and he realises she is not impressed, and he thinks he understands her reaction. Men create Synthias for their own amusement. They do not pause to consider how the women themselves will feel about the fate allotted to them. He is reminded of what the old man said to him.

He thinks now the song of the fish women expresses a longing of some sort, a desire for freedom perhaps, or for love, and that makes him think of poor Lisa again.

After a moment Cheryl says in a different tone, 'Okay,' and he knows she means that they have done the fountain, and she is ready now for something else.

From the lobby he takes them into the arcade where the shops are. Before they have gone very far Cheryl stops them outside the Synthia Store. It is the bottles of *Forever Young and Supple* in the window that have caught her attention.

'We need some more, Charlie,' she tells him simply, so he takes the two of them inside.

The shop may sell products for Synthias, but the customers and the sales assistants are all men. He thinks that if he ran the shop, he would staff it with Synthias, remembering the efficiency and professionalism of poor, lost Lisa. Perhaps he ought to give Synthia Corp his suggestion, but then he remembers he is shortly to become an outlaw and will be able to do no such thing.

The shop is very much larger than he thought at first and much larger than the Synthia Store on his own orbital. In addition to the range of care products and advertisements for the latest models there are all kinds of ornaments and accessories, as well as clothes. He sees that Poppy and Cheryl are staring around them wide-eyed at the items on display.

'We'll get some skin conditioner,' he says to Cheryl, 'but why don't you both have a look around first. Look at whatever you like.'

Cheryl looks at him as if he has suggested she get into the pool with the fish women.

'Go on,' he says, 'look at whatever you like. I'll be here in the shop too, but you don't have to stay with me. You can walk around by yourselves.'

He can see Poppy is excited by the idea, but Cheryl is still sceptical.

'Look,' he says, 'you can both spend one hundred Sens each, on whatever you want. It can be one thing or ten things that add up to a hundred, it's up to you.'

'You mean it, Charlie?' Cheryl asks him.

'Of course,' he says, 'and whatever you buy is yours.'

'It belong to us?' she asks him.

He nods. 'Of course,' he says again.

'You say Synthia not own anything,' she points out, 'only men can own things, you say.'

He remembers that he said just that. There is the suggestion of a smile on her lips, and he thinks she already knows what he will say, but he says it anyway.

'I was wrong,' he says, although he knows that from a legal perspective he was perfectly correct. 'I won't say it ever again.'

She kisses him quickly and then says, 'Come Poppy, before Charlie change mind.'

She takes Poppy's hand and leads her over to an area that displays ornaments for Synthias to wear in their ears, as well as bracelets, bangles, necklaces and probably other things too that Charlie cannot see from where he stands. He follows, but deliberately keeps his distance. He does not want to influence them or make them feel they have to please him with their choices.

'Excuse me, Sir,' a voice says behind him.

He turns. The man is one of the sales assistants. He has a small badge with the Synthia Store logo on his chest.

'Are those your Synthias?' the man asks, pointing discreetly at Poppy and Cheryl.

Charlie nods and says, 'They're just having a look around. I expect they'll want to buy something.'

'Yes,' the assistant says doubtfully. 'It's just that…' He stops, clasping his hands together uncertainly. Above the Synthia Store logo, the badge on the man's chest advertises his name as 'Rik'.

'It's just that we don't allow Synthias … well, not unaccompanied Synthias, in the store,' Rik says finally.

'They're not unaccompanied,' he tells Rik. 'I'm here.'

Rik looks unhappy, but Charlie gives the man a smile and moves away, but not rushing to catch up with the women. In fact, he goes back to the entrance and picks up a container for putting items in before they are paid for and then he slowly saunters after the Syns. Eventually, he catches up, having lingered as long as he can over the shelves of skin and hair care and various sanitising products that claim to keep a man's Syn clean inside and out.

"For wherever you go" one sign proclaims. It takes him a second or two to work out what it means. He wonders if he ought to buy some of the product, but he reasons that he and Cheryl have managed perfectly well without it. She keeps herself clean and fresh and she never smells anything other than lovely. He does not know what she does when she goes into the sanitation cubicle, but then until recently she had never seen him shower either.

He finds Poppy looking at a display head. It is just a head with enough neck and shoulders to display necklaces as well as ear ornaments. It looks surprisingly lifelike, and he sees Poppy wave her hand tentatively in front of its eyes.

'It's not alive,' he tells her.

She turns quickly. She had not known he was beside her and he has startled her.

'It's just an object to display the things that are for sale,' he explains.

She nods slowly and then puts a finger to the head's cheek. When it does not respond she turns and asks him, 'Am I alive?'

At first, he does not know what to tell her. It is an

interesting as well as a surprising question, and one that once again reminds him of his own ignorance. His instinct is to say that she is only a machine and that only men and biological women are alive, but that seems not only cruel but also at odds with his experience.

'Yes,' he tells her after a moment, 'of course you are.' Then more slowly he adds, a little surprised by his own words, 'I think that if you can ask the question, it means that you're alive.'

He is quite pleased with his answer, and he sees her thinking about it.

'But I'm only a machine,' she points out seriously.

It is clear she remembers what he said to Cheryl in his fit of temper the day before and he wishes he could recall the words, wishes he had never said them, but he thinks it is true nevertheless.

'I'm only a machine too,' he says eventually and she looks puzzled again.

'But you're a man,' she objects.

He nods, 'Yes, but I'm really just another kind of machine.'

She looks doubtful, so he holds his arm next to hers and then flexes it at the elbow and moves his hand and fingers. He sees her do the same, mimicking his actions.

'There are bones in my arm and blood flows around in there too,' he tells her, pointing with his other hand, 'but it's just part of a machine. It's very like your arm, but just made of different kinds of stuff.'

She frowns and looks down at her own arm again while she repeats the movements he made with his.

'If my heart stops beating,' he tells her, 'and my body stops working, that's the end of me.' He shrugs. 'No more Charlie, just as if I'd been deactivated.'

Poppy's eyes grow a little wider, as though she has not grasped the impermanent nature of men's existence until now.

Then with a sudden change of focus she turns and points to the ear ornaments. 'I like those,' she tells him.

He looks. 'Yes, they're pretty,' he agrees.

Then she asks him, 'Do I have holes?'

She holds her ear lobes between her thumb and forefinger for him to examine.

He looks. 'Yes, you do.'

'So I can wear those?' she asks, pointing at the ear ornaments again.

He nods. 'Yes, if you'd like to.'

'These?' she asks, pointing to a particular pair, a selection from the many that are on the display stand. He sees they are small and dainty. There are others that are longer, that hang down more, some with big hoops and rings, but these have a small and shiny cream sphere in the centre, surrounded by clear, glistening gemstones of some kind; glass presumably.

'I think they're lovely,' he tells her, 'but you choose the ones you like the most.'

'These,' she repeats, sticking to her original choice and he puts them into the container, explaining they will pay for them before they leave the shop.

He looks at the other customers peering at things

and weighing up whether to buy them. He wants to say, loudly enough for them all to hear, 'Why don't you go home and ask your Syns to come and choose.' He thinks they are missing out on so much by not doing so, but he keeps quiet. He does not know if his desire to make an exhibition of himself stems from his fear about what they are going to do later, or from the pleasure he feels at this moment.

Cheryl chooses a necklace and a bracelet and then, when Charlie has explained that they have quite a lot of Sens still to spend, they both choose some clothes, Cheryl a clinging dress and Poppy some trousers and a top. Both the Synthias seem delighted by it all and he cannot remember when he has ever enjoyed himself so much. He buys the skin and hair care products Cheryl says they need and a bag for Poppy, like the one Cheryl has, so that Poppy can carry her own things in it.

Further along the arcade they come to a shop selling various devices that a man might use with his Syn or by himself, things to enhance or bring about sexual fulfilment. Cheryl expresses an interest in going into the shop, but he does not want to. In the end she goes in on her own. An assistant, or perhaps the owner, comes out soon afterwards to speak to him.

Charlie explains that Cheryl just wants to look around and eventually the man goes back inside, apparently satisfied that Charlie takes full responsibility for Cheryl. After a while he sees Cheryl talking to the man near the back of the shop. He is showing her various objects he has for sale.

Poppy waits outside with him. She clings affectionately to his arm but is apparently unable to keep still. She smiles broadly from time to time, but why and about what he does not know. But he is not surprised; he feels much the same way.

When Cheryl comes out again she is quiet, but in answer to his question she says she is glad she went in and found it interesting. She takes his other arm.

Poppy asks Cheryl if she ought to have gone in with her.

Cheryl looks at her for a moment and then says carefully, 'It is better not to learn everything at once.'

He thinks Cheryl might be right.

They go into a store selling clothes for men and the two of them make suggestions about things he might wear, somewhat to the amusement of the assistants. Cheryl persuades him to make a couple of purchases, but he really only agrees in order to have a change of clothes.

The women are interested in everything and all of the many and various shops, but eventually he is forced to protest that this particular machine needs to sit down and needs some food, so they find somewhere for him to eat where the staff will also allow the women to sit with him while he does so.

All day he has been conscious of the time; the time they have been on the orbital and the time remaining before they go to do what they are here for. Cheryl is looking at his face now as he contemplates the food a waiter has just put before him.

'We still have plenty time, Charlie,' she tells him, correctly guessing his preoccupation, 'and you not think about it.'

'No,' he agrees.

'We have nice time,' she says, 'and I think, "Why we not go out before?"'

'I don't know,' he tells her with a wry grin.

He begins to eat and discovers he is hungry as well as simply in need of food.

23

Poppy is fascinated by the multiple reflections of herself, or perhaps it is the reflections of all three of them she is looking at. She turns repeatedly, as though hoping to catch one of the reflections doing something different, not behaving as it ought to, not following the lead given by herself or by her companions. She sees him looking at her, or she sees one of his reflections catching the eyes of one of hers. She smiles and he smiles back at her reflection. Then she turns to him, to see if this version of him is also smiling.

'These are not windows,' she says, indicating the walls of the car, 'they're mirrors.'

'Yes,' he agrees.

'But the colours are not the same,' she points out, holding one of her hands near its reflection. The reflection is a darker, more tanned version of the hand she holds in front of it.

'No,' he says, 'but they're both very pretty hands.'

'You like them?' she asks him seriously, considering them.

He nods. 'I do.'

'I like them too,' she decides and she smiles

again.

Cheryl is watching them. He thinks her tolerant expression suggests she finds them both a little silly, as if everything is new to him as well, and not only to Poppy, and in a way it is. Despite his anxiety about what they are soon to do, and the burden of the task itself, he feels different, lighter, happier, liberated in some way. It is as if the further they have travelled from his home and his old life, the greater his sense of this new freedom has become. His relationship with Cheryl has changed, has blossomed in some manner he does not fully understand, beyond the knowledge that the fact she is with him, that she cares about him, fills him with joy.

And there is Poppy too. There is the relief that comes from the absence of guilt, but it is more than that. He finds her innocence and evident joy at discovering and exploring the world infectious, although it makes him acutely aware of his responsibility towards her, his duty to look after and protect her. Whenever she smiles and gazes at him with those startlingly blue eyes it pierces him, makes him both wonder at and be a little anxious that there should be something so beautiful and fragile in a world he knows to be full of thoughtless cruelty and violence.

When the car stops, they get out and enter the private atrium. He sees Cheryl note the nameplate carefully. Then she entwines her arm in his and checks Poppy has done the same on his other side.

'Come,' she says softly. She has taken charge, has lent him some of her strength, and he thinks with her at his side he might indeed be able to accomplish what they have planned.

Then the three of them advance to the entrance together.

'Hello, Charlie,' Marie greets them uncertainly once she has opened the door. He notes there is to be no repeat this evening of the usual game about his name.

'It's nice to see you again, Marie,' he tells her and then he introduces his companions.

'You're not expected, Charlie,' Marie says.

She looks with interest at Cheryl and Poppy, but she is obviously uncomfortable about his arrival without an appointment, and he is sorry to be the cause of any difficulty for her.

'No,' he says gently, 'but don't worry. Sly will want to see me.'

The threesome step forward as a single entity and Marie is forced to step back and allow them to enter.

'We'll wait in the day room,' he announces and leads the way into the room before Marie has time to worry about what to do. He can hear no sounds from elsewhere in the apartment and he wonders where Sly is and what he is doing.

Marie follows them into the room.

'Charlie,' she pleads, 'you can't do this. I will get into trouble.'

He sees her lower lip trembles very slightly. She smells as lovely as ever and she is still wearing only the string of bells and her silk slippers, but it makes her seem vulnerable now rather than provocative. His body, however, is responding to her warmth and to her beauty even now, even with the feeling that his stomach has disappeared and has been replaced by a yawning chasm.

'I'll tell Sly it wasn't your fault,' he assures her. 'And I can't get into trouble because I'm dead.'

He sees her eyes widen, but failing to make any sense of this she reverts to her previous expression and simply looks worried. She is standing very close to him and he is looking down at her over her breasts, seeing the way the string of bells rest on her hips. He imagines how it would feel to press her body against his own, pulling her towards him with a hand on each of her buttocks. Her head would naturally tilt backwards, presenting her face to him and he would still that trembling lip, first with a finger and then with his mouth.

'What are you doing, Charlie?' she asks and at first he thinks she has followed his thoughts, or – worse – that he has actually begun to act out what he was imagining. 'I'm not only worried for myself,' she tells him.

'Please don't worry,' he tells her, meaning it. 'Just go and tell Sly we're here.'

She turns and goes out, giving them one last worried look before the doors slide closed and she is hidden from them.

Cheryl is looking around at the room and at its contents.

When Marie has gone, she says, 'Yes, this man clearly very rich, Charlie. He has many nice things.'

Poppy is walking around the edge of the room, and he realises she is trying to avoid treading on the rug that covers a large section of the floor. He has sometimes studied the design of the rug while seated and listening to Sly, but he looks at it again now with fresh interest. When your eyes merely glance over it, not really seeing it but thinking to yourself, 'there's a rug', it presents itself as mostly a kind of red, but there are many other colours in it and there is almost as much of another colour as there is of the red. Its colour is something like that of a food you might eat for breakfast. The effect is very rich and in sharp contrast to the dull and uniformly drab world he inhabits. The walls are not the simple utilitarian plastic that contain and define his own apartment. They are subtly coloured and matte rather than shiny, one wall a deeper shade of the same colour as the others.

'It's nice isn't it?' he says to Poppy, meaning the carpet, 'but it's meant to be walked on.'

'Really?' she queries. She tries placing one of her feet lightly on it and then she crouches and runs her fingers over the surface, feeling the texture of the short fibres and following the shapes of the design.

'It would be interesting to lie on,' she says, running the flat of her hand over the rug, adding uncertainly, 'without any clothes on.'

'Maybe,' he agrees with a smile. He has been tracing the shapes in his head, the way he has sometimes done when listening to Sly and not looking out of the window. Now he imagines lying on the rug with Poppy, without clothes on as she suggests. It would indeed be interesting, but as a man he knows the hardness of the floor would press into him uncomfortably and would hurt his elbows and his knees and he would quickly wish they were on a bed or something like one.

He hears the doors opening and turns to see Sly. Whatever Sly has been doing he looks as he always does and gives every appearance of being totally unruffled by their unexpected arrival. Perhaps he has been taking a shower for he looks fresh and scrubbed, although his hair is perfectly dry.

'Charlie,' Sly says, drawing the name out as he always does in greeting, 'this is an unexpected pleasure!' There is just the slightest emphasis on the penultimate word.

'Please don't blame Marie,' he tells Sly, 'we more or less forced our way in before she could decide what to do with us.'

He knows these words do not sound like him. They are something a character in one of the dramvids might say.

'Blame her?' Sly says with a frown. 'Why should I do that? I expect her to make you welcome.'

Sly appears to be using the same, artificial-sounding script and has clearly decided to meet their brazen arrival with a show of hospitality.

Before Charlie can gather his wits to say anything more, Sly says, only a fractionally less cordially, 'And you've brought some friends with you.'

He introduces the women and Sly says, 'Well, it's nice to meet you both,' but his eyes do not quite meet those of either Synthia.

'I promised them you would show them your window,' he tells their host.

'The window?'

'I've told them so much about it they wanted to see it for themselves.'

'Ah, yes, the window,' Sly says and they all turn in its direction, as though the word were a command of some kind.

'As you can see, the shutters are across it at the moment,' Sly says, as if this is the unexpected event this evening, not their sudden and uninvited appearance in the apartment.

Charlie says nothing.

'But we can certainly change that,' Sly says after a moment, rousing himself and crossing the room to pick up a control.

He follows Sly's movements with careful eyes. Sly touches an icon and the shutters begin to slide back, the machinery producing an audible hum in the apartment, and a threatening black hole begins to appear in the wall. It seems much larger than when it reveals the daytime planet below and now as it is revealed the window changes the whole feel of the room. Charlie can understand why a man might want to shut out that terrifying and heartless black, if only to escape perhaps the feeling that it is looking back in upon him.

'Come and take a look,' Sly says to the Synthias once the shutters have slid back completely.

Cheryl follows, but Poppy glances at Charlie, looking for her cue. He nods at her, and she joins Sly at the window.

Charlie hangs back, glancing around at the room. He knows where the alarm trips and the sensors are and where the cameras and the microphones are too, but there are no hidden weapons or anti-intruder devices in here according to the information on Gen's disc, nothing that Sly can activate remotely that might incapacitate any of them.

'As you can see, it's night on the surface,' Sly is telling the women, 'just as it is up here, so there's not as much to see as there is when it's daytime.'

'Are those lights?' Poppy asks him, pointing at something she can see.

Sly looks. 'Yes, that'll be a city,' he tells her. 'You know what a city is?'

She shakes her head, and Charlie sees Sly deciding how to explain it to her.

'Somewhere lots of men live in many buildings,' Sly explains, 'buildings like this apartment. There will be lights inside them and lights outside too.'

'Outside?' Poppy asks.

You're doing very well, Poppy, Charlie thinks. Just keep going.

'Yes,' Sly says, 'you can walk around on the surface down there without any protective suits or whatever, or so I'm told. They have lights outside so they can see their way around like we do in the hallways up here.'

Sly must have seen the interest in her face, for he adds, 'And you can look up at the sky.'

'Would they be able to see us looking down at them?' Poppy asks him.

Sly laughs. It sounds quite unforced, the sort of laugh a man might make when at ease.

'No, it's too far,' Sly tells Poppy, 'but they can

probably see the orbitals. They'd be just points of light though.'

'What could you see if you looked up from down there?' Poppy asks.

Sly considers this for a moment.

'Well, at the moment,' Sly says at last, 'you'd be able to see the stars and the orbital might look like just another of those, but in the day, I believe you'd see a kind of blue colour, or just clouds much of the time. That's what you see mostly when you look down.'

Poppy frowns. 'What are "clouds"?'

Sly starts to answer, but then he says, 'You'll have to come back again when it's daylight down there and I'll show you.'

'Thank you,' Poppy says politely, 'I'd like that.'

Sly looks at her and then he turns to look at his other guests. Perhaps he really forgot for a moment how things stand.

'Let me ask Marie to get you a drink, Charlie,' Sly says. 'I know I could do with one.'

Charlie hesitates. Then he says, 'Ask Marie to bring the things in here on a tray, and Cheryl can serve us.'

Sly looks puzzled for a just a fraction of a second and then he manages to look hurt.

'Oh, it's like that is it?' Sly says.

Charlie says nothing.

'Okay,' Sly agrees, 'we'll do it your way.'

Sly crosses the room towards the chairs where Charlie knows there is a device for summoning Marie. As Sly passes close to him something catches

Charlie's arm and there is a brief burning sensation. When he looks, he sees he has been cut. Blood now oozes from a long scratch on his forearm.

Sly reaches one of the chairs and fumbles for something in the cushions.

Then Sly turns and sees him examining his arm and says, 'Did I do that? How clumsy of me.'

The wound is not serious, and Charlie does not think he has been injected or poisoned with anything. It stings a little and it feels as though the initiative has passed to Sly again, or perhaps Sly has always been the one in control, but Charlie is trying to work out what Sly has done and why.

Sly gives a tight smile. 'It answers one question, doesn't it?'

'Which is?' he asks.

But before Sly can answer Marie is in the doorway.

'Bring in a couple of glasses, some ice and whatever else we need to fix a drink or two,' Sly tells her.

'You would like a drink for yourself and Mister Charlie?' Marie queries. 'I can do it for you.'

'Just the glasses and the ingredients,' Charlie tells her before Sly can reply. 'Bring it in on a tray and leave it over there. Cheryl will serve us.'

Marie looks from him to Sly and then back to him again. When Sly says nothing more she leaves without further comment.

'What question does this answer?' he asks Sly, wiping the blood from his arm with his hand.

'Why don't we let your Syns go and keep Marie

company,' Sly suggests, 'then we can talk properly.'

'I don't have any secrets from them,' Charlie says.

'Really?'

'I'd prefer them to stay.'

'As you wish,' Sly says, 'but why don't you come and take the weight off while we wait for our drinks?'

Charlie nods. 'Okay.'

He moves quickly and sits in the chair Sly usually occupies, but Sly merely shrugs and takes the other one.

'Not to doubt the veracity of anything our esteemed police force tells us,' Sly says conversationally once he is comfortable, 'but according to them you're a dead man, Charlie, although I must say you don't look that bad to me.'

Charlie remains silent.

'We both know the police have a tendency to say all kinds of things,' Sly continues, 'but they were quite definite about your state of health.'

Charlie sees no need to respond, not yet.

'So, when a man as is dead – blown to little pieces and scattered far and wide by all accounts – when that man turns up unannounced at another man's apartment,' Sly persists, 'that man is liable to ask himself some questions.'

Charlie waits.

'That man is liable to wonder, for example,' Sly goes on, 'if this unexpected visitor really is the recently departed friend he claims to be, rather than say, a synthetic, a synthetic sent by the upholders of the law with the intention of discovering whatever nasty and grubby bits of information they can, for their own frankly dubious and devious purposes.'

'You've seen that I bleed,' he tells Sly evenly.

'I have,' Sly agrees, 'and that suggests that you're not a synthetic, but…'

There is a knock and Marie enters with a tray of glasses and bottles and a bowl of ice.

'Put it over there, please,' Charlie tells her, 'on that piece of furniture.'

Marie looks to her owner for instruction, but receiving none she does as Charlie has asked.

'You may be interested to know that the piece of furniture in question is called a "credenza",' Sly says lightly as Marie sets down the tray, 'or it used to be a long time ago when it was made.'

He wonders if Sly's words are as casual as they seem: polite conversation or a code of some kind for Marie perhaps?

'It was also known as a "sideboard", I believe,' Sly adds.

Marie gives no visible sign that Sly's words mean anything to her.

'Is it very old?' Poppy asks.

'Several hundreds of years, I believe,' Sly tells her. 'If it isn't I was stupid enough to pay far more for it than was necessary.'

Marie is waiting for instruction so Charlie signals she should leave. She looks once again to Sly for guidance, but Sly simply waves her away.

'But I like it,' Sly says, meaning the item of furniture.

'Yes, it is nice,' Cheryl agrees, 'if you have room for it. If you have big room like this one.'

Sly looks at her. 'Your Syns are unusually chatty, Charlie,' he says, still looking at Cheryl.

Charlie says nothing and Sly addresses Cheryl directly, 'How do you think of this man? Is he your owner?'

'He is my man,' Cheryl tells him. 'He is good man.'

Sly nods. 'And what about you?' he asks, turning to Poppy, 'is he your owner?'

Poppy frowns, but says nothing.

'How do you regard him?' Sly asks her, adding for the avoidance of doubt, 'This man here.'

Sly points and Poppy smiles.

'I like him,' she says. 'I like him a lot.'

'Do you now?' Sly says. 'Well, that's nice. And what's his name again?'

'Charlie,' Poppy says, as if this is a game and the question is too easy.

'Why don't you fix us a drink, Cheryl?' Charlie says when Sly has finished with his questions.

Cheryl begins to sort out the drinks.

'To return to our hypothetical man,' Sly says, watching Cheryl while he talks, 'he might wonder other things too. Like why the police would say that his friend is dead when he is not, assuming the man has been convinced of this fact.'

'And has he been so convinced?'

'Yes,' Sly says thoughtfully, 'I think so and Marie seems to think so too, which is probably more significant. But it leaves the other questions hanging, doesn't it? Is this man still his friend or is he working with the police in some way? And if so to what end?'

'Was he your friend?'.

'Charlie!' Sly says, stung by the question. 'I thought so, and I'd like to think he still is.'

Charlie says nothing.

Sly asks him, 'How is it that you're not dead, by the way?'

He does not answer immediately and Sly says, 'I take it that you were on the shuttle?'

'I got off,' he says without adding to this explanation.

'Questions, questions,' Sly says slowly as though to himself. Then with a change of tone he asks more sharply, 'Why did you "get off" as you put it? Was it going the wrong way or something?'

'I realised it was a set up,' Charlie says, 'and that you were trying to kill me.'

Sly is good. The man looks both genuinely shocked and hurt by the accusation. Before Sly can respond, however, Cheryl hands him a drink, then she crosses to bring one over to Charlie. She does not look at Sly, but returns to stand beside the piece of furniture again.

'Now why would I want to kill you, Charlie?' Sly asks, looking thoughtfully at the drink Cheryl has given him.

'Because I know your secret,' Charlie says.

Sly's head comes up fast and he thinks that the man's eyes have a different look now. The silence is suddenly rather cold, as though the temperature in the room has dropped. Sly's eyes have grown sharper along with the air.

Sly says very quietly, 'It never occurred to me for a moment that you would ever use that knowledge against me. If I had thought you might, you wouldn't have known it in the first place.'

'And what about Tan and Nils?' he asks Sly. 'They knew too.'

He sees a flash of anger in Sly's eyes now and his face grows darker still.

'Of course they knew,' Sly says after a moment, the words coming from his mouth as if squeezed by force through a narrow aperture. 'They didn't only know, they shared my secret, and they were hardly likely to use it against me, were they?'

'Because they acquired her for you?'

Sly swears, his face an even darker shade now, darker like the reflection of Poppy's hand was in comparison to the original in the mirrors on the walls of the passenger tube car.

'What are you talking about, Charlie?' Sly asks him, apparently puzzled now as well as angry.

Charlie hesitates. The cold hand of doubt has reached up from the empty space where his stomach used to be. It has coiled itself around the back of his neck and is starting over the top of his head too, but he presses on anyway.

'You know who she is?' he says, 'don't you?'

Sly continues to look puzzled and then after a moment he laughs. The sound is so unexpected it rocks Charlie back in his chair, as if he has been hit by the shock wave from an explosion.

'You're talking about that woman I showed you

the last time you were here,' Sly says, still laughing, but without mirth. 'Aren't you?' Sly adds more quietly.

Charlie says nothing. He remembers his reaction to Kam on the shuttle and his judgement that the man ought to have been able to respond more swiftly to what another man told him, and he hears again the words given to him in his own sales training.

He has been so focussed on the woman that he has forgotten everything he learned. Sly, rather belatedly, now understands his preoccupation, but Sly had thought at first that he was talking about a very different secret, and he ought to have realised this. He is sorry too, because no matter what the man might have done or has tried to do to him, he would never have thought to use that particular information against the man. But he has to put the mistake behind him. He cannot afford to let it prevent him from listening more carefully from now on. His life might depend upon it. He has been taught that in general a man will only hear half of what you tell him, but a salesman must listen carefully to everything a man says as well as what he does not say. It is time to start putting his training into practice.

Sly is looking down at his drink again. He has not touched it.

'You do know about Tan and Nils?' Sly asks him quietly. 'Don't you?'

Charlie says nothing. He had not known. Perhaps it was rather slow of him, but he guesses the truth now.

'They didn't just work together,' Sly goes on in

the same quiet, rather sad way, 'they were...' Sly pauses and looks at him. Then he shrugs. 'Anyway, they were particular friends of mine.'

Sly looks down at his drink again. 'But it's that woman you're on about, isn't it?' Sly says. 'You've been obsessing about her.'

He nods and Sly studies him thoughtfully.

'As it happens,' he says after a moment, 'it was Tan and Nils that found her.'

Charlie waits. He waits a long time while Sly seems to be trying to analyse his drink by staring at it.

'We made the man an offer,' Sly says at last, 'something he couldn't refuse, but nothing too heavy. We didn't want to start any wars and I knew how carefully I had to go about it in order to keep it quiet. You're right about it needing to be kept secret. In fact, you can't have any idea how quiet it had to be kept. Anyway, it turned out that the man who had her didn't protest that much, not really, and he did quite well out of it, and I got her, the woman I showed you.'

'And you know who she is?' Charlie asks quietly.

Sly does not answer and merely sits for a moment contemplating his drink again.

'Do you know what an anomaly is, Charlie?' Sly asks him, speaking at last, but not answering the question.

Charlie remains silent.

'It's true,' Sly says slowly, 'she's the ultimate, the one every serious collector fantasises about. Owning her should be the final triumph of any man's collecting career.'

'And isn't it?'

'I showed her to you, Charlie, because – and I think you know this – I've always valued your opinion.'

Sly seems to be waiting for a response of some kind, so he nods.

'You saw right off that she was something special, didn't you?' Sly asks him.

He nods again.

'And you've seen some of my other biologicals, and they're about the best to be seen anywhere.'

Charlie nods again. 'Yes, they are,' he agrees.

'So you knew that she had a lot to live up to, but you could see straight away that this one was in a class of her own.'

Charlie nods again. He is unlikely to forget the impression the woman made on him.

'So you wondered what I'd paid for her,' Sly says.

'Of course,' he agrees readily.

'Right. So what do you think she's worth?' Sly asks him. 'Did you come up with a figure?'

When he remains mute, Sly says with feeling, 'Well? Come on, I think your knowledge of the market is as good as that of most men I know, so give me a figure.'

Charlie hesitates. 'She's priceless,' he says eventually.

'Yeah,' Sly agrees, 'bang on the money!'

Sly looks at his drink again and then at Cheryl.

Then Sly says, 'You see, the thing about collecting is you go for the rare ones, the really limited editions, the models where there are only one or two left or only a few to start with. You can look at the prices that they or similar ones have made in the past and you can get an idea what your own collection is worth. You try not to pay full price if you can, and if you're clever you keep them in original condition, keep them clean and mint, and they'll actually get more valuable the longer you own them. You can compare notes with other collectors if you're fairly sure of your security arrangements, one way or another.'

'And did you compare notes with anyone about her?'

Sly looks pained. 'Don't be stupid, of course not, and I never can, but I didn't go out and kill anyone to stop them talking about her. I didn't have to; the only ones who knew were you, and Tan and Nils.'

Sly lets this sink in before he adds, 'The bloke that owned her before won't know where she went. It wasn't exactly an eyes-open transaction as far as he was concerned, if you know what I mean.'

'So why is she an anomaly?'

'She doesn't fit,' Sly says simply, 'not when you think about it. She's not the same kind of thing. It's like, I don't know, a man collects a lot of China and then gets himself something made of glass.'

When Charlie lapses back into silence Sly asks him, 'Do you know what China is?'

Charlie shakes his head and Sly says, 'Well it doesn't matter. It's not glass is what I'm saying. It isn't the same thing at all, and in a way neither is she.'

Charlie must look unconvinced because Sly seems to feel the need to explain.

'She's a lovely woman, I'll give you that, and you're right – in so far as it's possible to be sure – she isn't farmed, however unlikely and impossible that may seem.' He shrugs. 'She isn't. And that makes her so rare that I personally can't think of a suitable comparison, even without... well, even without the provenance, the bona fides the man offered me that apparently suggest she is who I think you think she is. I can't judge the veracity of them, but I think she speaks for herself as it were. You thought so, didn't you?'

Charlie nods slowly.

'But is she China or is she glass?' Sly muses. 'Without a maker, how do we assess the craftsmanship? And is it craftsmanship or is it something else? Answer me that if you can.'

'She's a woman,' Charlie suggests.

'Oh, they're all women,' Sly says dismissively. 'These two every bit as much as she is.' He nods at Cheryl and Poppy. 'But we made these two, we used all our ingenuity and skill, perfected the techniques and the processes until we were good enough to make Poppy here, make her so she even seems to be breathing. She's a work of art. Personally, I don't lust after her, but I can appreciate the artistry that went into creating her.'

Sly is silent for a while, apparently studying Cheryl.

'But who made the woman that I showed you?' Sly asks, 'the one you've obviously been obsessing about since you saw her.'

'Interesting question don't you think?' Sly persists.

Charlie looks at Sly but remains silent.

'Oh, I know she's naturally reared,' Sly continues, 'and I know what that means, but you can't compare her with Poppy and say which of them is better, which is more skilful, or which of them is the more valuable? That's really what it comes down to. You can't even compare her to other biologicals. They're the work of careful genetics and commercial cloning. They're the product of selection and development, a finished item produced to a reproducible and repeatable specification. The growers may have started once with some natural raw material, but they've worked with it, perfected it and improved on it in all sorts of ways.'

Charlie has no response to make to any of this. He is just letting Sly talk.

Sly looks up now, his manner different again. 'I hope you don't mind my asking, but apart from the fact that you seem to think I tried to kill you, why are you here, Charlie? Why have you come? Are you here for revenge?'

There is a moment of silence again, and then Charlie says quietly, 'I want you to give the woman to me.'

Sly turns his head in his direction and then he laughs again. The sound disturbs Charlie, puts him on edge, just as the cut to his arm did.

'Do you now?' Sly says, still laughing, although his eyes remain cold and watchful.

When he says nothing more, Sly asks, 'And what would you do with her, Charlie? Would you run off with her to hide somewhere and live happily until the end of your natural? Is that it? Maybe you'd have a go at making babies with her. Personally, I think the idea is disgusting, but maybe you fancy it. You could create a string of little Charlies, or more of her.'

Charlie says nothing.

'But you'd be looking over your shoulder the rest of your life, Charlie,' Sly tells him. 'You wouldn't have the protection of the law behind you even if I gave her to you – and that isn't going to happen in case you really think it is – because you wouldn't be able to trust anyone. Every man would be a threat. You'd be left with sheer cunning and whatever physical strength you still had left in you to stop someone else stealing her. Until she gets old, of course, which I imagine she'll do with depressing speed once you reheat her. Then you'd finally be safe, because no one would want her, but would you?'

Charlie listens to all of this in silence. He has had similar thoughts himself, on those occasions when he has allowed himself to fantasise about a future for her in which he also figures. The only difference is that he knows now that he would still want her even when she was old, and he would be old himself.

'So,' Sly asks him with a shrug, 'What? What will you do with her? Do you think you can sell her and live to spend any of it? You're a fool if you do. Show her to another man, or even suggest that you have her or know where she is, and your days or hours will be numbered.'

He lets Sly finish and then he says quietly, 'I'd let her go.'

'Let her go?' Sly asks, his tone and his face suggesting frank incredulity. Sly is not acting now. 'You'd let her go?' he repeats.

'Yes.'

Charlie feels the eyes of Cheryl and Poppy on him too. They have not talked about what he plans to do with the woman once he has stolen her.

'It's not right for her to be kept locked up in suspended animation,' he tells Sly, 'or for her to be owned by someone.'

'Let her go where?' Sly asks him, his puzzlement apparently genuine. 'Are you going to just let her run around the orbital looking for somewhere to settle?'

'She must know where she came from,' Charlie suggests, but without real conviction. 'Maybe there are still more of her people living somewhere, people who will be glad to see her return.'

Sly regards him in silence for a while. Then he shakes his head. 'You know what your trouble is, Charlie?' Sly asks wearily.

Actually, he thinks he does know, but he lets Sly tell him.

'In a way I've always liked it about you, but what you are is weak and sentimental.'

Charlie merely shrugs. Cheryl has after all suggested much the same thing.

'There are worse failings, I suppose,' Sly muses, 'but it will be your undoing, mark my words. It really doesn't do to feel too much. You can't afford to make friends with other men either. It makes you vulnerable. They'll die on you some day even if they don't double cross you first.'

They sit in silence again until Sly says. 'Maybe I should kill you.'

'So you didn't book that shuttle for me?' Charlie says.

Sly merely sighs and then instead of answering he says, 'I wasn't entirely honest with you, Charlie, when I got you to do that little job for me.'

Before he can respond, Sly says, 'By the way, I take it that this is the Syn in question?' Sly gestures towards Poppy with the hand that holds the glass.

When Charlie does not react, Sly says, 'Don't worry, I'm not interested in taking her away from you. You obviously did a good job as it happens. It's a pity that it was a waste of time, but you showed initiative all the same.'

Charlie says nothing.

'Anyway, I can see she's cute. I'm sure you're quite smitten with her.'

'I wouldn't let any man harm either of them,' Charlie says quietly, glancing at Cheryl and Poppy.

Sly makes a rueful expression. 'It's amazing the strength of feeling we can develop for our Syns, isn't it?' he says. 'At least they'll never let us down.'

Then with a change of tone and as though rousing himself from some torpor Sly asks, 'Where are the things she was wearing when you took her out of the crate?'

When no one reacts, Sly says, 'She wasn't dressed like that!'

'Don't you like these clothes?' Poppy asks him.

'I couldn't care less what you wear,' Sly says, raising his voice, 'I want to know where the things are that you had on in the crate?'

Charlie is caught off guard by the question, but Cheryl says quietly, 'I have.'

Sly appears more alert and awake now than he has at any time since they arrived. 'Show me!' he barks now.

Cheryl picks up her bag and after a moment she brings out the dress and the shoes Poppy removed down in the dock. Charlie had forgotten about them and had not known that Cheryl had them with her.

Cheryl comes forward now and Sly stands to receive the items from her. He examines them carefully, rubbing the material of the dress between his fingers, holding it up to the light, and even putting it to his nose and sniffing it. With another man and in a different situation it might have appeared that Sly was searching for some lingering trace of Poppy herself or of the scent she wears. But Charlie knows it is unlikely to be that which has Sly so animated.

After a moment Sly throws the dress down and looks at the white satin shoes instead. He pulls out the lining and then forces off the low heel, hitting the shoe against the arm of the chair until it comes loose. Then he does the same with the second shoe. Then he sighs and sits down again. Whatever Sly was searching for – and it is obvious he was looking for something – he has evidently not found it in the things Cheryl gave him.

'What about the rest of the things?' Sly demands.

'What things?' he asks Sly.

He sees Sly look at Poppy and then close his eyes for a second.

'Something over her face,' Sly says, his eyes still closed, demonstrating with a hand what he means, 'something in her hair, and perhaps she was holding something.'

'Flowers,' Cheryl says.

'Yes!' Sly agrees readily. 'Where are the flowers?'

There is another silence and Sly looks at each of them in turn.

'Flowers are lost,' Cheryl tells him eventually.

Sly sits heavily. 'Lost,' he repeats without conviction. 'Of course they are.'

Charlie is struggling to understand what significance the flowers can possibly have. He thinks Sly might be simply trying to throw dirt in their eyes, to divert their attention, and his mind is racing as he tries to think what Sly might be planning.

'How lost?' Sly asks, eventually fixing his gaze on Poppy.

'What do you mean?' she asks him.

'How did you come to lose them?' he asks her with deliberate precision. 'Where did you lose them?'

Poppy is not intimidated. She simply shrugs. Then she says, 'I had them in the crate. Charlie and the other man asked me to change my clothes before we left the dock. I understand now that it was because they did not want me to look like a new Synthia, one that has just been delivered. They put the clothes I was wearing and the shoes in a bag, and when we got to the apartment, I did not have the flowers and they were not in the bag with the dress and the shoes.'

'Who is this "other man"?' Sly asks her.

Poppy shrugs. 'I don't know,' she says. 'He did not tell me his name.'

Most men believe a Syn is incapable of telling a lie, but Charlie has had ample proof recently that this is just a myth. Poppy looked straight at Sly as she spoke, and no man would have reason to doubt what she was saying. He has not coached her on this point, but he knows she likes the old man, and it seems she feels an instinctive desire to protect him.

'This other man, Charlie,' Sly asks, 'does he have the flowers?'

He shakes his head. 'No, I just left the flowers behind because it didn't occur to me they were important. Are they?'

Sly says nothing. Then he says, 'Important enough to kill a man for, maybe more than one.'

'How?' Charlie says. It seems the obvious question. 'Why are they important?'

Again, Sly does not answer. Instead, he finally lifts his glass to his lips, watching their reactions carefully as he does so.

'So,' Sly says, looking directly at Cheryl, 'what would happen to me were I stupid enough to drink this?'

Charlie starts to protest, but Sly stops him angrily, putting out a hand as though to hold him in his seat. 'Tell me,' he says directing his words to Cheryl again.

'It will make you sleep,' she tells him.

Sly gives a dry laugh, little more than a cough.

'Is that all?' Sly asks her. It sounds as if he does not care very much what happens to him.

24

'It's true I helped Luc to set up in business, Charlie,' Sly says. 'And he owed me money as a result, but that wasn't really important. That was just a hold I had over him.'

Charlie says nothing; he is listening very carefully instead. He knows Cheryl and Poppy are still observing closely everything that happens and they are listening too, Cheryl perfectly still at her station beside what Sly has called the Credenza. Poppy is moving casually about the room, seemingly without purpose or direction, occasionally moving in his vision across the blank stare of the window. He sees Sly watching her while he talks.

'Luc was a part of my operation,' Sly continues, 'and he was making me money. That's what really mattered. I wasn't worried about him repaying the debt, not immediately.'

'Go on,' Charlie says, when Sly's narrative seems in danger of drying up too soon.

Sly turns to him and raises an eyebrow. It is almost as though Sly was talking to himself and had forgotten his audience for a moment, but Charlie knows that is probably Sly's intention.

'The qualities that I admired in Luc began to

make him a liability,' Sly resumes after a moment. 'He's hungry and ruthless, traits which can be useful in a man put into the right situation, but he's greedy too and he's got altogether too full of himself.'

When Sly says no more for the moment, Charlie says, 'So stealing the Syn that he'd ordered was what? A slap across his face?'

'Yeah, not a bad analogy,' Sly nods, still holding the glass that Cheryl gave him. Sly looks down at it again now, apparently fascinated by the contents.

'But I didn't know what he was up to,' Sly says quietly, 'I didn't know just how big Luc was aiming to get or why he'd really ordered the Syn, and...' Sly sighs, 'that was before he killed two of my friends.'

'He killed Tan and Nils?'

'Yeah,' Sly agrees.

He would like to believe Sly, but something keeps him from doing so. The heavy sigh just before he uttered the throw-away line is a warning of sorts, a sub-conscious marker possibly that what was to follow was not really as casual, not as natural as Sly wanted it to appear, but there is something else, something Charlie cannot quite put his finger on, something that stops him from accepting the statement.

'Why did he kill them?' he asks.

'Do you know what pepper is, Charlie?' Sly asks him, apparently changing the subject instead of answering the question. 'I don't mean the stuff you put on your food. Pepper, scut, sizz, star dust, you pick your name for it. If you're a miner or just a con rotting in one of the penal colonies a little of that stuff makes everything bearable, for a while at least. Of course, it's highly addictive and it'll kill you sooner or later, but once you've tried it none of that matters. The only thing that matters is when you can get some more.'

Charlie has no direct experience with it, but he has an idea what Sly is referring to. Men talk about it, men who have not actually tried it themselves.

'For its own reasons the authorities have decided that pepper should be illegal,' Sly continues, 'which suits a lot of people just fine because it guarantees high profit margins for any man willing and able to supply it. It's a dirty business, but a man has to earn his Sens one way or another, doesn't he?'

Charlie decides this is a rhetorical question and needs no answer.

'Personally, I've always kept the business away from the orbitals,' Sly goes on without waiting for an answer. 'A man is only half human in a mining colony. The pay is good, but you have to live long enough to spend it, and if you're in a penal colony you probably don't have that many years anyway, so you might as well ease your life with a little pepper. But a man shouldn't mess on his own patch, that's always been my belief, and while the authorities will turn a blind eye to dealing in the more remote parts of the solar system it's not possible to lubricate the machinery in the same way here on the orbitals. It's much harder, very much harder to get the stuff in. Distribution almost takes care of itself, but getting the raw material on board in the first place is the problem. As I say, it's not a problem I've ever tried to solve, but young Luc is not just young, he's hungry and not prepared to listen to an old geezer like me. He thinks he knows better. It's like I said to you the last time we met, tell some men that something can't be done and they'll just ask how long it will take and what will it cost.'

Charlie thinks he has enough of the pieces now to make some kind of shape out of all this, or at least the shape that Sly wants him to see. The individual items that have been spinning around in his thoughts, apparently at random, are beginning to align themselves, to follow paths that hint at deeper truths, even if he cannot see them clearly yet.

'So that's where the flowers come in?' he suggests.

Sly looks up and raises his eyebrow at him shrewdly before nodding.

'Yeah, that's my guess now,' Sly agrees. 'It involved something that could be switched or added to the consignment in the shipping department just before the Syn was dispatched. That's where the contact is at Synthia Corp. I doubt the stuff is in the crate itself or the padding. That would be much more difficult; the crate with its padding has to be returned and surely the contact can't be sure of intercepting every empty crate that comes back. No, I think it has to be the flowers. You can mould the raw material for pepper into pretty much any shape you like and I guess you can colour it too, so it's probably not that hard to make it look like flowers. It's virtually odourless too.'

'And the shipment was valuable enough to go to

that kind of trouble?' Charlie asks.

'Valuable enough?' Sly gives another of his dry laughs, 'You could buy yourself a whole harem of Special Edition Syns like Poppy here – dozens of them – and a separate apartment to keep each of them in, with the profit from that shipment once it's processed and re-sold, and that's not including the margins that will be added as the product is cut and diluted and filtered down to the users. The raw material is extremely concentrated. A little really does go a very long way. The shipment was not some little deal on the side.'

Charlie thinks about his own desire to somehow make a lot of money, enough for a better future, sufficient money to allow him to break out of the apparently inevitable and limited course of his life. The truth is that he has never come up with any concrete ideas about how such a change in his circumstances might be realised. It has never been more than a hope, a fantasy. Vos, on the other hand, has apparently channelled his hunger into action.

'This deal is a game changer,' Sly tells him, 'even if he never manages to make it work a second time.' Sly shrugs. 'The cost of the Syn – the price Vos paid for Poppy here – is a mere bagatelle. If, that is, he can make it work a first time.'

An idea occurs to Charlie now. He does not know where it comes from, not exactly, it is just something that creates itself out of the small bits left lying around after Sly has done telling his story, and maybe it owes a little of its origin to something Lars said to him.

'Nils and Tan were a part of this deal,' he says, 'they played a role in setting it up.'

He sees Sly's face darken ominously, but Charlie finds the idea starting to make increasing sense to him.

'They connected up the players, didn't they?' Charlie presses. 'Vos knows a lot about the operation, but maybe not every part of it and it wouldn't have worked without input from Tan and Nils, for which they were paid handsomely.'

He sees Sly grow increasingly agitated as he speaks, and this tells him that he is close to the truth.

'Perhaps they didn't want to take a cut of any profits,' he says, remembering Lars telling him that Gel had reported that the two men had been spreading it about a bit before they died. 'Perhaps they just wanted their fee. Perhaps they thought it was safer for them that way.'

Sly is almost out of his chair now and seems to be holding himself back only with considerable effort.

'Charlie,' Sly begins, but it is little more than a growl. It is a warning and a threat, but there is another dimension to it, another sound in there that signals a different emotion, one that has been repressed but which will not be completely denied.

'That's why you killed them,' Charlie suggests now, oblivious to Sly's obvious distress, oblivious to the danger, 'not because of what they knew about the woman.'

Sly is breathing hard now.

'They killed themselves,' Sly says at last.

'They committed suicide? Surely there are easier

ways to do it...'

'Shut up, Charlie!' Sly shouts. 'That's enough.'

Sly sits again, breathing deeply, his eyes closed. Then he says, making an obvious effort to get a hold of himself, 'They betrayed me. Our long association, our friendship; all of that apparently counted as nothing. They betrayed me for a deal and a payoff. After all these years.'

Charlie says nothing for the moment, judging it wise to keep quiet. He has his answer.

There is a noise from somewhere beyond the room and then, at reduced volume and with a different tone, from closer at hand. The small screen that Sly normally has beside his chair, the one that Charlie now sits in, has come alive. It shows a view of the entrance. There are figures moving outside beyond the entrance and they are shouting, two of them anyway. The third man is on the ground and not moving, a fact likely connected to the many darts protruding from the man's immobile form.

'What's happening?' Sly asks rising from his chair. 'What are you up to?'

Charlie does not really have time to think. He just reacts and follows his instincts. He touches an icon on the screen and the shouting becomes louder. Now it can be heard just beyond the doors to the room.

'What have you done?' Sly growls, but before anyone can answer him the doors open, and Marie is pushed into the room in the company of two men.

'I couldn't stop them!' she says.

Charlie can see she is terrified, but whether of the intruders or of Sly he cannot tell. Of both perhaps.

One of the men has a dart protruding from his upper arm. Charlie has not seen either of the men before, but he has an idea who the uninjured man might be, the one who seems to be the boss, the one who kept back so that the other two suffered the onslaught of the anti-intruder devices. The man is short, about his own age, with dark, almost black hair and eyes to match. His clothes are expensive, a little flashy and not to Charlie's taste, but clearly not cheap. The man has a swagger about him, even now when he is angry and obviously in a state of shock.

It is clear that Luc Vos did not have the information about Sly's apartment and its defences that Gen had found for Charlie, and so Vos had not checked the status of the defences before approaching. Cheryl had carefully scrutinised the nameplate and seen that the entrance was not armed before they advanced. One has to know where to find the information, but it is there. He guesses Sly had not wanted to walk accidentally into any of his own traps and so included a status icon on the nameplate. Sly must have armed the entrance before coming into the day room after Marie informed him of their arrival.

Vos swears loudly at Sly, pacing the area of the room between the chairs and the window while the other man is still near the doors beside Marie, tentatively trying to pull the dart from his arm. The man has a knife like the one used by the man who attacked Lars, and Knife Man seems unwilling to put the weapon down, which is making the task of pulling the dart out even harder, but he has been lucky to have dodged all but one of the darts, or Knife Man would also be lying out there beyond the entrance to the apartment.

If Charlie had not let down the defences and opened the door, the other devices would probably have killed both Vos and Knife Man. Charlie's action was a split-second gamble, but it is too late to question the decision now.

Sly sits back in his seat, looking almost relaxed and he follows Sly's lead. It puts them at a disadvantage to the intruders, but it also signals confidence, or at least, that is what Charlie hopes.

'If you had told me you were coming, Luc,' Sly says calmly, 'we would have been ready to receive you.'

Vos is still breathing heavily and unable to stand still. 'You know that kind of thing is completely illegal,' he says, meaning the darts.

'I understand that you've had a few anti-intruder devices installed at your own place,' Charlie tells Vos easily before Sly can reply.

Information about Vos's private residence and the premises of his club is on the second of the two discs pulled from the dead Gen's pocket.

Vos turns to look in Charlie's direction and then glances more carefully around the room, apparently taking in his presence and that of the Syns for the first time.

'Who are you?' he asks aggressively. 'I haven't seen you before.'

Charlie pauses a moment before answering.

'I'm Cal, if you're really interested,' he says, 'but I don't see what it is to you.'

'Cal?' Vos repeats.

Vos narrows his dark, rather small eyes and regards him suspiciously. Then the little man says, 'So it was you that set Gen to snoop into my affairs?'

Charlie merely looks at Vos. He does not know for sure who requested the information, but he has an idea.

'It pays to be informed,' he tells Vos after a moment.

Vos looks as though he wants to kill him without further discussion, but lacking a weapon of his own Vos can only turn to Knife Man, but Knife Man has problems of his own: he has the dart in his arm. Vos is the one reacting now and with the element of surprise gone, the balance of power in the room has shifted a little, not much, but a little.

'It didn't work out very well for Gen, did it?' Vos says, contenting himself for the moment with words. 'Being informed, I mean, and he won't be sticking his nose into other men's affairs again. In fact, he won't be sticking something else into a Syn either.'

'So that was the clumsy message meant by the face on the table?' Charlie says slowly, deliberately revealing just how much he knows.

Vos says nothing more but looks about him again instead. Probably Vos expected to find Sly alone. He came with two men and that ought to have been sufficient, but one is already incapacitated, probably dead, and the numbers are even now – if you discount the women, as he guesses Vos certainly will.

'What can we do for you, Luc?' Sly asks him

pleasantly.

'Nice looking pair of Syns,' Vos says, ignoring Sly and looking at Poppy and Cheryl. Vos is trying to impose his own rhythm on the proceedings.

'But knowing you, Sly,' Vos adds, 'these are probably not what they seem, not under their skirts.'

Vos lifts the hem of Poppy's skirt and looks at the panties, stepping around to see the view from behind as well as from the front. 'This one looks like she ought to,' Vos says to no one in particular.

Vos takes a step towards Cheryl, but she says very firmly, 'You do not touch me, please.'

Vos looks surprised and advances no further.

'So, a feisty one?' Vos says, as if this is a great joke.

Nobody laughs.

Vos turns to Charlie, seeking an audience.

'You know that's why he has Marie here running around with just the bells on,' Vos asks him, gesturing towards Sly's house Synthia, 'don't you?'

Marie remains just inside the doors where Knife Man had pushed her. She still looks terrified and Charlie will have to check himself if either Vos or his henchman tries to hurt her.

'It's so we see that she's a real woman,' Vos says, when no one takes up the challenge of his question. 'So that we can see there are no nasty surprises up her skirt.'

Vos seems to think this is also a fantastic joke, but again nobody laughs.

'Was there something in particular?' Sly asks him with every show of patience.

'You know what I want,' Vos tells him.

Sly manages to look surprised. 'I do?' he says.

Vos is looking at Poppy now. He approaches her and she takes a step backwards.

'Shy are you?' Vos asks her. 'Not like the other one.'

'Touch her and you're a dead man,' Charlie tells Vos quietly.

Vos turns and regards him more carefully. 'Who did you say you are?' Vos asks.

Charlie says nothing.

'Who's this man?' Vos asks sharply, turning suddenly back to Poppy. 'What's his name?'

Poppy says, 'His name is Cal.'

Vos nods slowly.

Charlie guesses the man shares the common misconception that Synthias never lie.

'I've seen you before, darling,' Vos says to Poppy now. 'Not in the flesh, or not in whatever it is that you're made of, but in the catalogue, and in my dreams.'

Vos points to his head, and then with a leer, to his crotch. 'And in my dreams we've had such fun together, you and me.'

Poppy takes a further step away from the man. She looks at Vos with more distaste than fear.

'Very obliging and eager to please is what they told me you'd be,' Vos tells Poppy, matching her retreat with an advance towards her, adding, 'and with everything still to learn.'

'I don't know who you are,' Poppy tells him dismissively. 'I have never seen you before.'

'Doesn't the name Luc Vos mean anything to you?' the little man asks her.

The man's name had been the first thing she had said when they opened the crate, but Poppy does not even blink.

'Are you Luc?' she had asked and Charlie had found himself wishing he was.

She shakes her head now. 'No,' she says in answer to Vos' question. 'Should it?'

He thinks he sees doubt flick across the little man's face, but Vos is too full of himself to let anything like doubt cloud his thinking.

'Where are the flowers?' Vos asks Poppy suddenly, putting his face very close to hers.

Poppy pulls away as if his breath is bad and says. 'I don't have any flowers.'

'But you did have, didn't you?' Vos presses. 'You were supposed to give them to me,' he says speaking slowly and stressing each word as if he thinks she might not understand. 'You were supposed to give them to me just before I sampled the various pleasures a man might have with a Syn like you.'

Poppy looks at him as she might have done at the mess Charlie had made in his apartment when he vomited over the floor and the up-turned easy chair.

'It would have been your first experience of a man,' Vos says to her, 'and you were in for a treat, because I'm a real man.' He puts his hand to his crotch again.

Poppy looks puzzled. 'Do you mean you're not a synthetic? Is that what you mean?'

Vos looks a little startled and then suspicious.

'Why?' Vos asks her, 'have you tried it with a synthetic? I suppose Sly might think that's amusing, and he's not man enough to take you himself.'

'I have not tried it with any man,' Poppy says simply.

Vos blinks, but for the first time he seems to have nothing to say.

'The flowers,' Vos repeats eventually.

'Charlie was bringing them to me,' Sly says suddenly and Vos switches his attention from the Syn.

'He was bringing them with him on the shuttle,' Sly says wearily, 'when he had that unfortunate accident. I imagine the flowers have been reduced to very small pieces and flung into orbit.'

'Really, is that what you think?' Vos says lightly. 'Actually Charlie had nothing with him when he got on the shuttle or we wouldn't have been stupid enough to have caused it to vaporise so spectacularly.'

'Can you be sure of that?' Charlie asks Vos before Sly can say more.

'Oh, yes,' Vos says, turning back to him. 'Very sure. I had a man following him. We needed to be certain he got on board, so I know he had nothing with him.'

Vos looks round at Knife Man and the Syns, hoping for some reaction perhaps.

Getting none, Vos says, 'Set here planted the device.' Vos indicates Knife Man. 'I think you'll agree he did a good job?'

'I suppose he might get a free drink out of the

story one day,' Charlie tells Vos lazily, 'but if you're looking for applause, I'm afraid you've come to the wrong place. It was a clumsy way to kill a man.'

Vos looks annoyed. 'I just wanted you to understand we know the flowers weren't on the shuttle,' Vos tells him, 'however convenient an explanation that might be. And they weren't in Charlie's apartment either, but then your men had already searched it before we got there, hadn't they?' Vos says, turning back to Sly.

Sly nods fractionally.

'But I don't think Charlie ever had the flowers in the first place,' Vos continues conversationally. 'We had a chat with his mate at the dock, that useless excuse for a man who called himself Mat, you know him?'

Vos looks at Charlie, at Sly, and then at Charlie again. Charlie is careful not to blink and Sly manages to look as though he has no idea what Vos is talking about. Perhaps Sly really does not know about Mat.

When Sly remains silent, Charlie tells Vos, 'I never met the man. Was he important?'

'He claimed to have the flowers,' Vos says, 'but when we went to collect them they had got lost somehow. Imagine that! We tried to find out what had happened to them, but he preferred to make a hasty retreat down to the dock rather than tell us. Too hasty for his health, as it turns out.'

When no one says anything or shows surprise at this, Vos adds, 'In case you don't know, it's rather a long way down to the dock from his office and I think the speed of his descent proved too much. Once he reached the bottom anyway.'

Vos evidently finds the silence disconcerting, no doubt hoping for a better reception to this revelation.

'Once again, it sounds clumsy and unnecessarily messy,' Charlie says. 'I'm starting to see a pattern.'

Vos, getting increasingly annoyed, turns to Cheryl.

'Do you know where the flowers are?' Vos asks her, but not apparently expecting a reply, just playing for time. Then Vos turns to Knife Man and nods.

Set moves surprisingly quickly for a man with a dart in his arm and a quantity of his blood steadily spilling from the wound. Set goes to Sly and pushes the knife at Sly's neck, stopping the action fractionally before the knife touches the skin.

Vos appears satisfied, not realising that had Set put the knife to the neck of any of the three women the action would have produced a far better response. In fact, Vos could probably have had whatever he wanted if that had been his tactic.

'So,' the little man says, clearly feeling more powerful now, but still not quite sure which of the two men he should be questioning, 'one more time: where are the flowers?'

Vos pronounces the words as though in capital letters, with a pause between each of them.

'Because if that knife just touches the man's neck,' Vos adds, 'he'll only have seconds left to regret the way he has spent his sorry existence.'

Cheryl looks at Vos and then at Charlie. He keeps his face impassive. Charlie has no idea what Cheryl is thinking, but he sees she is about to act.

Cheryl says quietly, in answer to the little man's earlier question, 'I have.'

Vos turns quickly. 'Where?' he asks her. 'Where are the flowers?'

Cheryl picks up her bag and Charlie realises now what she intends.

With a glance at Vos, he says loudly to Cheryl, 'No!'

Cheryl ignores his shout, as he hoped, but instead of removing anything from the bag or giving it to Vos, she says, 'Here, Cal, you take.'

They had not expected Vos to be here, nor had they known anything about the significance of the missing flowers, but they had prepared for various eventualities.

Charlie glances again at Knife Man and the impossibly small distance between the edge of the weapon and Sly's throat. Then he sighs resignedly and stands to take the bag Cheryl is offering him, before Vos can reach for it himself.

'You know you won't get away with it,' he tells Vos. 'Even with the flowers you'll never get as far as selling any of the end product.'

'You let me worry about that,' Vos says, sensing victory. 'Just hand them over before Sly starts gasping for breath and his blood makes a mess of the rug.'

Charlie opens the bag and makes a show of looking at the contents. He moves slowly towards Vos as he does so, keeping his gaze on the inside of the bag as he edges forward.

Hans has told him that it might not work. He

stressed that he should wait a moment until it charges itself and that he should be as close as possible to his target before firing, because it might not work a second time, if it works at all. Charlie holds the bag level with his chest while he rummages inside. When he is almost within Vos's reach he looks up at the man and says, 'Here,' spitting out the single word with the full force of his disgust at what was done to Mat and to Lisa as well as to himself.

Hans has no reason to be apologetic about the weapon he made. Its effect on Vos is spectacular. There is no report, just a flash that seems to come from Vos's chest rather than from the bag. A part of Charlie's mind takes in the fact that the burst of energy has not even damaged the fabric of the bag. Vos is thrown backwards, locked in a sudden and violent spasm that propels the man's body upwards and away from Charlie before it collapses awkwardly onto the floor. The body twitches a little and then lies still.

The weapon does not have the sleek appearance of a mass-produced commercial device, but it has done what he wanted it to do. He experiences a brief elation at the look of surprise that flashed across the little man's features before the rictus of extinction replaced it, but now he feels sick, and he is shocked at the violence that resulted from the simple action of pressing the button on the handle of the device. He knows he does not really have what it takes to kill.

But there is no time to analyse what he has done. There is still the other man to deal with, and the knife. For a brief moment he has the advantage of surprise, but that will not last very long. He draws the weapon out of the bag.

The man with the knife and the dart in his arm watches him.

'That?' Set says with a mixture of surprise and disbelief when he sees what it is that just killed his boss.

'Yes,' Charlie says, 'this.'

He understands the man's reaction. It does look like an unlikely weapon.

'It was made by a friend of mine,' he tells Set. 'He told me that now he's old he can no longer rely on his physical strength. He says he isn't very worried about dying, but he wants to be able to protect the woman he loves, and he knows that if someone kills him before she dies the authorities will take her away.'

'How sweet,' Set says with a sneer.

'Move the knife and step away from Sly,' Charlie says, levelling the weapon at Knife Man's chest.

'I think not,' Set says calmly. 'If you blast me with that thing my arm will jerk, and your boss will be dead in seconds.'

'Okay,' Charlie says with a shrug, lowering the weapon. 'I was just interested to see what you would do.'

Set's face registers his surprise.

'You've been working for the wrong man,' Charlie tells Set. 'And where did that get you?'

Set does not reply, but Charlie did not really expect him to. Everyone knows there is no need to answer a rhetorical question, and sometimes it is best just to let a man talk.

'He got your pal out there killed,' Charlie says while Set regards him carefully, 'and now he's dead himself, and for what? He didn't even get to have the flowers. He bungled the whole deal.'

Set just continues what he is doing.

'Planting the device on the shuttle must have been tricky,' Charlie says. 'But Vos clearly undervalued you. He just used you as some sort of grunt, and he let you come here armed with just a knife!'

'It isn't just any knife,' Set says in his own defence.

'But you've got a dart in your arm and if we don't give you the antidote really soon the poison will kill you before you have a chance to bleed to death.'

He sees doubt and then fear in Set's expression. Perhaps the mention of the dart has made him aware of just how much his arm is hurting.

'It's up to you,' he tells Set, 'But I think it would be a waste of your potential for you to die in agony from a poison dart.'

'Maybe I'll just kill Sly anyway,' Set says, trying to use the injured arm to wipe away some of the sweat that is threatening to obscure his vision, but the pain makes Set wince, and he succeeds only in smearing blood on his face.

'It's fine with me if you kill Sly,' Charlie tells Set. 'It'll save me the trouble of doing it myself.'

'Charlie!' Sly manages to croak in protest.

Set turns. 'You're Charlie?' he asks with a frown.

'Yes,' Charlie says, unconcerned. 'You didn't

even get that job right.'

Set straightens himself and moves away from Sly warily, apparently re-evaluating the odds. Big mistake, but easy to make when you have a poison dart in your arm and you are steadily losing blood.

'How..?' Set begins to ask, but the question is truncated when Han's fears about his weapon not working a second time prove to be unfounded. The effect is no less spectacular this time, even from a greater distance.

Sly swears and then rubs at his neck.

'There isn't any antidote,' Sly says carefully, as if trying out his voice to see if it still works.

'I didn't even know about the poison,' he tells Sly. 'That was just a guess.'

'You took your time killing him,' Sly says, 'but otherwise you handled it very cleverly. Well done, but that was a bit too close for comfort at my age.'

Sly picks up his glass and empties it.

Sly sees Charlie's reaction and turns to look at Cheryl and Poppy. Then Sly clutches at his throat, his eyes wide with fear and panic.

'What have I done?' Sly asks, trying to make himself retch. 'Am I going to die?'

'It will make you sleep,' Cheryl tells him.

'Permanently, you mean?' Sly asks her.

'It is drug you give to woman before you prepare her to go in freezer,' Cheryl tells him carefully. 'It is sedative only.'

Sly looks as though he is going to try to run from the room, but he sits in the chair a little heavily instead.

'Charlie told me about you,' Sly says to Cheryl. 'He said you were beautiful, but he left out everything else.'

'What do you mean?' she asks him.

'You have the cunning and courage of a man,' Sly says, his voice already a little slurred.

Sly's eyes close and then flick open again before he asks, 'Are you going to kill me, Charlie?'

'No,' he says. 'You'll be okay, but you're going to sleep for a while, maybe for a long time.'

'Charlie...' Sly begins, and then the man is still, head lolling against the back of the chair, arms hanging limply at his sides, and it is suddenly very quiet in the room. Sly's open-mouthed breathing is the only sound, while the black beyond the window looks silently in at them all.

'Will he really be okay?'

Charlie had forgotten about Marie. She looks frightened and absurdly naked.

25

He leaves Cheryl and Poppy in the day room to keep an eye on Sly. He is not worried that Sly will come round, not with the dose they have given him, but there is a risk he might vomit and choke. Then he asks Marie to take him to see Sly's biological specimens. She hesitates at first, perhaps trying to decide where her loyalties lie and he wonders for a moment if she is going to refuse to cooperate. Then she merely nods.

'This way, Charlie,' Marie says.

The room seems much smaller than he expects, smaller than it appears on the plans, but much of the space is occupied by the suspender units, which account for one wall of the room, arranged in four stacks, three units high, extending from floor to ceiling. Each unit has a window in the front and a screen to display data, and the room is alive with the humming of fans and motors, the bank of machinery radiating an almost palpable energy.

'Which one is the woman Sly showed me the last time I was here?' he asks eagerly, 'You know the one I mean?'

Marie looks at him for a moment and then points to one of the units in the second row from the bottom.

He crouches so that his face is level with the window and peers in through the glass. The interior of the unit, about the size of the crate Poppy had been dispatched in, is bright, bathed in a shadow-less blue light from panels in the top, sides and bottom. The woman is horizontal, with her head towards him and her feet pointed away towards the far end. She is securely strapped to a padded board by a kind of webbing that criss-crosses most of her body. Under the webbing she is naked, just as she had been when he first saw her. She lies with her back to the board, but the board is slowly rotating. The movement is too slow to see at first, but as he watches he sees the woman shift position very slightly as the board turns and the orbital's gravity tugs at her. The weight of the woman's body presses her against the webbing a little tighter as she rotates until she is once more horizontal but face down now with the board above her. Her breasts are flattened and a little distorted in this position as the weight of her body presses them into the webbing. Her immobile face, not very far from his own, also subtly changes shape as she rotates. Her eyes are held closed with soft pads kept in place with tape, while bands across her forehead and chin secure her head. There is a large tube in her mouth and others are connected to needles in her hands and arms. Wires too are connected to small pads at various points on her body, the wires and the tubes secured to the webbing and fed to the back of the unit. The woman's skin has apparently been covered with some kind of milky ointment or cream and it is slightly blue in the lights of the unit, but he thinks she looks every bit as beautiful as she had the first time he saw her, even though her face and body are severely foreshortened at present by the angle of his view.

She looks peaceful rather than merely inert, and he finds it hypnotic watching her as she makes her slow rotation. His own breathing has become so shallow that it has almost ceased, and time has slowed for him too. He could crouch there a long time like that just looking in at her, except that his knees and thighs are beginning to complain.

It is hard to believe that she is really here, just the other side of the window, the woman that every man thinks about, the subject of so many stories and fantasies, a woman worth more money than anything else he can think of, probably more than the cost of an orbital.

The woman, like all Sly's biologicals, is in 'prime condition'. That means young, he reminds himself. She is still young; old enough to be sexually mature perhaps, but comparatively young. He wonders how many years she can be awake, eating, walking and breathing before she will start to show signs of ageing. The commercial growers talk about 'delayed ageing' and a 'maximum service life' once the women they grow have reached maturity, but exact timeframes are rarely spelled out. This woman is naturally reared and so there is nothing to go by. A man buying her and planning to keep her for himself, might wonder how much each year of her life not spent in suspended animation would cost him. Every hour – each day certainly – would cost more than almost anything Charlie has ever purchased. It would be more than the price of his apartment.

He puts a hand to the window of the unit. He thinks it feels a little cold to the touch, but he can see that it is double-layered, and no doubt effectively insulated. When the woman has turned a complete revolution – or perhaps it has been several, for he has lost track of time – and is once more on her back he straightens up.

He glances at the other units. 'Are they all in use?' he asks and Marie nods.

'How long will it take to get the woman out and awake enough so that she can walk again?'

He is thinking not only about how long it will be before the woman is conscious enough for them to leave, but also how long it will be before Sly can be installed in her place.

'The time it takes to wake them up depends on how long they have been in there,' Marie tells him, confirming what he has already learned for himself. 'She was put in no more than a few days ago, but even so it is not quick.'

'You do know how to work these things?' he asks her, realising that he ought to have ascertained the answer to that beforehand.

'Yes, Charlie, it was one of my tasks to look after the sleeping women.'

'What did Sly say about this one?' he asks her. 'Did he say she was special?'

She hesitates. 'He told me that I must take particular care of her,' she says gravely. 'He told me that she is more valuable than all the others, and that if...'

'If what?' he asks when she hesitates and then says no more.

'Sly said he would deactivate me if I let anything happen to her.'

He is shocked and he tells her, 'I won't let that happen.'

She smiles sadly. 'But you won't be here, Charlie, when he discovers she is missing.'

He has no answer to that at present. He can only think about the immediate future and for now that means just one thing: taking Isabelle from the suspender unit. He asks Marie to start the process of waking the woman up. Then he watches while she puts delicate fingers to icons and looks carefully at the values and figures that appear on the display panel as it cycles through its various states. Several of the indicators have a zero value.

'She's okay?' he asks anxiously when he can keep silent no longer.

Marie nods.

'What are these?' he asks, pointing at the display where the readings are empty. 'They're not a problem?'

Marie reads from the panel. 'Her heart is not beating, she isn't breathing, the oxygen level in her blood is zero.' She turns to him and adds, 'There is only the conserving fluid circulating in her,' then she turns back to the screen and reads from the remaining items he had indicated, 'There are no by-products indicating metabolism or cell decay.'

He exhales. 'So that's all good?'

'Yes, Charlie.' She touches the panel again and when the woman is lying on her back once more, he sees that the rotation has stopped.

'Her temperature will gradually return to a little closer to normal and then we can replace the fluid with blood,' Marie tells him. 'I think she will be ready to wake sometime tomorrow or perhaps the next day.'

She notices his expression and adds, 'It is not safe to hurry the process, Charlie.'

'Okay, it will have to take what it takes,' he says, trying to suppress his impatience. 'Can we keep Sly sedated until the unit is free?' he asks.

She looks surprised, perhaps only now fully understanding what he plans. Then she nods, 'Yes, it is better that way. The women are deprived of food and drink before they go in. We can start to prepare Sly before we take the woman out.'

He says, 'Some of these women must have been here when you arrived.'

'Yes, most of them were bought before Sly bought me.'

He thinks that Sly showed him a total of four of the twelve currently stored here. He looks at the array of units again and shakes his head, not quite able to get his mind around what he is seeing, what these units represent.

'These women are like me,' he says slowly. 'I mean, they're not men, obviously, but they have bodies that are really the same kind as mine, in most ways.'

He is thinking that although it is bodies that are

stored in the units, there are lives stored here too, yet not stored perhaps, only arrested. Surely a life cannot be stored?

'Does that sound silly?' he asks Marie when she does not respond. He is unable to read her expression.

The blue lights and the whirring and humming machinery are real to him, they are part of his experience, but this moment is not part of the lives of the women. They are effectively outside time and in that sense they are both alive and not alive. It is a difficult concept, and his mind seems unable to fully grasp it. He shrugs.

Marie has been watching him. 'I understand, Charlie,' she says. 'Synthias are only copies, copies of them.' She points at the array of women. 'They are the real women.'

The lights from the units are reflected in highlights in her eyes. He realises that she has misunderstood the nature of his thoughts.

'That isn't what I meant,' he says, taking her gently by the shoulders. 'You're just as real as they are.'

She looks at him doubtfully and he struggles to find the right words. It is the first time he has dared to touch her, but the moment is not the one he imagined.

'You're just as alive,' he tells her, remembering what he said to Poppy. He sees her studying his face and he thinks later that what he wanted to tell her is that she is every bit as precious as the women stored in this room, that her life is as important even as that of the woman he has come to rescue, but at this moment all his thoughts are clouded by the knowledge that they have begun to wake her up; they have begun to reheat a goddess.

Some sense makes him turn and he sees that Poppy has joined them and is looking at the units with interest. She approaches and looks into one of the windows at the level of her eyes. Then she watches the woman inside as she makes her slow rotation.

'Which of them is the one?' she asks.

He knows what she means, and he points. Poppy crouches and looks for a while at the woman, her face immobile, the bluish light making her look for a moment very like the woman inside.

'So, she is sleeping?' Poppy asks.

He nods. 'Yes, but it's a very deep kind of sleep.'

Poppy watches the woman again for a moment and then she says, 'Is she dreaming, do you think?'

It is a good question. 'No,' he decides after a moment, 'I don't think she's doing anything while she's in there, not even dreaming. She's not dead, but she's not really alive either, not at the moment.'

Poppy stands again, the action graceful and lithe, with no suggestion that her thighs or her knees complain.

Poppy says, 'Cheryl wants you to come back to the day room for a moment.'

He checks that Marie knows what she is to do and then he follows Poppy out, leaving the twelve women to their dreamless state.

As they reach the doors to the day room something flies from a corner of the lobby, catching him by surprise and throwing him violently against the wall. The impact knocks the breath from him, hurting his shoulder and elbow, and before he can recover, he is seized again and propelled back onto the wall, his head this time colliding with it before the rest of his body does. He is dazed for a moment, but when he opens his eyes again the face of his attacker is frighteningly close, Jan's face, contorted with fury and hatred. He must have seen that his master is incapacitated. Perhaps he thinks that Sly is dead.

The safety mechanisms installed in all femdroids have been bypassed in Jan, removed when the Syn was adapted and given his new masculine identity because Sly wanted Jan not just as a lover, but as a bodyguard too. There is a safe word and speaking it will persuade Jan that the man who utters it is a friend, but Charlie is struggling to remember what it is.

He tries to push Jan away, but the synthetic is too strong. Unable to free himself from Jan, he spins around in order to dash the synthetic against the wall. He feels the impact through his own arms and for a moment Jan loosens his grip, but before Charlie can get away, Jan seizes his arms and throws him to the floor.

Charlie has seen men fight often enough and has been involved in physical contests of strength himself. Men use their fists generally, at least to start with, throwing punches until the men are either pulled apart or one of them acknowledges defeat and backs off. Jan seems intent on simply breaking him, destroying his body as one might try to break up a machine or an object.

He manages to land on his side, his shoulder and

arm taking the fall, but the impact fills him with pain and stuns him. Then as he begins to struggle to his feet, Jan leaps on him again and propels him against the far wall. He succeeds in butting Jan with his head, using the force of the impact in his favour, but it appears to have little impact on the synthetic.

Jan is immensely strong, but no heavier than Cheryl or Poppy and as they hit the wall and bounce off it, Charlie manages to continue the movement sufficiently to spin them both so that they fall to the floor. By luck or judgement, Charlie finds himself on top, but Jan is attempting to strangle him now.

He clasps the synthetic's wrists and forces Jan's arms away from him, trying to wrest them back until they are on the floor either side of Jan's head, but ultimately the synthetic is too strong, and the hands begin to move back up towards his throat.

'Jan, stop!' he manages to grunt, but Jan only renews his struggling, the fury on his face undiminished.

Charlie's mind is still trying to dredge up the safe word. He thinks it is something ordinary, or maybe it is a name. Jan bends his arms now until he has enough leverage to succeed in rolling them both over until their positions are reversed and Charlie is underneath him. Then Jan's hands find Charlie's throat and begin to compress it with an iron grip. The pain is incredible, and the blood begins to pound in his head.

The safe word is something like 'sleep', he thinks. No, that is not it, but it is a word he has heard recently. Someone spoke it just now. He knows that it has to be a word that a man will not be likely to use if attacked by the synthetic.

Dream. Yes, that is it. He tries to say the word, but he finds that he can make no sound.

He clutches at Jan's fingers, desperately trying to peel them from his throat, but he cannot budge them even a little and he knows that his strength will soon start to ebb away. As he begins to lose consciousness, he registers a sudden swift movement. Something swings rapidly in front of him, from left to right, and Jan's head disappears. The fingers on his throat relax their grip and he rolls onto his side, unable to do more, curled around the pain and sucking in air in ragged gasps. He can feel Jan's body on him, limp and lifeless and then it too is gone.

When he opens his eyes, he finds himself staring at Jan's face once more, but the head ends now in a tangle of connectors and torn material below the neck. The eyes are sightless and frozen, the vengeful expression gone, the features slack and motionless.

'Charlie, you okay?' Cheryl is asking him.

Then he is pulled into a sitting position, and he is looking into the beautiful but anxious face of his Synthia.

'Charlie, you okay,' she says again, but it seems to be a statement now rather than a question.

He nods. On the floor to his right, Jan's body lays where Cheryl has thrown it. To his left, behind Jan's head, is the thing Cheryl used to part the head from the body. It is the vertical stand of a lamp he remembers from the day room. It is almost as tall as Cheryl, its diameter about the same as a man's thigh at the bottom and of a man's wrist at the top where it swells into the part that glows when it is illuminated. The base must still be in the day room. From its position on the floor, it appears that the heavy end of the stand was the part that collided with Jan's head when Cheryl swung it at him.

He pulls her to him and kisses her gently.

'You okay, Charlie?' she repeats, and he nods again, still unable to speak.

'Jan!' a voice calls suddenly, a voice filled with shock and dismay. He pulls away from Cheryl sufficiently to see that Marie has come from the room of sleeping women, drawn no doubt by the sounds of the struggle. She has her hands to her face.

'No!' she cries more quietly, taking in the scene.

She approaches Jan's body, but then appears to change her mind and goes to the head instead. Then she stops again and looks back at the body without touching the head. Finally, hesitantly, she reaches out a hand.

'Jan,' she repeats more softly, gently caressing the cheek of the severed head. It lies now in a small pool of system fluid that has leaked from the broken tubes that spill out of the jagged neck. Marie appears torn by conflicting responses to the grisly object, both repulsed and attracted to it. He thinks she probably sees the head both as it is now and as she remembers it, in its proper place and animated by what had been Jan. Growing bolder she caresses the cheeks and the forehead and then presses her fingers to the mouth and the slightly parted lips.

Then she turns to Charlie and asks dully, 'What

happened?'

'He tried to kill Charlie,' Cheryl tells her. 'I stop him.'

'He attacked you,' Marie nods as if unsurprised, addressing Charlie rather than the other Synthia. 'He was very loyal to Sly. He was his...' She stops. 'I don't know how to describe it, but he was the master's Synthia, his special friend.'

She looks from the head to the body. 'Sly was much more important to Jan than I was. He treated me almost the way Sly did, but I….'

Marie stops, saying no more and Charlie says nothing. His throat is sore, but he has no idea what he would say if he could speak.

'Sly never wanted to have sex with me,' Marie adds. She looks at Charlie and at Cheryl now, but it is not clear whether she is speaking to them or to the remains of Jan. 'Sly never touched me. Jan had no reason to be jealous.'

'I'm sorry,' Charlie says to her, his voice no more than a painful croak.

He is sorry not only for the destruction of Jan, but for all of it: her life as a Synthia, as Sly's property. These women have been created to desire men, to need them, no matter how badly they are treated by them. Of course, it suits men's purpose, and that is what men have made them for, but somehow it is also a form of cruelty perhaps, to make Synthias so dependent on their creators. It is true that men themselves are like that, needing women – or other men – needing another to satisfy their desires and to make them feel whole, to make their lives complete.

Yet that is different, surely; it is just how men are. No one has made them that way.

Poppy stands a little apart from the rest of them. She looks anxious and unsure what to do.

Marie shrugs now, gathering herself. 'It's not your fault, Charlie,' she tells him.

He forgets for a moment that she does not know what he has been thinking; she does not mean that all of it – the whole situation, the nature of the Synthias that men create for themselves and the lives they live – that it is not all his responsibility. Yet, perhaps that is exactly what she means.

'I not sorry,' Cheryl says defiantly. 'He was going to kill my man.'

'It's Okay,' Marie tells her gently. 'I'm glad you stopped Jan from hurting Charlie.'

Cheryl moves her hand towards Marie's, and then after what seems like a moment's indecision, she places it on top. The action is very brief and he might have missed it, but a look passes between the two Synthias.

'Come, Charlie,' Cheryl says, rousing herself. 'I want to see the Lost Princess. I want to see why she so important.'

She helps him to his feet and the four of them return to the suspender units. Poppy points out the woman and Cheryl crouches as Charlie and then Poppy had done and looks in through the window. She looks for a long time, almost as motionless as the woman within.

'So,' she says eventually, 'this is woman.' It is hard to tell from her tone what she is thinking.

He nods. 'Yes,' he says. His throat still hurts when he speaks. 'She's the one.'

Cheryl makes a face and nods and then turns once more to the window.

'You are real woman,' she says quietly, as though repeating it to herself or perhaps she is speaking to the woman on the other side of the glass.

Then Cheryl straightens up and looks around the room. Without saying anything more she goes quickly to the other door, not the one through which they entered. He has paid it no attention until now and is trying to remember from the plans where it leads. Cheryl appears determined to find out, or perhaps she already knows what is on the other side.

'No, Cheryl, don't!' Marie says quickly when she sees what Cheryl is doing.

Cheryl looks at her. 'No?'

Marie shakes her head. 'No, Cheryl, it's better if you don't go in there.'

He can see that this does not deter Cheryl. If anything, Marie's words have merely piqued her interest, as they have his own.

'What's in there?' he asks Marie, but before she can answer him Cheryl has opened the door, and he sees lights coming on in the space beyond.

Cheryl goes through the door, but before she has taken more than a couple of steps into the room she stops and they hear her say quietly, 'Oh!'

He and Poppy follow in order to see for themselves whatever it is that Cheryl has found.

The room is probably the same size as the one they have just left, but there are no suspender units to occupy the space and so it appears much larger. The women in here do not need freezing in order to preserve their beauty. They merely stand motionless, lined up around the edges of the room. Of course, they are all exquisitely beautiful for Sly has assembled a selection of the very best examples of their kind ever produced by any company, and here they are just as they were on the day they were dispatched by their makers. Each of them is secured to the wall by a kind of bracket around the waist.

Marie has come to the doorway and regards them solemnly.

Charlie is excited at seeing such a magnificent collection, but Cheryl's reaction is very different.

'And they stay in here, in dark?' she says quietly, turning to Marie, 'Like this?'

Marie simply nods.

'How long?' Cheryl asks her. 'For what time they have been here?'

'Some of them were here long before Sly bought me,' Marie tells her from the doorway, 'but he never let me go into this room, not that I ever wanted to.'

The bank of suspender units radiates a kind of energy of its own, and together with the hum of the fans, the motors and the lights, they fill the space next door with a kind of living presence, even if the women inside the units are not technically alive. In this room the motionless and silent Synthias create a totally different atmosphere. It is difficult to describe, but he feels it no less strongly. In this room there is a profound sense not just of life in suspension, but of life extinguished. The air feels as if it has not been disturbed in a very long time. It is dead and stale.

'It is like being in crate,' Cheryl says in a low voice to Poppy and Poppy shivers and nods.

'Are they… asleep?' Charlie asks and he feels the eyes of his three companions on him.

He shrugs defensively. 'I'm only a man,' he says.

Cheryl says, 'It is best to think of nothing when you have nothing to do or see, or when you trapped like this against wall.'

Then she claps her hands and addressing the motionless women, she says loudly, 'Time to wake up.'

He sees the eyes of the Synthias open almost in unison. They begin to look around them, as though indeed waking from a kind of deep sleep. Then they start tentatively moving their bodies, extending their arms and legs, but still fixed to the wall they are unable to move around.

'How do we open these?' Cheryl asks Marie, tugging at one of the brackets that secures the nearest Synthia.

'Only Sly can unlock them,' Marie tells her timidly. 'He has to put his hand here.'

She extends an arm into the room to reach a panel on the wall near the door. It appears that she is unwilling to step into the room itself, even now when Sly will not know.

Cheryl looks at the panel and says, 'Come, Poppy, we bring Sly in here.'

'Don't worry,' Cheryl says to the femdroids that line all four walls of the room, 'We come back and get you out.'

'Cheryl, wait,' he says, putting out an arm to restrain her as she and Poppy turn to leave. 'What are you doing?'

Cheryl frowns. 'It is obvious, Charlie,' she says. 'We must unlock them from wall.'

'But then what?' he asks her, his voice still hoarse and painful. 'Are we going to just let them wander about the apartment?'

'No, Charlie,' she says patiently. 'We take them with us.'

He puts his hands to his head in renewed frustration and exasperation. 'We can't!' he says. 'That's impossible. We have something more important to do. We have to get the woman away from the apartment and off the orbital. That won't exactly be easy, and we can't have all these Syns coming too!'

It is too absurd an idea to even need dismissing. It is so obviously not possible that he struggles to find words to explain why it is a ridiculous idea.

'We'll fill up a shuttle on our own!' he tells her, saying the first thing that comes into his head.

Cheryl looks unimpressed and unconvinced.

'Charlie,' she says, 'you say you have to get Lost Princess, you have to steal her. You say you cannot explain why; you just have to. I understand, and Poppy and I we help. Now Cheryl have to bring these Synthias. They cannot stay. It is same thing.'

'But it's not the same,' he protests.

'I not argue, Charlie,' Cheryl says firmly, 'but it is same thing. Cheryl just have to. Come Poppy.'

Poppy makes no comment and follows Cheryl

from the room. She does not even check with him whether she should do what Cheryl is asking.

He simply watches them go. He has no idea what to do about it, but he has to try to reason with Cheryl somehow. She has to see it is ridiculous to think they can take all these Syns with them. It is impossible. He scans the room, making a quick count. There are sixteen of them!

He sighs. They are lovely, and yes, it is a shame for them to be simply stored like this, like decorative objects, but he can hardly be expected to save every woman, can he?

'What's your name?' he asks the nearest femdroid, knowing this is foolish and that he should simply turn out the lights and close the door. She blinks at him, but says nothing. He thinks she is a genuine Synthia, a Limited Edition Special, or one of the highest specification premium range at the very least. She is lovely, but she appears unable or unwilling to speak to him.

He asks her neighbour the same question and receives the same response.

'Why aren't they talking?' he asks Marie, realising now that it is odd that none of them have made any sound. They have not even asked who these strangers are or what they are doing.

'Sly has told them that if he hears any of them speak, he will deactivate them,' Marie says quietly.

'He wouldn't do that,' he objects, 'they're all far too valuable.'

'They don't know that,' Marie tells him, 'and he might, as a warning to the others.'

'Nonsense,' he says, with more conviction than he feels, wondering privately if Marie might be right. Perhaps it really is fear of deactivation that is keeping them quiet, has kept them silent during the years they have been in this room, for some of them must have been here many years.

'Why didn't he want them to talk?' he asks Marie.

'He says it disturbed him, hearing them talking to each other.'

While he is still wondering about Sly's reasoning he hears sounds from the adjoining room and Marie moves aside to let Cheryl and Poppy get past her. They are carrying Sly between them, Cheryl at his shoulders and Poppy with her hands under his folded knees. Charlie gets out of their way, and they step backwards and sideways and then forwards again until they have Sly's body near the panel Marie pointed out to them.

'Charlie, you put Sly's hand on panel,' Cheryl instructs, her own hands still under Sly's arms.

'We need to talk about this,' he tells her.

'No, Charlie,' she says, 'we not talk. You just put hand on panel.'

He thinks now would be a good time to argue with her, while she is encumbered with the unconscious man, but he does as she instructs and lifts Sly's right hand. It hangs limply from the arm, but the arm and the hand together are surprisingly heavy. He tries to rotate the hand until it will sit flat on the panel, but he cannot make it reach.

'You'll have to lift him higher,' he tells Cheryl.

She does so without complaint, and he manages to get the hand flat on the panel. Nothing happens at first, but after he has tried a couple of times, the panel glows and he hears the brackets unlocking all around the room with an audible click.

'We lay Sly on floor in room next door,' Cheryl instructs Poppy, and they carry him out again.

'Put him here,' Marie instructs them, and he sees she has pulled down a kind of table or board from the wall, clearly designed for the purpose, although he guesses it has never held a man before.

Then he watches Sly's collection of Synthias as they respond to their new freedom. Unsurprisingly, many of them appear to be stiff and so unused to movement that they are a little unsteady when they try to step forward away from the wall. They peer down at themselves and at each other. When they look up at him, he smiles. It is just the natural reaction of a man who suddenly finds himself in a room full of beautiful women. He is more than a little in awe of the woman next door, but he knows Synthias, and he is comfortable with them. They have only ever been good to him, although the presence of so many of them all at once is disorientating and makes him a little giddy.

'My name's Charlie,' he tells them as they cluster around him, 'and Cheryl is right, we're not going to leave you here in the dark fixed to the wall. You deserve better. And you can talk. Sly can't hurt you now.'

It feels good presenting himself as the agent of their deliverance, but he knows that in reality he would probably have left them here just as they were. Not probably, he would have, because nothing must get in the way of his mission. The knowledge makes him sad and ashamed, but how will he feel if he fails to get the woman away because they have all of these Synthias with them?

'Hello, Charlie,' one of them says, the first of them brave enough to break the habit of silence. She is dressed in an outfit very similar to the one Poppy had been wearing in the crate, complete with something over her face and flowers in her hair. In fact, many of them are dressed in variations of this outfit, in white with matching shoes. Some have short skirts that puff out over layers of some lacy, gauzy material. Others have dresses that are figure-hugging, but in the same general vein: white and lacy or satin. None of the outfits are the kind of thing a man would dress his femdroid in once he has taken delivery of her – unless, like Sly, he is just a collector and only wants to own rather than to actually use the Syn in the way their designers intend.

Now that they are moving about he can smell faintly the perfume that was applied to their skin when they were packaged, together with an equally faint but lingering reminder of the smell that had come from Poppy's crate when he and Hans opened it, the odour of 'newness' as he thinks of it. It comes from the folds of their clothes and from the veils and the flowers they wear in their hair and perhaps from their limbs too.

The other Synthias begin to speak now, speaking to him and to each other. They touch his arm and shoulder, put fingers gently to his hand and then to his face, as though to satisfy themselves that he is real, is really here and not only a fantasy or something they are dreaming.

'Are you our new owner?' one asks him. She has long, fair hair done up in two plaits either side of her head. Her eyes are very blue as she looks at him.

'No,' he tells her, shaking his head. 'I think Cheryl is.'

The Synthia frowns. No doubt she believes that only men can own anything. It is after all what the law says. The law says that he owns Cheryl and can tell her what to do. It says that he has total power over her, but as all men know, the law is often mistaken.

In truth, he is happy to let her take charge at the moment. He knows better than anyone that he has never been cut out to be a hero. He is happy just to be surrounded by all these Synthias who for the present will hang upon his every word and do whatever he asks them to do without question.

26

It is essentially a problem of refuse disposal. Seeing it in those terms feels callous, as though he is inured to killing and to death, but that is what it comes down to: how to dispose of the refuse. It is a problem he knows will not solve itself, but for the moment he is trying not to think about it.

It is Marie who reminds him it is something he cannot ignore.

'What about the bodies, Charlie?' she asks him.

She is removing tubes from the body of the woman and for a moment he is confused.

'The bodies?' he asks stupidly.

'You can't just leave them,' she says. 'They will decompose.'

It still takes him a moment to catch on. His mind is filled with thoughts about the woman and her body, of suspended animation, how it works and what its short or medium term effects might be.

'Oh,' he says, catching on at last, 'those bodies. You mean the two from the day room.'

Cheryl and Poppy have moved them and laid them neatly side by side in the main lobby, but he knows this is merely a temporary position for them. He has to come up with a long-term solution. Or two solutions.

'Don't forget the one outside,' Marie reminds him.

Three solutions then.

He wonders if you can store dead men in suspender units. Possibly, but it does not really matter because all the units are in use, or soon will be. Isabelle has been removed from her unit this morning and she now lies on another pull-down table like the one Sly rests on. Sly will soon be going into the unit she has left vacant, so unless they re-heat another three women there is nowhere they can put the dead men, even if it is a viable solution. He does not like to ask Marie if it would work, partly because he fears the answer. If she says it is possible he would be under pressure to take more women out, and it will be even more difficult to get away if they have to take another three women with them.

When he first conceived his crazy idea he envisaged that it would be just the woman and himself making their escape and finding somewhere to hide. He had worried for a while that he could not leave Cheryl behind because she would be able to tell the authorities what he planned and what he had done. Astonishingly, he did not understand from the outset that whatever happens he can never leave Cheryl. He does not know why he has not always seen that he cannot be parted from her. It might be stupid and perhaps it is only because he is weak and sentimental, but he knows now that his Syn is more precious to him than anything else ever can be. He just hopes that Cheryl never suspected that he planned to leave her. It feels like an incredible betrayal when he considers it now, even if he only did it carelessly and thoughtlessly in the privacy of his head. He can try to put it down to the effect that the woman had on him, but that gives him very little comfort.

And now, of course, he cannot abandon Poppy. He thought at first it was because he is weak, but he is beginning to understand that he cannot sacrifice any woman in order to rescue another one, not even in order to rescue Isabelle. She is special and precious, but so are they all. So there are the four of them to worry about. Five perhaps, if Marie wants to come with them.

Five, if Cheryl had not thrown her spanner in the works. Sixteen spanners in fact.

He still thinks it is going to be extremely difficult to take them all with them, but he can see that Cheryl is not going to change her mind. He understands it would be wrong to simply leave them as they were and when he thinks about it now he sees that theirs was a situation almost too horrible to comprehend. A man would have gone mad left in the dark like that for months and years at a time, forbidden even to talk to one another – leaving aside the physical problems a man would have experienced. And of course, now they are free and roaming about the apartment they are becoming individuals, with names and distinct personalities. Like Poppy, they are starting to belong to him – to use Cheryl's word – even if only until they are able to choose something better for themselves. If Cheryl asked him now to choose which of them he will leave behind he knows he could not leave any of them.

The previous evening Cheryl discovered another room and another facet of Sly's collecting. The room contained clothes, shoes and accessories for femdroids, all of them in unused and as-new condition like the Syns themselves. The items are all special or limited edition pieces of clothing, shoes or complete outfits. They are not the kind of thing a man would ordinarily find for sale in the Synthia Store and Sly has carefully stored them under protective wrappings on hangers or in their original packaging.

Cheryl was astonished, so much so that she had been uncharacteristically quiet for a moment. He did not understand the source of her surprise at first. He knew Sly was a collector, but Cheryl pointed out that Marie appeared to have nothing to wear.

'Why she run around apartment naked when her owner have all these clothes?' she asked him when she found her voice again. 'Why, Charlie? It make no sense.'

So he tried to explain why Sly would have kept them as he did, rather than allow any of the Syns to wear them. He knows Cheryl is still puzzled about the point of collecting things in this way – things that are meant to be used – even though he did his best to explain to her that Sly simply wanted to own them and hoped that the items would increase in value. Allowing a Syn to wear the clothes would immediately decrease their value.

Cheryl simply said, 'Hmm.'

He is starting to understand what that means now, just as he thinks he is also starting to see the world –

brief glimpses at least – through Cheryl's eyes.

Cheryl invited the Synthias she liberated to help themselves to whatever they fancied from Sly's collection, with the result that the Syns that now wander about the apartment are attired in a wide variety of outfits in many different styles. None of them has elected to stay in the outfit they were dispatched in, the ones in which they were incarcerated in 'that room' as Cheryl refers to it.

He has managed to push Marie's reminder about the bodies to the back of his mind again while his thoughts wander. He is watching with quiet fascination now as Marie tenderly washes the woman's body, sponging the eyes and wiping the face, lifting each hand in turn to clean the fingers and then in between, before turning the hand to wipe the palms.

'They have to be washed before they go in and when they come out,' Marie tells him without looking up.

She has already washed Sly's body with a disinfecting solution. Naked now, he lies on the table that Cheryl and Poppy put him on the evening before. There is a tube in his arm like the ones in the body of the woman.

'They have to be cleaned inside too,' Marie adds.

He must look puzzled for she adds, 'They cannot have food left inside. If it does not go bad it will become dried out and solid.'

He decides he need not ask what had been involved in cleaning the inside of Sly's body. His breakfast is still fresh in his mind, and he wants to keep it in his stomach where it belongs. He concentrates instead on what Marie is doing now, watching her working so methodically and delicately on the woman. He had been drawn here this morning by his excitement about seeing Isabelle and he wanted to learn how far she was towards waking up, but he finds that he is enjoying this easy intimacy with Marie. He would have wanted to be here whoever the body was on the table. There is a companionable quality about the long silences while she works and he simply watches. He has fantasised about her, but the reality – the real Marie, rather than the one he lusted after – is different, more complicated and much nicer.

While the Synthias had excitedly looked through the collection of clothing that Cheryl had found, he had picked out a short tunic-style dress and taken it to Marie. For some reason the style as well as the colour made him think it would suit her. She thanked him and she had looked pleased when he gave it to her, but she is not wearing it this morning. She is wearing only her silk slippers.

'You're not wearing the dress?' he says.

'I don't want to make it dirty,' she tells him. 'The chemicals I used on Sly might stain it.' She shrugs and smiles a little self-consciously, briefly looking down at herself. 'I can sponge my body if I get any of it on me.'

Despite his fascination with the woman on the table Charlie decides it is better to stop his mind thinking about sponging Marie's body before it goes too far with the idea. His mind tends to do that sort of thing if left to itself.

'You're not wearing the bells,' he points out, his attention having been drawn to her middle.

She looks at him and says, 'No,' her mouth tightly set.

For a moment she works in silence, starting now on the woman's legs. Her gentle movements have a soothing, calming effect on him. Or maybe it is the room itself, or the woman on the table. Whatever it is, his breathing has slowed almost to nothing as it had the day before when he looked in through the small window of the unit.

'No,' Marie repeats, 'I'm not wearing the bells and I will never wear them again, now that I don't have to.'

She looks at him and he nods slowly. Then she resumes her work.

When he came into the room this morning it was obvious to him that Marie had worked for much of the night, caring for her two charges, one on his way to temporary oblivion, the other in the process of reanimation and waking. He did not tell her to do any of this. He only asked her to wake the woman up and prepare Sly to go into the suspender unit in her place. He had no idea what was entailed or that there was so much work involved. He asked her to do something, and she is simply carrying out his instructions, patiently, skilfully and without complaint. He tells himself there is nothing surprising about it, but he feels humbled nevertheless.

His mind reverts to the woman on the table. He has been interested in the various tubes and wires that were connected to the woman while she was in the unit and he watched carefully as Marie removed most of the remaining ones. Only two are left now, one connected to a vein in the woman's arm and one that trails from between her legs. He is particularly interested in this last one and for some time he has been wanting to ask Marie about its purpose.

Unable now to contain his interest any longer he asks, 'What's this tube for?'

Marie appears surprised, surprised that he needs to ask.

'It's for urine,' she says. There is the suggestion of a smile at the corners of her mouth. Then her eyes flick to his crotch.

'She makes water like you, Charlie,' she says.

Marie shows him that she has already inserted its corollary into Sly. In retrospect this is something he would have preferred not to have drawn to his attention.

Isabelle is still asleep, or unconscious, he is unsure which. Marie told him that she can be woken in a few hours but warned him that she will remain groggy and weak for some hours and even days after that. He would like to put a hand to the woman while she lies motionless like this, to feel her skin and to stroke her hair, but he does not like to touch her in the presence of Marie, and it seems inappropriate when she is so carefully bathing the woman.

'The bodies, Charlie,' she reminds him gently.

He nods and makes a noise of unenthusiastic assent. He thinks that it is only natural that he tries to forget he has killed two men, and not only because of the problem of disposing of their bodies. He woke in the night to the realisation of what he has done. He had been torn then between a desire to go out into the lobby and see for himself that the two men are really dead, and to try to think of something else entirely and go back to sleep as quickly as possible.

He slept in the day room with Cheryl and Poppy, on a bed they made up for themselves. Poppy suggested they simply sleep on the rug, but Cheryl told her that men need more 'softness'. Marie offered to change the bedding in Sly's bedroom, but he has no wish to even enter that room.

A couple of the other Synthias joined them in the day room sometime during the night, but he has the impression that most of them are enjoying their new freedom too much to want to settle. They are making up for lost time by talking incessantly.

Before they retired Cheryl suggested that he has the pick of so many Synthias now he might find it hard to decide which of them to sleep with. He assured her that he only wanted to sleep with her, but he is unsure whether she had been serious in her suggestion. He slept between Cheryl and Poppy – having had sex with neither of them – and would not have wanted it any other way, but that did not stop him imagining as he settled down what it would be like to have sex with Marie or with any of Cheryl's new cohort of femdroids.

He must have been tired because despite all of that he quickly fell asleep and woke only the once, and even the knowledge of what he had done had not kept him awake very long.

When he does think about the issue, he finds his thoughts running in the same endless circles. It is true that the two men tried to kill him. Indeed, they thought themselves already successful in this and Vos died without discovering the truth. So surely he cannot really be blamed for killing them. He reasons that any man in his place would do the same. And if he had not been there and stopped them they might have killed Sly. On the other hand, he was the one who lowered the defences and let them in.

Then again, if Sly had not asked him to steal Poppy then none of this would have happened, and perhaps if Sly had known what Vos was really up to he would not have asked him to do it. And if Charlie had never had the tip that there was a wealthy collector over on Orbital C with whom he might be able to do some lucrative business then he would never have met Sly in the first place.

And most of all, if Sly had not shown him the woman... But none of this makes any difference. It neither excuses nor exonerates his actions, and it does not change the problem: what is he going to do about the bodies?

Marie raises an eyebrow at him while she works and he knows she is nudging him again. He has acknowledged her words, but has not stirred to actually do anything about the problem.

'Okay,' he says and without wondering if it is the right thing to do he plants a careful kiss on her cheek and leaves her to her task.

27

After lunch the previous day he took Cheryl and Poppy to Orbital C's park. Now, just short of twenty-four hours later, the intervening time feels more like a week than the span of a single day. In that time, they have confronted Sly, Charlie has killed two men and Cheryl has drugged a third before saving Charlie's life. In the past when he has looked back over similar periods of time, he has found that he can think of nothing that has occurred.

He has been into the park on Orbital C once before, but it was only a brief visit, a moment snatched from a day when he had more important things to do, and he had been on his own. For most of his life he has been used to doing everything on his own, except perhaps for sex, and even this he sometimes did on his own before he purchased Cheryl. He knows well enough though that experiences are more pleasurable when a man has someone to share them with, and he thought his Synthias would be every bit as impressed and surprised by the park as he had been. The visit had also been a part of their reconnaissance, somewhere on the orbital they might hide perhaps, should it prove necessary.

He told the Syns there are plants in the park and Cheryl wondered if she might find a plant like the one she left with Will. He watched that scene with a pang of regret, sorry for the way his plans have disrupted Cheryl's life, forcing her from the apartment they shared and now obliging her to part with the only possessions she cares about, the plant and the fish. Cheryl has not complained, but he knows she did not part with them lightly.

At first, he thought Cheryl was simply going to ask Will to look after the items, but she made a gift of them to the old woman. It was a nice gesture, even if Cheryl realised she is unlikely to be able to come back to claim them. Instead of asking the old couple to look after the plant and the fish for her, Cheryl gave them to Will to thank her for being so kind to the three of them. He had seen how fascinated the old woman was by these living things and is sure Cheryl realised this too. It is true that Will and Hans were extraordinarily helpful and hospitable, and he guesses he has his 'lovely ladies' to thank for that. They are easy to like.

Will did not want them to leave and the hug she gave Cheryl was fierce and long. Afterwards Will hurriedly dabbed at her face with her hands as she released the other woman.

Orbital C's park is full of a great variety of plants, none of them exactly like Cheryl's, many of them far too large to keep in an apartment. They towered over the heads of the three of them, causing them to look up and to take in the fact there was no ceiling above them. There was only empty space all the way to the centre of the orbital and beyond that to whatever is on the opposite side, but that was too distant for them to see and, confusingly, although it felt as though it ought to be above them, whatever it is, is down, not up from the middle of the orbital.

There were large areas in the park where some plant with small thin leaves grew like a continuous carpet over the floor. They were careful to keep to the paths, but they saw men walking on the green rug, and Charlie experimented by placing one foot on the leaves, noting how they sprang back again when he lifted his shoe.

The park was filled with colour, even if the predominant one was green. The air too was different, unlike the atmosphere in the rest of the orbital. It was warm and humid and heavy with strange and unfamiliar aromas and scents.

They passed a man using a tool of some kind, something with a long handle with which he seemed to be collecting up leaves and flowers fallen from the plants above. Poppy asked the man what he was doing and the man looked a little startled at being addressed in this way by a woman. He checked with Charlie that it was okay to speak to the Syn before answering her question.

The man explained what was obvious, that he was collecting up fallen leaves and flowers from under the plants.

'If I left them they would begin to decompose,' the man told Poppy.

He explained to her quite patiently what that meant and why it would be a problem. The problem being that they would produce carbon dioxide as they rot.

'That's a gas,' the man explained. Then with a glance at Charlie he added, 'like the air that your owner and me are breathing.'

Poppy looked unimpressed. 'Would that be bad?' she asked.

The man looked her over for a moment, probably in order to confirm that she really was a Syn and not a biological.

'Well, it wouldn't bother you, little lady,' the man said, 'but it's poisonous to men, and to biological women too.'

Poppy nodded slowly and the man added, 'Keeping the air fit for men to breathe is a full-time job on an orbital.'

'What do you do with the stuff after you collect it up?' Poppy asked, and Charlie thought it was a good question. They did not go into the park for the express purpose of finding ways of disposing of a body, but it was one of the things they had discussed beforehand, just in case that too proved necessary, depending upon the outcome of their actions later that day.

The man seemed very happy talking to Poppy and he told her his name was Bob, and when they were all introduced, he took the three of them to the park's waste disposal area. It was really just a freight tube stop, but it also has a direct connection to the orbital's waste system.

Every apartment has a connection too, via a chute into which waste can be put. The chute works using a vacuum or negative pressure, and waste that is fed into it, like uneaten food for example, is whisked away, eventually to be deposited… where? Charlie had not known. He had never even thought about it.

Bob seemed to think Charlie would know, but Bob was happy to explain it to Poppy, just so long as she went on looking at him with those lovely blue eyes and speaking to him in her clear and musical voice. Bob was bent over and no taller than Poppy, and she was looking so young, so clean and fresh, while his face was age-worn and wrinkled like his hands. His overalls were baggy on a body that appeared to have lost much of its former bulk.

Charlie did not listen very carefully to the man's explanation about the problem of treating the waste once it is collected. However, he was interested in the machine that Bob showed them.

The waste chutes in the apartments are much too small to put a body in. Perhaps that is deliberate; otherwise men might be killing each other on a regular basis and disposing of the bodies by putting them into the waste chutes.

Poppy innocently suggested to the park employee that the chute that takes away the dead and unwanted parts of the plants in the park must be much larger than the chute in an apartment and she pointed to a pile of thick and woody stalks that lay nearby. The stalks – Bob called them 'branches' – were as thick as a man's arm.

'Actually, no,' Bob told Poppy with a grin, 'it's the same size, but this machine here chops the branches into very small pieces and they get sucked away into the duct in no time at all.'

The machine was a friendly green colour. It had a large funnel or hopper, the top high enough so they could not look into it. Below that was some kind of large motor and machinery which produced a loud whining noise when Bob switched it on to demonstrate how it worked, feeding one of the branches into the hopper.

Poppy said, 'Oh,' when she heard the man's explanation and again when he demonstrated how it gobbled up the branch. Just the sharp, splintering noises that the machine made were horrible. It was not necessary to see the actual smashing up of the waste to understand what was happening.

When the machine was switched off again Bob smiled, evidently pleased by Poppy's response.

'It would be rather a shame,' he said with a leer, 'but we could put you in there, little lady, and the machine would have no difficulty in chewing you up into pieces no bigger than my thumbnail here. Then you'd be sucked in to be recycled along with these branches.'

Poppy's eyes grew large at this, and she shivered, making Bob laugh again in a way that made Charlie uneasy.

Cheryl exchanged a look with Charlie behind Poppy's back and he guessed that she was thinking what he was. The idea of it was horrible. He did not like Bob so much then, but he liked the idea of putting the body of a man into the machine still less.

'We will have to go at night,' Cheryl tells him now, 'when men not working.'

He says nothing. He is remembering the sounds

of splintering and smashing the machine made when the branch had gone in, and his mind is supplying the additional squelching and sucking sounds that might be added if a man were put into it. He is unsure if he can do it once, let alone three times.

'It is no good getting squeamish,' Cheryl says, accurately reading his thoughts. 'It is too late to worry about the bodies. They already dead.'

Poppy looks as though she likes the idea no more than he does and he takes one of her hands and squeezes it.

'You don't have to come with us,' he tells her.

He does not like the idea of Cheryl being involved either. It is risky as well as an unpleasant task and he does not want to expose either of them to the danger.

'Maybe I should go on my own,' he tells them.

Cheryl raises an eyebrow. 'There are three bodies, Charlie,' she says. 'I think it better if Poppy and I help. You not so strong, Charlie.'

He cannot argue with her. He doubts he would manage to lift one body into the hopper on his own and lifting the second and third body would almost certainly prove impossible. His women look dainty and feminine as they sit at the table with him, but he knows they are stronger than he is. Their legs are powerful as well as slender and graceful under the short, flared skirts they are wearing.

'Okay,' he agrees at last, but his thoughts as he looks at Cheryl now are a long way from the park and the gruesome task they have been considering. He is wondering if there is somewhere private in the apartment that he and Cheryl can go when he has finished eating.

Cheryl raises her eyebrows a fraction, once again reading his thoughts, and then she rises from her seat and slides around the table. When she is beside him, she lays her fingers lightly on his hand and then slides them up his arm as she continues past him, apparently intent on leaving the room. Her hand continues idly up over his shoulder and neck to his face, where it lingers on his cheek for a moment. Then she and her hand are gone.

He turns and finds her looking back at him from the doorway. She shrugs and gives him a little smile.

'Come,' she says, 'if you finished eating?'

He has, and he gets up to follow her.

'Where are we going?'

Instead of answering she puts her arm through his. 'Not far.'

She leads him past the room he knows is Sly's bedroom and he is relieved for he does not wish to go in there, however illogical his feelings about it are. She opens a door into another space further along the passage and then closes it behind them. There is a sort of low bed here with a collection of pillows in various sizes. The bed is large and appears to take up much of the room, but the walls are curved in a way that makes it hard to judge the exact size and shape of the space they contain. Perhaps he is simply tired, but it is difficult for his mind to get any sort of fix on the boundaries of the room. Only the bed is really clear to him, and he likes the look of it. He tries to pull Cheryl down onto it with him, but she resists.

'What is it?' he asks.

Cheryl has picked up a controller of some kind from one of the pillows and now she touches an icon. The lights are extinguished and in the sudden, near total dark he can see the stars. They are sharp and clear and both very far away and very close at the same time. The walls have somehow become a wrap-around window without edges, the stars extending over their heads too. The effect is dizzying, and it reminds him of his experience in the suit after he left the shuttle.

Cheryl takes his hand and pulls him down and snuggles into him.

'What you think, Charlie?' she asks quietly, her mouth very close to his neck.

'It's impressive,' he says after a moment. 'What is it?'

She puts a finger to his lips. 'Don't talk, Charlie,' she tells him, 'just lie back with Cheryl.'

He needs no persuading to do that.

'You like the stars, Charlie?' she asks him after a moment, even though she has told him not to talk.

'I like you,' he tells her, nuzzling his face into her neck.

He kisses her and then runs his hand up her leg under the skirt and she gives a little shiver of excitement and kisses him again with renewed passion. Her eagerness, her own obvious pleasure in their sex together is becoming almost as important to him as his own, greatly adding to his satisfaction. He finds himself doing things with the intention of pleasing her and not simply himself.

Afterwards he must have slept. When he wakes the stars have gone and a flickering light makes him blink and shield his eyes. Cheryl is very still beside him, her body curved into his, strands of her hair partially covering her face. The light falls in a patchy formation on their naked skin and looking up he sees that it is filtered through the leaves and branches of tall plants. Around them is a living green carpet similar to the one they saw in the park, but it is darker and less green around the bed in the shade of the tall plants. Beyond where they lay, the green falls gently away from them into a distance that surely extends far beyond the room, the apartment and even the orbital itself, green as far as he can see under the bright light. He hears water running and turns his head to where it flows between the green in a kind of irregular channel whose sides are the same dark brown of the ground around the plants in the park. The water flows from a higher level somewhere behind them, making a pleasant chuckling and gurgling sound, its surface reflecting the light from above in dancing points that glint almost too brightly to look at. The light is hot as well as bright, and it is only the shade of the leaves above their heads and the air that moves over them that is keeping them cool. The moving air caresses his skin and tugs at his hair as though there are fans directed at them, but he cannot see the walls or the ceiling, or any other details of the room, only this wide and open space. He wonders if Cheryl programmed it to appear this way when they woke again, but then his thoughts return to the woman, and he wonders if she is awake now. He gently disentangles himself from Cheryl, puts on his clothes and slips from the room.

As he nears 'the room of the sleeping women' as Cheryl has christened it, he hears voices, and he enters to find both Poppy and Marie standing beside the fold-down table on which the woman lies.

Poppy looks up, her face bright with an excited smile.

'She's awake,' Poppy says.

When he looks, he sees that the woman is restrained by bands at her wrists and ankles.

'What are these?' he asks, turning to Marie. 'Why is she tied down?'

'It's for her safety,' Marie tells him quickly. 'As she starts to come round and gets stronger there is a danger she may fall off the table, and then if she stands too soon she may fall and injure herself.'

'Oh,' he says, only a little reassured, his tone sceptical.

Poppy is gently sponging the woman's mouth and the side of her face.

'She has just…' Poppy indicates what she means with a graphic gesture using her hand and her open mouth.

'It's normal for them to vomit,' Marie tells him. 'It will last for a few hours. We have given her a few sips of water. That is all she can have at the moment.'

The woman's eyes are closed.

'Has she… I mean, is she speaking?' he asks.

Poppy nods. 'Yes, she wanted to know who I was.'

'You were here when she woke up?' he asks.

'Yes,' Poppy tells him with obvious pleasure. 'I saw her open her eyes.'

He wanted to be here himself. It is a moment he has thought about again and again, but he was asleep with Cheryl. He is a little annoyed that he was not here when she came to, and he is irrationally irritated by Poppy's involvement, that she had been here rather than him, that she is the one sponging the woman's mouth rather than Marie or himself, but her evident excitement and interest quickly soothes and smooths his feelings. He kisses Poppy's cheek, sorry now for the way he reacted.

'It is exciting isn't it?' he tells her.

Poppy smiles and nods happily and he sees Marie look at him. He thinks she saw his initial reaction, even if Poppy did not. She probably heard the aggressive tone of his question about the restraints. He is disappointed with himself and wonders why he so often responds in this way.

He thinks Marie looks different now and then sees she is wearing the dress he picked out for her.

'You're wearing the dress,' he says and she moves back for him to see, turning to her left and right.

'You like it?' he asks and she nods.

'Yes, it's nice to wear clothes, but it will take time to get used to, and I'm worried about getting the dress dirty.'

'We can clean it or find you another one,' he tells her and then he looks again at Isabelle and sees that her eyes are open and that she is looking directly at him.

He moves in closer, standing between Poppy and Marie, and the woman's eyes follow him. He thinks she flinches slightly as he approaches her, but perhaps he only imagines it.

He is suddenly ridiculously tongue-tied and finds he does not know what to say to her.

'Hello,' he says eventually. Then he adds, 'I'm Charlie.'

Isabelle does not respond and her eyes begin to close again. When they re-open they are a little unfocused. Then they snap into focus again and he thinks she recognises him now. Her expression changes, her face no longer so relaxed and slack. He sees her swallow and assumes she is trying to speak.

'How long?' she asks. Her voice is a little croaky, as his sometimes is in the morning if he has been drinking the night before and has stayed up late, but he is still excited to hear it. He thinks, if nothing else, I have heard her speak, and she spoke to me.

But he does not know what she means. How long what?

Then, catching her meaning, he says, 'Only a few days. It's only a few days since you were put in the suspender unit.'

She closes her eyes again, turning her head towards the wall, apparently uninterested. Then she turns back to face him.

'Why did you wake me up?' she asks flatly.

He has no idea what to say and Poppy and Marie look at him expectantly.

'Why?' he repeats, stupidly.

'To get you out,' he says at last.

Poppy and Marie are still looking at him and he wonders if his words are coming out right.

'I want to rescue you,' he tells Isabelle. 'To get you away from here.'

He cannot tell how she receives the news. He imagined she would be excited or relieved, or both, at finally being set free.

'I'm going to set you free,' he says, thinking this is what he meant to say all along.

Now she frowns. 'You were there,' she says.

Speaking seems an effort for her and Marie says, 'She will be very weak, Charlie. Maybe we should let her rest now.'

'You were there,' Isabelle repeats. 'The other man showed me to you, on that rotating platform, under the lights.'

'Yes,' he agrees, pleased she remembers him. He pulls his shirt open and shows her the fading bruise. 'You gave me this.'

'I was aiming for your face,' she says. 'I'm sorry I missed.'

Then, closing her eyes, she turns away from him again and he looks from Poppy to Marie, unsure what to think.

Poppy says, 'When she wakes up again, I will tell her you're a nice man, that you are very kind and I like you. Then she'll want to be your friend.'

The woman on the table starts to sit up, her mouth open and he sees her stomach heave. Marie has a small bowl ready and holds it for the woman while she dry retches. Isabelle produces only a little yellow bile she tries to spit from her mouth, but it dribbles down her cheek and chin and Poppy quickly sponges it for her. There are beads of sweat on the woman's forehead.

'She'll be okay, Charlie,' Marie tells him, seeing his anxious expression. 'It's normal. She'll feel better in a few hours.'

'Do you want some more water?' Poppy asks the woman and after a moment Isabelle nods. She sips at the water Poppy offers her and then lies back again with her eyes closed, her face turned away from them again.

28

Sufficient light spills from inside the car to confirm that this is the right stop, but the waste area itself, beyond the faintly illuminated platform, is concealed in a deep and daunting darkness. He suggests in a whisper that they prop the car doors open, thinking it will provide some illumination at least, and it will keep the car there at the park, something which might be useful if they need to make a quick departure. He leaves the women with the body and walks tentatively into the blackness looking for something suitable to wedge inside the car.

He insisted that they bring only one of the dead men with them on this first trip. He dislikes the idea of being encumbered with more than they can carry between them, in case something goes wrong. Cheryl protested that it will mean more journeys, but he also has an irrational feeling that bad as it would be to be caught with a dead man, it would somehow be very much worse to be discovered with three.

There proved to be a freight tube stop close to the service entrance to Sly's apartment and he guesses this is the way Sly brought in his collection pieces. Loading the body into the car had been straightforward; they saw no one and both the hallway and the tube were silent. There are no seats in the freight car and so they travelled standing, holding on to cleats in the wall. The bright, white light from the overheads in the car, at a time when his body tells him he should be sleeping, made his eyes feel dry and sore.

He is glad he has not tried to perform this task alone, and not simply because he almost certainly lacks the physical strength required to carry the body and then to lift it into the machine. He has no particular fear of dead bodies, but he found himself continually checking the dead man while they travelled in the car, certain the body had opened an eye or moved in some way.

Cheryl told him, 'He is just dead body, Charlie. He very cold and stiff and is not going to give trouble.'

He knows this is true, but in the eerie quiet of the night a man's mind grows less rational, is prone to all kinds of fancies that it would find easy to dismiss in the morning.

If at all possible, he hopes they can manage their task without putting on the floodlights in the ceiling of the waste area. They will be making enough noise without also filling the night with light, but after the harsh light inside the tube car it is hard to make out anything in this near impenetrable black. Then his foot catches against an object, nearly tripping him, and he decides it is a substantial branch like the one Bob showed them the previous day. It is heavy, but he thinks it might be the right length to keep the doors apart so they are almost completely open.

He drags the branch back to the car, but it proves to be too narrow and too irregular to block both the inner and outer doors, but he discovers that if he wedges one end against an inner door and the other against the opposite outer door it keeps them both open, for the moment at least. He keeps a careful eye on the branch while the Synthias carry the body out. He remembers what happened to Tan and he is anxious that the same thing should not happen to one of them.

Cheryl and Poppy begin to shuffle the body forward now, into the dark. They know that once they are inside the waste area the space is large, but the shadows thrown by the light from the tube car create huge shapes that look menacing and solid but which prove to be unreal, while it hides other objects that prove all too solid and immovable.

'Over here,' he calls, finally seeing the shape of the machine they want.

'We put him down for moment,' Cheryl says and she and Poppy lay the body on the floor. It is the body of the man who died outside and it still has several darts protruding from it. They proved difficult to pull out and so they simply left the remaining ones in place.

'How we do this?' Cheryl asks and he tells her to keep her voice down. He is becoming increasingly nervous and jumpy, fearing they will be discovered at any moment.

'There is no one here, Charlie,' she tells him patiently. 'It is night and all men are sleeping.'

'Not all men.'

'We are here to do job, not to talk, Charlie,' Cheryl says and something about the way she says this makes him wonder if she is feeling anxious too.

'Bob turned the machine on before he put the branch in,' Poppy points out.

'Yes,' he agrees, 'that's a good point.'

He feels around the body of the machine where he thinks the switch ought to be. He does not find it, but the machine starts, and the sudden noise is astonishing in the quiet.

'The button is here,' Poppy says. Her memory, of course, is better than his.

'If they not hear that,' Cheryl points out, 'they not hear me talking, Charlie.' Then she says, 'Come, Poppy, we lift either side and put body in head first.'

He is breathing into his cupped hands while the women lift the body up, a nervous gesture he is not even conscious of. He just wants them to get it done and get out again as quickly as possible.

When they have the body upright with its back to the machine Cheryl tells him, 'Now you help lift legs, Charlie.'

They lift the body between them until it topples backwards into the hopper and falls, and they are suddenly relieved of its weight. He is ready for the ghastly sounds that must surely follow, but the whining noise of the motor does not change.

'What's wrong?' he asks. 'Why isn't it working?'

Cheryl says, 'We see.'

She puts her arms around Poppy's waist and lifts her up. 'Can you see problem?' she asks her.

'I can feel one of the legs,' Poppy says, her voice

sounding faint and far off. 'It's caught. The body is hanging from one of the darts.'

'Can you free it?' he asks her.

'No,' Poppy tells him.

Cheryl lowers Poppy to the ground.

'We need something stand on,' Cheryl says.

They spread out, feeling in front of them with their hands and feet. He finds what appears to be a crate and carries it back to the machine. Cheryl tests it with her foot and then climbs onto the crate and Poppy joins her.

'I lift you,' Cheryl says and starts to lift Poppy over the hopper.

He finds the stop button and presses it, his hands shaking. The thought of Poppy falling by accident into the machine while it is running is too awful to consider.

'There,' he hears Poppy say.

'Why machine stopped?' Cheryl asks.

Poppy is standing beside her on the crate again now.

He says nothing. He presses the start button and the machine makes a noise, but the sound does not build up into the loud whine it made before. It only hums loudly.

'Machine is jammed,' Cheryl announces after a moment. 'We have to lift body up again. Then you start machine, Charlie, and we drop body.'

He hits the stop button and the humming ceases.

But before Cheryl can lift Poppy up again he pleads, 'Let me do it. Come down Poppy,' he tells her, 'It's too dangerous.'

'Charlie, you heavier than Poppy,' Cheryl tells him patiently, 'and she is stronger.'

He sighs. 'Okay, but be very careful,' he tells them.

'Oh, yes, be careful, Poppy,' Cheryl says, adding with considerable irony. 'That is good idea; why we not think of it?'

Cheryl lifts Poppy again and Charlie sees her hanging over the edge of the hopper, her head and chest inside it, hidden from view. Her skirt is up and he can see the white panties clearly in the dim light, and it makes her look frail and feminine.

After a moment he hears Poppy call from inside the hopper, 'Okay.'

'Turn on machine, Charlie,' Cheryl instructs.

'Just hold on to Poppy as tightly as you can,' he tells Cheryl. Then he starts the machine. This time it begins to make the deafening whine it did before.

Cheryl says, 'Okay, Poppy, you let go now.'

Then two things happen simultaneously: the machine begins to make the kind of smashing and splintering noises it had done with the branch, and Poppy screams.

A spasm of pain pierces him, and his body is suddenly full of ice, each piece like a splinter of bone.

'What's happened?' he screams, even before the echo of Poppy's cry has died completely away.

He sees Poppy standing on the crate again now beside Cheryl. Poppy has her hands over her face.

'What's the matter?' he shouts.

Cheryl ignores him; she is talking to Poppy and trying to examine her face.

Then he hears Poppy say quietly, 'It's okay, I'm not hurt.'

'Pieces of body shot up and hit Poppy in face,' Cheryl tells him, 'but she say she is not hurt.'

'Is she sure?'

'Yes, Charlie, she is sure.'

He was so scared that something had happened to Poppy he hardly heard the awful noises of the man being smashed and chopped. They seem to have stopped now and the machine is just making its loud, even whine again, so he switches it off.

As the noise dies down he hears a man shouting, 'Hey, you over there! What are you doing?'

He hurriedly helps the two women down from the crate.

'Hold it right there!' the voice calls.

He thinks he can see the man now, or rather he sees a beam of light from a hand-held lamp or torch. The light is approaching from the freight tube stop and then the man himself is silhouetted for a moment in the light spilling from the open doors of the car. He holds the torch in one hand and something in the other that looks like a baton. The shape of his silhouette suggests he is one of the security guards that patrol the lobby and the other public spaces on the orbital. If the man is a guard he also has a side arm as well as the baton and his will not be a home-made device like the one Hans gave him, and he will be able to fire as often as he wishes without waiting for it to re-charge or worrying if it will work a second time.

They have crept around to the far side of the

machine now, away from the tube stop and towards the park side. The man will not be able to see them where they are, but the guard will find them sooner or later. He puts his head out around the side of the machine. He does not see the man or the sweeping beam of the torch and wonders where the guard has gone.

Then the floodlights in the ceiling come on, blinding them.

'We run, Charlie,' Cheryl whispers.

She is probably right; if they are momentarily blinded by the lights the guard will be too. They head for the doors they came through yesterday with Bob, the ones that lead out into the park. As they run he is thinking that the guard no longer needs the hand-held light. That means he has a hand free to use the weapon as well as the baton. He reaches the doors and tries the pull them apart. He has seen that they slide open on tracks and with some doors if you start to open them it activates the mechanism and they work automatically. These are either locked or they do not operate that way.

'Find the switch,' he tells the others, although he can see they are already looking for it, one on each side of the doors.

Suddenly the door comes alive and he feels intense heat radiate from it.

Poppy screams again, but then quickly says, 'I'm okay.'

The guard has fired at them and missed. He has hit the doors instead, but the guard might not miss a second time. The doors are now slightly parted, perhaps because of the energy from the shot and with a little effort he finds he can move them a fraction. The sound of the guard running behind them helps him redouble his efforts. Cheryl pulls at the other door and finally they open sufficiently for the three of them to squeeze through into the dark of the park.

He tries to remember what had been out there in the daylight.

Poppy says, 'This way.'

She takes his hand and they run forward, Cheryl on Poppy's other side, trusting that Poppy knows what she is doing.

'Here,' she says suddenly and they stop running.

He has his hands out in front of him, still not able to see anything, but he feels low branches and leaves around him and the ground underneath his feet is now soft and slightly uneven. Hands clutch at him and pull him through some soft fronds just as the beam from the torch sweeps the ground behind him.

Looking out through the plants he can see the lighted shape of the open doors of the waste area, a narrow rectangle in the black that appears nearer than he expected. A shape crosses the rectangle as the beam of the torch sweeps the ground slowly left and right. The guard seems to be going away from them now.

'We keep off the path,' Cheryl whispers, 'and make no noise.'

Then Poppy is tugging at him and he takes her hand again. Moving more slowly now they continue to follow Poppy's lead. She seems to be able to see where she is going. Once or twice small branches or large leaves hit his face and he has to be careful not to cry out.

They hear the guard shouting again, but his voice appears to be quite distant now. It seems to get closer for a moment and he thinks this is a second voice, that another guard has joined the search, but the next time the man calls it is further away again.

Then bright light makes him shield his eyes with his free hand and as he squints down at the ground he sees light from the open doors that lead out of the park. He stumbles behind Cheryl and they are in the main lobby.

Fortunately, the lobby is quiet, the only sound the ceaseless rush and hiss of the water in the fountain. There are no security guards to be seen. Perhaps the one normally stationed in the lobby has joined the one that found them in the park.

'We should go to the passenger tube,' he says, but Cheryl holds him back.

'Take off shoes, Charlie,' she instructs.

He looks down at his feet and sees that his shoes are covered with the dark ground that lies under the plants in the park. Their shoes have left a visible trail on the marble of the lobby floor. The trail runs from where they stand all the way back to the doors of the park.

Shoes in hand, they get in a car at the passenger tubes. He starts to give Sly's apartment as their destination, but at the last moment he gives another number instead. He does not know if this will really cover their tracks, but it cannot hurt. They can take a second car to the apartment.

He looks at the three of them in the mirrors. Poppy has something spattered on her face and down the front of her blouse. Despite the bronze tint it looks very like blood, and there are some pieces of something else, more solid, like particles of food dropped by a man not paying attention while he ate. But she looks unharmed and she has done well in guiding them out of the park. He squeezes their hands and smiles in turn at each of them.

'Well done, Poppy,' he says.

She smiles with obvious pleasure, despite the gruesome stains and the organic matter on her face. She knows she has done well.

'You're both wonderful,' he says when he can think of nothing else to say.

'We not go back, Charlie,' Cheryl says gravely after a moment. 'We need different solution for other two bodies.'

He does not argue with her, he has no wish to go back either, but when they reach the apartment they find they have a different problem. There is only one body waiting for them now, not two.

29

'We left the bodies here in the lobby,' he says, looking from Cheryl to Poppy, 'Right?'

He knows there is always a possibility he remembers things differently from the women, but he feels quite certain about this. Neither Syn replies.

'Didn't we?' he presses, feeling increasingly agitated.

Cheryl shrugs. 'Yes, Charlie,' she agrees carefully, 'we left bodies here, but now there is only one.'

'Yes, I think we can all see that,' he tells her.

The man with the dart in his arm is still here, lying quietly as any dead person ought to. The body that had been Vos has gone. No one seems to know how; it has just gone.

They have spoken to the other Syns, most of whom are in the day room playing a game of some kind that appears to have them all quite excited, but they claim to know nothing about the missing body. He found two Syns reading in Sly's study and Cheryl found the remaining pair in the room of illusions, as he has come to think of it. They were lost in an underwater world with fish and other creatures swimming around them. Cheryl says they were using a couple of the pillows to hide behind whenever a particularly large and threatening creature came towards them. Like the others, they looked blank when asked about the missing body.

'A body can't…' Poppy asks, 'I mean it can't walk on its own, can it?' Her expression suggests she finds the idea a little terrifying.

'No,' he tells her firmly. 'Dead men don't walk around. Somebody must know what's happened to it. The body didn't go off somewhere by itself!'

None of them says anything.

'I mean, we checked they were both dead,' he says, looking around at Marie and then at Poppy and Cheryl, 'didn't we?'

When none of them answers he shakes his head and says. 'That's so obvious I don't need to ask.'

'Who is "we", Charlie?' Cheryl says patiently.

'You two moved them from the day room,' he says, hearing the accusation in his words. 'You and Poppy,' he adds for clarity.

'Yes, we moved them,' Cheryl agrees, 'and they not give us any trouble.'

He looks at Marie.

She shakes her head. 'I didn't touch them. I was busy with Isabelle and Sly.'

'We saw you shoot him with the weapon,' Poppy says. 'That made him dead, didn't it?'

He had seen the man jerk backwards after he fired the weapon at him, and afterwards he had lain very still. The blast of energy from the weapon and its effect upon Vos had been quite spectacular, but he did not actually check for a pulse in the body afterwards.

Probably he ought to have done so, but he had other things on his mind. So it is possible that Vos was only stunned, has only been unconscious all this time. He feels the hair on the top of his head shift at the idea. He would have felt better if he had someone to blame for this latest cock up, but he knows that it is unfair to suggest that any of this is the Synthias' fault.

'We need to find him,' he says, resigned to the fact that it was his mistake, but increasingly alarmed. 'At once. He mustn't get away.'

'He couldn't have got out of the apartment,' Marie says reasonably. 'The doors are locked.'

'Then he is still here,' Cheryl says.

'So the body is a "he" again?' Poppy asks slowly, her eyes wide. 'It's not dead?'

'No, maybe not,' he agrees, 'not now.'

'Not now?' Poppy repeats, looking unhappy about this whole dead/not dead thing.

'I mean, not before either. We… I, just assumed he was dead.'

'Look on bright side, Poppy' Cheryl says quietly. 'At least we don't have to put him in machine in park.'

'If he's still in the apartment, what's he doing?' Marie asks, also now sounding less than happy about this development.

'We have to find him,' he says, 'and quickly, but we should search in pairs. He may be dangerous.'

'I go with Poppy,' Cheryl suggests, 'and you go with Marie, but maybe we not kill him unless very necessary, Charlie. I think we have enough bodies already.'

He is more concerned that Vos might kill or injure one of them, but as a practical suggestion he knows that not killing Vos if it can be avoided is a good one. Then they can put him in one of the suspender units along with Sly. It would be worth taking another woman out in order to solve the problem of what to do with his body, and he has started to grow curious about the sleeping women as well as concerned about leaving them, but there is no time to think about them now.

'You start with the back entrance and work back from there,' he tells Cheryl. 'We'll start from this end of the apartment.'

His first question when they got back to the apartment had been, 'How is she?' He did not need to say who he meant.

'She's getting stronger, Charlie,' Marie told him.

'Is she talking?'

Marie's expression told him more than her words. 'A little,' Marie said.

He wanted to go to see her immediately, but he was unable to ignore this new problem. It was here for them to see as soon as they came in, or more accurately, it was not here when it ought to have been.

'We'll start with the collection rooms,' he says now, unable to leave seeing Isabelle for a moment longer.

When they enter the room Isabelle is also missing, no longer on the pull-down treatment table. The restraints are undone and the tube that was in her arm trails from the wall, slowly dripping some fluid from its end that has formed a tiny pool on the padded surface.

'Where is she?' he asks.

Marie only shakes her head, her eyes wide. 'I don't know, Charlie.'

'You don't know? Was she still restrained?'

'Yes, I told you, Charlie,' she says defensively, 'it was for her safety...'

'I understand that,' he assures her, 'but it means that she didn't leave on her own.'

He puts his hands on his head. It is what he always does when he has no idea what to do.

'We'll find her, Charlie,' Marie says, tentatively putting her hand on his arm.

'We'd better,' he tells her.

She looks terrified and he remembers the threat Sly had made, that he would deactivate her if she let anything happen to this woman.

'It's not your fault,' he says quickly, taking the hand she had put on his arm and holding it. 'You've looked after her very well.'

Marie searches his face. She still looks anxious, but there is not time now to do anything except find Isabelle.

They look first in the adjoining room where until recently Sly's Synthias were stored. They do not find either Isabelle or Vos here, so they try the room where Cheryl discovered Sly's collection of clothes and accessories. The room is a mess, with discarded clothing piled on the floor and heaped onto the shelves together with still unused items, but there is no one hiding here.

On their way out again, Poppy almost collides with them.

'He's in the kitchen, Charlie!' she says urgently. 'Come quickly.'

In the kitchen they find Vos, as Poppy has said. They find Isabelle too. Vos has an arm around her to stop her from escaping, and to take some of her weight, suggesting she is still a little unsteady on her feet. Vos has the knife that Set had been carrying pressed to her throat. Cheryl is in the doorway, keeping her distance. She stands as though she is relaxed and uninterested in what is happening, but he sees the intensity of her stare as she studies Vos and the knife.

His first reaction is a fierce anger as well as terror, but he does his best to force both of those back down again, knowing they will not help him, but they feel like unwholesome food or drink his stomach is anxious to expel.

'There you are!' he says to Vos. 'You had us worried.'

He tries to keep his voice relaxed and steady, but to his own ears the fear it contains is evident.

'Don't try anything,' Vos warns him. 'Just stay back, you and the Syns, or she'll be dead before you can catch her and stop her falling to the floor.'

Charlie takes in the physical details of the situation without appearing to do so. Vos is standing on the other side of the table, with his back to the work area and the sink. There are cupboards on the wall behind the man. There is nothing there that might help, but it limits Luc's room for manoeuvre.

'You must have a mighty headache,' he tells Vos, trying to appear unconcerned at finding him here with Isabelle.

'What do you mean?' Vos asks him.

'You must have bumped your head pretty hard because you were out for a long time.'

He knows that he has to play to his own strengths. He has limited experience at fighting, but he is quite good at talking. It is after all what he does to earn his commission.

'Who bumped their head?' Vos asks, his eyes narrowed with suspicion.

'You did,' Charlie tells him. 'I think you must have had a seizure or something, Luc. One minute you were standing there and the next you fell backwards, and I think you hit your head because you were suddenly out cold, pal.'

Charlie is in danger of sounding like Lars. He does not think his friend would mind too much and he wishes Lars was here now because he would know what to do, would know instantly how to handle this, but there is no one to help him. It is down to him.

He is thinking he had not brought the weapon out of the backpack before he fired it at Vos. He fired through the material and only took the weapon out after Vos was already on the floor, presumed dead. He hopes there is a chance he can bluff his way through this. Either way, it is all he can come up with at the moment.

'I have a pain in my chest,' Vos says slowly, 'as well as a headache.'

Luc's tone suggests that he holds Charlie

responsible for these things, but it gives him hope.

'Well, my guess is you had a heart attack,' Charlie nods sympathetically. 'I think you should take it easy.'

'Yeah,' Vos says. 'That would suit you, wouldn't it?'

Charlie shrugs. 'It doesn't matter to me, but if you've had a heart attack you ought to get medical attention really soon. I can get Marie to take a look at you.'

'Yeah,' Vos says again. 'Thanks for the advice.'

'So, what do you want?' Charlie asks, pulling out a chair from the table to sit on.

'Stay where you are!' Vos barks.

Charlie does the shrugging thing again. 'Okay,' he says, 'but to repeat the question, what do you want, Luc?'

When Vos says nothing, he decides the man is weighing up his alternatives, and the odds.

'Why don't you put the woman down,' Charlie suggests. 'She's just come out of the freezer and she's liable to be a bit weak.'

'So you can kill me again?' Vos says, but he thinks the man's words lack total conviction.

'Why would I want to kill you?' he asks, making every effort to appear surprised at the suggestion. 'And what do you mean "again"?'

'So I really just fell down yesterday?'

Charlie nods, as though the matter is of no real consequence. 'Yeah, and I must say you did a very good job of looking dead afterwards.'

Vos makes a noise that could mean many things.

'But it wasn't yesterday,' he tells Vos.

'What do you mean?'

'It was the day before yesterday,' Charlie says. 'Like I said, you've been out a long time.'

He hopes this might confuse Vos some more. The knife is fractionally less close to Isabelle's neck now. Vos has not let his guard down yet, but there are beads of sweat on his forehead and the man really does not look well. Isabelle's face is expressionless, and it is hard to tell if she is properly conscious. She seems to be putting more weight on Luc's arm now, leaning away from the man and the knife. He hopes this is deliberate.

'So where's Sly?' Vos asks.

'He had to go out to attend to some business,' Charlie says offhandedly. 'Why don't you put the woman down and have a drink. You can wait for Sly to come back before you go if you want to speak to him.'

He thought that sitting down would make him appear relaxed and unconcerned because it would make it harder for him to react if Vos tries to make a move. They both know there is no mileage in actually cutting the woman, but he cannot afford to let Vos know just how desperate he is to prevent it from happening. He has not got as far as sitting, but the chair is out from under the table now, with its back towards him. He thinks this could be useful, unless it simply gets in his way if he ever has a chance to make a grab for Isabelle, Vos or the knife.

'What about the flowers?' Vos asks. 'I seem to remember you were going to give them to me before… before I fell down.'

Charlie nods. 'Yeah. They're here if you want them.'

Vos looks like a man who does not know what to believe any more. Being dead for nearly thirty-six hours could do that to a man, he supposes.

'Now I think about it,' Charlie suggests reasonably, 'maybe you had some kind of reaction to the flowers. You know that in a really concentrated form like that star dust can do that to a man.'

Vos looks sceptical. 'You don't say?'

The man's scepticism is unsurprising; Charlie is making it up as he goes along, but he thinks it sounds plausible.

'I'm told that just a whiff will do it if you're sensitive enough,' he tells Vos.

He is used to making up things that will help tip a potential customer towards making a purchase, and it sounds genuine, even to himself, but Vos says nothing. Maybe Vos thinks there might be some truth in what he is saying, or maybe Vos knows that sometimes you just let a man talk.

'You ever try star dust yourself?' he asks Vos.

'Do I look that stupid?' Vos says. The sweat is dripping from the man's forehead now and running into his eyes. Vos is trying to blink it away. He cannot use his hands because they are both busy.

'Cheryl here will get the flowers if that's what you want,' he tells Vos, 'but it might be a good idea if she puts them in a bag for you. If you're that sensitive and get another reaction like that you may not survive it.'

'You'll full of such good ideas, aren't you?' Vos says, but he does not quite manage to pull off the tone of snide sarcasm he probably hopes for. His voice is weakening and the man's eyes appear less focussed.

Charlie is trying not to keep looking at the knife or at Isabelle's throat.

'I'm going to sit down, even if you're not,' he says and before Vos can react he sits on the chair he has pulled out. This puts him closer to Vos. There is just the table between them now.

'I told you to stay standing,' Vos says, but that does not work as a threat on its own and they both know it.

'Why don't you sit down as well and we can have a drink while Cheryl gets the flowers.'

Vos says nothing.

'Be a good Syn and go and get the man his flowers,' Charlie says, speaking to Cheryl who he knows is waiting in the doorway.

'Okay,' she agrees without expression, and after a moment's hesitation she leaves.

'But put them in a bag,' he calls after her. It gives him an opportunity to look back at the door. He cannot see either Marie or Poppy, but he thinks they must be just outside.

When he turns back again Vos has lowered the knife and is using it to support some of his weight by pressing it to the table. When Vos sees Charlie looking at him again he raises it threateningly before putting it once more to Isabelle's throat.

Charlie notices that the knife has left a deep cut in the surface of the table.

'You better not be trying anything,' Vos says, visibly swaying a little on his feet.

'Put the woman down and sit down before you fall down,' he tells Vos, adding 'You're obviously unwell.'

'She's coming with me,' Vos says, gesturing to Isabelle with the knife and Charlie flinches and has to struggle very hard not to act too soon. It is clear that Vos thinks the endgame is in sight.

'The woman and the flowers,' Vos says.

Charlie fights down the terror and does the shrugging thing again. He thinks he is getting good at it.

Cheryl reappears. She has a smart-looking bag that is probably from Sly's collection of accessories. It certainly looks expensive. Charlie stands as Cheryl arrives and takes the bag from her. Then he opens it and looks inside before making to hand it to Vos.

'Wait!' Vos says, recoiling.

Charlie cannot tell if this is because Vos fears it is a trick of some kind or because the man really thinks it might have been the flowers that caused him to pass out. Then again, perhaps Vos has a subconscious memory of the backpack and what had come out of it at his chest.

'Show me,' Vos says more quietly, nodding his head at the bag.

Charlie opens the bag and holds it so that Vos can see the contents. Inside are a bouquet of flowers and a circle of similar flowers that until recently were on the head of one of Sly's Synthias.

'Okay,' Vos nods. It does not seem to occur to

him that these might not be the flowers he wants.

Charlie casually lays the bag on the table in front of Vos.

'I should still see a medic as soon as you can,' he tells Vos, 'if you won't let Marie take a look at you.'

Now Vos is faced with a decision. If Vos wants to pick up the flowers he has to take the knife away from the woman's throat. He sees the effort Vos is making, trying to decide what to do. He is watching for some tiny tell-tale flicker in the man's face that will signal a decision.

Vos lowers his eyes to the bag, and Charlie takes that as his cue.

Vos moves the hand with the knife, and then without letting go of the weapon he uses two fingers of the same hand to try to pick up the bag. The movement appears to take place in slow motion although it is really just a quick snatching action. But Charlie is already moving before Vos lowers his arm, and long before the man's fingers reach the bag. He whips up the chair he had been sitting on a moment ago and jabs the legs at Vos, trapping the arm that holds the knife and the bag, and forcing the arm behind Vos, in a direction that it does not like. Vos winces and drops both items. Then, before Vos can get his arm out from the legs of the chair, Charlie hits the man in the face left-handed. He is surprised he manages to make the blow connect with his target. He is also surprised how much it hurts when his knuckles make contact with Vos' nose and cheekbone.

Luc's head goes back until it hits the cupboards behind him and his feet slip forwards on the floor. As he is struggling to regain his balance, Isabelle rotates out of his grip and continues the turn in a full circle, twisting the man's arm up behind his back. It is a neat move, but Vos is already sinking, apparently determined not to let the blood from his nose hit the floor before he does. Weak as he is, Vos cries out in pain as Isabelle twists his arm up behind him and then collapses into unconsciousness again.

'Let's get him restrained on one of those tables in the suspender room,' Charlie says, raising his voice and directing it to Cheryl and the other two he knows must be just beyond the open door.

Then he pulls the table back to clear a way for them to carry the man out.

'You're not going to kill him?' Isabelle asks him.

'No, we're going to put him to sleep. He can go in a freezer unit as soon as we've got another woman out.'

Isabelle looks unimpressed. 'It would be easier to kill him. I'll do it if you don't want to.'

'I've killed him once already' he tells her. 'And it's less messy this way. We won't have to get rid of his body this time.'

Isabelle merely raises an eyebrow.

'You look better,' he says more gently when he realises who he is talking to, and suddenly he is tongue-tied again.

'Cheryl, will you help me carry him?' he says, turning away from Isabelle before she can see his awkwardness.

He puts his hands under Vos' arms and Cheryl picks up his legs, her hands under the knees. They take a couple of shuffling steps towards the door, Vos sagging between them, and then Cheryl calls for Poppy.

'We will do it, Charlie,' she says, putting the man's legs down. 'We are becoming expert moving bodies.'

He smiles. 'Okay, thanks.'

He is aware that Isabelle is watching him.

'Do you need to sit down?' he asks her. 'If you're still a bit weak?'

'So you can tie me up too?' she asks.

'No,' he says, 'that's not really my thing.'

She gives him a slightly pitying look and he thinks his attempt to be casual has not really worked quite as he hoped. In the silence he is aware of Cheryl and Poppy carrying Vos out and he can hear Marie giving them directions about what to do with him.

'Maybe you want some clothes,' he suggests, trying not to look at Isabelle now that he is conscious of her nakedness. He has only seen her without clothes and he has got so used to Marie's habitual nudity that he did not give it any thought until now.

She merely looks at him, apparently trying to decide if he is harmless or another threat.

'And we can ask Marie if you're allowed any food,' he says.

'Allowed?' she queries. 'What do I have to do to earn food?'

'I mean, if it's safe for you to eat,' he explains carefully. 'Marie's the expert. I don't really know anything about suspended animation or its effects, or...'

He stops, aware he is talking too much.

'I'm Charlie,' he says, holding out his hand to her.

'I know,' she says, without taking his hand. 'You already told me that.'

'And you're...' he stops. It sounds incredible and he is afraid of what she might say. 'And you're Isabelle?'

She raises her eyebrows. Then she lowers her shoulders. 'Does it matter?' she asks him.

He thinks about this. He is disconcerted and does not know what to make of her.

'Not really, I suppose,' he says slowly. 'I mean, you can go free whoever you are. I don't think any man should own you. But you're not farmed, are you? You're not a commercial clone.'

She looks at him. She is very still, almost like a Synthia. Her chest rises and falls gently like Poppy's does. Otherwise it is only her eyes that move as she looks at him. Then she puts out a hand to steady herself, holding the back of the chair he has just used to disable Vos.

'Sit down,' he tells her gently. 'And then you can decide if you want the clothes or the food first.'

She sits on the chair and he sees she is really still quite weak.

'Have you been… you know, frozen,' he asks her, 'many times before?'

'How many is "many"?' she asks. Then she says, 'It's only the waking up that's horrible. Otherwise it's better to be unconscious. You don't feel anything then.'

'Don't say that,' he says.

'Why not?'

'Because I'm going to help you.'

'Help me do what exactly?'

'I'm going to help you get back to wherever you came from. Help you get wherever you want to go.'

'Really,' she says dully. 'I'm sure you're going to sell me to whoever will pay you the most. And if not, you're just hoping to use me yourself before you sell me.'

'No,' he says.

'No?'

'No,' he repeats firmly. 'Ask the others if you don't believe me.'

'The others?' she says, looking genuinely puzzled. 'What others? I've only seen your toys so far.'

He frowns. 'What do you mean?' he asks, although he thinks he knows very well what she means.

'These pretty machines you have running around,' she says, gesturing beyond the kitchen, 'the artificial beings doing your dirty work when they're not pleasuring you sexually.'

He does not know what to say.

'You don't know anything about them,' he tells her finally. 'You wouldn't say that if you did. I'm more in awe of them everyday.'

'Yes, how clever you men are,' she says.

'I don't mean that,' he tells her quietly, 'I don't mean that at all.'

He looks up and sees Poppy in the doorway. She

is staring at Isabelle and when she sees him looking at her she lifts her shoulders and then lets them fall.

'You can come in,' he tells her.

She smiles with obvious pleasure and comes forward to stand in front of Isabelle.

'Are you okay?' Poppy asks her.

'What does that mean?' Isabelle says in the same flat way she has been speaking to Charlie.

'He didn't hurt you?' Poppy asks her.

Charlie wonders if Poppy understands Isabelle's mood.

'I was frightened when I saw the knife so close to you,' Poppy tells her.

Isabelle studies Poppy, looking her up and down. Then she says, 'What's that on your face and your clothes?'

Poppy presses her lips together. 'It's bits of body,' she says ruefully, 'the machine spat them out at me when we put the body in.'

'Do you have a lot of bodies?' Isabelle asks her, turning to include Charlie in the question.

'Only one now,' Poppy says, 'now that the man who attacked you isn't dead anymore.'

Isabelle says nothing.

'I don't think he's a very nice man,' Poppy says.

'Charlie, you mean?'

'No!' Poppy says, clearly puzzled as well as surprised by Isabelle's question, 'The man who attacked you!'

Isabelle nods slowly and Poppy says, 'He was supposed to be my owner, but I'm glad he isn't. I think he's horrid.'

'So who is your owner?' Isabelle asks her.

Again Poppy looks surprised. 'Charlie!' she says. 'He's a nice man and I think you're going to like him too, but he says he isn't going to be your owner.' Then she adds doubtfully, 'He says no one is.'

Isabelle appears to see that Poppy struggles with this idea.

'And did Charlie tell you to tell me all this?' she asks Poppy.

'No,' Poppy says simply. She raises her shoulders and lets them fall again, clearly perplexed. 'Why would he?'

Isabelle says nothing.

Poppy is quiet for a second too, but her excitement soon resurfaces.

'Marie says that you can have something to eat now,' she tells Isabelle.

The woman looks sceptically at the stuff on Poppy's face and down the front of her top.

'I have to change my clothes and wash this stuff off,' Poppy explains quickly, seeing Isabelle's expression, 'but would you like me to make some food for you when I've done that?'

Watching the two of them, he very much hopes Isabelle will say yes.

He says, 'I'll leave you two together. I need to go and see how Marie is doing with Vos.'

As he is leaving Poppy is saying. 'You can come with me if you like and choose some clothes while I clean myself.'

Poppy is clearly fascinated by the woman and he thinks it would be nice if the two of them become friends.

To his surprise, he finds Marie working on not one man, but two. It is clearly to be a night full of surprises, but maybe it is already morning; he does not know.

'I thought I should check,' Marie says, seeing him come in, 'after what you said. The man has a pulse, but it's very weak.'

He blows his cheeks out. He has not killed anyone after all. Not yet at least.

'I think we have to get the dart out of his arm,' Marie tells him. 'There's the poison and I think the wound's infected. I have given him a drug for that.'

Charlie puts his hand to the man's forehead. For a dead man he is rather hot. The body they took to the park was cold he reminds himself, very cold. He is certain of that. The man had a dozen darts in him, but it would be a shame to have gone to all that trouble if he was not dead after all, quite apart from the horrible idea that they might have killed a man by accident, and unnecessarily.

'And the other one?' he asks now, looking up.

He is pleased to see that Vos is restrained, even though he does not appear conscious.

'I think he will be okay,' Marie says, 'but you know I'm not a doctor.'

He nods.

'I've started to prepare two of the women to come out of the units,' she tells him. 'I hope that's what you wanted?'

He assures her that it is. 'Yes, of course. Thank you. We couldn't have done any of this without your help.'

Marie has her head down, working intently on the flesh around the dart in Knife Man's arm, the man Vos had called Set.

Then he says, 'I hope Sly realised how lucky he was to have you.'

She makes no reply at first.

'I suppose I still belong to him, Charlie,' she says after a moment. He imagines that she picked up on his use of the past tense in describing her relationship to Sly. He sees her eyes flick to the suspender unit in which her owner now slowly rotates. He thinks Sly is technically still alive, even if he is not still living in the normal sense, and probably Marie does too. Assuming that Sly is successfully reanimated one day they have merely arrested his life and cut his time line in two. He thinks it probably best if the two of them do not meet again, but it is interesting to think that when Sly's time line is restarted Charlie might be older, perhaps much older than Sly is now.

'Do you want to belong to Sly?' he asks Marie.

Her head shoots up to look at him. 'No, Charlie, but I don't have a choice, do I?'

Her words start as a statement, but she appears to end them as a question. His mouth is dry now and he hesitates before speaking.

'I'd like you to come with us,' he tells her. 'I thought you needed to stay here to look after these.' He indicates the suspender units. 'Maybe you do, I don't know, but I'd like you to come. I think you know that.'

'Would you be my owner then?' she asks him.

The tone of her voice gives nothing away about her view of the matter either way.

'No one needs to own you,' he tells her. 'You can own yourself.'

'Someone has to own a Synthia in order to protect her,' she says, 'to stop other men just taking her away.'

'Then I'll steal you and be your owner,' he tells her firmly, 'if you'd like that.'

It was once one of his fantasies. He thinks about it differently now, but he likes her much more, not less. He does not want to own her, not in the sense meant by the laws of commerce, but he will do his best to protect her and keep her safe.

'So it's my choice?' she asks in the same neutral tone.

'Yes, of course,' he tells her.

She makes no reply and carries on working. Then she asks him to hold the end of the dart.

'You can pull it when I tell you,' she says.

He thinks she is smiling to herself while she works now, but she is still concentrating upon what she is doing, and he marvels as he has before at the combination of her skill, dedication and tenderness. In the old days, before his world became so upended and strange, Marie was just a woman who let him in and greeted him and served drinks when her owner asked her to. He thought her lovely, but he had not known her, not at all. He had not guessed at her many skills or the hidden depths to her personality and character. He is only beginning to get to know her now, and he knows he will miss her keenly if she decides to stay when they finally leave.

He has intervened in Marie's life as surely as he has changed the course of Poppy's existence and he has to make sure that it does not end badly for either of them as a result of his actions or his mistakes, or for any of Cheryl's Synthias.

He knows now that they will have to discuss what they should do about the other sleeping women. The Syns, and Isabelle too, they all have a right to be involved in whatever decision they make. The responsibility of it all would feel like an impossible burden to carry if he did not know that Cheryl is here to help him. And Marie too. He kisses her gently on the cheek and goes to find Cheryl.

Cheryl is in the day room where the game is still going on. She does not appear to be joining in, but she is giving advice and her verdict as to whether the moves made by the players themselves are within the rules, whatever they are.

When she sees him come in she breaks away and comes to him and she puts her arms around his neck.

'Are you sleepy, Charlie?' she asks.

He realises suddenly that he is. They have been up all night, and it is only adrenaline that has kept him going.

He nods and she smiles. She removes her arms from his neck and gently pulls his arm, gesturing for him to follow her and he needs no further persuading. She leads him to the room of illusions again. There are three Syns already in there and he would have simply looked for somewhere else to sleep, but when Cheryl asks them to go they leave without complaint.

'Thanks,' he tells them and they go out with timid smiles and close the door behind them.

He has a lot on his mind, but with Cheryl smoothing his hair and caressing his face he falls asleep very quickly.

30

He wakes suddenly, his heart thudding in his chest, convinced something is very wrong. Cheryl is still beside him; she appears to be asleep, her body completely relaxed, one of her arms thrown over him. He lifts his head and listens to see if a noise has roused him, but he can hear nothing and the room of illusions is heavily soundproofed, so it is unlikely to have been that.

He dreamt that someone was leaving the apartment through the front entrance. He saw a figure cross the lobby and open the door and then go out. There was something furtive about the actions of the figure in his dream. It must have been a dream, but it was very vivid and it seems more, not less real to him now that he is awake.

He lifts Cheryl's arm and rises. He is still fully dressed. He even has his shoes on because he had been too tired to take them off. At the door he hears Cheryl begin to stir. She is asking what he is doing, but he does not have time to answer her. He hurries down the passageway, headed for the lobby. There seems to be no one about and there is certainly no one in the lobby. He tries the switch for the outer door and finds it already unlocked. He thinks that if the doors are unlocked the anti-intruder devices will not be activated, and he is certain someone has just gone out this way.

He opens the door with a mounting sense of urgency and then runs through the outer atrium to the passenger tube stop, where he sees the doors to a car just closing. He sprints forward and jams his arm and then his foot into the narrow opening before it fully closes. He knows he can lose a hand or a foot, but something tells him that everything depends upon his opening the doors and getting into the car before it can depart. He tugs at the doors with both hands as hard as he can, straining until he can feel the veins standing out on his head and his body begins to shake with the effort. Finally, they begin to open, and he leaps in, his muscles so strained and fatigued he can barely control them.

There is someone in the car and he knows at once who it is. He thinks he knew all along who was leaving the apartment, but it is a second or two before his eyes confirm the person's identity. Isabelle is wearing men's clothes, either his or possibly some of Sly's. They are too big for her and have the same baggy quality as Bob's overalls. She has a cap on and she has it down over her face. Her hair must be pinned up and contained underneath.

He sits next to her on the bench.

'What are you doing?' he asks her, beginning now to regain his breath.

'What does it look like?' she asks him.

He thinks she does not seem too disconcerted that he has caught up with her.

He shrugs. 'I don't know. I was asleep and I dreamt you were leaving. I saw it while I was asleep,' he says, still perplexed that he should have done so, 'I saw you cross the lobby and go out the door.'

She looks at him for a moment before she says, 'I'm escaping,' and she turns her face away from him and looks at his reflection in the bronzed mirrors instead.

'But...,' he protests weakly, stopping because he has no idea what to say.

He thinks he is not yet fully awake. Her face is turned from him, and he is looking at the back of her head now and then at her reflection.

'But we're going to escape together,' he says eventually.

'Then your idea of escaping is different to mine,' she tells him, turning to address his face directly, rather than his reflection.

He absorbs this for a while. Then he says, 'How far will you get on your own?'

'I don't know,' she says, 'but I have to try.'

'But you don't have any money and who's going to help you? You don't even have an owner they can return you to.'

She says nothing and does not try to refute his objections.

'And where will you go?'

She turns to look at him again, frowning. 'You think I'm going to tell you?'

He must look as hurt as he feels, for she makes a face and then shakes her head at him.

'You stand a better chance of getting away if we

go together,' he tells her.

'Really,' she says flatly.

'I don't just mean with me, I mean with Cheryl and Marie and Poppy, and the others. They're clever and we might manage it with their help.'

She looks sceptical, so he says, 'Cheryl's already save my life, and I wouldn't have got this far without her help.'

'This far with what?' she asks him.

He sighs. 'With freeing you,' he says simply. 'You may not believe me, but after I saw you I couldn't get the idea out of my head. It would have been easier to go on with my life as it was, with Cheryl, but I couldn't, I couldn't get you out of my head, or the expression on your face after you kicked me.'

Now her expression is simply one of pity he thinks, but he does not care. It has never been about him, not really. She shakes her head again, apparently in disbelief.

'It's almost original, I suppose,' she tells him. 'But nothing I've ever experienced says I should trust you.'

'I understand that,' he says.

'No, you don't,' she says quietly and rather wearily. 'You can't begin to understand. Not even a little.'

'Okay, but I was going to say I understand now about when I first saw you.'

'What?' she asks, 'what do you understand about it?'

'I deserved the kick.'

'I was aiming for your face.'

He shrugs. 'If it had been a man, if it had been me on that stand, restrained like you were, naked...' he shrugs again and sighs, 'powerless to stop whatever was going to happen, and then you'd come along and… and did what I did to you, treated me like...'

'What?' she asks again. 'If it had been you, what?'

'You're right: I can't imagine,' he admits, 'not really. I would have hated it. I'd be so angry and ashamed…'

He stops and she continues to look at him. When he has his thoughts in order again he says, 'Men are never treated like that. It's horrible even to think about. To be so... I don't know how I would ever get over it.'

'You obviously thought it was all right at the time,' she points out.

He nods. 'Yes. But you gave me that look.'

'What look?'

'Sort of defiant,' he says, 'like you were angry. You had your hands clenched into fists as though you wanted to follow up the kick with a punch or two.'

'And you were surprised?'

'Yes,' he admits, 'not now, but then, yes, I was. You are a woman, and we were just admiring you, assessing you. It's what men do.'

They sit in silence for a while and he thinks, 'It's true: it's what we men do.'

She says, 'Good speech.'

'I'm trying to explain,' he says.

She nods.

'I'd want to kill someone if I was treated that way.'

'I thought you were good at that, with all the bodies you've been getting rid of.'

'No, I'm not even good at that. I haven't actually killed anyone, and I'm glad.'

She is looking at him and suddenly he feels that it is hopeless. It is only now that he has said the words that he really begins to understand and he does not know why she should trust him. But he has to try.

'Please come back with me,' he says. 'I think you need us and we certainly need you.'

'You need me for what?'

'You can show us where to go,' he says.

'Where to go for what?'

'Where you come from perhaps. Somewhere...' he lifts his shoulders and lets them fall, as he has seen Poppy do. 'Maybe just somewhere different, somewhere where women are not owned by men.'

'You think there is somewhere like that?'

'Yes,' he says. 'There has to be.'

'And what are we going to do when we get there? When we get to this better place?'

He says nothing for a moment. Then he says, the idea coming to him almost as he says it, 'We could make babies.'

She laughs. She laughs quite freely and it is lovely to hear, although he does not like being the one she is laughing at.

'Oh, Charlie,' she says when she has finished laughing, and she shakes her head at him.

'What's wrong with that?' he asks her. 'You're a

naturally-reared woman.'

'You think that's what I want?'

She turns her head away from him, looking again at his reflection.

'It's illegal to make women who are fertile,' he explains, thinking she might not understand, 'or else men would be able to make more women for themselves.'

'That's what you think?' she asks, turning back to him, her expression somewhere between puzzlement and mirth. 'You think that's why they create them like that?'

'Every man knows it,' he says.

She shakes her head again. 'It's so they're always available for sex.'

She must see his puzzled expression because she says, 'Being fertile can be inconvenient, for the woman and... and for the men who want to "use" them.'

He must look puzzled still for she adds, 'I'm not going to explain it to you.'

Then, before he can think of a reply, she says, 'Apart from anything else, you're an artificially engendered male, Ex-U gestation, essentially just another clone. I don't know if you're fertile.'

'No, you've got that wrong,' he tells her patiently. 'It's the cloned women who are infertile.'

'You can believe that if you like,' she says, apparently unconcerned by his explanation.

He just looks at her. He is shocked by her suggestion.

'In the end you're not so very different from your

cloned women, Charlie,' she says. 'The companies that grow you don't own you, not in the same way you own your women, but you pay your makers for creating you, you pay for it your whole life.'

He struggles to understand what she means. 'In the tax we pay, you mean?'

She nods. 'I imagine they make back the cost many times over.'

It is hard for him to absorb this into his understanding of his own identity. It threatens to make his life as accidental and as arbitrary, as dependent on the whim of others as that of Cheryl or Poppy, or Will, but he cannot think about it now. There is only one thing that he cares about: persuading her to come back with him.

She looks at her own reflection again for a while, or perhaps she is simply turned away from him.

The car tells them they have reached the stop for the main lobby, and it comes to a halt and the doors open, but she does not immediately get up. He thinks about taking her to see the fountain, but there will be a better time for that, and in truth he is starting to feel differently about it. When he thinks of the fish women now, he is conscious they are condemned to spend their lives trapped in the pool, on display for the amusement and entertainment of the men who pass, most of whom do not even give the fountain a second glance. He knows there is some lesson to be learned from the fountain, that it represents a fact or aspect of reality that until now has eluded him.

Isabelle is looking at him again. She seems to be waiting for something, something from him.

'Please come back with me,' he says quietly, 'then when we're ready, we'll all try to escape together.'

'I'm trying to escape from you too, Charlie, don't you understand?'

'You'll be stronger by then,' he tells her.

She sighs. 'What happens if I just get out now and go my own way?'

'You'll probably be captured by some man or group of men, or the police will take you in and when they can't find your owner or they realise that you're not a commercial clone they'll pass you around and then try to sell you. Probably you'll end up the property of some very wealthy or very powerful official.'

'Is that your problem?'

'I'd be sorry, very sorry and it would be a waste,' he says. 'It would be a shame to throw away a chance at escaping, even if in the end we don't make it and we all get captured. You won't be any worse off if it happens that way.'

She pulls a face. 'You know what you are?'

'Yes, I do know,' he tells her, nodding.

'What?' she asks, looking genuinely interested in his answer.

'I'm weak and sentimental.'

She laughs again. 'Yes, probably, but I was going to say that you're a dreamer.'

'Is that worse?' he asks.

She nods. 'Much worse.'

Then she sighs again and looks at him, looking deep into his eyes, scanning his face and assessing his expression. He holds her gaze and thinks not just how lovely she is, but how young she is and how much he does not want her to be captured again. He thinks the future he outlined for her if she gets out now is all too likely and he cannot bear the idea of it, or the thought he has not done enough to prevent it.

'Okay,' she says at last, 'I'll come back with you.'

He smiles. It is not a conscious or a controlled gesture. It is just something his face does because he is so relieved and suddenly very happy.

'Don't look at me like that,' she says fiercely, 'or I'll get out now, even if I have to kill you.'

From the pocket of her jacket she produces the knife, the one that Vos had had at her throat.

'Don't think I won't use it,' she tells him.

'I believe you,' he says, and he does.

'So don't ever try to double cross me.'

'I won't, I really won't, but I can't promise I won't smile at you; I can't help it.'

She shakes her head. 'You men are hopeless,' she says, but not altogether unkindly he thinks.

He gets up and presses the button to close the doors and tells the car to return to the apartment. When he sits down again he is careful not to sit so close to her it will make her feel uncomfortable, although his instinct is to put an arm around her and hold her. He thinks she looks tired and small. Her body has lost most of the tension, the alert watchfulness it exhibited when he first got in beside her.

She is silent on the return journey, but she does

not turn her head away from him and turns to him more than once to study his face again.

When the car stops, he gets out first and then reaches in and offers her his hand. She looks at it, and he wonders if she is thinking, as he is, of the first time he saw her, when he had simply taken her hand and examined it in the way that men do with the items on display in the Synthia Store.

Eventually, when he has begun to think that she will ignore his gesture, she reaches out her arm and takes his hand. It is the first time they have touched since she was taken out of the suspender unit. Her eyes meet his and he thinks her expression has softened.

'Everything's going to be all right,' he tells her, and he gently squeezes her hand.

He looks towards the entrance to the apartment and sees Cheryl waiting for them by the door, and he is certain that what he has said is true: everything will be all right.

31

The apartment feels lifeless and sterile, despite the artwork and the rugs and the various ornaments, and as he slowly works his way around it the quiet seems to press into his ears as though the air pressure is set too high. There is evidence of money everywhere he looks, the trappings of a wealth beyond anything he could dream of, let alone ever aspire to. The size of the apartment alone – even without its impressive list of appointments and features – has redefined for him what it means to be rich. He knows that a policeman's salary is relatively modest, but in comparison to this it feels as though he works for nothing. Yet, none of it seems real somehow. It is more like a display, an illustration of some kind, rather than a place where a man actually lives, or had done so until recently. It does not feel like a crime scene either, not like any that he has ever encountered.

As he stands in each of the rooms, he tries to imagine what had gone on during that month. He knows that Charlie has to have been here for that length of time, but there is no evidence now of his presence. Apparently, this is how they found it. Everything has been cleaned and tidied away, almost obsessively so and to the point of sterility. It is difficult even to find any trace of the man who had lived here for twelve years before Charlie's arrival.

He recalls the conversation he had had with the young man who had just been rescued, tries to imagine him here with the others, and with the women, but fails. He knows now that he had seriously underestimated the man. It is just short of three months since he interviewed Charlie in the infirmary back on his own orbital, but somehow it feels as though that meeting belongs to a different time. He tries to imagine where the man might be now, trying to dismiss the wish that he was there too, assuming they are all still together.

The opulence of the apartment evokes no jealousy in him, only a wonder at the distance between his own life and that of the man who owned it, but he would swap places in an instant with the man who left this apartment seven weeks ago together with the women. It is that which evokes envy in him: that and his growing certainty about what it is that Charlie has done, what he has really done that is, not simply the daring theft of an entire collection of rare and extremely valuable Syns and biologicals – a crime that most men accept Charlie committed, even if it is not yet officially recognised as such.

He sighs, and after a final glance at the huge window he leaves the day room and goes to stand again in the room where the three men slowly rotate within the bank of humming and gently whirring machinery. It is the only part of the apartment that feels alive, although it is the machinery that is animated, not the men inside.

He turns at a sound behind him, but it is not a ghost, not some lingering trace of Charlie and the women, but his contact with the police force here on C, the man who has let him in. Technically, Wes has been allowed this visit because two of the men are from his home orbital – although all three are wanted by his force in connection with a string of crimes – but Wes suspects that the bizarre nature of the situation had something to do with the invitation. No one quite knows how to handle it, but there is a natural desire to display the evidence.

'When do you think a decision is likely?' he asks his contact.

Wes and Abe share the same rank, but the conditions under which the two men work are very different, and cooperation between the police forces on the two orbitals is at an all-time low. Wes felt this in the slight awkwardness that was evident when the two of them shook hands after he stepped off the shuttle, and it is present still in the way that Abe stands a little way off as they converse in this confined space.

Abe shrugs. 'Who knows,' he says.

'No man would voluntarily have himself frozen,' Wes states, voicing the thoughts of most men acquainted with the case.

Abe shrugs again. 'There's the document found beside the units,' he says. 'It isn't simple to prove that the men didn't write it themselves.'

Wes nods slowly. He knows the details. He wanted to know if Abe's force knows any more than his.

'Men are putting themselves into suspended animation,' Abe points out, 'those that can afford it.'

Wes nods again, although he finds the idea more than strange.

'Some hope that when they're reheated science will have progressed enough that they can live forever. Others are just the victim of religious beliefs.'

Wes has the idea that Abe has given this speech before, as he has surely given this tour to others before Wes. He has allowed Wes to wander through the apartment on his own. That may have been because he wanted to show that he trusted another police officer, or it may just have been another sign of the distance between their respective forces.

'That could be why the owner got rid of all his women,' Abe suggests now. 'It could have been some kind of religious re-evaluation of his life maybe, and you know what they're saying about his… tastes.'

Wes nods again, but says nothing. He has his own ideas, but he is not about to share them with Abe. In any case, he doubts that Abe believes any of this any more than he does. Abe is a man as well as a police officer. On both counts he is unlikely to accept that these three men went into the freezer willingly.

'Anyway,' Abe says more confidentially, his voice a little lower now, as though afraid that his employers might be listening, 'the Orbital's management company isn't going to admit that this is evidence of a crime. It would be too damaging. The owner of the apartment was – or will be again, according to how you define his present status – a very wealthy and powerful man. What would it do for the Orbital's reputation if it was known that he had been put into one of his own suspender units while he was robbed of his extremely valuable collection of women and who knows what else?'

Wes maintains his silence, but he recognises that here at least Abe is being candid, that this is the true nature of the dilemma and why the legal arguments continue unresolved, while the life of these three men remains suspended.

Abe has started to look like a man who has somewhere to go, and Wes knows that his time at the apartment is at an end, but he has something else he wants to do. He is debating whether to admit this and trust that Abe will humour him as a fellow officer or if he should conceal it and come up with an excuse for spending time on his own before he leaves the orbital.

He sees Abe having some kind of internal debate of his own and thinks it is probably about the extent to which he needs to offer hospitality before he puts the visitor back on the shuttle. If things were better, he would probably invite Wes back to headquarters, but Wes thinks that unlikely at present. He makes a decision and guesses it will help Abe out.

'Is it okay with you if I have a wander around the shops and maybe visit the park before I return?' he asks. 'I know you'll feel responsible for me until I leave, but I haven't had an opportunity to sightsee. You probably take it all for granted, but you know what we men from B are like.'

He makes a joke of it, using a little self-deprecation to boost the other man's self-esteem, and to ease any feelings of guilt that Abe might feel about showing a lack of hospitality.

Abe does a good job of concealing his relief. 'Yes, of course,' he agrees. 'I'll come back with you to the main lobby and take leave of you there.'

The next day, back on his home orbital and behind his desk once more, Wes writes up his notes. The atmosphere of the apartment still haunts him, but he sticks to the facts, scanty as they are. Then he opens the file and plays again the recordings he has spliced together in chronological sequence. He wishes there were recordings from the apartment, but they have all been wiped, by Charlie presumably, so these are all he has, the only tangible evidence.

He watches again as Charlie, flanked by two Syns, approaches the booking desk where he purchases tickets for the shuttle from C over to the Hub: tickets for two men, nineteen Syns and eleven biologicals. That would have been extremely unusual in itself, but all of the women were to travel in the cabin with the men, not in the pressurised freight hold. He would like to be able to see the face of the ticket clerk when he receives this news, but the camera does not even show the back of his head and unfortunately Wes does not have the authority to interview the man.

Although Wes has seen these images many times already, he is still a little dazzled by the inviting smiles and flashing eyes of the Syns as they approach the desk, the one with the curly blonde hair and the startlingly blue eyes and the other whose eyes are like black diamonds. He imagines it must have been the same for the ticket clerk.

There is a second man at the desk, a man who arrived with Charlie and the Syns, but he stands a little too far to the camera's left to be clearly seen. Only his shoulder and occasionally an arm resting on the counter can be seen, in a posture that suggests that he had stood with his face angled away from the clerk. Wes fills in the remaining details from the later recordings made by other cameras and pictures him with his cap well down over his head, his clothes a little too large and baggy.

There is no sound with the recording, but Wes knows that Charlie gave his name as 'Bob', a man who works in the park on Orbital C. Wes suspected this was not a matter of chance, nor simply because Charlie wanted to cover his tracks. So the previous day, after Abe had left him beside the fountain in the lobby, Wes tracked down the real Bob. He had been raking up leaves under the plants when Wes found him and he had been happy to talk. Wes showed him a still from this part of the recording and Bob recognised the Syns, had recognised them immediately, but was less sure about Charlie. Bob particularly remembered the one with the curly hair and talked freely about the things he would like to do with her. He had not known that he was talking to a policeman, of course, and in any case, Wes had been there in an unofficial capacity, without permission from the orbital's own force, and against the explicit orders of his own superior. But Wes had felt compelled to follow up the lead. It was basic police work, and he has learned something interesting from Bob even if he has no proof that it is a related crime. Officially, no crime has been committed, but Wes has it recorded in his own file as destruction of evidence and a probable clue to the whereabouts of a missing man, a man named Jed. It is surely not a coincidence that the second man in the group had given his name as this Jed.

One of the very few things about the identity of that individual that Wes is able to prove is that he is not Jed. Apart from anything else, Jed was much bigger and heavier and much older, and Wes now has a pretty good idea where Jed's remains are, even if it will be impossible to prove.

Had Charlie wanted them to know about Jed? Was it the action of a man so convinced that he would never be caught that he was teasing the police? Somehow Wes thinks not, but he would be hard pressed to explain the reason for this belief in a court.

The next section of the footage shows the group passing through to the airlock, where the IDs of the Syns are scanned and the growers' marks and serial numbers of the biologicals are read. Then the last camera shows the group entering the shuttle. The women appear lively and talkative, a fact confirmed by the only other passenger that Wes has been able to track down and interview. The man said that the trip had been like none he has ever known and that the atmosphere on board was like a kind of party. He said in his testimony that because the two men who were with the Syns were several rows in front of him, he had felt it safe to chat to the Syn seated beside him.

He said she seemed happy to talk. When Wes asked him, the man admitted that he had asked the Syn where they were going, but told Wes that she had said she did not know.

Not all of the Syns look so carefree, Wes notes. The two who went to the desk with Charlie and one other, wear more serious and watchful expressions, and they help to shepherd the others onto the shuttle and into their seats, and they assist the others fastening harnesses. One of these Wes knows is the only Syn registered to Charlie, the one with the black-diamond eyes, apparently known as 'Cheryl'. Cheryl can be seen visibly counting the women before she takes her own seat, presumably to ensure that they are all safely aboard.

The camera continued to record during the flight itself, but the system is set to keep footage from the flight only in the event of unusual or untoward events. He has been told by the force's technical department that it is now impossible to recover the recording made on the trip.

He knows that there is footage of the passengers alighting at the other end, at the Hub, but Wes does not have access to it. He would like to travel to the Hub to view it and to interview anyone who had any dealings with the passengers. He would dearly like to know where the group went afterwards, but he has no jurisdiction on the Hub and can point to no officially recognised crime that he is investigating that will justify a request to either his superiors or the force on the Hub itself to do so. This is just one extremely frustrating hurdle that he can see no way over at present.

When the footage ends, he goes to the stills and enlargements he has made, and in particular to those of the mysterious second 'man'. He has viewed these more times than he can remember, but they still give him a frisson of excitement whenever he studies them. Something had bothered him about this second man the very first time he had seen the images. Now he is certain. It is not simply the face, or the fact that the individual seems so eager to conceal it under the cap, it is also the fact that this individual does not display the behaviour normal for a man when interacting with women. He – if that is what he is – is never seen taking charge or exercising authority over the women in the group. Wes has discounted the idea that this is due to his youth. He is sure now it is more than that. In his notes on the footage Wes has recorded the observation that the man behaves as though the women are his equal.

The thing that Wes cannot be completely sure of is the identity of this woman, or rather, to be accurate, he has not yet found a way to prove what he believes, what he is convinced of without the slightest shred of doubt. Somehow his trip over to C the previous day – his talk with Bob as well as the visit to the apartment – has only added to this conviction. He had already believed that what drove Charlie to act was not greed, not the prospect of the financial reward to be gained from selling the women he has taken, an action that most men are confident will finally get him caught.

Everyone's attention is on the women they can see, on the obvious. But Wes is sure that the real prize, what Charlie was after, has completely escaped them.

He has found that the question, 'Who is the second man, Charlie's unknown accomplice?' provokes little more than a shrug. What does it matter?

Most men are ready to admit that Charlie was clever and daring, but Wes cannot help smiling to himself when he thinks what they would say if they knew the truth.

'What are we looking at?'

The voice startles him, and he turns a little guiltily to see his superior officer. He has come into the office without Wes hearing him.

'Don't tell me,' his superior says a little testily, relieving Wes of the necessity of answering. 'I can guess.'

The man has the rank of Captain, but unless he is in trouble about something, Wes knows him as Eli, a mark of their familiarity with each other.

Wes remains quiet and his superior sighs. Then he settles heavily into the chair beside Wes.

'Okay, so tell me about it,' Eli says with something like resignation. 'I can see that you're still obsessed with the case, even after your visit yesterday. So, why this face? Do you know now who he is?'

Wes hesitates and Eli makes a kind of growling noise in his throat and says, 'He looks very young, and…'

He frowns.

'And what?' Wes asks when his superior says no

more.

'Well, he's not exactly… masculine is he? Not a man's man, if you know what I mean.'

Wes nods his head, and Eli says, 'I mean, you might say that it's a beautiful face.'

Wes says nothing and Eli adds quickly, 'I hope you're not, I mean, tell me you don't have some kind of…'

'No,' Wes says quickly. 'You know me better than that.'

'Good,' Eli says, 'I hope so.'

Wes puts his hand on the image on the screen now, an enlargement of just the head, his hand blocking out the cap that threatens to obscure the face.

Eli tilts his head to the left and then the other way, looking at the image now through half-closed eyes.

'Hmm,' he says. 'You're not suggesting…' he breaks off, but Wes says nothing, letting him make the jump.

When Eli remains quiet Wes says, 'It's also the behaviour.'

'Kind of effeminate, you mean?'

'No,' Wes says, and he explains what he has noticed about the interaction of this man and the women in the group. Perhaps it is not surprising that Eli is not convinced by this explanation.

Eli sighs again.

Wes shows him some more of the still images, images that show the face from various angles, some with less shadow than others.

Then Eli stops him. 'There, that one, keep it there,' he says, and he puts his own hand over the cap.

'He never removes the cap?' Eli asks, and Wes shakes his head.

'Hmm,' his superior says again.

Wes knows the man well enough to know that this means something like, 'I don't like it, but you may have a point.'

'Okay, here's a question for you,' Eli says.

'I'm listening.'

'In a group that already includes so many women, women that sit in the cabin with the men rather than travel in the hold, women that draw plenty of attention to themselves, why would Charlie want this one to try to conceal her identity? Why doesn't he simply let her grower's mark and serial number be read like the others? Why does he get her to try to pass as a man instead? According to you it can't be because she's been stolen, because they've all been stolen.'

'All except one.'

'Okay, all except the one you say is actually registered to Charlie.'

'You agree she's not a man?' Wes asks him and Eli just sighs again.

'For the sake of argument?' Wes persists.

Eli nods reluctantly. Then he says, 'Well?' to draw attention to the fact that Wes has not yet answered his own question. 'Do you have a theory?'

Wes hesitates. Then he says, 'I do.'

'Are you going to share it?'

Wes hesitates again before he says quietly, 'This woman doesn't have a serial number.'

Eli is silent for a moment. 'Why not? Has it been damaged?' he asks. 'Some kind of accident due to rough play?'

'No,' Wes says carefully. 'She never had one.'

Eli looks puzzled, then he frowns, and he says slowly, 'Now wait a minute, you're not suggesting…'

'That's she's naturally reared?' Wes supplies at last when his superior does not finish whatever he had been going to say.

Eli sighs even louder and shakes his head. 'Tell me you're not suggesting that,' he begs. 'Please, no, not that.'

Wes says nothing.

Eli whistles softly and looks at Wes. 'You are suggesting that, aren't you?' he says.

Wes is careful to say nothing, and they sit in silence for a while.

At last Eli says, 'It seems fairly certain that, legal technicalities aside, there's a crime here. Unless that man really gave Charlie the women, which seems hard to believe, this is theft on a grand scale, in broad daylight, clever and daring and maybe you admire him for it, but if what you're suggesting is true this is a crime almost without parallel.'

Wes is of the opinion that it is best to continue to say nothing for the moment and let his superior work his way through it.

'And you're saying that he did it on his own,' Eli adds. 'We don't have to work out the identity of the accomplice because he didn't have one?'

Wes tries to convey with his expression he knows how much of a mental stretch it is. Privately, he thinks about the Syns who had assisted the others, shepherding them onto the shuttle, helping them fasten their harnesses, and about Cheryl counting the women before taking her seat. Perhaps Charlie had not really done it alone, but the idea is too fantastic, and he is not about to suggest it to his superior.

'You're talking about the biggest theft in history!' Eli protests.

'Apart from the first time,' Wes says quietly.

'The first time?' Eli queries.

Then, when he has worked it out, Eli says, 'Oh, yes, I see what you mean, but I suppose that her… her mother might have sold her.'

The unfamiliar word sits awkwardly in the captain's mouth, as though he is uncertain of its pronunciation.

Wes looks doubtful.

'But I agree it's not very likely,' Eli says. He puts his hand on the screen again, obscuring the cap. Wes can see that Eli is beginning to come to terms with the idea.

'A remarkable face, when you allow it's a woman,' Eli says, almost to himself, 'quite remarkable.'

'Yes,' Wes agrees, judging it safe to say this much.

'I'd give a great deal to meet her,' Eli says quietly.

'So would most men,' Wes nods, and the two men sit in silence, looking at the face on the screen.

'Hmm,' Eli says quietly.

It is almost no more than an exhalation this time and Wes makes no comment. He sees his superior's face slowly soften as he gazes for long moments at the screen. Wes has a pretty good idea what he feels.

'Do you really think it's possible?' Eli asks eventually. 'That it's her, I mean?'

His tone is not that of the senior policeman questioning his subordinate. He is not seeking Wes' professional opinion on the strength of the evidence. It is more like a cry from the heart.

The End

Printed in Great Britain
by Amazon

43174536R00248